ROBERT WILSON

Robert Wilson was born in 1957. A graduate of Oxford University, he has worked in shipping and advertising in London and trading in West Africa. He is married and divides his time between England, Spain and Portugal.

He was awarded the CWA Gold Dagger for Fiction for his fifth novel, *A Small Death in Lisbon*.

Visit www.AuthorTracker.co.uk for exclusive updates on Robert Wilson.

Also by Robert Wilson

The Company of Strangers
A Small Death in Lisbon

JAVIER FALCON NOVELS
The Blind Man of Seville
The Silent and The Damned

BRUCE MEDWAY NOVELS
A Darkening Stain
Blood Is Dirt
The Big Killing
Instruments of Darkness

ROBERT WILSON

The Hidden Assassins

HARPER

Harper
An imprint of HarperCollins*Publishers*
77–85 Fulham Palace Road,
Hammersmith, London W6 8JB

www.harpercollins.co.uk

This paperback edition 2007
4

First published in Great Britain by
HarperCollins*Publishers* 2006

A catalogue record for this book is
available from the British Library

ISBN-13: 978 0 00 720292 8
ISBN-10: 0 00 720292 X

Set in Meridien by Palimpsest Book Production Ltd
Grangemouth, Stirlingshire

Printed and bound in Great Britain by
Clays Ltd, St Ives plc

For Jane and my mother
and
Bindy, Simon and Abigail

ACKNOWLEDGEMENTS

This book would have been impossible without extensive research in Morocco, especially to see how all levels of Moroccan society are reacting to the friction between Islam and the West. I would like to thank Laila for her hospitality and for introducing me to people from all walks of life. They gave me valuable insights into the Arab world's point of view. I must stress that although all opinions are faithfully represented, none of the characters in this book remotely resembles any real person, alive or dead. They are all figments of my imagination and were generated to perform their functions in my story.

As always, I would like to thank my friends Mick Lawson and José Manuel Blanco for putting me up and putting up with me. They made the Seville end of my research for this book a lot easier. My thanks to the Linc language school in Seville and my teacher Lourdes Martinez, for doing her best to improve my Spanish.

I have been published by HarperCollins for just over ten years and I think it fitting that after a decade of hard work on my behalf I should thank my editor, Julia Wisdom, who has not only offered perceptive advice about my books and brought them successfully to the market place, but has also been one of my greatest in-house proponents.

Finally I would like to thank my wife, Jane, who has helped me with my research, spurred me on through the long months of writing, and been my first, and unflagging, reader and critic. Some think that being a writer is hard, but spare a thought for the writer's wife, who while working and supporting has to watch much writhing and torment and is rewarded with scant praise and little compensation for the horrors she must witness. You'd only do it for love and I thank her for it and return it doubled.

Turning and turning in the widening gyre
The falcon cannot hear the falconer;
Things fall apart; the centre cannot hold;
Mere anarchy is loosed upon the world,
The blood-dimmed tide is loosed, and everywhere
The ceremony of innocence is drowned;
The best lack all conviction, while the worst
Are full of passionate intensity.

'The Second Coming' W.B. YEATS

And now, what will become of us without the barbarians?
Those people were a kind of solution.

'Waiting for the Barbarians' CONSTANTINE CAVAFY

The West End, London – Thursday, 9th March 2006

'So, how's your new job going?' asked Najib.

'I work for this woman,' said Mouna. 'She's called Amanda Turner. She's not even thirty and she's already an account director. You know what I do for her? I book her holidays. That's what I've been doing all week.'

'Is she going somewhere nice?'

Mouna laughed. She loved Najib. He was so quiet and not of this world. Meeting him was like coming across a *palmerie* in the desert.

'Can you believe this?' she said. 'She's going on a pilgrimage.'

'I didn't know English people went on pilgrimages.'

Mouna was, in fact, very impressed by Amanda Turner, but she was much keener to receive Najib's approbation.

'Well, it's not exactly religious. I mean, the reason she's going isn't.'

'Where is this pilgrimage?'

'It's in Spain near Seville. It's called La Romería del Rocío,' said Mouna. 'Every year people from all over

Andalucía gather together in this little village called El Rocío. On something called the Pentecost Monday, they bring out the Virgin from the church and everybody goes wild, dancing and feasting, as far as I can tell.'

'I don't get it,' said Najib.

'Nor do I. But I can tell you the reason Amanda's going is not for the parading of the Virgin,' said Mouna. 'She's going because it's one big party for four days – drinking, dancing, singing – you know what English people are like.'

Najib nodded. He knew what they were like.

'So why has it taken you all week?' he asked.

'Because the whole of Seville is completely booked up and Amanda has loads, I mean loads, of requirements. The four rooms have all got to be together . . .'

'Four rooms?'

'She's going with her boyfriend, Jim "Fat Cat" Maitland,' said Mouna. 'Then there's her sister and *her* boyfriend and two other couples. The guys all work in the same company as Jim – Kraus, Maitland, Powers.'

'What does Jim do in his company?'

'It's a hedge fund. Don't ask me what that means,' said Mouna. 'All I know is that it's in the building they call the Gherkin and . . . guess how much money he made last year?'

Najib shook his head. He made very little money. So little it wasn't important to him.

'Eight million pounds?' said Mouna, dangling it as a question.

'How much did you say?'

'I know. You can't believe it, can you? The lowest paid guy in Jim's company made five million last year.'

2

'I can see why they would have a lot of require-ments,' said Najib, sipping his black tea.

'The rooms have all got to be together. They want to stay a night before the pilgrimage, and then three nights after, and then a night in Granada, and then come back to Seville for another two nights. And there's got to be a garage, because Jim won't park his Porsche Cayenne in the street,' said Mouna. 'Do you know what a Porsche Cayenne is, Najib?'

'A car?' said Najib, scratching himself through his beard.

'I'll tell you what Amanda calls it: Jim's Big Fuck Off to Global Warming.'

Najib winced at her language and she wished she hadn't been so eager to impress.

'It's a four-wheel drive,' said Mouna, quickly, 'which goes a hundred and fifty-*six* miles an hour. Amanda says you can watch the fuel gauge going down when Jim hits a hundred. And you know, they're taking four cars. They could easily fit in two, but they have to take four. I mean, these people, Najib, you cannot believe it.'

'Oh, I think I can, Mouna,' said Najib. 'I think I can.'

The City of London – Thursday, 23rd March 2006

He stood across the street from the entrance to the underground car park. His face was indiscernible beyond the greasy, fake fur-lined rim of the green parka's hood. He walked backwards and forwards, hands shoved deep down into his pockets. One of his trainers was coming apart and the lace of the other dragged and flapped about the sodden frayed bottom of his faded jeans, which seemed to suck on the wet pavement. He was muttering.

He could have been any one of the hundreds of unseen people drawn to the city to live at ankle height in underground passages, to scuff around on cardboard sheets in shop doorways, to drift like lost souls in the limbo of purgatory amongst the living and the visible, with their real lives and jobs and credit on their cards and futures in every conceivable commodity, including time.

Except that he *was* being seen, as we are all being seen, as we have all become walkers-on with bit parts in the endlessly tedious movie of everyday life. Often in the early mornings he was the star of this grainy black-and-white documentary, with barely an extra in sight and only the sporty traffic of the early traders and Far East fund managers providing any action. Later, as the sandwich shops opened and the streets filled with bankers, brokers and analysts, his role reverted to 'local colour' and he would often be lost in the date or the flickering numbers of time running past.

Like all CCTV actors, his talent was completely missable, his Reality TV potential would remain undiscovered unless, for some reason, it was perceived that his part was crucial, and the editor of everyday life suddenly realized that he had occupied the moment when the little girl was last seen, or the young lad was led away or, as so often happens in the movies, briefcases were exchanged.

There was none of that excitement here.

The solitary male or female (under the hood not even that was clear) moved in the tide of extras, sometimes with them, sometimes against. He was extra to the extras and, worse than superfluous, he was getting in the way. He did this for hour after hour, week after week, month after . . . He was only there for a month. For four weeks he muttered and shuffled across the cracks in the pavement opposite the underground car park and then he was gone. Reality TV rolled on without him, without ever realizing that a star of the silent screen had been in its eye for just over 360 hours.

Had there been a soundtrack it would not have helped. Even if a mike had been placed within the horrible greasy hood of the parka it would have clarified nothing. All that would have registered was the mutterings of a marginalized moron, telling himself the colour, model and registration number of apparently

5

random cars and the time they passed his patch of pavement. It was surely the obsessive work of a lunatic.

What sort of sophisticated surveillance equipment would have been able to pick up that the eyes deep inside the darkness of the hood were only choosing cars that went into the underground car park of the building across the street? And even if there was equipment that could have made that connection, would it also have been able to discover that the stream of uninteresting data was being recorded on to the hard disk of a palm-sized dictaphone in the inside pocket of the parka?

Only then would the significance of this superfluous human being have been realized and the editor of everyday life, if he was being attentive that morning, might have sat up in his chair and thought: Here we have a star in the making.

1

Dead bodies are never pretty. Even the most talented undertaker with a genius for *maquillage* cannot bring the animation of life back to a corpse. But some dead bodies are uglier than others. They have been taken over by another life form. Bacteria have turned their juices and excretions into noxious gas, which slithers along the body's cavities and under the skin, until it's drum tight over the corruption within. The stench is so powerful it enters the central nervous system of the living and their revulsion reaches beyond the perimeter of their being. They become edgy. It's best not to stand too close to people around a 'bloater'.

Normally Inspector Jefe Javier Falcón had a mantra, which he played in the back of his mind when confronted by this sort of corpse. He could stomach all manner of violence done to bodies – gunshot craters, knife gashes, bludgeon dents, strangulation bruises, poisoned pallor – but this transformation by corruption, the bloat and stink, had recently begun to disturb him. He thought it might just be the psychology of decadence, the mind troubled by the slide to the only possible end of age; except that this wasn't the ordinary decay of death. It was to do with the corruption of the body – the heat's rapid transformation of a slim girl into a stout middle-aged matron or, as in the case of this body that they were excavating from the rubbish of the landfill site beyond the outskirts of the city, the metamorphosis of an ordinary man to the taut girth of a sumo wrestler.

The body had stiffened with rigor mortis and had come to rest in the most degrading position. Worse than a defeated sumo wrestler tipped from the ring to land head first in the front row of the baying crowd, his modesty protected by the thick strap of his *mawashi*, this man was naked. Had he been clothed he might have been kneeling as a Muslim supplicant (his head even pointed east), but he wasn't. And so he looked like someone preparing himself for bestial violation, his face pressed into the bed of decay underneath him, as if unable to bear the shame of this ultimate defilement.

As he took in the scene Falcón realized that he wasn't playing his usual mantra and that his mind was occupied by what had happened to him as he'd taken the call alerting him to the discovery of the body. To escape the noise in the café where he'd been drinking his café solo, he'd backed out through the door and collided with a woman. They'd said '*Perdón*', exchanged a startled look and then been transfixed. The woman was Consuelo Jiménez. In the four years since their affair Falcón had only had a glimpse of her four or five times in crowded streets or shops and now he'd bumped into her. They said nothing. She didn't go into the café after all, but disappeared quickly back into the stream of shoppers. She had, however, left her imprint on him and the closed shrine in his mind devoted to her had been reopened.

Earlier the Médico Forense had stepped carefully through the rubbish to confirm that the man was dead. Now the forensics were concluding their work, bagging anything of interest and removing it from the scene. The Médico Forense, still masked up and dressed in a white boiler suit, paid his second visit to the victim. His eyes searched and narrowed at what they found. He made notes and walked over to where Falcón was standing with the duty judge, Juez Juan Romero.

'I can't see any obvious cause of death,' he said. 'He didn't die from having his hands cut off. That was done afterwards. His wrists have been very tightly tourniqueted. There are no contusions around the neck and no bullet holes or knife wounds. He's been scalped and I can't see any catastrophic damage to the skull. He might have been poisoned, but I can't tell from his face, which has been burnt off with acid. Time of death looks to be around forty-eight hours ago.'

Juez Romero's dark brown eyes blinked over his face mask at each devastating revelation. He hadn't handled a murder investigation for more than two years and he wasn't used to this level of brutality in the few murders that had come his way.

'They didn't want him recognized, did they?' said Falcón. 'Any distinguishing marks on the rest of the body?'

'Let me get him back to the lab and cleaned up. He's covered in filth.'

'What about other body damage?' asked Falcón. 'He must have arrived in the back of a refuse truck to end up here. There should be some marks.'

9

'Not that I can see. There might be abrasions under the filth and I'll pick up any fractures and ruptured organs back at the Forensic Institute once I've opened him up.'

Falcón nodded. Juez Romero signed off the *levantamiento del cadáver* and the paramedics moved in and thought about how they were going to manipulate a stiffened corpse in this position into a body bag and on to the stretcher. Farce crept into the tragedy of the scene. They wanted to cause as little disturbance as possible to the body's noxious gases. In the end they opened up the body bag on the stretcher and lifted him, still prostrate, and placed him on top. They tucked his wrist stumps and feet into the bag and zipped it up over his raised buttocks. They carried the tented structure to the ambulance, watched by a gang of municipal workers, who'd gathered to see the last moments of the drama. They all laughed and turned away as one of their number said something about 'taking it up the arse for eternity'.

Tragedy, farce and now vulgarity, thought Falcón.

The forensics completed their search of the area immediately around the body and brought their bagged exhibits over to Falcón.

'We've got some addresses on envelopes found close to the body,' said Felipe. 'Three have got the same street names. It should help you to find where he was dumped. We reckon that's how he ended up in that body position, from lying foetally in the bottom of a bin.'

'We're also pretty sure he was wrapped in this –' said Jorge, holding up a large plastic bag stuffed with a grimy white sheet. 'There's traces of blood from his severed hands. We'll match it up later . . .'

'He was naked when I first saw him,' said Falcón.

'There was some loose stitching which we assume got ripped open in the refuse truck,' said Jorge. 'The sheet was snagged on one of the stumps of his wrists.'

'The Médico Forense said the wrists were well tourniqueted and the hands removed after death.'

'They were neatly severed, too,' said Jorge. 'No hack job – surgical precision.'

'Any decent butcher could have done it,' said Felipe. 'But the face burnt off with acid *and* scalped . . . What do you make of that, Inspector Jefe?'

'There must have been something special about him, to go to that trouble,' said Falcón. 'What's in the bin liner?'

'Some gardening detritus,' said Jorge. 'We think it had been dumped in the bin to cover the body.'

'We're going to do a wider search of the area now,' said Felipe. 'Pérez spoke to the guy operating the digger, who found the body, and there was some talk of a black plastic sheet. They might have done their postmortem surgery on it, sewed him up in the shroud, wrapped him in the plastic and then dumped him.'

'And you know how much we love black plastic for prints,' said Jorge.

Falcón noted the addresses on the envelopes and they split up. He went back to his car, stripping off his face mask. His olfactory organ hadn't tired sufficiently for the stink of urban waste not to lodge itself in his throat. The insistent grinding of the diggers drowned out the cawing of the scavenging birds, wheeling darkly against the white sky. This was a sad place even for an insentient corpse to end up.

Sub-Inspector Emilio Pérez was sitting on the back

of a patrol car chatting to another member of the homicide squad, the ex-nun Cristina Ferrera. Pérez, who was well built with the dark good looks of a 1930s matinée idol, seemed to be of a different species to the small, blonde and rather plain young woman who'd joined the homicide squad from Cádiz four years ago. But, whereas Pérez had a tendency to be bovine in both demeanour and mentality, Ferrera was quick, intuitive and unrelenting. Falcón gave them the addresses from the envelopes, listing the questions he wanted asked, and Ferrera repeated them back before he could finish.

'They sewed him into a shroud,' he said to Cristina Ferrera as she went for the car. 'They carefully removed his hands, burnt his face off, scalped him, but sewed him into a shroud.'

'I suppose they think they've shown him some sort of respect,' said Ferrera. 'Like they do at sea, or for burial in mass graves after a disaster.'

'Respect,' said Falcón. 'Right after they've shown him the ultimate disrespect by taking his life and his identity. There's something ritualistic and ruthless about this, don't you think?'

'Perhaps they were religious,' said Ferrera, raising an ironic eyebrow. 'You know, a lot of terrible things have been done in God's name, Inspector Jefe.'

Falcón drove back into the centre of Seville in strange yellowing light as a huge storm cloud, which had been gathering over the Sierra de Aracena, began to encroach on the city from the northwest. The radio told him that there would be an evening of heavy rain. It was probably going to be the last rain before the long hot summer.

12

At first he thought that it might be the physical and mental jolt he'd had from colliding with Consuelo that morning which was making him feel anxious. Or was it the change in the atmospheric pressure, or some residual edginess left from seeing the bloated corpse on the dump? As he sat at the traffic lights he realized that it ran deeper than all that. His instinct was telling him that this was the end of an old order and the ominous start of something new. The unidentifiable corpse was like a neurosis; an ugly protrusion prodding the consciousness of the city from a greater horror underneath. It was the sense of that greater horror, with its potential to turn minds, move spirits and change lives that he was finding so disturbing.

By the time he arrived back at the Jefatura, after a series of meetings with judges in the Edificio de los Juzgados, it was seven o'clock and evening seemed to have come early. The smell of rain was as heavy as metal in the ionized air. The thunder still seemed to be a long way off, but the sky was darkening to a premature night and flashes of lightning startled, like death just missed.

Pérez and Ferrera were waiting for him in his office. Their eyes followed him as he went to the window and the first heavy drops of rain rapped against the glass. Contentment was a strange human state, he thought, as a light steam rose from the car park. Just at the moment life seemed boring and the desire for change emerged like a brilliant idea, along came a new, sinister vitality and the mind was suddenly scrambling back to what appeared to be prelapsarian bliss.

'What have you got?' he asked, moving along the window to his desk and collapsing in the chair.

'You didn't give us a time of death,' said Ferrera.

'Sorry. Forty-eight hours was the estimate.'

'We found the bins where the envelopes were dumped. They're in the old city centre, on the corner of a cul-de-sac and Calle Boteros, between the Plaza de la Alfalfa and the Plaza Cristo de Burgos.'

'When do they empty those bins?'

'Every night between eleven and midnight,' said Pérez.

'So if, as the Médico Forense says, he died some time in the evening of Saturday 3rd June,' said Ferrera, 'they probably wouldn't have been able to dump the body until three in the morning on Sunday.'

'Where are those bins now?'

'We've had them sent down to forensics to test for blood traces.'

'But we might be out of luck there,' said Pérez. 'Felipe and Jorge have found some black plastic sheeting, which they think was wrapped around the body.'

'Did any of the people you spoke to at the addresses on the envelopes remember seeing any black plastic sheeting in the bottom of one of the bins?'

'We didn't know about the black plastic sheeting when we interviewed them.'

'Of course you didn't,' said Falcón, his brain not concentrated on the details, still drifting about in his earlier unease. 'Why do you think the body was dumped at three in the morning?'

'Saturday night near the Alfalfa . . . you know what it's like around there . . . all the kids in the bars and out on the streets.'

'Why choose those bins, if it's so busy?'

'Maybe they know those bins,' said Pérez. 'They knew

that they could park down a dark, quiet cul-de-sac and what the collection times were. They could plan. Dumping the body would only take a few seconds.'

'Any apartments overlooking the bins?'

'We'll go around the apartments in the cul-de-sac again tomorrow,' said Pérez. 'The apartment with the best view is at the end, but there was nobody at home.'

A long, pulsating flash of lightning was accompanied by a clap of thunder so loud that it seemed to crack open the sky above their heads. They all instinctively ducked and the Jefatura was plunged into darkness. They fumbled around for a torch, while the rain thrashed against the building and drove in waves across the car park. Ferrera propped a flashlight up against some files and they sat back. More lightning left them blinking, with the window frame burnt on to their retinae. The emergency generators started up in the basement. The lights flickered back on. Falcón's mobile vibrated on the desktop: a text from the Médico Forense telling him that the autopsy had been completed and he would be free from 8.30 a.m. to discuss it. Falcón sent a text back agreeing to see him first thing. He flung the mobile back on the desk and stared into the wall.

'You seem a little uneasy, Inspector Jefe,' said Pérez, who had a habit of stating the obvious, while Falcón had a habit of ignoring him.

'We have an unidentified corpse, which could prove to be unidentifiable,' said Falcón, marshalling his thoughts, trying to give Pérez and Ferrera a focus for their investigative work. 'How many people do you think were involved in this murder?'

'A minimum of two,' said Ferrera.

'Killing, scalping, severing hands, burning off features

with acid . . . yes, why did they cut off his hands when they could have easily burnt off his prints with acid?'

'Something significant about his hands,' said Pérez.

Falcón and Ferrera exchanged a look.

'Keep thinking, Emilio,' said Falcón. 'Anyway, it was planned and premeditated and it was important that his identity was not known. Why?'

'Because the identity of the corpse will point to the killers,' said Pérez. 'Most victims are killed by people –'

'Or?' said Falcón. 'If there was no *obvious* link?'

'The identity of the victim and/or knowledge of his skills might jeopardize a future operation,' said Ferrera.

'Good. Now tell me how many people you really think it took to dispose of that body in one of those bins,' said Falcón. 'They're chest high to a normal person and the whole thing has got to be done in seconds.'

'Three to deal with the body and two for lookout,' said Pérez.

'If you tipped the bin over to the edge of the car boot it could be done with two men,' said Ferrera. 'Anybody coming down Calle Boteros at that time would be drunk and shouting. You might need a driver in the car. Three maximum.'

'Three or five, what does that tell you?'

'It's a gang,' said Pérez.

'Doing what?'

'Drugs?' he said. 'Cutting off his hands, burning off his face . . .'

'Drug runners don't normally sew people into shrouds,' said Falcón. 'They tend to shoot people and there was no bullet hole . . . not even a knife wound.'

'It didn't seem like an execution,' said Ferrera, 'more like a regrettable necessity.'

Falcón told them they were to revisit all the apartments overlooking the bins first thing in the morning before everybody went to work. They were to establish if there was black plastic sheeting in any of the bins and if a car was seen or heard at around three in the morning on Sunday.

Down in the forensic lab, Felipe and Jorge had the tables pushed back and the black plastic sheet laid out on the floor. The two large bins from Calle Boteros were already in the corner, taped shut. Jorge was at a microscope while Felipe was on all fours on the plastic sheet, wearing his custom-made magnifying spectacles.

'We've got a blood group match from the victim to the white shroud and to the black plastic sheet. We hope to have a DNA match by tomorrow morning,' said Jorge. 'It looks to me as if they put him face down on the plastic to do the surgery.' He gave Falcón the measurements between a saliva deposit and some blood deposits and two pubic hairs which all conformed to the victim's height.

'We're running DNA tests on those, too,' he said.

'What about the acid on the face?'

'That must have been done elsewhere and rinsed off. There's no sign of it.'

'Any prints?'

'No fingerprints, just a footprint in the top left quadrant,' said Felipe. 'Jorge has matched it to a Nike trainer, as worn by thousands of people.'

'Are you going to be able to look at those bins tonight?'

'We'll take a look, but if he was well wrapped up I don't hold out much hope for blood or saliva,' said Felipe.

'Have you run a check on missing persons?' asked Jorge.

'We don't even know if he was Spanish yet,' said Falcón. 'I'm seeing the Médico Forense tomorrow morning. Let's hope there are some distinguishing marks.'

'His pubic hair was dark,' said Jorge, grinning. 'And his blood group was O positive . . . if that's any help?'

'Keep up the brilliant work,' said Falcón.

It was still raining, but in a discouragingly sensible way after the reckless madness of the initial downpour. Falcón did some paperwork with his mind elsewhere. He turned away from his computer and stared at the reflection of his office in the dark window. The fluorescent light shivered. Pellets of rain drummed against the glass as if a lunatic wanted to attract his attention. Falcón was surprised at himself. He'd been such a scientific investigator in the past, always keen to get his hands on autopsy reports and forensic evidence. Now he spent more time tuning in to his intuition. He tried to persuade himself that it was experience but sometimes it seemed like laziness. A buzz from his mobile jolted him: a text from his current girlfriend, Laura, inviting him to dinner. He looked down at the screen and found himself unconsciously rubbing the arm which had made contact with Consuelo's body in the entrance of the café. He hesitated as he reached for the mobile to reply. Why, suddenly, was everything so much more complicated? He'd wait until he got back home.

The traffic was slow in the rain. The radio news commented on the successful parading of the Virgin of Rocío, which had taken place that day. Falcón crossed the river and joined the metal snake heading north. He sat at the traffic lights and scribbled a note without thinking before filtering right down Calle Reyes Católicos. From there he drove into the maze of streets where he lived in the massive, rambling house he'd inherited six years ago. He parked up between the orange trees that led to the entrance of the house on Calle Bailén but didn't get out. He was wrestling with his uneasiness again and this time it was to do with Consuelo – what he'd seen in her face that morning. They'd both been startled, but it hadn't just been shock that had registered in her eyes. It was anguish.

He got out of the car, opened the smaller door within the brass-studded oak portal and went through to the patio, where the marble flags still glistened from the rain. A blinking light beyond the glass door to his study told him that he had two phone messages. He hit the button and stood in the dark looking out through the cloister at the bronze running boy in the fountain. The voice of his Moroccan friend, Yacoub Diouri, filled the room. He greeted Javier in Arabic and then slipped into perfect Spanish. He was flying to Madrid on his way to Paris next weekend and wondered if they could meet up. Was that coincidence or synchronicity? The only reason he'd met Yacoub Diouri, one of the few men he'd become close to, was because of Consuelo Jiménez. That was the thing about intuition, you began to believe that everything had significance.

The second message was from Laura, who still wanted to know if he would be coming for dinner that night; it would be just the two of them. He smiled at that. His relationship with Laura was not exclusive. She had other male companions she saw regularly and that had suited him . . . until now when, for no apparent reason, it was different. Paella and spending the night with Laura suddenly seemed ridiculous.

He called her and said that he wouldn't be able to make dinner but that he would drop by for a drink later.

There was no food in the house. His housekeeper had assumed he would go out for dinner. He hadn't eaten all day. The body on the dump had interrupted his lunch plans and ruined his appetite. Now he was hungry. He went for a walk. The streets were fresh after the rain and full of people. He didn't really start thinking where he was going until he found himself heading round the back of the Omnium Sanctorum church. Only then did he admit that he was going to eat at Consuelo's new restaurant.

The waiter brought him a menu and he ordered immediately. The pan de casa arrived quickly; thinly sliced ham sitting on a spread of salmorejo on toast. He enjoyed it with a beer. Feeling suddenly bold he took out one of his cards and wrote on the back: *I am eating here and wondered if you would join me for a glass of wine. Javier.* When the waiter came back with the revuelto de setas, scrambled eggs and mushrooms, he poured a glass of red rioja and Javier gave him the card.

Later the waiter returned with some tiny lamb chops and topped up his glass of wine.

'She's not in,' he said. 'I've left the card on her desk so that she knows you were here.'

Falcón knew he was lying. It was one of the few advantages of being a detective. He ate the chops feeling privately foolish that he'd believed in the synchronicity of the moment. He sipped at his third glass of wine and ordered coffee. By 10.40 p.m. he was out in the street again. He leaned against the wall opposite the entrance to the restaurant, thinking that he might catch her on the way out.

As he stood there waiting patiently he covered a lot of ground in his head. It was amazing how little thought he'd given to his inner life since he'd stopped seeing his shrink four years ago.

And when, an hour later, he gave up his vigil he knew precisely what he was going to do. He was determined to finish his superficial relationship with Laura and, if his world of work would let him, he would devote himself to bringing Consuelo back into his life.

2

Consuelo Jiménez was sitting in the office of her flag-
ship restaurant, in the heart of La Macarena, the old
working-class neighbourhood of Seville. She was in a
state of heightened anxiety and the three heavy shots
of The Macallan, which she'd taken to drinking at this
time of night, were doing nothing to alleviate it. Her
state had not been improved by bumping into Javier
early in the day and it had been made worse by the
knowledge that he'd been eating his dinner barely ten
metres from where she was now sitting. His card lay
on the desk in front of her.

She was in possession of a terrible clarity about her
mental and physical state. She was not somebody who,
having fallen into a trough of despair, lost control of
her life and plunged unconsciously into an orgy of
self-destruction. She was more meticulous than that,
more detached. So detached that at times she'd found
herself looking down on her own blonde head as the
mind beneath stumbled about in the wreckage of her
inner life. It was a very strange state to be in: physically in good shape for her age, mentally still very

focused on her business, beautifully turned out as always, but . . . how to put this? She had no words for what was happening inside her. All she had to describe it was an image from a TV documentary on global warming: vital elements of an ancient glacier's primitive structure had melted in some unusually fierce summer heat and, without warning, a vast tonnage of ice had collapsed in a protracted roar into a lake below. She knew, from the ghastly plummet in her own organs, that she was watching a prefiguration of what might happen to her unless she did something fast.

The whisky glass travelled to her mouth and back to the desk, transported by a hand that she did not feel belonged to her. She was grateful for the ethereal sting of the alcohol because it reminded her that she was still sentient. She was playing with a business card, turning it over and over, rubbing the embossed name and profession with her thumb. Her manager knocked and came in.

'We're finished now,' he said. 'We'll be locking up in five minutes. There's nothing left to do here . . . you should go home.'

'That man who was here earlier, one of the waiters said he was outside. Are you sure he's gone?'

'I'm sure,' said the manager.

'I'll let myself out of the side door,' she said, giving him one of her hard, professional looks.

He backed off. Consuelo was sorry. He was a good man, who knew when a person needed help and also when that help was unacceptable. What was going on inside Consuelo was too personal to be sorted out in an after-hours chat between proprietor and manager.

This wasn't about unpaid bills or difficult clients. This was about . . . everything.

She went back to the card. It belonged to a clinical psychologist called Alicia Aguado. Over the last eighteen months Consuelo had made six appointments with this woman and failed to turn up for any of them. She'd given a different name each time she'd made these appointments, but Alicia Aguado had recognized her voice from the first call. Of course she would. She was blind, and the blind develop other senses. On the last two occasions Alicia Aguado had said: 'If ever you *have* to see me, you must call. I will fit you in whenever – early morning or late at night. You must realize that I am always here when you need me.' That had shocked Consuelo. Alicia Aguado knew. Even Consuelo's iciest professional tone had betrayed her need for help.

The hand reached for the bottle and refilled the glass. The whisky vaporized into her mind. She also knew why she wanted to see this particular psychologist: Alicia Aguado had treated Javier Falcón. When she'd run into him in the street, it had been like a reminder. But a reminder of what? The 'fling' she'd had with him? She only called it a fling because that's what it looked like from the outside – some days of dinners and wild sex. But she'd broken it off because . . . She writhed in her chair at the memory. What reason had she given him? Because she was hopeless when in love? She turned into somebody else when she got into a relationship? Whatever it was, she'd invented something unanswerable, refused to see him or answer his calls. And now he was back like an extra motivation.

She hadn't been able to ignore a recent and more worrying psychological development, which had started to occur in the brief moments when she wasn't working with her usual fierce, almost manic, drive. When distracted or tired at the end of the day sex would come into her mind, but like a midnight intruder. She imagined herself having new and vital affairs with strangers. Her fantasies drifted towards rough, possibly dangerous men and assumed pornographic dimensions, with herself at the centre of almost unimaginable goings on. She'd always hated porn, had found it both disgustingly biological and boring, but now, however much she tried to fight it with her intelligence, she was aware of her arousal: saliva in her mouth, the constriction of her throat. And it was happening again, now, even with her mind apparently engaged. She kicked back her chair, tossed Aguado's card into the gaping hole of her handbag, lunged at her cigarettes, lit up and paced the office floor, smoking too fast and hard.

These imaginings disgusted her. Why was she thinking about such trash? Why not think about her children? Her three darling boys – Ricardo, Matías and Darío – asleep at home in the care of a nanny. In the care of a nanny! She had promised that she would never do that. After Raúl, her husband, their father, had been murdered she had been determined to give them all her attention so that they would never feel the lack of a parent. And look at her now – thinking of fucking while they were at home in another person's care. She didn't deserve to be a mother. She tore her handbag off the desk. Javier's card fluttered to the floor.

She wanted to be out in the open, breathing the rain-rinsed air. The five or six shots of The Macallan she'd drunk meant that she had to walk up to the Basilica Macarena to get a taxi. To do this she had to pass the

Plaza del Pumarejo, where a bunch of drunks and addicts hung out all day, every day, and well into the night. The plaza, under a canopy of trees still dripping from the earlier storm, had a raised platform with a closed kiosk at one end and at the other, near the shuttered Bodega de Gamacho, a group of a dozen or so burnt-out cases.

The air was cool around Consuelo's bare legs, which were numbed by the whisky. She had not considered how obtrusive her peach-coloured satin suit would be under the street lamps. She walked behind the kiosk and along the pavement by the old Palacio del Pumarejo. Some of the group were standing and boozing, gathered around a man who was talking, while others slumped on benches in a stupor.

The wiry central figure in a black shirt open to the waist was familiar to Consuelo. His talk to this unsavoury audience was more of an oration, because he had a politician's way with words. He had long black hair, eyebrows angled sharply into his nose and a lean, hard, pockmarked face. She knew why the group around him hung on his words and it had nothing to do with the content. It was because under those satanic eyebrows he had very bright, light green eyes, which stared out of his dark face, alarming whoever they settled on. They gave the powerful impression of a man who had quick access to a blade. He drank from a bottle of cheap wine, which hung by his side with his fore-finger plugged into its neck.

A month ago, while Consuelo was waiting to cross the road at a traffic light, he'd approached her from behind and muttered words of such obscenity that they'd entered her mind like a shiv. Consuelo had remonstrated loudly when it happened. But, unlike the usual perpetrators, who would slink off into the crowds of shoppers, ignoring her, he'd got up close and silenced her with those green eyes and a quick wink, that made her think he knew something about her that she, herself, did not.

'I know your sort,' he'd said, and touched the corner of his mouth with the point of his tongue.

His bravado had paralysed her vocal cords. That and the horrible little kiss he'd blown her, which found its way to her neck like a horsefly.

Consuelo, distracted by these memories, had slowed to a halt. A member of the group spotted her and jerked his head in her direction. The orator stepped towards the railing holding the bottle up, letting it dangle from his forefinger.

'Fancy a drink?' he said. 'We haven't got any glasses, but I'll let you suck it off my finger if you want.'

A low, gurgling laugh came from the group, which included some women. Startled, Consuelo began walking again. The man jumped off the raised platform. The steel tips on the heels of his boots hammered the cobbles. He blocked her path and started to dance an extremely suggestive Sevillana, with much pelvic thrusting. The group backed him up with some flamenco clapping.

'Come on, Doña Consuelo,' he said. 'Let's see you move. You look as if you've got a decent pair of legs on you.'

She was shocked to hear him use her name. Terror slashed through her insides, tugging something strangely exciting behind it. Muscles quivered in the backs of her thighs. Disparate thoughts barged into each other in her mind. Why the hell had she put herself in such a position? She wondered how rough his hands would be. He looked strong – potentially violent.

The sheer perversity of these thoughts jolted her back to the reality. She had to get away from him. She veered off down a side street, walking as fast as her kitten heels would permit on the cobbles. He was behind her, steel tips leisurely clicking.

'Fucking hell, Doña Consuelo, I only asked you for a dance,' he shouted after her, a mocking inflexion on her title. 'Now you're leading me astray down this dark alley. For God's sake, have some self-respect, woman. Don't go showing your eagerness so early on. We've barely met, we haven't even danced.'

Consuelo kept going, breathing fast. All she had to do was get to the end of the street, turn left and she'd be at the gates of the old city and there would be traffic and people . . . a taxi back to her real life at home in Santa Clara. An alley appeared on her left, she saw the lights of the main road through the buildings leaning into each other. She darted down it. Shit, the cobbles were wet and all over the place. It was too dark and her heels were slipping. She wanted to scream when his hand finally landed on her shoulder, but it was like in those dreams where the need to yell the neighbourhood awake produced only a strangled whimper. He pushed her towards the wall, whose whitewash hung off in brittle flakes, and crackled as her cheek made contact. Her heart thundered in her chest.

'Have you been watching me, Doña Consuelo?' he said, his face appearing over her shoulder, the sourness of his winy breath in her nostrils. 'Have you been keeping a little eye out for me? Perhaps . . . since you lost your husband your bed's been a bit cold at night.'

She gasped as he slipped his hand between her bare legs. It *was* rough. An automatic reflex clamped her thighs shut. He sawed his hand up to her crotch. A voice in her head remonstrated with her for being so stupid. Her heart walloped in her throat while her brain screamed for her to say something.

'If it's money you want . . .' she said, in a voice that whispered to the flaking whitewash.

'Well,' he said, pulling his hand away, 'how much have you got? I don't come cheap, you know. Especially for the sort of thing you like.'

He took her handbag off her shoulder, flipped it open and found her wallet.

'A hundred and twenty euros!' he said, disgusted.

'Take it,' she said, her voice still stuck under her thyroid.

'Thank you, thank you very much,' he said, dropping her handbag to his feet. 'But that's not enough for what you want. Come back with the rest tomorrow.'

He pressed against her. She felt his obscene hardness against her buttocks. His face came over her shoulder once more and he kissed her on the corner of her mouth, his wine and tobacco breath and bitter little tongue slipping between her lips.

He pushed himself away, a gold ring on his finger flashed in the corner of her eye. He stepped back, kicked her handbag down the street.

'Fuck off, whore,' he said. 'You make me sick.'

The steel tips receded. Consuelo's throat still throbbed so that breathing was more like swallowing without being able to achieve either. She looked back to where he'd gone, confused at her escape. The empty cobbles shone under the yellow light. She pushed away from the wall, snatched up her handbag and ran, slipping and hobbling, down the street to the main road where she hailed a cab. She sat in the back with the city floating past her pallid face. Her hands shook too much to light the cigarette she'd managed to get into her mouth. The driver lit it for her.

At home she found money in her desk to pay for the taxi. She ran upstairs and checked the boys in their beds. She went to her own room and stripped off and looked at herself in the mirror. He hadn't marked her. She showered endlessly, soaping and resoaping herself, rinsing herself again and again.

She went back to her desk in her dressing gown and sat in the dark, feeling nauseous, head aching, waiting for dawn. When it was the earliest possible acceptable moment, she phoned Alicia Aguado and asked for an emergency appointment.

3

Juez Esteban Calderón was not on business. The urbane and highly successful judge had told his wife, Inés, that he was working late before going to dinner with a group of young state judges who had come down from Madrid on a training course. He *had* worked late and he *had* gone to the dinner, but he'd excused himself early and was now taking his favourite little detour down the side of the San Marcos church to reach 'the penthouse of promise', which overlooked the church of Santa Isabel. He usually enjoyed smoking a cigarette at the edge of the small, floodlit plaza, looking from within the darkness at the fountain and the massive portal of the church. It calmed him after long days spent with prosecutors and policemen and kept him out of the way of some bars around the corner, which were frequented by colleagues. If they saw him there it would get back to Inés and there'd be awkward questions. He also needed a few moments to rein in his quivering sexual tension, which started every morning when he woke up and imagined the long coppery hair and mulatto skin of his Cuban girlfriend, Marisa

31

Moreno, who lived in the penthouse just visible from where he was sitting.

His cigarette hissed in a puddle where he'd tossed it, half smoked. He took off his jacket. A breeze sprayed droplets of water from the orange trees on to his back, and he caught his breath at the lash of its sudden chill. He kept to the wall of the church until he was in the darkness of the narrow street. His finger hovered over the top button of the entry phone as an accumulation of half thoughts made him hesitate: subterfuge, infidelity, fear, sex, dizziness and death. He scratched at the air above the button; these unusual thoughts made him feel that he was on the brink of something like a great change. What to do? Either step over the edge or fall back. He swallowed some thick, bitter saliva from his fast smoking. The sensuality of the lash of raindrops across his back reached that nexus of nerves in the base of his spine. The unease disappeared. His recklessness made him feel alive again and his cock leapt in his pants. He hit the buzzer.

'It's me,' he said, to the crackle of Marisa's voice.

'You sound thirsty.'

'Not thirsty,' he said, clearing his throat.

The two-man lift didn't seem to have enough air and he started panting. Its stainless steel panels reflected the absurd shape of his arousal and he rearranged himself. He brushed back his thinning hair, loosened his flamboyant tie and knocked on her door. It opened a crack and Marisa's amber eyes blinked slowly. The door fell open. She was wearing a long, orange silk shift, which nearly reached the floor. It was fastened with a single amber disc between her flat breasts. She kissed him and slipped a cube of ice from between her lips into his confused mouth and something like a firework went off in the back of his head.

She held him at bay with a single finger on his sternum. The ice cooled his tongue. She gave him an appraising look, from crown to crotch, and admonished him with a raised eyebrow. She took his jacket and hurled it into the room. He loved this whorish stuff she did, and she knew it. She dropped to her haunches, undid his belt and tugged his trousers and underpants down, then eased him profoundly into the coolness of her mouth. Calderón braced himself in the doorframe and gritted his teeth. She looked up at his agony with wide eyes. He lasted less than a minute.

She stood, turned on her heel and strode back into her apartment. Calderón pulled himself together. He didn't hear her hawking and spitting in the bathroom. He just saw her reappear from the kitchen, carrying two chilled glasses of cava.

'I thought you weren't coming,' she said, looking at the thin, gold wafer of watch on her wrist, 'and then I remembered my mother telling me that the only time a Sevillano wasn't late was for the bulls.'

Calderón was too dazed to comment. Marisa drank from her flute. Twenty gold and silver bracelets rattled on her forearm. She lit a cigarette, crossed her legs and let the shift slip away to reveal a long, slim leg, orange panties and a hard brown stomach. Calderón knew that stomach, its paper-thin skin, hard wriggling muscularity and soft coppery down. He'd laid his head on it and stroked the tight copper curls of her pubis.

'Esteban!'

He snapped out of the natural revolutions of his mind.

'Have you eaten?' he asked, nothing else coming to him, conversation not being one of the strengths of their relationship.

'I don't need any feeding,' she said, taking a shelled brazil nut from a bowl, and putting it between her hard, white teeth. 'I'm quite ready to be fucked.'

The nut went off in her mouth like a silenced gun and Calderón reacted like a sprinter out of the blocks. He fell into her snake-like arms and bit into her unnaturally long neck, which seemed stretched, like those of African tribal women. In fact for him, that was her attraction: part sophisticate, part savage. She'd lived in Paris, modelling for Givenchy, and travelled across the Sahara with a caravan of Tuaregs. She'd slept with a famous movie director in Los Angeles and lived with a fisherman on the beach near Maputo in Mozambique. She'd worked for an artist in New York, and spent six months in the Congo learning how to carve wood. Calderón knew all this, and believed it because Marisa was such an extraordinary creature, but he didn't have the first idea of what was going on in her head. So, like a good lawyer, he clung to these few dazzling facts.

After sex they went to bed, which for Marisa was a place to talk or sleep but not for the writhings and juices of sex. They lay naked under a sheet with light from the street in parallelograms on the wall and ceiling. The cava fizzed in glasses balanced on their chests. They shared an ashtray in the trough between their bodies.

'Shouldn't you have gone by now?' said Marisa.

'Just a little bit longer,' said Calderón, drowsy.

'What *does* Inés think you're doing all this time?' asked Marisa, for something to say.

'I'm at a dinner . . . for work.'

'You're just about the last person in the world who should be married,' she said.

'Why do you say that?'

'Well, maybe not. After all, you Sevillanos *are* very conservative. Is that why you married her?'

'Part of it.'

'What was the other part?' she asked, pointing the cone of her cigarette at his chest. 'The more interesting part.'

She burnt a hair off one of his nipples; the smell of it filled his nostrils.

'Careful,' he said, feeling the sting, 'you don't want ash all over the sheets.'

She rolled back from him, flicked her cigarette out on to the balcony.

'I like to hear the parts that people don't want to tell me about,' she said.

Her coppery hair was splayed out on the white pillow. He hadn't been able to look at her hair without thinking of the other woman he'd known with hair of the same colour. It had never occurred to him to tell anybody about the late Maddy Krugman except the police in his statement. He hadn't even talked to Inés about that night. She knew the story from the newspapers, the surface of it anyway, and that was all she'd wanted to know.

Marisa raised her head and sipped from her flute. He was attracted to her for the same reason that he'd been attracted to Maddy: the beauty, the glamour, the sexiness and the complete mystery. But what was he to her? What had he been to Maddy Krugman? That was something that occupied his spare thinking time. Especially those hours of the early morning, when he woke up next to Inés and thought that he might be dead.

'I don't really give a fuck why you married her,' said Marisa, trying a well-tested trick.

'Well, that's not what's interesting.'

'I'm not sure I need to know what *is* interesting,' said Marisa. 'Most men who think they're fascinating only ever talk about themselves . . . their successes.'

'This wasn't one of my successes,' said Calderón. 'It was one of my greatest failures.'

He'd made a snap decision to tell her. Candour was not one of his strongest suits; in his society it had a way of coming back on you, but Marisa was an outsider. He also wanted to fascinate her. Having always been the object of fascination to women he'd understood completely, he had the uncomfortable feeling of being ordinary with exotic creatures like Maddy Krugman and Marisa Moreno. Here, he thought, was an opportunity to intrigue the intriguers.

'It was about four years ago and I'd just announced my engagement to Inés,' he said. 'I was called to a situation, which looked like a murder-suicide. There were some anomalies, which meant that the detective, who, by a coincidence, happened to be the ex-husband of Inés, wanted to treat it as a double murder investigation. The victim's neighbours were American. The woman was an artist and stunningly beautiful. She was a photographer with a taste for the weird. Her name was Maddy Krugman and I fell in love with her. We had a brief but intense affair until her insane husband found out and cornered us in an apartment one night. To cut a long and painful story short, he shot her and then himself. I was lucky not to get a bullet in the head as well.'

They lay in silence. Voices came up over the balcony rail from the street. A warm breeze blew at the voile curtains, which billowed into the room, bringing the smell of rain and the promise of hot weather in the morning.

'And that's why you married Inés.'

'Maddy was dead. I was very badly shaken. Inés represented stability.'

'Did you tell her you'd fallen in love with this woman?'

'We never talked about it.'

'And what now . . . four years later?'

'I feel nothing for Inés,' said Calderón, which was not quite the whole truth. He did feel something for her. He hated her. He could hardly bear to share her bed, had to steel himself to her touch, and he couldn't understand why. He had no idea where it came from. She hadn't changed. She had been both good to him and for him after the Maddy incident. This feeling of dying he had when he was with her in bed was a symptom. Of what, he could not say.

'Well, Esteban, you're a member of a very large club.'

'Have you ever been married?'

'You *are* joking,' said Marisa. 'I watched the soap opera of my parents' marriage for fifteen years. That was enough to warn me off that particular bourgeois institution.'

'And what are you doing with me?' asked Calderón, fishing for something, but not sure what. 'It doesn't get more bourgeois than having an affair with a state judge.'

'Being bourgeois is a state of mind,' she said. 'What you do means nothing to me. It has no bearing on us. We're having an affair and it will carry on until it burns out. But I'm not going to get married and you already are.'

'You said I was the last person in the world who should be married,' said Calderón.

'People get married if they want to have kids and fit into society, or, if they're suckers, they marry their dream.'

'I didn't marry *my* dream,' said Calderón. 'I married everybody else's dream. I was the brilliant young judge, Inés was the brilliant and beautiful young prosecutor. We were the "golden couple", as seen on TV.'

'You don't have any children,' said Marisa. 'Get divorced.'

'It's not so easy.'

'Why not? It's taken you four years to find out that you're incompatible,' said Marisa. 'Get out now while you're still young.'

'You've had a lot of lovers.'

'I might have been to bed with a lot of men but I've only had four lovers.'

'And how do you define a lover?' asked Calderón, still fishing.

'Someone I love and who loves me.'

'Sounds simple.'

'It can be . . . as long as you don't let life fuck it up.'

The question burned inside Calderón. Did she love him? But almost as soon as it came into his mind he had to ask himself whether he loved her. They cancelled each other out. He'd been fucking her for nine months. That wasn't quite fair, or was it? Marisa could hear his brain working. She recognized the sound. Men always assumed their brains were silent rather than grinding away like sabotaged machinery.

'So now you're going to tell me,' said Marisa, 'that you can't get a divorce for all those bourgeois reasons – career, status, social acceptance, property and money.'

That *was* it, thought Calderón, his face going slack in the dark. That was *precisely* why he couldn't get a divorce. He would lose everything. He had only just scraped his career back together again after the Maddy debacle. Being related to the Magistrado Juez Decano de Sevilla had helped, but so had his marriage to Inés. If he divorced her now his career might easily drift, his friends would slip away, he would lose his apartment and he would be poorer. Inés would make sure of all that.

'There is, of course, a bourgeois solution to that,' said Marisa.

'What?' said Calderón, turning to look at her between her upturned nipples, suddenly hopeful.

'You could murder her,' she said, throwing open her hands, easy peasy.

Calderón smiled at first, not quite registering what she had said. His smile turned into a grin and then he laughed. As he laughed his head bounced on Marisa's taut stomach and it bounced higher and higher as her muscles tightened with laughter. He sat up spluttering at the brilliant absurdity of her idea.

'Me, the leading Juez de Instrucción in Seville, killing his wife?'

'Ask her ex-husband for some advice,' said Marisa, her stomach still contracting with laughter. 'He should know how to commit the perfect murder.'

4

Manuela Falcón was in bed, but not sleeping. It was 5.30 in the morning. She had the bedside light on, knees up, flicking through *Vogue* but not reading, not even looking at the pictures. She had too much on her mind: her property portfolio, the money she owed to the banks, the mortgage repayments, the lack of rental income, the lawyer's fees, the two deeds due to be signed this morning, which would release her capital into beautifully fluid funds of cash.

'For God's sake, relax,' said Angel, waking up in bed next to her, still groggy with sleep and nursing a small cognac-induced hangover. 'What are you so anxious about?'

'I can't believe you've asked that question,' said Manuela. 'The deeds, *this* morning?'

Angel Zarrías blinked into his pillow. He'd forgotten.

'Look, my darling,' he said, rolling over, 'you know that nothing happens, even if you think about it *all* the time. It only happens . . .'

'Yes, I know, Angel, it only happens when it happens.

But even you can understand that there's uncertainty *before* it happens.'

'But if you don't sleep and you churn it over in your head in an endless washing cycle it has no effect on the outcome, so you might as well forget about it. Handle the horror if it happens, but don't torture yourself with the theory of it.'

Manuela flicked through the pages of *Vogue* even more viciously, but she felt better. Angel could do that to her. He was older. He had authority. He had experience.

'It's all right for you,' she said, gently, 'you don't owe six hundred thousand euros to the bank.'

'But I also don't own nearly two million euros' worth of property.'

'I own one million eight hundred thousand euros' worth of property. I owe six hundred thousand to the bank. The lawyer's fees are . . . Forget it. Let's not talk about numbers. They make me sick. Nothing has any value until it's sold.'

'Which is what you're about to do,' said Angel, in his most solid, reinforced concrete voice.

'Anything can happen,' she said, turning a page so viciously she tore it.

'But it tends not to.'

'The market's nervous.'

'Which is why you're selling. Nobody's going to withdraw in the next eight hours,' he said, struggling to sit up in bed. 'Most people would kill to be in your position.'

'With two empty properties, no rent and four thousand a month going out?'

'Well, clearly I'm looking at it from a more advantageous perspective.'

Manuela liked this. However hard she tried, she couldn't get Angel to participate in her catalogue of imagined horrors. His objective authority made her feel quite girlish. She hadn't yet got to the point of recognizing what their relationship had become, how it fitted with her powerful needs. All she knew was that Angel was a colossal comfort to her.

'Relax,' said Angel, pulling her to him, kissing the top of her head.

'Wouldn't it be great to be able to compress time and just *be* in tomorrow evening now,' she said, snuggling up to him, 'with money in the bank and the summer free?'

'Let's have a celebratory dinner at Salvador Rojo tonight.'

'I was thinking that myself,' she said, 'but I was too superstitious to book it. We could ask Javier. He could bring Laura so you can have someone to flirt with.'

'How very considerate of you,' he said, kissing her head again.

When Angel and Manuela had met it seemed that the only thing holding her life together was her legal battle over Javier's right to have inherited the house in which he was living. They'd met in her lawyer's office, where Angel was sorting out his late wife's estate. As soon as they'd shaken hands she'd felt something cave in high up around her stomach and no man had ever done that to her before. They left the lawyer's office and went for a drink and, having never looked at older men, having always gone for 'boys', she immediately saw the point. Older men looked after you. You didn't have to look after them.

The more she found out about Angel the more she

fell for him. He was a phenomenally charming man, a committed politician (sometimes a little *too* committed), right wing, conservative, a Catholic, a lover of the bulls, and from an established family. In politics he'd been able to broker agreements between fanatically opposed factions just because neither party wanted to be disliked by him. He'd been 'someone' in the Partido Popular in Andalucía but had quit in a fury over the impossibility of getting anything to change. Recently he'd joined forces, in a public relations capacity, with a smaller right-wing party called Fuerza Andalucía, which was run by his old friend, Eduardo Rivero. He contributed a political column for the *ABC* newspaper and was also their highly respected bullfight commentator. With all these talents at his disposal it hadn't taken him long to bring Javier and Manuela back together again.

'All energy expended on court cases like yours is negative energy,' Angel had told her. 'That negative energy dominates your life, so that the rest of it has to go on hold. The only way to restart your life is to bring positive energy back into it.'

'And how do I do that?' she'd asked, looking at this huge source of positive energy in front of her with her big brown eyes.

'Court cases use up resources, not just financial ones, but physical and emotional ones, too. So you have to be productive,' he said. 'What do you want from your life at the moment?'

'That house!' she'd said, despite being pretty keen on Angel right then, too.

'It's yours, Javier has offered it to you.'

'There's the small matter of one million euros . . .'

'But he hasn't said you can't have it,' said Angel.

'And it's much more productive to make money in order to buy something you really want, than to throw it away on useless lawyers.'

'He's not useless,' she said, and ran out of steam.

There were a few thousand other reasons she had stacked up against Angel's stunningly simple logic, but the source of most of them was her miserable emotional state, which was not something she wanted to peel back for him to see. So, she agreed with him, sold her veterinary practice at the beginning of 2003, borrowed money against the property she had inherited in El Puerto de Santa Maria and invested it in Seville's booming property market. After three years of buying, renovating and selling she had forgotten about Javier's house, the court case and that hollow feeling at the top of her stomach. She now lived with Angel in a penthouse apartment overlooking the majestic, tree-lined Plaza Cristo de Burgos in the middle of the old city and her life was full and about to be even sweeter.

'How did it go last night?' asked Manuela. 'I can tell you wound up on the brandy.'

'Gah!' said Angel, wincing at some gripe in his intestines.

'No smoking for you until after coffee this morning.'

'Maybe my breath could become a cheap form of renewable energy,' said Angel, fingering some sleep out of his eye. 'In fact everyone's breath could, because all we do is spout hot, alcoholic air.'

'Is the master of positive energy getting a little bit bored with his cronies?'

'Not bored. They're my friends,' said Angel, shrugging. 'It's one of the advantages of age that we can tell each other the same stories over and over and still laugh.'

'Age is a state of mind, and you're still young,' said Manuela. 'Maybe you should go back to the commercial side of your public relations business. Forget politics and all those self-important fools.'

'And finally she reveals what she thinks of my closest friends.'

'I like your friends, it's just . . . the politics,' said Manuela. 'Endless talk but nothing ever happens.'

'Maybe you're right,' said Angel, nodding. 'The last time there was an event in this country was the horror of 11th March 2004, and look what happened: the whole country pulled together and by due process of democracy kicked out a perfectly good government. Then we bowed down to the terrorists and pulled out of Iraq. And after that? We sank back into the comfort of our lives.'

'And drank too much brandy.'

'Exactly,' said Angel, looking at her with his hair exploded in all directions. 'You know what someone was saying last night?'

'Was this the interesting bit?' she said, teasing him on.

'We need a return to benevolent dictatorship,' said Angel, throwing up his hands in mock exasperation.

'You might find yourselves out on a limb there,' said Manuela. 'People don't like turmoil with troops and tanks on the streets. They want a cold beer, a tapa and something stupid to watch on TV.'

'My point entirely,' said Angel, slapping his stomach. 'Nobody listened. We've got a population dying of decadence, so morally moribund that they no longer know what they want, apart from knee-jerk consumption, and my "cronies" think that they'll be *loved* if they do these people the favour of mounting a coup.'

'I don't want to see you on television, standing on a desk in Parliament with a gun in your hand.'

'I'll have to lose some weight first,' said Angel.

Calderón came to with a jolt and a sense of real panic left over from a dream he could not recollect. He was surprised to see Marisa's long brown back in the bed beside him, instead of Inés's white nightdress. He'd overslept. It was now 6 a.m. and he would have to go back to his apartment and deal with some very awkward questions from Inés.

His frantic leap from the bed woke Marisa. He dressed, shaking his head at the slug trails of dried semen on his thigh.

'Take a shower,' said Marisa.

'No time.'

'Anyway, she's not an idiot – *so* you tell me.'

'No, she's not,' said Calderón, looking for his other shoe, 'but as long as certain rules are obeyed then the whole thing can be glossed over.'

'This must be the bourgeois protocol for affairs outside marriage.'

'That's right,' said Calderón, irritated by her. 'You can't stay out all night because that is making a complete joke out of the institution.'

'What's the cut-off point between a "serious" marriage and a "joke" one?' asked Marisa. 'Three o'clock . . . three thirty? No. That's OK. I think by four o'clock it's ridiculous. By four thirty it is a complete joke. By six, six thirty . . . it's a farce.'

'By six it's a tragedy,' said Calderón, searching the floor madly. 'Where is my *fucking* shoe?'

'Under the chair,' said Marisa. 'And don't forget your camera on the coffee table. I've left a present or two on it for you.'

He threw on his jacket, pocketed the camera, dug his foot into his shoe.

'How did you find my camera?' he asked, kneeling down by the bed.

'I went through your jacket while you were asleep,' she said. 'I come from a bourgeois family; I kick against it, but I know all the tricks. Don't worry, I didn't erase all those stupid shots of your lawyers' dinner to prove to your very intelligent wife that you weren't out all night fucking your girlfriend.'

'Well, thanks very much for that.'

'And I haven't been naughty.'

'No?'

'I told you I left some presents on the camera for you. Just don't let her see.'

He nodded, suddenly in a hurry again. They kissed. Going down in the lift he tidied himself up, got everything tucked away and rubbed his face into life to prepare for the lie which he practised. Even he saw the two micro movements of his eyebrows, which Javier Falcón had told him was the first and surest sign of a liar. If he knew that, then Inés would know it, too.

No taxis out at this early hour of the morning. He should have called for one. He set off at a fast walk. Memories ricocheted around his mind, which seemed to dip in and out of his consciousness. The lie. The truth. The reality. The dream. And it came back to him with the same sense of panic he'd had on waking in

Marisa's apartment: his hands closing around Inés's slim throat. He was throttling her, but she wasn't turning puce or purple and her tongue wasn't thickening with blood and protruding. She was looking up at him with her eyes full of love. And, yes, she was stroking his forearms, encouraging him to do it. The bourgeois solution to awkward divorces – murder. Absurd. He knew from his work with the homicide squad that the first person to be grilled in a murder case was the spouse.

The streets were still wet from last night's rain, the cobbles greasy. He was sweating and the smell of Marisa came up off his shirt. It occurred to him that he'd never felt guilty. He didn't know what it was other than a legal state. Since he'd been married to Inés he'd had affairs with four women of whom Marisa had lasted the longest. He'd also had one-night stands or afternoons with two other women. And there was the prostitute in Barcelona, but he didn't like to think of that. He'd even had sex with one of these women whilst having an affair with another as a married man, which must make him a serial philanderer. Except it didn't feel like philandering. There was supposed to be something enjoyable about philandering. It was romantic, wasn't it . . . in the eighteenth-century sense of the word? But what he'd been doing was not enjoyable. He was trying to fill a hole, which, with every affair, grew bigger. So what was this expanding void? Now that would be a thing to answer, if he could ever find the time to think about it.

He slipped on a cobble, half fell, scuffed his hand on the pavement. It pulled him out of his head and on to more practical business. He'd have to have a shower as soon as he got in. Marisa was in his sinuses.

48

Maybe he should have had a shower before he left, but then there would have been the smell of Marisa's soap. Then another revelation. What did he care? Why the grand pretence? Inés knew. They'd had fights – never about his affairs, but about ridiculous stuff, which was a cover for the unmentionable. She could have got out. She could have left him years ago, but she'd stayed. That was significant.

The graze on his hand was stinging. His thoughts made him feel stronger. He wasn't afraid of Inés. She could strike fear into others. He'd seen her in court. But not him. He had the upper hand. He fucked around and she stayed.

His apartment block on Calle San Vicente appeared before him. He opened the door with a flourish. He didn't know whether it was the conclusion he'd arrived at, his stinging hand or the fact that he tripped up on the stairs because the decorators, those idle sods, had pushed their dustsheets to one side rather than clearing them away – but he began to feel just a little bit cruel.

The first-floor apartment was silent. It was 6.30 a.m. He went to his study and emptied the pockets of his suit on to his desk in the dark. He took off his jacket and trousers and left them on a chair and went to the bathroom. Inés was asleep. He stripped off his pants and socks, threw them in the laundry basket and showered.

Inés was *not* asleep. She lay with her shiny, dark eyes blinking in the sepia light as morning crept through the louvred shutters. She had been awake since 4.30 a.m. when she'd found her husband's side of the bed vacant. She'd sat up in bed, arms folded across her flat chest, her brain seething. She'd run the marathon of her thoughts for two hours, her insides molten with rage at the humiliation of finding his undented pillow. But then she would suddenly feel weak at the thought of facing this latest demonstration of his infidelity, because that's what it was – a demonstration.

In those hours she realized that the only area of her life that was functioning was her work, which now bored her. Not that the work had changed in any way, but her perspective had. She wanted to be a wife and mother. She wanted to live in a big old house with a patio, inside the city walls. She wanted to go for walks in the park, meet her friends for lunch, take her children to see her parents.

None of that had happened. After the American bitch had been removed from the scene, she and Esteban had come together, had, in her mind, grown closer. She had stopped using contraceptives without telling him, wanting to surprise him, but her periods kept coming with plodding regularity. She'd gone for a check-up and been pronounced a perfectly healthy female of the species. After sex one morning she'd saved a sample of his sperm and taken it for a fertility test. The result was that he was a man of exceptional virility. Had he known, he would have framed the result and hung it next to their wedding photograph.

The sale of her apartment had gone through quickly. She'd banked the money and started looking for her dream home. But Esteban loathed the houses that she wanted to buy and refused to look at them. The property market boomed. The money she'd got for her apartment now looked paltry. Her dream became an impossibility. They lived in his very masculine, aggressively modern apartment on the Calle San Vicente and he became angry if she tried to change a single detail. He wouldn't even let her put a chain on the door, but that was because he didn't want to have to be let in by her reeking of sex after a night out.

Their sex life began to falter. She knew he was having affairs from the tireless grind of his lovemaking and the paucity of his ejaculations. She tried to be more daring. He made her feel foolish, as if her proposed 'games' were ridiculous. Then suddenly he'd taken up her offer to 'play games' but given her debasing roles, seemingly inspired by internet porn. She subjected herself to his ministrations, hiding her pain and shame in the pillow.

At least she wasn't fat. She inspected herself minutely in the mirror every day. It satisfied her to see the deflation of her bust, her individual ribs and her concave thighs. Sometimes she would feel dizzy in court. Her friends told her she'd never get pregnant. She smiled at them, her pale skin stretched tight over her beautiful face, her aura frighteningly beatific.

Inés was toying with the idea of a massive confrontation when she heard Esteban put his key in the lock. Her stick-thin forearms seemed to have grown more hair and they made her feel curiously weak. She sank down into the bed and pretended to be asleep.

She heard him empty his pockets and go to the bathroom. The shower came on. She ran barefoot to his study, saw his suit and sniffed it over like a dog: cigarettes, perfume, old sex. Her eyes were riveted to the digital camera. She touched it with her knuckle. Still warm. She burned to know what was on its memory. The shower door rolled open. She ran back to bed and lay with her heart beating fast as a cat's.

His weight tipped her feather-light frame in the bed. She waited for his breathing to settle into the pattern that she knew was his sleep. Her heart slowed. Her mind cooled. She slid out of the bed. He didn't move. In the study she pressed the camera's quick-view button and caught her breath as a miniature Marisa appeared on the screen. She was naked on the sofa, legs apart, hands covering her pubis. Inés pressed again. Marisa naked, kneeling and looking backwards over her shoulder. The whore. She pressed again and again and only found her husband's alibi of the judges' dinner. She went back to the whore. Who was she? The black bitch. She had to know.

Inés's laptop was in the hall. She took it into the kitchen and booted it up. In the grey-bar time she went back to his study and scoured the shelves for the download lead. Back to the kitchen. Opened up the camera, plugged in the lead, connected it to her laptop. Total concentration.

The icon appeared on the screen. The software automatically loaded. She clicked on 'import' and clenched her fist as she saw she was going to have to download fifty-four shots to get the ones she wanted. She stared at the screen, willing it to process faster. She heard only the breathing of the computer's fan and the flickering of the hard disk. She didn't hear the bedclothes stir. She didn't hear his bare foot on the wooden floor. She didn't even hear his question properly.

His voice did turn her round. She was conscious of her cotton nightdress on the points of her shoulders, its hem brushing the tops of her thighs, as she took in the full-frontal nudity of her husband standing in the frame of the kitchen door.

'What's going on?' he asked.

'What?' said Inés, her eyes unable to look anywhere other than his treacherous genitals.

He repeated his question.

The adrenaline spike was so powerful she wasn't sure that her heart could cope with the sudden surge.

After nearly twenty years' experience in the criminal element Calderón could recognize terror when he saw it. The wide eyes, the mouth neither open nor closed, the paralysed facial muscles.

'What's going on?' he asked, for a third time but with no sleep in his voice, pure weight.

'Nothing,' she said, keeping her back to the laptop, but unable to stop the reflex action of her arms fanning out to prevent him from seeing her laptop.

Calderón swept her aside, not roughly, but she was so light she had to stop her fragile ribs from cracking against the edge of the black granite work surface. He saw his camera, the lead, the thumbnails of the lawyers' dinner appearing in the photo library. And then plink, plink. Two shots of Marisa: *My present to you*. It was embarrassing, incriminating and worse: it was the little boy being found out.

'Who is she?' asked Inés, her finger ends white against the black granite.

His look was murderous and in no way offset by the ridiculousness of his nudity.

'Who is she, that you can stay out all night, leaving your wife alone in the marital bed?'

The words incensed him, which was Inés's calculation. Her fear had vanished. She wanted something from him – his concentrated attention.

'Who is she, that you can whore with her until six in the morning, in defiance of your marital vows?'

Another calculated sentence, using some of the oratory she employed in court.

He turned on her, with the slow intent of an animal who's found a rival on his territory. The thickness around his belly, the shrivelled penis, the slim thighs should have made him laughable, but his head was dipped down and his eyes looked up from under his brow. His rage was palpable. Still Inés couldn't help herself. The taunts leapt from her lips.

'Do you fuck her like you fuck me? Do you make her shout with pain?'

Inés did not finish because she was unaccountably on the floor, with her feet pedalling against the white marble tiles, trying to fight air back into her lungs. She focused on his toes, the knuckles crimped as they gripped. He kicked her. His big toe invaded her kidney. She bit on air. She was shocked. It was the first time he'd ever hit her. She'd provoked him. She'd wanted a reaction. But she had been shocked by his restraint. She'd thought he would lash out, backhand her across the face to shut that taunting uxorial mouth, fatten her lip, bruise her cheek. She wanted to wear the badge of his violence to show the world what he was really like and draw some daily remorse from him until the damage faded. But he'd hit her under the arch of her ribs, kicked her in the side.

Her chest creaked as she found the motor memory to breathe again. She felt her husband's hand at the back of her head, stroking. You see, he did love her. Now for the remorse and the tenderness. This was just another fling . . . But he wasn't stroking her, he was reaching into her hair, he was sheafing it. His nails dug into her scalp. He shook her head as if she were a dog, caught by the scruff, and stood up from his crouch. She hadn't found her feet and she hung from his hand. He dragged her from the kitchen, hauled her down the corridor and flung her at the bed. She bounced and rolled off to the side. Three strides and he was on her again. She scrambled under the bed.

It hadn't worked out as she'd thought. His hand reached for her under the bed, grabbing at her night-dress. She flinched away from it. His face appeared, hideous with rage. He stood up. His feet moved off. She watched them, as if they were loaded weapons. They left the room. He swore and slammed the door. Her scalp burned. Her fear was overriding all other emotions. She couldn't scream, she couldn't cry.

Under the bed was good. There were childhood memories of safety, of observing in secrecy, but they couldn't contain her confusion. Her brain lunged at what she wanted to be certainties, but they wouldn't support her. Instead she found herself trying to accommodate his behaviour. She had proved his infidelity to him. She had humiliated him. He was angry because he felt guilty. That was natural. You lashed out at the one you loved. That was it, wasn't it? He didn't want to be whoring with that black bitch. He just couldn't help himself. He was an alpha male, a virile, high-octane performer. She shouldn't be so hard on him. She held on to her side and squeezed her eyes shut at a jab of pain in her kidney.

The door swung open, the feet came back into the room. His presence made her shrink. He took fresh socks and pants from the drawer and put them on. He stepped into a pair of trousers and took a crisp, white shirt, ironed by the laundry where he still sent his clothes. He shook it out and drove his arms into the sleeves, shot the cuffs. He whipped a crimson tie into a perfect knot. He was efficient, vigorous and precise. He rammed those brutal feet into a pair of shoes, threw on a jacket – his savagery now perfectly disguised.

'I'm working late tonight,' he said, his tone back to normal.

The apartment door clicked shut. Inés crawled out from under the bed and flopped against the wall. She sat with her legs splayed out, her hands helpless by her sides. The first sob jolted her away from the wall.

5

Falcón came to in the profound darkness of his shuttered bedroom. He lay there in his private universe, contemplating last night's events. After the disappointment at Consuelo's restaurant the drink with Laura had gone better than expected. They'd agreed to see each other as friends. She was only a little offended that he was ending their affair with, as he'd told her, no other prospect in sight.

He showered and put on a dark suit and white shirt and folded a tie into his pocket. He had meetings planned all morning after he'd been to see the Médico Forense. It was a morning of shimmering brilliance, with not a cloud in the sky. The rain had cleansed the atmosphere of all that puzzling electricity.

A temperature gauge outside in the street told him it was 16°C while the radio warned that a great heat was about to descend on Seville and by evening they should expect temperatures in excess of 36°C.

The Forensic Institute was next to the Hospital de la Macarena behind the Andalucían Parliament, which itself looked across the road to the Basilica de la

Macarena, just inside the old city walls. At 8.15 a.m. Falcón was early, but the Médico Forense had already arrived.

Dr Pintado had the file open on his desk and was reminding himself of the detail of the autopsy. They shook hands, sat down and he resumed his reading.

'What I concentrated on in this case,' he said, still scanning the pages, 'apart from the cause of death, which was straightforward – he was poisoned with potassium cyanide – was giving you as much help as possible on the identification of the body.'

'Potassium cyanide?' said Falcón. 'That's not exactly in keeping with the ruthlessness of the post-mortem operations. Was it injected?'

'No, ingested,' said Pintado, other things on his mind. 'The face . . . I might be able to help you with that, or rather I have a friend who is interested in helping. You remember I was telling you about a case I handled in Bilbao, where they made a facial model from a skull found in a shallow grave?'

'It cost a fortune.'

'That's right, and you don't get resources like that for any old murder.'

'So how much does your friend cost?'

'He's free.'

'And who is he?'

'He's a sort of sculptor, but he's not that interested in the body, just faces.'

'Would I have heard of him?'

'No. He's strictly amateur. His name is Miguel Covo. He's seventy-four years old and retired,' said Pintado. 'But he's been working with faces for nearly sixty years. He builds them out of clay, makes moulds for wax, and carves them out of stone, although that's quite a recent development.'

'What's he proposing and why is it free?'

'Well, he's never done this kind of thing before, but he wants to try,' said Pintado. 'I let him take a plaster cast of the head last night.'

'OK, so there's no decision,' said Falcón.

'He'll make up a half-dozen models, do some sketches and then start working up the face. He'll paint it, too, and give it hair – real hair. His studio can give you the creeps, especially if he likes you and introduces you to his mother.'

'I've always got on well with mothers.'

'He keeps her in a cupboard,' said Dr Pintado. 'Just a model of her, I mean.'

'It would be cruel to keep a woman in her nineties in a cupboard.'

'She died when he was small, which was when his fascination with faces started. He wanted the photographs of her to be more real. So he recreated her. It was the only time he fashioned a body. She's in that cupboard with real hair, make-up, her own clothes and shoes.'

'So, he's weird, too?'

'Of course he is,' said Pintado, 'but likeably weird. You might not want to invite him to dinner with the Comisario and his wife, though.'

'Why not?' said Falcón. 'It would make a change from the opera.'

'Anyway, he'll call you when he has something, but . . . not tomorrow.'

'What else have you got?'

'It's all helpful, but not as helpful as a physical image,'

said Pintado. 'I worked with a guy who did forensics on mass graves in Bosnia and I learnt a bit from him. The first thing is dental. I've made a full set of digital X-rays and notes about each tooth. He's had extensive orthodontic work done to get the teeth all straight and looking perfect.'

'How old is this guy?'

'Mid forties.'

'And normally you'd have that sort of work done in your early teens.'

'Exactly.'

'And there wasn't a lot of orthodontic work being done in Spain in the mid seventies.'

'Most likely it was done in America,' said Pintado. 'Apart from that, there's nothing much else to go on, dentally. He's had no major work done, and only a molar missing on the lower right side.'

'Have you found any distinguishing marks on the outside of the body – moles, birthmarks?'

'No, but I did come across something interesting on his hands.'

'Forgive me, Doctor, but . . .'

'I know. They were severed. But I checked the lymph nodes to see what was deposited there,' said Pintado. 'I'm sure our friend had a small tattoo on each hand.'

'I don't suppose there's a snapshot of it in the lymph node?' asked Falcón.

'Lymph nodes are quite clever about killing bacteria and neutralizing toxins, but their talent for recreating images from tattoo ink, introduced into the bloodstream via the hand, is extremely limited. There was a trace of ink and that was all.'

'What about surgery?'

'There's good news and bad there,' said Pintado. 'He's had surgery, but it was a hernia operation, which is just about the world's most common procedure. His was also the most common type of inguinal hernia, so he has a scar on the right side of his pubis. I'd guess it was about three years old, but I'll get one of the vascular surgeons to come over and confirm that for me. Then we'll take a look at the mesh they used to patch the hernia and hopefully he'll be able to tell me who supplied it, then you can find the hospitals *they* supply . . . and, I know, it's going to take a lot of work and time.'

'Maybe he had that done in America as well,' said Falcón.

'Like I said: good news and bad.'

'What about his hair?' asked Falcón. 'They scalped him.'

'He had hair that was at least long enough to cover his collar.'

'How do you get that?'

'He's been on the beach this year,' said Pintado, turning some photographs around for Falcón to look at. 'You can see the tan lines on his arms and legs, but if you turn him over you don't see any tan line at the back of his neck. In fact, if you look, it's quite white compared to the rest of his back, which to me means that it rarely sees the sun.'

'Would you describe him as "white"?' asked Falcón. 'His skin colour didn't look Northern European to me.'

'No. He's olive-skinned.'

'Do you think he was Spanish?'

'Without doing any genetic testing, I would say that he was Mediterranean.'

'Any scars?'

'Nothing significant,' said Pintado. 'He'd sustained a fracture to his skull, but it's years old.'

'Anything interesting about the structure of his body that would give us an idea of what he did?'

'Well, he wasn't a bodybuilder,' said Pintado. 'Spine, shoulder and elbows indicate a deskbound, sedentary life. I'd say that his feet didn't spend much time in shoes. The heels are more splayed than usual, with a lot of hardened skin.'

'As you said, he liked the sun,' said Falcón.

'He also smoked cannabis and I would say he was a regular user, which could be thought of as unusual in someone in his mid forties,' said Pintado. 'Kids smoke dope, but if you're still doing it in your forties it's because it's your milieu . . . you're an artist, or a musician, or hanging out with that sort of crowd.'

'So he's a desk worker with long hair, who spent time in the sun, not wearing shoes, and smoking dope.'

'A hard-working hippy.'

'They might have been like that in the seventies, but it's not the profile of a modern-day drug smuggler,' said Falcón. 'And potassium cyanide would be an unusual method of execution for people with 9mm handguns in their waistbands.'

The two men sat back from the desk. Falcón flicked through the photographs from the file hoping that something else might jump out at him. He was already thinking about the university and the Bellas Artes, but he didn't want to confine himself at this early stage.

In this momentary silence the two men looked up at each other, as if they were on the brink of the same idea. From beyond the grey walls of the Facultad de

Medicina came the unmistakable boom of a significant explosion, not far away.

Gloria Alanis was ready for work. By this time she would normally be on her way to her first client meeting, thinking how much, as it receded in the rear-view mirror, she hated the drab seventies apartment block where she lived in the barrio of El Cerezo. She was a sales rep for a stationery company but her area of operation was Huelva. On the first Tuesday of every month there was a meeting of the sales team at the head office in Seville, followed by a team-building exercise, a lunch and then a mini-conference to show and discuss new products and promotions.

It meant that for one day during the month, she could put breakfast on the table for her husband and two children. She could also take her eight-year-old daughter, Lourdes, to school, while her husband delivered their three-year-old son, Pedro, to the pre-school which was visible from the back window of their fifth-floor apartment.

On this morning, instead of hating her apartment, she was looking down on the heads of her children and husband and feeling an unusual sensation of warmth and affection early in the week. Her husband sensed this, grabbed her and pulled her on to his lap.

'Fernando,' she said, warning him, in case he tried anything too salacious in front of the children.

'I was thinking,' he whispered in her ear, his lips tickling her lobe.

'It's always dangerous when you start doing that,' she said, smiling at the children, who were now interested.

'I was thinking there should be more of us,' he whispered. 'Gloria, Fernando, Lourdes, Pedro and . . .'

'You're crazy,' she said, loving those lips on her ear, saying these things.

'We always talked about having four, didn't we?'

'But that was before we knew how much two cost,' she said. 'Now we work all day and still don't have enough money to get out of this apartment or take a holiday.'

'I have a secret,' he said.

She knew he didn't.

'If it's a lottery ticket, I don't want to see it.'

'It's not a lottery ticket.'

She knew what it was: wild hope.

'My God,' he said, suddenly looking at his watch. 'Hey, Pedro, we've got to get going, man.'

'Tell us the secret,' said the children.

He lifted Gloria up and put her on her feet.

'If I tell you that, it's not a secret any more,' he said. 'You have to wait for the secret to be revealed.'

'Tell us now!'

'This evening,' he said, kissing Lourdes on the head and taking Pedro's tiny hand.

Gloria went to the door with them. She kissed Pedro, who was staring at his feet, and not much interested. She kissed her husband on the mouth and whispered on his lips:

'I hate you.'

'By this evening you'll love me again.'

She went back to the breakfast table and sat opposite Lourdes. There were another fifteen minutes before they had to leave. They spent a few minutes looking at one of Lourdes' drawings before going to the window.

Fernando and Pedro appeared below in the car park in front of the pre-school. They waved. Fernando held Pedro above his head and he waved back.

Having delivered the boy to school, Fernando walked off between the apartment blocks to the main road to catch the bus to work. Gloria turned back into the room. Lourdes was already at the table working on another drawing. Gloria sipped her coffee and played with her daughter's silky hair. Fernando and his secrets. He played these games to keep them amused and their hopes up that they would eventually be able to buy their own apartment, but the property prices had exploded and they now knew that they would be renting for the rest of their lives. Gloria was never going to be anything other than a rep and, though Fernando kept saying he was going to take a plumbing course, he still needed to make the money he did as a labourer on the construction site. They'd been lucky to find this apartment with such a cheap rent. They were lucky to have two healthy children. As Fernando said: 'We might not be rich, but we *are* lucky and luck will serve us better than all the money in the world.'

She didn't immediately associate the shuddering tremor beneath her feet with the booming crash that came from the outside world. It was a noise so loud that her rib cage seemed to clutch at her spine and drive the air out of her lungs. The coffee cup jumped out of her hand and broke on the floor.

'MAMÁ!' screamed Lourdes, but there was nothing for Gloria to hear, she saw only her daughter's wide-eyed horror and grabbed her.

Terrible things happened simultaneously. Windows shattered. Cracks and giant fissures opened up in the walls. Daylight appeared where it shouldn't. Level horizons tilted. Doorframes folded. Solid concrete flexed. The ceiling crowded the floor. Walls broke in half. Water spurted from nowhere. Electricity crackled and sparked under broken tiles. A wardrobe shot out of sight. Gravity showed them its remorselessness. Mother and daughter were falling. Their small, fragile bodies were hurtling downwards in a miasma of bricks, steel, concrete, wire, tubing, furniture and dust. There was no time for words. There was no sound, because the sound was already so loud it rendered everything else silent. There wasn't even any fear, because it had all become grossly incomprehensible. There was just the sickening plummet, the stunning impact and then a vast blackness, as of a great receding universe.

'What the fuck was that?' said Pintado.

Falcón knew exactly what it was. He'd heard an ETA car bomb explode when he was working in Barcelona. This sounded big. He kicked back his chair and ran out of the Institute without replying to Pintado's question. He punched the Jefatura's number into his mobile as he left. His first thought was that it was something in the Santa Justa station, the high-speed AVE arriving from Madrid. The railway station was less than a kilometre away to the southeast of the hospital.

'*Diga*,' said Ramírez.

'There's been a bomb, José Luis . . .'

'I heard it even out here,' said Ramírez.

'I'm at the Institute. It sounded close. Get me some news.'

'Hold it.'

Falcón ran past the receptionist, the mobile pressed

to his ear, listening to Ramírez's feet pounding down the corridor and up the stairs and people shouting in the Jefatura. The traffic had stopped everywhere. Drivers and passengers were getting out of their cars, looking to the northeast at a plume of black smoke.

'The reports we're getting,' said Ramírez, panting, 'is that there's been an explosion in an apartment block on the corner of Calle Blanca Paloma and Calle Los Romeros in the barrio of El Cerezo.'

'Where's that? I don't know it. It must be close because I can see the smoke.'

Ramírez found a wall map and gave rapid instructions.

'Is there any report of a gas leak?' asked Falcón, knowing this was wildly optimistic, like the so-called power surge on the day of the London underground bombings.

'I'm checking the gas company.'

Falcón sprinted through the hospital. People were running, but there was no panic, no shouting. They had been training for this moment. Everyone in a white coat was making for the casualty department. Orderlies were sprinting with empty trolleys. Nurses ran with boxes of saline. Plasma was on the move. Falcón slammed through endless double doors until he hit the main street and the wall of sound: a cacophony of sirens as ambulances swung out into the street.

The main road was miraculously clear of traffic. As he crossed the empty lanes he saw cars pulling up on to pavements. There were no police. This was the work of ordinary citizens, who knew that this stretch of road had to be kept clear to ferry the wounded. Ambulances careered down the street two abreast, whooping and delirious, with lights flashing queasily, in air that was filling with a grey/pink dust and smoke that billowed out from behind the apartment blocks.

At the crossroads bloodstained people stumbled about on their own or were being carried, or walked towards the hospital with handkerchiefs, tissues and kitchen roll held to foreheads, ears and cheeks. These were the superficially wounded victims, the ones sliced by flying glass and metal, the ones some distance from the epicentre, who would never make it into the top flight of disaster statistics but who might lose the sight in an eye, or their hearing from perforated eardrums, bear facial scars for the rest of their lives, lose the use of a finger or a hand, never walk again without a limp. They were being helped by the lucky ones, those who didn't even have a scratch as the air whistled with flying glass, but who had the images burned on to their minds of someone they knew or loved who had been whole seconds before and was now sliced, torn, bludgeoned or broken.

In the blocks of flats leading up to Calle Los Romeros, the local police were evacuating the buildings. An old man in bloody pyjamas was being led by a boy, who had realized his importance. A young man holding a crimson-flashed towel to the side of his head stared through Falcón, his face horribly partitioned by rivulets of blood, coagulating with dust. He had his arm around his girlfriend, who appeared unhurt and was talking at full tilt into her mobile phone.

The air, more dust-filled by the moment, was still splintering to the sound of breaking glass as it fell from high shattered windows. Falcón called Ramírez again and told him to organize three or four buses to act as improvised ambulances to ferry the lightly wounded from all these blocks of apartments down the road to the hospital.

'The gas company have confirmed that they supply buildings in that area,' said Ramírez, 'but there's been no report of a leak and they ran a routine test on that block only last month.'

'For some reason this doesn't feel like a gas explosion,' said Falcón.

'We're getting reports that a pre-school behind the destroyed building has been badly damaged by flying debris and there are casualties.'

Falcón pressed on up through the walking wounded. There were still no signs of serious damage to buildings, but the people floating around, calling and looking for family members in the spaces at the foot of the emptying apartment blocks were phantasmal, dust-covered, not themselves. The light had turned strange, as the sun was scarfed by smoke and a reddish fog. There was a smell in the air, which was not immediately recognizable to anyone who didn't know war. It clogged the nostrils with powdered brick and concrete, raw sewage, open drains and a disgusting meatiness. The atmosphere was vibrant, but not with any discernible sound, although people were making noise – talking, coughing, vomiting and groaning – it was more of an airborne tinnitus, brought about by a collective human alarm at the proximity of death.

Lines of fire engines, lights flashing, were backed up all the way to Avenida San Lazaro. There wasn't a pane of intact glass in the apartment buildings on the other side of Calle Los Romeros. A bottle bank was sticking out of the side of one of the blocks like a huge green plug. A wall that ran down the street opposite the stricken building had been blown on to its back and cars were piled up in a garden, as if it was a scrapyard. The torn stumps of four trees lined the road. Other vehicles parked on Calle Los Romeros were buried under rubble: roofs crumpled, windscreens opaque, tyres blown out, wheel trims off. There were clothes strewn everywhere, as if there'd been a laundry drop from the sky. A length of chain-link fencing hung from a fourth-floor balcony.

Firemen had clambered up the nearest cascade of rubble and had their hoses trained on the two remaining sections of what had been a complete L-shaped building. What was now missing was a twenty-five-metre segment from the middle of it. The colossal explosion had brought down all eight floors of the block, to form a stack of reinforced concrete pancakes to a height of about six metres. Framed by the ragged remains of the eight floors of apartments, and just visible through the mist of falling dust, was the roof of the partially devastated pre-school and the apartment blocks beyond, whose façades were patched with black and gaping glassless windows. A fireman appeared on the edge of a broken room on the eighth floor and in the war-torn air made a sign to show that the building was now clear of people. A bed fell from the sixth floor, its frame crunched into the piled debris, while its mattress bounced off wildly in the direction of the pre-school.

On the other side of the rubble, further down Calle Los Romeros, was the Fire Chief's car but no sign of any officers. Falcón walked along the collapsed wall and made his way around the block to see what had happened to the pre-school. The end of the building closest to the explosion had lost two walls, part of the roof had collapsed and the rest was hanging, ready to drop. Firemen and civilians were propping the roof, while unblinking women stared on in appalled silence, hands holding their faces as if to stop them from dropping off in disbelief.

On the other side, at the entrance to the school, it was worse. Four small bodies lay side by side, their faces covered with school pinafores. A large group of men and women were trying to control two of the mothers of the dead children. Covered in dust they were like ghosts, fighting for the right to go back to the living. The women were screaming hysterically and clawing madly against hands trying to prevent them from reaching the inert bodies. Another woman had fainted and was lying on the ground, surrounded by people kneeling to protect her from the swaying and surging crowd. Falcón looked around for a teacher and saw a young woman sitting on a mat of broken glass, blood trickling down the side of her face, weeping uncontrollably, while a friend tried to console the inconsolable. A paramedic arrived to give her wounds some temporary dressing.

'Are you a teacher?' asked Falcón, of the woman's friend. 'Do you know where the mother of the fourth child is?'

The woman, dazed, looked across at the collapsed apartment block.

'She's in there somewhere,' she said, shaking her head.

Only firemen moved around inside the pre-school, their boots crunching over debris and glass. More props came in to support the shattered roof. The Fire Chief was in an undamaged classroom at the back of the school, giving a report to the Mayor's office on his mobile.

'All gas and electricity to the area has been cut off and the damaged building has been evacuated. Two fires have been brought under control,' he said. 'We've pulled four dead children out of the pre-school. Their classroom was in the direct path of the explosion and took its full force. So far we've had reports of three other deaths: two men and a woman who were walking along Calle Los Romeros when the explosion occurred. My men have also found a woman who seems to have died from a heart attack in one of the apartment blocks opposite the destroyed building. It's too difficult to say how many wounded there are at the moment.'

He listened for a moment longer and closed down the phone. Falcón showed his ID.

'You're here very early, Inspector Jefe,' said the Fire Chief.

'I was in the Forensic Institute. It sounded like a bomb from there. Is that what you think?'

'To do that sort of damage, there's no doubt in my mind that it was a bomb, and a very powerful one at that.'

'Any idea how many people were in that building?'

'I've got one of my officers working on that at the moment. There were at least seven,' he said. 'The only thing we can't be sure of is how many were in the mosque in the basement.'

'The mosque?'

'That's the other reason why I'm sure this was a

bomb,' said the Fire Chief. 'There was a mosque in the basement, with access from Calle Los Romeros. We think that morning prayers had just finished, but we're not sure if anyone had left. We're getting conflicting reports on that from the outside.'

6

Desperation had brought Consuelo to Calle Vidrio early. The children were being taken to school by her neighbour. Now she was sitting in her car outside Alicia Aguado's consulting room, getting cold feet about the emergency appointment she'd arranged only twenty-five minutes earlier. She walked the street to calm her nerves. She was not someone who had things wrong with her.

At precisely 8.30 a.m., having stared at the second hand of her watch, chipping away at the seconds – which showed her how obsessive she was becoming – she rang the doorbell. Dr Aguado was waiting for her, as she had been for many months. She was excited at the prospect of this new patient. Consuelo walked up the narrow stairs to the consulting room, which had been painted a pale blue and was kept at a constant temperature of 22°C.

Although Consuelo knew everything about Alicia Aguado, she let the clinical psychologist explain that she was now blind due to a degenerative disease called retinitis pigmentosa and that as a result of this disability

74

she had developed a unique technique of reading a patient's pulse.

'Why do you need to do that?' asked Consuelo, knowing the answer, but wanting to put off the moment when they got down to work.

'Because I'm blind I miss out on the most important indicators of the human body, which is physiognomy. We speak more to each other with our features and bodies than we do with our mouths. Think how little you would glean from a conversation just by hearing words. Only if someone was in an extreme state, such as fear or anxiety, would you understand what they were feeling, whereas if you have a face and body you pick up on a whole range of subtleties. You can tell the difference between someone who is lying, or exaggerating, someone who's bored, and someone who wants to go to bed with you. Reading the pulse, which I learnt from a Chinese doctor and have adapted to my needs, enables me to pick up on nuance.'

'That sounds like an intelligent way of saying that you're a human polygraph.'

'I don't just detect lies,' said Aguado. 'It's more to do with undercurrents. Translating feeling into language can defeat even the greatest of writers, so why should it be any easier for an ordinary person to tell me about their emotions, especially if they're in a confused state?'

'This is a beautiful room,' said Consuelo, already shying away from some of the words she'd heard in Aguado's explanation. Undercurrents reminded her of her fears, of being dragged out into the ocean to die of exhaustion alone in a vast heaving expanse.

'There was too much noise,' said Aguado. 'You know how it is in Seville. Noise was becoming so much of a distraction for me, in my state, that I had the room double-glazed and soundproofed. It used to be white, but I think my patients found white as intimidating as black. So I opted for tranquil blue. Let's sit down, shall we?'

They sat in the S-shaped lovers' seat, facing each other. She showed Consuelo the tape recorder in the armrest, explaining that it was the only way for her to review her consultations. Aguado asked her to introduce herself, give her age and any medication she was on so that she could check it was recording properly.

'Can you give me a brief medical history?'

'Since when?'

'Anything significant since you were born – operations, serious illnesses, children . . . that sort of thing.'

Consuelo tried to drink the tranquillity of the pale blue walls into her mind. She had been hoping for some miraculous surgical strike on her mental disturbances, a fabulous technique to yank open the tangled mess and smooth it out into comprehensible strands. In her turmoil it hadn't occurred to her that this was going to be a process, an intrusive process.

'You seem to be struggling with this question,' said Aguado.

'I'm just coming to terms with the fact that you're going to turn me inside out.'

'Nothing leaves this room,' said Aguado. 'We can't even be heard. The tapes are locked up in a safe in my office.'

'It's not that,' said Consuelo. 'I hate to vomit. I would rather sweat out my nausea than vomit up the problem. This is going to be mental vomiting.'

'Most people who arrive at my side are here because

of something intensely private, so private that it might even be a secret from themselves,' said Aguado. 'Mental health and physical health are not dissimilar. Untreated wounds fester and infect the whole body. Untreated lesions of the mind are no different. The only difficulty is that you can't just show me the infected cut. You might not know what, or where, it is. The only way for us to find out is by bringing things from the subconscious to the surface of the conscious mind. It's not vomiting. It's not expelling poison. You bring perhaps painful things to the surface, so that we can examine them, but they remain yours. If anything, it's *more* like sweating out your nausea than vomiting.'

'I've had two abortions,' said Consuelo, decisively. 'The first in 1980, the second in 1984. Both were performed in a London clinic. I have had three children. Ricardo in 1992, Matías in 1994 and Darío in 1998. Those are the only five occasions I have been in hospital.'

'Are you married?'

'Not any more. My husband died,' said Consuelo, stumbling over this first obstacle, used to obfuscation of the fact, rather than natural openness. 'He was murdered in 2001.'

'Was that a happy marriage?'

'He was thirty-four years older than me. I didn't know this at the time, but he married me because I reminded him physically of his first wife, who had committed suicide. I didn't want to marry him, but he was insistent. I only agreed when he said that he would give me children. Quite soon after the marriage he found out, or allowed himself to realize, that my likeness to his wife stopped at the physical. We still stayed

77

together. We respected each other, especially in business. He was a diligent father. But as for loving me, making me happy . . . no.'

'Did you hear that?' asked Aguado. 'Something outside. A big noise, like an explosion.'

'I didn't hear anything.'

'I know about your husband's case, of course,' said Aguado. 'It was truly terrible. That must have been very traumatic for you and the children.'

'It was. But it's not directly linked to why I'm sitting here,' said Consuelo. 'That investigation was necessarily intrusive. I was a prime suspect. He was a wealthy, influential man. I had a lover. The police believed I had a motive. My life was turned inside out by the investigation. Nasty details of my past were revealed.'

'Such as?'

'I had appeared in a pornographic movie when I was seventeen to raise money to pay for my first abortion.'

Aguado forced Consuelo to relive that ugly slice of her life in great detail and didn't let her stop until she'd explained the circumstances of the next pregnancy, with a duke's son, which had led to the second abortion.

'What do you think of pornography?' asked Alicia.

'I abhor it,' said Consuelo. 'I especially abhorred my need to be involved in it, in order to find the money to terminate a pregnancy.'

'What do you think pornography is?'

'The filming of the biological act of sex.'

'Is that all?'

'It is sex without emotion.'

'You described quite strong emotions when you were telling me –'

'Of disgust and revulsion, yes.'

'For your partners in the movie?'

'No, no, not at all,' said Consuelo. 'We were all in the same boat, us girls. And the men needed us to perform. It's not a highly sexually charged atmosphere on a porn set. We were all high on dope, to help us get over what we were doing.'

Consuelo's enthusiasm for her account waned. She wasn't getting to the point.

'So who were these strong feelings of anger aimed at?' asked Aguado.

'Myself,' said Consuelo, hoping that this partial truth might be enough.

'When I asked you what pornography was, I don't believe you were telling me what *you* actually thought,' said Aguado. 'You were giving me a socially acceptable version. Try answering that question again.'

'It's sex without love,' said Consuelo, hammering the chair. 'It's the *antithesis* of love.'

'The antithesis of love is hate.'

'It's self-hate.'

'What else?'

'It's the desecration of sex.'

'What do you think of men and women being filmed having sex with multiple partners?' asked Aguado.

'It's perverted.'

'What else?'

'What do you mean, "what else"? I don't know *what else* you want.'

'How often have you thought about the movie since it came to light in your husband's murder investigation?'

'I forgot about it.'

'Until today?'

'What's that supposed to mean?'

'This isn't a social situation, Sra Jiménez.'

'I realize *that*.'

'You mustn't be concerned with what I think of you in that respect,' said Aguado.

'But I don't know what you're trying to get me to admit.'

'Why are we talking about pornography?'

'It was something that came to light in my husband's murder investigation.'

'I asked you whether your husband's murder had been traumatic,' said Aguado.

'I see.'

'What do you see?'

'That the movie coming to light was more traumatic for me than my husband's death.'

'Not necessarily. It was bound up in a traumatic event, and in that highly emotionally charged period it made its mark on you.'

Consuelo struggled in silence. The tangled mess was not unravelling but becoming even more confused.

'You've made appointments with me several times recently and you've never appeared for them,' said Aguado. 'Why did you come this morning?'

'I love my children,' said Consuelo. 'I love my children so much it hurts.'

'Where does it hurt?' asked Aguado, leaping on to this new revelation.

'You've never had children?'

Alicia Aguado shrugged.

'It hurts me in the top of my stomach, around my diaphragm.'

'Why does it hurt?'

'Can't you ever just accept something?' said Consuelo. 'I love them. It hurts.'

'We're here to examine your inner life. I can't feel it or see it. All I have to go on is how you express yourself.'

'And the pulse thing?'

'That's what raises the questions,' said Aguado. 'What you say and what I feel in your blood don't always match up.'

'Are you telling me I *don't* love my children?'

'No, I'm asking you why you say it hurts. What is causing you the pain?'

'*Joder!* It's the fucking love that hurts, you stupid bitch,' said Consuelo, tearing her wrist away, ripping her blabbing pulse out from under those questioning fingertips. 'I'm sorry. I'm really sorry. That was unforgivable.'

'Don't be sorry,' said Aguado. 'This is no cocktail party.'

'You're telling me,' said Consuelo. 'Look, I've always been very firm about telling the truth. My children will confirm that.'

'This is a different type of truth.'

'There is only *one* truth,' said Consuelo, with missionary zeal.

'There's the real truth, and the presentable truth,' said Aguado. 'They're often quite close together, but for a few emotional details.'

'You've got me wrong there, Doctor. I'm not like that. I've seen things, I've done things and I've faced up to them all.'

'That *is* why you're here.'

'You're calling me a liar and a coward. You're telling me I don't know who I am.'

'I'm asking questions, and you're doing your best to answer them.'

'But you've just told me that what I'm saying and what you're feeling in my pulse don't match. Therefore, you are calling me a liar.'

'I think we've had enough for today,' said Aguado. 'That's a lot of ground to have covered in the first session. I'd like to see you again very soon. Is this a good time of day for you? The morning or late afternoon is probably the best time in the restaurant business.'

'You think I'm coming back for any more of this shit?' said Consuelo, heading for the door, swinging her bag over her shoulder. 'Think again . . . blind bitch!'

She slammed the door on the way out and nearly went over on her heel in the cobbled street. She got into her car, jammed the keys into the ignition, but didn't start the engine. She hung on to the steering wheel, as if it was the only thing that would stop her falling off the edge of her sanity. She cried. She cried until it hurt in exactly the same place as it did when she was watching her children sleeping.

Angel and Manuela were sitting out on the roof terrace in the early-morning sunshine, having breakfast. Manuela sat in a white towelling robe examining her toes. Angel blinked with irritation as he read one of his articles in the *ABC*.

'They've cut a whole paragraph,' said Angel. 'Some stupid sub-editor is making my journalism look like the work of a fool.'

'I can hear myself getting fat,' said Manuela, barely thinking, her whole being consumed by the business that was to take place later that morning. 'I'm going to have to spend the rest of my life in a tracksuit.'

'I'm wasting my time,' said Angel. 'I'm just messing about, writing drivel for idiots. No wonder they cut it.'

'I'm going to paint my nails,' said Manuela. 'What do you think? Pink or red? Or something wild to distract people from my bottom?'

'That's it,' said Angel, tossing the newspaper across the terrace. 'I'm finished with this shit.'

And that was when they heard it: a distant, but significant, boom. They looked at each other, all immediate concerns gone from their minds. Manuela couldn't stop herself from saying the obvious.

'What the hell was that?'

'That,' said Angel, getting to his feet so suddenly that the chair collapsed beneath him, 'was a large explosion.'

'But where?'

'The sound came from the north.'

'Oh shit, Angel! Shit, shit, shit, shit, shit!'

'What?' said Angel, expecting to see her with red nail polish all over her foot.

'It can't possibly have slipped your mind already,' said Manuela. 'We've been up half the night talking about it. The two properties in the Plaza Moravia – which is north of where we're standing now.'

'It wasn't *that* close,' said Angel. 'That was outside the city walls.'

'That's the thing about journalists,' said Manuela, 'they're so used to having their fingers on the pulse that they think they know everything, even how far away an explosion is.'

'I'd have said . . . Oh my God. Do you think that was in the Estación de Santa Justa?'

'That's east,' she said, pointing vaguely over the rooftops.

'North is the Parliament building,' he said, looking at his watch. 'There won't be anybody there at this time.'

'Apart from a few expendable cleaners,' said Manuela.

Angel stood in front of the TV, flicking from channel to channel, until he found Canal Sur.

'We have some breaking news of a large explosion to the north of Seville . . . somewhere in the area of El Cerezo. Eyewitnesses say that an apartment block has been completely destroyed and a nearby pre-school has been badly damaged. We have no reports of the cause of the explosion or the number of casualties.'

'El Cerezo?' said Angel. 'What's in El Cerezo?'

'Nothing,' said Manuela. 'Cheap apartment blocks. It's probably a gas explosion.'

'You're right. It's a residential area.'

'Not every loud noise you hear has to be a bomb.'

'After March 11th and the London bombings, our minds move in natural directions,' said Angel, opening up a street map of Seville.

'Well, you're always wanting something to happen and now it has. You'd better find out if it was gas or terrorism. But, whatever you do, Angel, don't give –'

'El Cerezo is two kilometres from here,' he said, cutting through her rising hysteria. 'You said it yourself, it's a cheap residential area. It's got nothing to do with what you're trying to sell in the Plaza Moravia.'

'If that was a terrorist bomb, it doesn't matter where it went off . . . the whole city will be nervous. One of my buyers is a foreigner making an investment. Investors react to this kind of thing. Ask me, if you like – I *am* one.'

'Did the Madrid property market crash after March 11th?' asked Angel. 'Keep calm, Manuela. It was probably gas.'

'The bomb could have detonated accidentally while they were preparing it,' she said. 'They might have blown themselves up because they realized that they were about to be raided by the police.'

'Call Javier,' said Angel, stroking the back of her neck. 'He'll know something.'

Falcón called his immediate boss, the Jefe de Brigada de Policía Judicial, Comisario Pedro Elvira, to give his initial report that the Fire Chief was almost certain this level of destruction was caused by a significant bomb, and gave the number of casualties so far.

Elvira had just come out of a meeting with *his* boss, Seville's most senior policeman, the Jefe Superior de la Policía de Sevilla, Comisario Andrés Lobo, who had appointed him to lead the entire investigative operation. He also confirmed that the Magistrado Juez Decano de Sevilla had just appointed Esteban Calderón as the Juez de Instrucción in charge of directing the investigation. Three companies had been contacted to supply demolition crews to start removing the rubble and to work with rescue teams, who were already on their way, to try to find any survivors as quickly as possible.

Falcón made a number of requests: aerial photography, before the huge crime scene became too contaminated by the rescue and demolition operation. He also asked for a large police presence to cordon off nearly a square kilometre around the building, so that they could investigate every vehicle in the vicinity. If it was a bomb, it had to have been transported and the vehicle could still be there. When they started searching suspect vehicles they would also need a team of forensics and a unit from the bomb squad. Elvira confirmed everything back to him and hung up.

The Fire Chief was a man in his moment. He'd trained for this terrible day and brought the immediate calamity under control in less than ninety minutes. He accompanied Falcón to the edge of the destruction. On the way he ordered a crew of firemen to stop work on supporting the roof of the destroyed classroom so that the bomb squad could see how the explosion had affected the building. He talked Falcón through the architecture of the destroyed apartment block and how enormous the explosion must have been to blow out the four main supporting pillars for that section. The effect of that would have brought the sudden and phenomenal weight of all the reinforced concrete floors on to the skin walls between each storey. There would have been an accumulative weight and acceleration as each level fell from a greater and greater height.

'Nobody could have survived that collapse,' he said. 'We're praying for miracles here.'

'Why are you so certain that this couldn't have been a gas explosion?'

'Apart from the fact that there's been no reported leak, and we've only had to deal with two small fires, the mosque in the basement is in daily use. Gas is heavier than air and would accumulate at the lowest point. A large enough quantity of gas couldn't have accumulated without anybody noticing,' he said. 'Added to that, the gas would have had to collect in a big enough space before exploding. Its power would be dissipated. Our main problem would have been incendiary, rather than destruction. There would have been a massive fireball, which would have scorched the whole area. There would have been burns victims. A bomb explodes from a small, confined source. It therefore has far more concentrated destructive power. Only a very large bomb, or several smaller bombs, could have taken out those reinforced concrete supporting pillars. Most of the dead and injured we've seen so far have been hit by flying debris and glass. All the windows in the area have been blown out. It's all consistent with a bomb blast.'

At the edge of the destruction the light was bruised and sickly yellow. The pulverized brick and concrete formed a fine dust, which clogged the throat and nostrils with the stench of decay. From within the stacked floors came the repetitive, desperate sounds of mobile phone jingles, the same customized tunes begging to be answered. Here, rather than being an irritant, they had personality. The Fire Chief shook his head.

'It's the worst thing,' he said, 'listening to someone else's hope fading away.'

Falcón almost jumped as his own mobile vibrated against his thigh.

'Manuela,' he said, walking away from the Fire Chief.

'Are you all right, little brother?' she asked.

'Yes, but I'm busy.'

'I know,' she said. 'Just tell me one thing. Was it a bomb?'

'We've had no confirmation –'

'I don't want the official communiqué,' she said. 'I'm your sister.'

'I don't want Angel running off to the *ABC* with a quote from the Inspector Jefe at the scene.'

'This is for my ears only.'

'Don't be ridiculous.'

'Just tell me, Javier.'

'We think it was a bomb.'

'Fuck.'

Falcón hung up in a fury without saying goodbye. Men, women and children had died and been injured. Families had been destroyed, along with homes and possessions. But Manuela still needed to know which way the property market was going to tip.

7

A figure sprinted between Falcón and the Fire Chief as he closed down his mobile. The man stumbled into the rubble at the foot of the fallen building, picked himself up and ran at the stacked pancakes of the reinforced concrete floors. His scale was strangely diminished by the vastness of the collapse. He seemed like a puppet as he dithered to the left and right, trying to find a purchase point in the tangle of cracked concrete, bristling steel rods, ruptured netting and shattered brick.

The Fire Chief shouted at him. He didn't hear. He plunged his hands into the wreckage, swung his body up and hooked his leg over a thick steel rod, but he was a horribly human mixture of crazed strength overwhelmed by futility.

By the time they got to him he was hanging helpless, his palms already torn and bloody, his face distorted by the rawness of his pain. They lifted him off his ghastly perch, like soldiers removing a comrade from the wire of the front line. No sooner had they got him down than he recovered his strength and lunged at the building once more. Falcón had to tackle him around the legs to hold him back. They scrabbled over the rubble, like an ancient articulated insect, until Falcón managed to crawl up the man's body and clasp his arms to his chest.

'You can't go in there,' he said, his voice rasping from the dust.

The man grunted and flexed his arms against Falcón's embrace. His mouth was wide open, his eyes stared into the mangled mess of the building and sweat beaded in fat drops on his filthy face.

'Who do you know who is in there?' asked Falcón.

On the back of the man's grunting came two words – wife, daughter.

'Which floor?' asked the Fire Chief.

The man looked up at them blinking, as if this question demanded some complicated differential calculus.

'Gloria,' said the man. 'Lourdes.'

'But which floor?' asked the Fire Chief.

The man's head went limp, all fight gone. Falcón released him and rolled him on to his back.

'Do you know anybody else in there, apart from Gloria and Lourdes?' asked Falcón.

The man's head listed to one side, and his dark eyes took in the damaged end of the pre-school. He sat up, got to his feet and trod robotically through the rubble and household detritus between the apartment block and the pre-school. Falcón followed. The man stood at the point where there should have been a wall. The classroom was a turmoil of broken furniture and shards of glass, and on the far wall fluttering in a breeze were children's paintings – big suns, mad smiles, hair standing on end.

The man's feet crunched through the glass. He tripped and fell heavily over a twisted desk, but righted himself immediately and made for the paintings. He pulled one off the wall and looked at it with the intensity of a collector judging a masterpiece. There was a tree, a sun, a high building and four people – two big, two small. In the bottom right-hand corner was a name written in an adult hand – Pedro. The man folded it carefully and put it inside his shirt.

The three men went into the main corridor of the school and out through the entrance. The local police had arrived and were trying to clear a path for the ambulance to remove the four bodies of the dead children taken from the destroyed classroom. Two of the mothers kneeling at the feet of their children gave a hysterical howl at this latest development. The third mother had already been taken away.

A woman with a thick white bandage on the side of her face, through which the blood underneath was just beginning to bloom, recognized the man.

'Fernando,' she said.

The man turned to her, but didn't recognize her.

'I'm Marta, Pedro's teacher,' she said.

Fernando had lost the power of speech. He took the painting out of his shirt and pointed at the smallest figure. Marta's motor reflexes seemed to malfunction and she couldn't swallow what was in her throat, nor articulate what was in her mind. Instead her face just caved in and she only managed to squeeze out a sound of such brutality and ugliness that it left Fernando's chest shuddering. It was a sound uncontrolled by any civilizing influence. It was grief in its purest form, before its pain had been made less acute by time or more poignant by poetry. It was a dark, guttural, heaving clot of emotion.

Fernando was not affronted. He folded the painting up and put it back in his shirt. Falcón led him by the arm to the four small bodies. The ambulance was backing up, the rest of the crowd had been squeezed out of the scene. Two paramedics appeared with two body bags each. They worked quickly because they knew the situation would be better with those pitiful bodies removed. Falcón held Fernando around the shoulders as the paramedics uncovered each body and placed it in a body bag. He had to remind Fernando to breathe. At the third body Fernando's knees buckled and Falcón lowered him to the ground, where he fell forward on to all fours and crawled around, like a poisoned dog looking for a place to die. One of the paramedics shouted and pointed. A TV cameraman had come around the back, through the pre-school, and was filming the bodies. He turned and ran before anybody could react.

The ambulance moved off. The ghostly crowd surged after it and gave up, with a final spasm of grief, before dissolving into groups, with the bereaved women supported from all sides. Television journalists and their cameramen tried to force their way in to talk to the women. They were rebuffed. Falcón pulled Fernando to his feet, pushed him back into the pre-school out of sight, and went to find a policeman to keep journalists away.

Outside a journalist had found a young guy in his twenties, with a couple of bloody nicks in his cheek, who'd been there when the bomb exploded. The camera was right in his face, inches away, the proximity giving the pictures their urgency.

'. . . straight after it happened, I mean, the noise . . . you just can't believe the loudness of that noise, it was so loud I couldn't breathe, it was like . . .'

'What was it like?' asked the journalist, an eager young woman, stabbing the microphone back into his face. 'Tell us. Tell Spain what it was like.'

'It was like the noise took away all the air.'

'What was the first thing you noticed after the explosion, after the noise?'

'Silence,' he said. 'Just a deathly quiet. And, I don't know whether this was in my head or it actually happened, I heard bells ringing . . .'

'Church bells?'

'Yes, church bells, but they were all crazy, as if the shock waves of the explosion were making them ring, you know, at random. It made me sick to hear it. It was as if everything had gone wrong with the world, and nothing would be the same.'

The rest was lost in the clatter and thump of a helicopter's rotor blades, thrashing away at the dust in the air. It went up higher, to take in the whole scene. This was the aerial photography Falcón had ordered up.

He posted a policeman at the entrance of the school, but found that Fernando had disappeared. He crossed the corridor to the wrecked classroom. Empty. He called Ramírez as he crashed through the broken furniture.

'Where are you?' asked Falcón.

'We've just arrived. We're on Calle Los Romeros.'

'Is Cristina with you?'

'We're all here. The whole squad.'

'All of you come round to the pre-school now.'

Fernando was back at the wall of rubble and collapsed floors. He threw himself at it like a madman. He tore at the concrete, bricks, window frames and hurled them behind him.

'. . . rescue teams working on this side,' roared Ramírez, over the noise of the helicopter. 'There are dogs in the wreckage.'

'Get over here.'

Fernando had grabbed at the steel netting of a shattered reinforced concrete floor. He had his feet braced against the rubble. His neck muscles stood out and his carotid arteries appeared as thick as cord. Falcón pulled him off and they fought for some moments, tripping and floundering about in the dust and rubble until they were ghosts of their former selves.

'Have you got Gloria's phone number?' roared Falcón.

They were panting in the choking atmosphere, their sweating faces caked with grey, white and brown dust, which swirled around them from the chopper's blades.

The question transfixed Fernando. Despite hearing all these mobile phones ringing, his mind was so paralysed with shock, he hadn't thought of his own. He ripped it out of his pocket. He squeezed life into the starter button. The helicopter moved off, leaving an immense silence.

Fernando blinked, his brain fluttering like torn flags, trying to remember his PIN. It came to him and he thumbed in Gloria's number. He stood up from his kneeling position and walked towards the wreckage. He held a hand up as if demanding silence from the world. From his left came the faint, tinny sound of some Cuban piano.

'That's her,' he roared, moving left. 'She was on this side of the building when . . . when I last saw her.'

Falcón got to his feet and made a futile attempt to dust himself down just as his homicide squad turned up. He stayed them with his hand and moved towards the tinkling piano, which he recognized as a song called 'Lágrimas Negras' – Black Tears.

'She's there!' roared Fernando. 'She's in there!'

Baena, a junior detective from Falcón's squad, ran back and fetched a rescue team with a dog. The team pinpointed the spot from where the ringing tone was coming and managed to get Fernando to tell them that his wife and daughter had been on the fifth floor. They gave him steady looks when he released that information. In the face of his radiant hope not one of them had the heart to tell him that the fall, with three storeys coming down on top, meant that, at this moment, they were praying only.

'She's in there,' he said, to their still, expressionless faces. 'That mobile is always with her. She's a sales rep. "Lágrimas Negras" was her favourite song.'

Falcón nodded to Cristina Ferrera and they guided Fernando back to the pre-school and got a nurse to clean him up and dress his cuts. Falcón called the homicide squad into the school latrines. He washed his hands and face and looked at them in the mirror.

'This is going to be the most complicated investigation that any of us have ever been involved in, and that includes me,' said Falcón. 'Nothing is straightforward in terrorist attacks. We know that from what happened on March 11th in Madrid. There are going to be a lot of people involved – the CNI's intelligence agents, the CGI's antiterrorist squad, the bomb disposal teams and us – and that's just on the investigative side. What we've got to do is keep it clear in our minds what we, as the homicide squad, are trying to achieve. I've already asked for a police cordon to keep the site clear for us.'

'They're in place,' said Ramírez. 'They're working on getting the journalists out.'

Falcón turned to face them, shaking his wet hands.

'By now you all know that there was a mosque in the basement of that block. Our job is not to speculate on what happened and why. Our job is to find out who went into that mosque, and who came out, and what went on inside it in the last twenty-four hours, and then forty-eight hours, and so on. We do that by talking to every possible witness we can find. Our other crucial task is to find out about every vehicle in the vicinity. The bomb was big. It would have had to be transported to this place. If that vehicle is still here, we have to find it.

'At the moment the first task is going to be difficult, with all the occupants of the apartments evacuated from their buildings. So our priority is to identify all vehicles and their owners. José Luis will divide you up and you will search every sector, starting with cars closest to the collapsed building. Cristina, you'll stay with me for the moment.

'And remember, everybody here is suffering in some way, whether they've lost somebody or seen them injured, whether they've had their home destroyed or their windows smashed. You've got a heavy workload and you're going to be under a lot of pressure, with or without the media on your backs. You'll get more information by being sensitive and understanding than by treating this as the usual process. You're all good people, which is why you're in the homicide squad – now go out there and find out what happened.'

They filed out. Ferrera stayed behind. Falcón washed his hair under the tap and then wiped his face and hands.

'His name is Fernando. His wife and daughter were in the collapsed apartment block, his son was one of the children killed in the blast. Find out if he has any other family and, if not, any close friends. Not anybody will do. He left home after his breakfast to find out, half an hour later, that he's lost everything. When it comes home to him, he's going to lose his mind.'

'And you want me to stay with him?'

'I can't afford that. I want you to make sure he's safely delivered into the hands of a trauma team, who should be along any minute. He needs his predicament explained, he's lost the ability to articulate. He'll want to stay here until the bodies are found. But don't lose track of him. I want to know where he ends up.'

They left the latrines. A bomb squad team was picking its way through the shattered classroom, like mineral fossickers looking for valuable rocks. They filled polypropylene sacks with their finds. There were two more teams outside, working furiously so that the machinery could move in to start the demolition task and the search for survivors.

Cristina Ferrera went into the classroom where the nurse was just finishing dressing Fernando's cuts. She knew why Falcón had chosen her for this job. The nurse was doing her best with Fernando, but he wasn't responding, his brain was teeming with bigger, darker fish. The nurse finished and packed up. Cristina asked her to send someone from a trauma team as soon as possible. She sat on a chair by the blackboard, at some distance from Fernando. She didn't want to crowd him, even though it was obvious that he was living inside his head at an intensity that excluded the outside world. Grief darkened, as quickly as hope lightened, his face, like clouds passing over fields.

'Who are *you*?' he asked, after some minutes, as if noticing her for the first time.

'I'm a policewoman. My name is Cristina Ferrera.'

'There was a man before. Who was he?'

'That was my boss, Javier Falcón. He's the Inspector Jefe of the homicide squad.'

'He's got some work on his hands.'

'He's a good man,' said Ferrera. 'An unusual man. He'll get to the bottom of it.'

'We all know who it is, though, don't we?'

'Not yet.'

'The Moroccans.'

'It's too early to say.'

'You ask around. We've all thought about it. Ever since March 11th we've watched them going in there and we've been waiting.'

'Into the mosque, you mean? The mosque in the basement.'

'That's right.'

'They're not all Moroccans who go to mosques, you know. Plenty of Spaniards have converted to Islam.'

'I work in construction,' he said, uninterested in her balanced approach. 'I put together buildings like that. Much better buildings than that. I work with steel.'

'In Seville?'

'Yes, I build apartments for rich young professionals . . . that's what I'm told anyway.'

Fernando's head had been turned upside down and now he was trying to put the furniture straight. Except that, occasionally, he noticed the furniture's emptiness and it tipped his mind back into the abyss of loss and grief. He tried to talk about building work but got lost in moments of imagination as he saw his wife and daughter falling through steel and concrete. He wanted to get out of himself, out of his body and head and into . . . where? Where could the mind go for respite? A helicopter battering the air overhead knocked his thoughts into another pattern.

'Do you have children?' he asked.

'A boy and a girl,' she said.

'How old?'

'The boy's sixteen. The girl's fourteen.'

'Good kids,' he said; not a question, more of a hope.

'They're both being difficult at the moment,' she said. 'Their father died about three years ago. It's not been easy for them.'

'I'm sorry,' he said, but wanting her tragedy to bury his own for a while. 'How did he die?'

'He died of a rare type of cancer.'

'That's hard for your kids. Fathers are good for them at that age,' he said. 'They like to try things out on their mothers to give themselves the confidence to rebel against the world. That's what Gloria told me, anyway. They need fathers to show them it's not as easy as they think.'

'You might be right.'

'Gloria says I'm a good father.'

'Your wife . . .'

'Yes, my wife,' he said.

'Can you tell me about your own kids?' she asked.

He couldn't. There were no words for them. He measured them out with a hand up from the floor, he pointed out of the window at the destroyed apartment block, and finally he pulled the painting out from his shirt. That said it all – sticks and triangles, a tall rectangle with windows, a round green tree and behind it a massive orange sun in a blue sky.

A colossal crane arrived, preceded by a bulldozer, which cleared the land in between the destroyed block and the pre-school. Two tipper trucks manoeuvred around the back of the crane and a digger began to scoop rubble and dump it in the tippers. In the cleared land the crane settled its feet and a team of men in yellow hard hats began preparing the rig.

Around the front of the building, on Calle Los Romeros, a change of clothes had arrived from the Jefatura for Falcón. The rest of the homicide squad were busy working with the local police, identifying vehicles and their owners. Comisario Elvira had turned up in full uniform and was being given a tour of the site by the Fire Chief. As he moved around, his assistant called all the team leaders involved in the operation to a meeting in one of the classrooms in the pre-school. As the entourage headed for the pre-school a woman approached Elvira and gave him a list with twelve names on it.

'And who are these people?' asked Elvira.

'They are the names of all the men in the mosque at the time of the explosion not including the Imam, Abdelkrim Benaboura,' she said. 'My name is Esperanza.

I'm Spanish. My partner, who is also Spanish, was in the mosque. I represent the wives, mothers and girlfriends of these men. We are in hiding. The women, especially the Moroccan women, are scared that people may think that their husbands and sons were in some way responsible for what has happened. There's a mobile number on the back of the list. We would ask you to call us when you have some news of their . . . of anything.'

She moved away, and the pressure of time and lack of personnel meant that Elvira let her go unfollowed. Calderón made his way through the crowd to Falcón.

'I didn't realize it was you, Javier,' he said, shaking him by the hand. 'How did you get into that state?'

'I had to stop someone from throwing himself into the wreckage to rescue his wife and daughter.'

'So, this is the big one,' said Calderón, not bothering to engage with what Falcón had said. 'It's finally happened to us.'

They continued to the school, where the police, judges, fire brigade, bomb squad, rescue services, trauma units, medical services and demolition gangs were all represented. Elvira made it clear that nobody was allowed to say a word until he had delivered the plan of action. To focus their attention he asked the leader of the bomb squad to give a brief report on the initial analyses of fragments from the blast. They showed that the apartment block had been devastated by a bomb of extraordinary power, most probably situated in the basement of that section of the building, and whose explosive was probably of military, rather than commercial, quality. This expert opinion silenced the assembled company completely and Elvira was able to hammer out a co-ordinated plan in about forty minutes.

At the end of the meeting Ramírez headed Falcón off as he was making for the latrines to change his clothes.

'We've got something,' he said.

'Talk me through it while I change.'

As soon as he was dressed, Falcón found Comisario Elvira and Juez Calderón, and asked Ramírez to repeat what he'd just told him.

'In the immediate vicinity of the building, excluding vehicles buried in the rubble, we've found three stolen cars plus this van,' said Ramírez. 'It's parked right outside the pre-school here. It's a Peugeot Partner, registered in Madrid. There's a copy of the Koran on the front seat. We can't see in the back because it's a closed van and the rear windows have been shattered, but the owner of the vehicle is a man called Mohammed Soumaya.'

8

The car park was directly behind the destroyed building and next to the pre-school. There were some trees, which provided a canopy to a sitting area near Calle Blanca Paloma on one side and a five-storey apartment block on the other. There was only one access road to the car park. While Calderón, Elvira, Falcón and Ramírez made for the Peugeot Partner, Elvira's assistant logged on to the police terror suspects list and entered Mohammed Soumaya's details. He was in the lowest risk category, which meant that he had no known connections to any body, organization or persons with either terror or radical Islamic background. The only reason he was on the list was that he fitted the most basic terrorist profile: under forty years of age, a devout Muslim and single. Elvira's assistant entered the names from the list of all the men in the mosque at the time of the explosion, which had been given by the Spanish woman, Esperanza. There was no Mohammed Soumaya among them. He patched the names through to the CNI – the Spanish intelligence agency.

Two breakdown vehicles were working in the car

park to remove cars whose owners had been identified and screened. Most of these cars had windows smashed and bodywork damage from flying debris. The Peugeot Partner's two rear windows were opaque with shattered glass and the rear doors were dented. The side windows were clear and the windscreen, which had been facing away from the explosion, was intact. The copy of the Koran, a new Spanish edition, was visible on the front passenger seat. Two forensics in white hooded boiler suits and latex gloves were standing by. There was a discussion about booby traps and a bomb squad team was called over, along with a dog handler. The dog found nothing interesting around the car. The underside and engine compartment were inspected and found clear. The bomb squad man picked the glass out of one of the smashed rear windows and inspected inside. The rear doors were opened and shots taken of the empty interior and its carpeted floor. A fine, crystalline, white powder, which covered an area of about 30 cm by 20 cm, had been spilled on the floor. The excited sniffer dog leapt in and immediately sat down by the powder. One of the forensics took a hand-held vacuum cleaner with a clear plastic flask attached and hoovered up the powder. The flask was removed from the vacuum cleaner, capped and given an evidence number.

The forensics moved round to the front of the car and bagged the new copy of the Koran, whose spine was unbroken. In the glove compartment they found another copy of the Koran. This was a heavily used Spanish translation, with copious notes in the margins; it proved to be exactly the same edition as the one found on the front seat. This was bagged, as were the vehicle documents. Falcón took a note of the ISBN and bar codes of both books. Under the passenger seat was an empty mineral water bottle and a black cotton sack, which contained a carefully folded green-and-white sash whose length was covered in Arabic writing. There was also a black hood with eye and mouth holes.

'Let's not get too excited until we've had an analysis of that powder in the back,' said Calderón. 'His occupation is "shop owner", it could just as easily be sugar.'

'Not if my dog sat down next to it,' said the bomb squad man. 'He's never wrong.'

'We'd better get in touch with Madrid and have someone visit Mohammed Soumaya's home and business premises,' said Falcón, and Ramírez moved off to make the call. 'We want detail about his movements over the last forty-eight hours, as well.'

'You're going to have a job on your hands just to find all these people who had a view of this car park, and the front and rear of the destroyed building,' said Calderón. 'As the bomb squad guy said, it was a big bomb, which means a lot of explosive arrived here, possibly in small lots and maybe from a number of different suppliers, and at different times.'

'We're going to need to know whether the mosque, or any of the people in the mosque, were the subject of surveillance by the CGI's antiterrorist squad or the CNI's intelligence agents and, if they were, we'd like that information,' said Falcón. 'And, by the way, where are they? I didn't see anybody from the CGI in that meeting.'

'The CNI are on their way down here now,' said Elvira.

'And the CGI?' asked Calderón.

'They're in lockdown,' said Elvira, quietly.

'What does that mean?' said Calderón.

'It will be explained to us when the CNI get here,' said Elvira.

'How much longer will it be before the fire brigade and the bomb squad can declare all these apartment blocks surrounding the destroyed building safe?' asked Falcón. 'At least if people can come back to their homes we've got a chance of building up our information quickly.'

'They know that,' said Elvira, 'and they've told me that they should be letting people back in within the next few hours, as long as they don't find anything else. In the meantime a contact number's been issued to the press, TV and radio for people to call in with information.'

'Except that they don't know of the Peugeot Partner's importance yet,' said Falcón. 'We're not going to get anywhere until people get back into their apartments.'

The Mayor, who'd been stuck in traffic as the city had ground to a halt, finally arrived in the car park. He was joined by ministers of the Andalucían Parliament, who had just come from the hospital where they'd been filmed talking to some of the victims. A gaggle of journalists had been allowed through the police cordon and they gathered around the officials, while camera crews set up their equipment, with the destruction providing the devastating backdrop. Elvira went across to the Mayor to give his situation report and was intercepted by his own assistant. They talked. Elvira pointed him across to Falcón.

'Only three of the twelve names given to us on that list appear on the terror suspect database,' said the assistant, 'and they're all in the lowest risk category.

Five of the twelve were over sixty-five. Morning prayers isn't such a popular time with the young, as most people have to get to work.'

'Not exactly the classic profile of a terrorist cell,' said Falcón. 'But then we don't know who else was in there yet.'

'How many under the age of thirty-five?' asked Calderón.

'Four,' said the assistant, 'and of those, two are brothers, one of whom is severely disabled in a wheelchair, and another is a Spanish convert called Miguel Botín.'

'And the remaining three?'

'Four, including the Imam, who isn't on the list the woman gave us. He's fifty-five and the other three are in their forties. Two of them are claiming disability benefit from the state after suffering industrial accidents, and the third is another Spanish convert.'

'Well, they don't sound like a special forces unit, do they?' said Calderón.

'There is one interesting point. The Imam is on the terror suspect database. He's been in Spain since September 2004, arriving from Tunis.'

'And before that?'

'That's the point. I don't have the clearance for that level of information. Maybe the Comisario does,' he said, and went to rejoin the media scrum around the Mayor.

'How can somebody be in a low-risk category and yet have a higher level of clearance for his history?' asked Ramírez.

'Let's look at the certainties, or the almost certainties,' said Juez Calderón. 'We have a bomb explosion, whose epicentre seems to be the mosque in the basement of the building. We have a van belonging to Mohammed Soumaya, a low-risk category terrorist – who we are not sure was in the building at the time of the blast. His van bears traces of explosive, according to the bomb squad dog. We have a list of twelve people in the mosque at the time, plus the Imam. Only three, plus the Imam, make it on to a list of low-risk category terror suspects. We are investigating the deaths of four children in the pre-school and three people outside the apartment block at the time of the explosion. Anything else?'

'The hood, the sash, the two copies of the Koran,' said Ramírez.

'We should get all those notes in the margins of the used copy of the Koran looked at by an expert,' said Calderón. 'Now, what are the questions we want answered?'

'Did Mohammed Soumaya drive this van here? If not, who did? If that powder is confirmed as explosive then what was it, why was it being gathered here, and why did it detonate?' said Falcón. 'While we wait to hear from Madrid about Soumaya we'll build up a picture of what happened in and around this mosque over the last week. We can start by asking people whether they remember this van arriving, how many people were in it, did they see it being unloaded and so on. Can we get a shot of Soumaya?'

Ramírez, who was on the phone again, trying to sort out someone to look at the copy of the Koran, nodded and twirled an index finger to show that he was on to it. A policewoman came from the wreckage site and informed Calderón that the first body in the collapsed building had been found – an old woman on the eighth floor. They agreed to reconvene in a couple of hours. Ramírez came off the phone as Cristina Ferrera arrived from the pre-school.

It was agreed that Ramírez would continue working on the vehicle identification with Sub-Inspector Pérez, Serrano and Baena. Falcón and Cristina Ferrera would start trying to find the occupants of the five-storey apartment building with the best view of the car park where the Peugeot Partner had been left. They went down the street towards the police cordon where a group of people had gathered, waiting to be able to get back into their apartments.

'How was Fernando by the time you left him?' asked Falcón. 'I didn't catch his surname.'

'Fernando Alanis,' she said. 'He was more or less under control, considering what had happened to him. We've exchanged numbers.'

'Has he got anybody he can go to?'

'Not in Seville,' she said. 'His parents are up north and too old and sick. His sister lives in Argentina. His wife's family didn't approve of the marriage.'

'Friends?'

'His life was his family,' she said.

'Does he know what he's going to do?'

'I've told him he can come and stay with me.'

'You didn't have to do *that*, Cristina. He's not your responsibility.'

'You knew I'd offer though, didn't you, Inspector Jefe?' she said. 'If the situation demanded it.'

'I was going to put him up at my place,' said Falcón. 'You've got to go to work, the kids . . . you don't have any room.'

'He needs a sense of what he's lost,' she said. 'And who'd look after him at your place?'

'My housekeeper,' said Falcón. 'You won't believe me, but I really did not intend for that to happen.'

'We have to pull together or we let them win by falling apart,' she said. 'And you always choose me for this type of work – once a nun always a nun.'

'I don't remember saying that.'

'But you remember thinking it, and didn't you say that we weren't just foot soldiers in the fight against crime,' said Ferrera, 'but that we're here to help as well. We're the crusading detectives of Andalucía.'

'José Luis would laugh in your face if he heard you say that,' said Falcón. 'And you should be very wary of using words like that in *this* investigation.'

'Fernando was already accusing "the Moroccans",' she said. 'Ever since March 11th they've been watching them go into that mosque and wondering.'

'That's the way people's minds naturally work these days, and they like to have their suspicions confirmed,' said Falcón. 'We can't take their prejudices into this investigation. We have to examine the facts and keep them divorced from any natural assumptions. If we don't, we'll make the sort of mistakes they made right from the beginning in the Madrid bombings when they blamed ETA. Already there are confusing aspects to the evidence that we've found in the Peugeot Partner.'

'Explosives, copies of the Koran and a green sash and black hood don't sound confusing to me,' said Ferrera.

'Why two copies of the Koran? One brand-new

cheap Spanish edition and the other heavily used and annotated, but exactly the same edition.'

'The extra copy was a gift?'

'Why leave it in full view on the front seat? This is Seville, people usually leave their cars completely empty,' said Falcón. 'We need more information on these books. I want you to find out where they were bought and if there was a credit card or cheque used.'

He tore the page from his notebook with the ISBNs and bar codes, recopied them and gave Ferrera the torn page.

'What are we trying to find out from the occupants of this apartment block?'

'Keep it simple. Everybody's in shock. If we can find witnesses we'll bring them to this car park, ask whether they saw the Peugeot Partner arrive, if they saw anybody getting out of it, how many, what age and if they took anything out of the back.'

At the police cordon Falcón called out the address of the apartment block. An old man in his seventies came forward and a woman in her forties with a bruised face and a plastered arm in a sling. Falcón took the old man, Ferrera the woman. As they passed the entrance to their block a bomb squad man and a fireman confirmed that the building was now clear. Falcón showed the old man the Peugeot Partner and took him back up to his third-floor apartment, where the living room and kitchen were covered in glass, all the blinds in shreds, the chairs fallen over, photographs on the floor and the soft furniture lacerated, with brown foam already protruding from the holes.

The old man had been lying on his bed in the back of the apartment. His son and daughter-in-law had already left for work, with the kids, who were too old for the pre-school, so nobody had been hurt. He stood in the midst of his wrecked home with his left hand shaking and his old, rheumy eyes taking it all in.

'So you're here on your own all day,' said Falcón.

'My wife died last November,' he said.

'What do you do with yourself?'

'I do what old guys do: read the paper, take a coffee, look at the kids playing in the pre-school. I wander about, talk to people and choose the best time to smoke the three cigarettes I allow myself every day.'

Falcón went to the window and pulled the ruined blinds away.

'Do you remember seeing that van?'

'The world is full of small white vans these days,' said the old man. 'So I can't be sure whether I saw the same van twice, or different vans in two separate instances. On the way to the pharmacy I saw the van for the first time, driving from left to right down Calle Los Romeros, with two people in the front. It pulled into the kerb by the mosque and that was it.'

'What time?'

'About ten thirty yesterday morning.'

'And the next time?'

'About fifteen minutes later on the way back from the pharmacy I saw a white van pull into the parking area, but not in that spot. It was on the other side, facing away from us, and only one guy got out.'

'Did you see him clearly?'

'He was dark. I'd have said he was Moroccan. There are a lot of them around here. He had a round head, close-cropped hair, prominent ears.'

'Age?'

'About thirty. He looked fit. He had a tight black T-shirt on and he was muscled. I think he was wearing jeans and trainers. He locked the car and went off through the trees to Calle Blanca Paloma.'

'Did you see the van when it arrived in the position it is now?'

'No. All I can tell you is that it was there by six thirty in the evening. My daughter-in-law parked next to it. I also remember that when I went for coffee after lunch the van had left its position on the other side. There aren't so many cars during the day, except for the ones belonging to teachers lined up in front of the school, so I don't know how, but I noticed it. Old guys notice different things to other people.'

'And there were two men when it was going along Calle Los Romeros?'

'That's why I can't be sure if it was the same van.'

'On which side of the van did your daughter-in-law park her car?'

'To the left as we're looking at it,' said the old man. 'Her door was blown open by the wind and knocked into it.'

'Did the van move again at all?'

'No idea. Once people are around me I don't notice a thing.'

Falcón took the daughter-in-law's name and number and called her as he walked upstairs. He talked her through the conversation he'd just had with her father-in-law and asked her if she'd had a look at the van when her door had knocked into it.

'I checked it, just to make sure I hadn't dented it.'

'Did you glance in the window?'

'Probably.'

'Did you see anything on the front passenger seat?'

'No, nothing.'

'You didn't see a book?'

'Definitely not. It was just a dark seat.'

Ferrera was coming out of the fourth-floor apartment as he hung up. They went downstairs in silence.

'Was your witness injured in the blast?' asked Falcón.

'She *says* she fell down the stairs last night, but she's got no bruises on her arms or legs, just the ones on her face,' said Ferrera angrily. 'And she was scared.'

'Not of you.'

'Yes, of me. Because I ask questions, and one question leads to another, and if any of it somehow gets back to her husband it's another reason for him to beat her.'

'You can only help the ones that want to be helped,' said Falcón.

'There seems to be more of it about these days,' said Ferrera, exasperated. 'Anyway, she did see the van arrive in its current position. There's a woman on the same shift at the factory where she works, who lives in one of the blocks further down her street. They meet for a chat under the trees on Calle Blanca Paloma. They walked past the van at 6 p.m. just as it had arrived. Two guys got out. They were talking in Arabic. They didn't take anything out of the back. They went up to Calle Los Romeros and turned right.'

'Descriptions?'

'Both late twenties. One with a shaved head, black T-shirt. The other with more of a square head, with black hair, cut short at the sides and combed back on top. She said he was very good looking, but had bad

114

teeth. He wore a faded denim jacket, white T-shirt, and she remembers he had very flashy trainers.'

'Did she see the van move again from that position?'

'She keeps an eye on this car park, looking out for when her husband comes home. She said it hadn't moved by the time he came in at 9.15 p.m.'

The police were letting people through the cordon so that they could get back into their homes to start clearing up the damage. There was a large crowd gathered outside the chemist's at the junction of Calle Blanca Paloma with Calle Los Romeros. They were angry with the police for not letting them back into any part of the block attached to the destroyed building, which was still too dangerous. Falcón tried talking to people in the crowd, but they couldn't give a damn about Peugeot Partners.

Pneumatic drills started up on the other side of the block. Falcón and Ferrera crossed Calle Los Romeros to another apartment building, whose glass was more or less intact. The apartments on the first two floors were still empty. On the third floor a child led Falcón into a living room, where a woman was sweeping up glass around a pile of cardboard boxes. She had moved in at the weekend but the removal company hadn't been able to deliver until yesterday. He asked his question about the white van and the two guys.

'Do you think I'd be sitting on the balcony watching the traffic with all this lot to unpack?' she said. 'I've had to give up two days' work because these people can't deliver on time.'

'Do you know who was in here before you?'

'It was empty,' she said. 'Nobody had been living

here for three months. The letting agency on Avenida San Lazaro said we were the first to see it.'

'Was there anything left here when you first arrived?' asked Falcón, looking out of the living-room balcony on to Calle Los Romeros and the rubble of the destroyed building.

'There was no furniture, if that's what you mean,' she said. 'There was a sack of rubbish in the kitchen.'

'What sort of rubbish?'

'People have been killed. *Children* have been killed,' she said, aghast, pulling her own child to her side. 'And you're asking me what sort of *rubbish* I found here when I moved in?'

'Police work can seem like a mysterious business,' said Falcón. 'If you can remember noticing anything it might help.'

'As it happens, I had to tie the bag up and throw it out, so I know that it was a pizza carton, a couple of beer cans, some cigarette butts, ash and empty packets and a newspaper, the *ABC*, I think. Anything else?'

'That's very good, because now we know that, although this place was empty for three months, somebody had been here, spending quite some time in this apartment, and that could be interesting for us.'

He crossed the landing to the apartment opposite. A woman in her sixties lived there.

'Your new neighbour has just told me that her apartment had been empty for the last three months,' he said.

'Not quite empty,' she said. 'When the previous family moved out, about four months ago, some very smart businessmen came round, on maybe three or four occasions. Then, about three months ago, a small van turned up and unloaded a bed, two chairs and a table. Nothing else. After that, young men would turn up in pairs, and spend three or four hours at a time during the day, doing God knows what. They never spent the night there, but from dawn until dusk there was always someone in that apartment.'

'Did the same guys come back again, or were they different every time?'

'I think there might have been as many as twenty.'

'Did they bring anything with them?'

'Briefcases, newspapers, groceries.'

'Did you ever talk to them?'

'Of course. I asked them what they were doing and they just said that they were having meetings,' she said. 'I wasn't that worried. They didn't look like druggies. They didn't play loud music or have parties; in fact, quite the opposite.'

'Did their routine change over the months?'

'Nobody came during Semana Santa and the Feria.'

'Did you ever see inside the apartment when they were there?'

'In the beginning I offered them something to eat, but they always very politely refused. They never let me inside.'

'And they never let on about what these meetings were about?'

'They were such straight, conservative young men, I thought they might be a religious group.'

'What happened when they left?'

'One day a van arrived and took away the furniture and that was it.'

'When was that?'

'Last Friday . . . the second of June.'

117

Falcón called Ferrera and told her to keep at it while he went to talk to the letting agency down the street on Avenida de San Lazaro.

The woman in the letting agency had been responsible for selling the property three months ago and renting it out at the end of last week. It had not been bought by a private buyer but a computer company called Informáticalidad. All her dealings were through the Financial Director, Pedro Plata.

Falcón took down the address. Ramírez called him as he was walking back up Calle Los Romeros towards the bombed building.

'Comisario Elvira has just told me that the Madrid police have picked up Mohammed Soumaya at his shop. He lent the van to his nephew. He was surprised to hear that it was in Seville. His nephew had told him he was just going to use it for some local deliveries,' said Ramírez. 'They're following up on the nephew now. His name is Trabelsi Amar.'

'Are they sending us shots of him?'

'We've asked for them,' said Ramírez. 'By the way, they've just installed an Arabic speaker in the Jefatura, after receiving more than a dozen calls from our friends across the water. They all say the same thing and the translation is: "We will not rest until Andalucía is back in the bosom of Islam."'

'Have you ever heard of a company called Informáticalidad?' asked Falcón.

'Never,' said Ramírez, totally uninterested. 'There's one last bit of news for you. They've identified the explosive found in the back of the Peugeot Partner. It's called cyclotrimethylenetrinitramine.'

'And what's that?'

'Otherwise known as RDX. Research and Development Explosive,' said Ramírez, in a wobbly English accent. 'Its other names are cyclonite and hexogen. It's top-quality military explosive – the sort of thing you'd find in artillery shells.'

9

Ferrera had found one occupant who'd given her a sighting of the Peugeot Partner late yesterday afternoon, Monday 5th June. The van had stopped on Calle Los Romeros, opposite the mosque, and two men had unloaded four cardboard boxes and some blue plastic carrier bags. The only description of the men was that they were young and well built and were wearing T-shirts and jeans. The boxes were heavy enough that they could only be carried one at a time. Everything was taken into the mosque. Both men came out and drove away in the van. Falcón told her to keep looking for witnesses and if necessary to go down to the hospital.

Back in the car park the Mayor and the deputies from the Andalucían Parliament had gone and Comisario Elvira and Juez Calderón were coming to the end of an impromptu press conference. Another body had been found on the seventh floor. The rescue workers had not made contact with anybody alive in the rubble. Pneumatic drills were being used to expose the steel netting in the reinforced concrete floors and oxyacetylene torches and motorized cutters were breaking up the floors into slabs. These slabs were being lifted away by the crane and put into tippers. With each piece of information given, more questions came at them. Elvira was visibly irritated by it all, but Calderón was playing at the top of his game and the journalists loved him. They were more than happy to concentrate on the good-looking, charismatic Calderón when finally Elvira took his leave and headed into the pre-school, where they'd set up a temporary headquarters in the undamaged class-rooms at the back.

The journalists recognized Falcón and came after him, preventing him from following Elvira. Microphones butted his face. Cameras were thrust between heads. What's the name of the explosive again? Where did it come from? Are the terrorists still alive? Is there a cell still operating in Seville? What have you got to say about the evacuations in the city centre? Has there been another bomb? Has anybody claimed responsibility for the attack? Falcón had to force his way out of the scrum and it took three policemen to push the journalists back from the pre-school entrance. Falcón was straightening himself up in the corridor when Calderón burst through the roaring crowd at the gates.

'*Joder*,' he said, remaking his tie, 'they're like a pack of jackals.'

'Ramírez just told me about the explosive.'

'They keep asking me about that. I haven't heard anything.'

'The common name is RDX or hexogen.'

'Hexogen?' said Calderón. 'Wasn't that what the Chechen rebels used to blow up those apartment blocks in Moscow back in 1999?'

'The military use it in artillery shells.'

'I remember there was some scandal about the Chechens using recycled explosives from a government scientific research institute, which had been bought by the mafia, who then sold it to the rebels. Russian military ordnance being used to blow up their own people.'

'Sounds like a typical Russian scenario.'

'It's not going to be easy for you,' said Calderón. 'Hexogen can come from anywhere – Russia, a Muslim Chechen terrorist group, an arms dump in Iraq, any Third World country where there's been a conflict, where ordnance has been left behind. It might even be American, this stuff.'

Falcón's mobile vibrated. It was Elvira, calling them into a meeting with the Centro Nacional de Inteligencia and the antiterrorist squad of the Comisaría General de Información.

There were three men from the CNI. The boss was a man in his sixties, with white hair and dark eyebrows and a handsome, ex-athlete's face. He introduced himself only as Juan. His two juniors, Pablo and Gregorio, were younger men, who had the bland appearance of middle managers. In their dark suits they were barely distinguishable, although Pablo had a scar running from his hairline to his left eyebrow. Falcón was uncomfortably aware that Pablo had not taken his eyes off him since he'd walked into the room. He began to wonder whether they'd met before.

There was only one representative from the antiterrorism unit of the CGI. His name was Inspector Jefe Ramón Barros, a short, powerfully built man, with close-cropped grey hair and perfect teeth, which added a sinister element to his brutal and furious demeanour.

Comisario Elvira asked Falcón to give a résumé of

his findings so far. He started with the immediate aftermath of the bomb and moved on quickly to the discovery of the Peugeot Partner, its contents, and the times it was seen by witnesses in the car park.

'We've since discovered that the fine white powder taken from the rear of the van is a military explosive known as hexogen, which my colleague, Juez Calderón, has told me was the same type of explosive used by Chechen rebels to blow up two apartment blocks in Moscow in 1999.'

'You can't believe everything you read in the newspapers,' said Juan. 'There's considerable doubt now that it was the Chechen rebels. We're not great believers in conspiracy theories in our own back yard, but when it comes to Russia it seems that anything is possible. There is a natural inclination, after such a catastrophic attack as this, to make comparisons to other terrorist attacks, to look for patterns. What we've learnt from the mistakes we made after March 11th is that there *are* no patterns. It's the government's business to quell panic by offering some kind of order to a terrified public. It's our job to treat every situation as unique. Carry on, Inspector Jefe.'

None of the Sevillanos liked this patronizing little speech and they looked at the CNI man in his expensive loafers, lightweight suit and stiff, heavy, silvery tie and decided that the only thing he'd said that didn't mark him out as a typical visiting Madrileño was his admission of a mistake.

'If it wasn't Chechen rebels, who was it?' asked Calderón.

'Not relevant, Juez Calderón,' said Juan. 'Proceed, Inspector Jefe.'

'It might be interesting from the point of view of sources for the hexogen,' said Calderón, who was not a man to be brushed off easily. 'We've found a van with traces of explosive and Islamic paraphernalia. The Chechens are known to have access to Russian military ordnance and have the sympathy of the Muslim world. In most people's minds those rebels were responsible for the destruction of the Moscow apartment blocks. If any of these connections have been proven invalid by the intelligence community, then perhaps the Inspector Jefe should know about them now. The source of the explosives will be an important area of his investigation.'

'*His* investigation?' said Juan. '*Our* investigation. This is going to be a concerted effort. The Grupo de Homicidios is not going to crack this case on its own. This hexogen will have been imported. The CNI has the international connections to find out where it came from.'

'Nevertheless,' said Calderón, embarking on some of his own pomposity, 'this is where the investigation begins, and if the Inspector Jefe is about to pursue an avenue of enquiry with incorrect or misleading information, then perhaps he should be told.'

Calderón was aware that this *was* irrelevant in terms of information for the purposes of the investigation, but he also knew that a demonstration of power was required to put Juan in his place. Calderón was the leading Juez de Instrucción and he was not going to have his authority undermined by an outsider, especially a Madrileño.

'We cannot be certain,' said Juan, exasperated by the posturing, 'but a theory is being given credibility that the Russian Security Service, the FSB, were *themselves*

124

responsible for the outrage, and that they successfully managed to frame the Chechens. Just prior to the explosion Putin had become director of the FSB. The country was in turmoil and there was the perfect opportunity for a power play. The FSB provoked a war in Chechnya and Dagestan. The prime minister lost his job and Putin took over at the beginning of 1999. The Moscow apartment explosions gave him the opportunity to start a patriotic campaign. He was the fearless leader who would stand up to the rebels. By the beginning of 2000, Putin was acting president of Russia. The hexogen used by the FSB was supposed to have come from a scientific research institute in Lubyanka where the FSB has its headquarters. As you can see, Juez Calderón, my explanation does not help us very much here, but it does illustrate how very quickly the world can become a dangerous and confusing place.'

Silence, while the Sevillanos considered the reverberations of the explosion in their own city to places like Chechnya and Moscow. Falcón continued his briefing about the Peugeot Partner, the two men seen unloading goods for the mosque, the men believed to have been in the mosque at the time of the explosion, and the latest revelations about the owner of the vehicle and his nephew, Trabelsi Amar, who had borrowed it.

'Anything else?' asked Juan, while Elvira's assistant entered the name of Trabelsi Amar into the terrorist suspects database.

'Just one thing to clear up before I continue with the investigation,' said Falcón. 'Did the CNI or the CGI have the mosque under surveillance?'

'What makes you think that we might have done?' asked Juan.

Falcón briefed them on the mysterious, well-dressed young men from Informáticalidad, who had frequented the nearby apartment over the past three months.

'That is not the way *we* would run a surveillance operation and I've never heard of Informáticalidad.'

'What about the antiterrorism unit, Inspector Jefe Barros?' asked Elvira.

'We did not have the mosque under active surveillance,' said Barros, who seemed to be restraining great anger under preternatural calm. 'I've heard of Informáticalidad. They're the biggest suppliers of computer software and consumables in Seville. They even supply us.'

'One final question about the Imam,' said Falcón. 'We're told he arrived here from Tunis in September 2004 and that he is in the lowest risk category for terrorist suspects, but his history required a higher authority for clearance.'

'His file is incomplete,' said Juan.

'What does that mean?'

'As far as we know, he's clean,' said Juan. 'He has been heard to speak out against the cold-blooded, indiscriminate nature of the Madrid bombings. We understand from his visa application that part of the reason he came to Seville was to attempt a healing of the wounds between the Catholic and Muslim communities. He saw that as his duty. We were only concerned about gaps in his history that we could not fill. These gaps occurred in the 1980s, when a lot of Muslims went to Afghanistan to fight with the mujahedeen against the Russians. Some returned radicalized to their homes in the 1990s and others later became the Taliban. The Imam would have been in his thirties at the time and therefore a prime candidate. In the end, the Americans vouched for him and we allowed him a visa.'

'So this bomb has killed a potential sympathizer, five men over the age of sixty-five, a man under thirty-five who was in a wheelchair, two Spanish converts and two men in their forties collecting disability benefits, which leaves only two under the age of thirty-five, able-bodied and of North African origin,' said Elvira. 'Can the CNI offer a theory as to why this strangely mixed group of people who, we have just been told, were not under active surveillance, should be storing high-quality military explosive and why it should have been detonated?'

Silence. The grinding gears of the machinery outside reached them. The thunder of rubble dropping into empty tippers, the hiss and scream of hydraulics, the low roar of the crane's unwinding cable, all punctuated by the pneumatic drills' staccato stabbing, reminded these men of the purpose of their meeting and the disaster that had befallen this city.

'Trabelsi Amar is not on any terrorist suspect database and he's an illegal alien,' said Elvira's assistant, breaking the silence.

'Do you believe that explosives could have been stored in the mosque without the knowledge of the Imam?' asked Calderón.

'There's an outside chance that he didn't recognize what it was,' said Juan. 'As you know, hexogen looks like sugar. The trace left on the floor indicates that the packaging wasn't exactly hermetically sealed. It's possible that the explosive was in those cardboard boxes, which the Inspector Jefe has told us were seen being unloaded yesterday.'

'But for the hexogen to actually explode would require a detonator,' said Falcón. 'From the way in which they were moving it around it must be a stable product.'

'It is,' said Juan.

'Then that means they must have been working on making bombs and accidentally detonated it,' said Falcón. 'I doubt they could be doing that in secret in a mosque of that size, with thirteen other people in it. I haven't seen the plans, but it can't be more than ten by twenty metres.'

'So the Imam is complicit in that scenario,' said Juan. 'We'll have to talk to the Americans about Abdelkrim Benaboura and we'll find a photo ID and a history for Trabelsi Amar.'

'If Soumaya is identifying Amar as his nephew, then that doesn't sound to me like deep terrorist cover. He's probably got photographs,' said Falcón. 'We have to consider the possibility that this van was not being driven by him. It could have been stolen or, for whatever reason, given to another party to transport goods to Seville. Trabelsi Amar's function could have been simply to provide a van, which would not be reported stolen.'

'We'll make sure the CGI in Canillas communicate with the local police in Madrid, who are interviewing Mohammed Soumaya,' said Juan, which sounded like he was undermining Inspector Jefe Barros, who was still boiling in silence. 'It's one of the complications of these terrorist operations that the people we know about are active only in so far as they use up our time and resources. As was the case with March 11th, where none of the operatives were known terrorists or had

128

any links to known radical Islamic organizations. They came out of nowhere to perform their tasks.'

'But you're in a better position now than you were then,' said Elvira.

'Since 9/11 and the evidence of connections made by Islamic terrorist cell members in Spain . . .'

'You mean al-Qaeda members?' said Elvira.

'We don't like to use the name al-Qaeda because it implies an organization with a hierarchy along Western lines. This is not the case,' said Juan. 'It's useful for the media to have this name to hang on Islamic terrorism, but we don't use it in the service. We have to remind ourselves not to be complacent. As I was saying: since 9/11 and the evidence of connections made by Islamic terrorist cell members in Spain with the perpetrators of the Twin Towers and Washington DC attacks, there has been considerable stepping up of activities.'

'But, as you say, there seems to be an unending stream of young operatives who you don't know about and who can be organized at a distance to perform terrorist acts,' said Calderón. 'That, surely, is the problem?'

'As you've seen from the investigations into the London bombings, there is extraordinary co-operation between all the secret services,' said Juan. 'Our proximity to North Africa makes us vulnerable but gives us opportunities as well. In the two years since the Madrid train bombings we have achieved considerable penetration into Morocco, Algeria and Tunisia. We hope to improve our ability to pick up sleeping cells by intercepting the signals that might eventually activate them. We are not perfect, but neither are they. You don't hear about our successes, and it's too early to say whether we are dealing here with one of our failures.'

'You said that "in this scenario the Imam is complicit",' said Falcón. 'Does this mean you are looking at other scenarios?'

'All we can do is prepare ourselves for eventualities,' said Juan. 'In the last two years we have been examining a domestic phenomenon, which first came to light on the internet. I hesitate to call this phenomenon a group, because we have found no evidence of organization, or communication, for that matter. What we have found are newsletter pages on a website called www.vomit.org. This was thought to be an American site because it first appeared in the English language, but the CIA and MI5 have just recently told us they now believe VOMIT stands for Victimas del Odio de Musulmanos, Islamistas y Terroristas.'

'What's the content of the newsletter?'

'It's an updated list of all terrorist attacks carried out by Islamic extremists since the early 1990s. It gives a short account of the attack, the number of victims, both dead and injured, followed by the number of people directly affected by the death or injury of a person close to them.'

'Does that mean they are contacting the victims' families?' asked Elvira.

'If they are, the victims seem to be unaware of it,' said Juan. 'Victims get approached by the media, the government, the social services, the police . . . and, as yet, we haven't found anyone who has been able to tell us that they've been contacted by VOMIT.'

'Did this start in 2004 after the Madrid bombings?' said Elvira.

'The British first came across the pages in June 2004. By September 2004 it also included Muslim on Muslim attacks, such as suicide bombings against police recruiting offices in Iraq, and since the beginning of 2005 there has also been a section on Muslim women who have been the victims of honour killings or gang rapes. In these cases, they only report on the type of attack and number of victims.'

'Presumably the posting of these pages on the web is completely anonymous,' said Calderón, who didn't wait for an answer. 'There must have been a Muslim reaction to this, surely?'

'The Al Jazeera news channel did a piece on these web pages back in August 2004 and there was a huge internet response in which various Arab-sponsored websites enumerated Arab victims of Israeli, American, European, Russian, Far Eastern and Australian aggression. Some of them were extreme and went back in history to the Crusades, the expulsion of the Moors from Spain and the defeat of the Ottoman empire. None of the websites came up with as powerful a banner as VOMIT, and a lot of them couldn't resist spouting an agenda, so although they were read avidly in the Arab world, they didn't penetrate the West at all.'

'So what makes you think that VOMIT has gone from being a passive, unorganized internet phenomenon into an active, operational entity?' asked Falcón.

'We don't,' said Juan. 'We review their web pages daily to see if there's any incitement to violence, disrespect shown to Islam, or attempts at recruitment to some kind of cause, but there's nothing except the clocking up of attacks and their victims.'

'Have you spoken to victims of the Madrid bombings?' asked Falcón.

'There is no common theme of vengeance amongst them. The only anger was directed at our own politicians and not against North Africans in general, or Islamic fanatics specifically. Most of the victims recognized that many Muslims had also been killed in the bombings. They saw it as an indiscriminate act of terror, with a political goal.'

'Did any of them know about VOMIT?'

'Yes, but none of them said they would seek membership if it existed,' said Juan. 'However, we do know that there is anger out there from fanatical right-wing groups with strong racist views and anti-immigration policies. We are keeping an eye on them. The police handle their violent activities at a local level. They are not known to have a national organization or to have planned and carried out attacks of this magnitude.'

'And religious groups?'

'Some of these fanatically right-wing groups have religious elements, too. If they advertise themselves in any way, we know about them. What concerns us is that they might be learning from their perceived enemies.'

'So the other possible scenario – that this was an organized attack against a Muslim community – is based solely on what? That it's about time there was a reaction against Islamic terrorism?' asked Calderón.

'Each terrorist atrocity is unique. The circumstances that prevail at the time make it so,' said Juan. 'At the time of the March 11th attack, Aznar's government were *expecting* an ETA attempt to disrupt the forthcoming elections. A couple of months earlier on

Christmas Eve 2003 two bombs of 25 kilos each had been discovered on the Irún–Madrid intercity train. Both bombs were classic ETA devices and had been set to explode two minutes before their arrival in the Chamartín station. Another ETA bomb was found on the track of the Zaragoza–Caspe–Barcelona line, which was set to explode on New Year's Eve 2003. On 29th February 2004, as everybody in this room knows, the Guardia Civil intercepted two ETA operatives in a transit van which contained 536 kilos of Titadine, destination Madrid. Everything was pointing to a major attack on the railway system prior to the elections on 14th March 2004, which would be planned and carried out by ETA.'

'That was the information, and the extrapolation from it was sent to the government by the CNI,' said Calderón, keen to stick it in.

'And it was wrong, Juez Calderón. *We were wrong,*' said Juan. 'Even after listening to the tapes of the Koran found in the Renault Kangoo van near the Alcalá de Henares station, and the discovery of the detonators not previously used by ETA, and the fact that the explosive was not Titadine, as customarily used by ETA, but Goma 2 ECO, we still couldn't believe that ETA was *not* behind it. *That* is the very point I am making, and it is why we should consider all scenarios in this present attack and not allow our minds to harden around a core of received opinion. We must work, step by step, until we have the unbreakable line of logic that leads to the perpetrators.'

'We can't leave people in the dark while we do this,' said Calderón. 'The media, the politicians and the public need to know that something is happening, that their safety is assured. Terror breeds confusion –'

'Comisario Elvira, as leader of this investigation, has that responsibility, as do the politicians. Our job is to make sure that they have the right information,' said Juan. 'We've already started looking at this attack with a historical mind – the apartment bombs in Moscow, the discovery of Islamic paraphernalia in a white van – and we can't afford to do that.'

'The media already knows what was found in the Peugeot Partner van,' said Calderón. 'We cannot prevent them from drawing their conclusions.'

'*How* do they know that?' asked Juan. 'There was a police cordon.'

'We don't know,' said Calderón, 'but as soon as the vehicle was removed and the journalists allowed into the car park, Comisario Elvira and I were fielding questions about the hexogen, the two copies of the Koran, a hood, the Islamic sash, and plenty of other stuff that wasn't even in the van.'

'There were a lot of people out in that car park,' said Falcón. 'My officers, the forensics, the bomb squad, the vehicle removal men, were all in the vicinity of that first inspection of the van. Journalists do their job. The cameras were supposed to be kept away from the bodies of the children in the pre-school, but one guy found his way in there.'

'As we've seen before,' said Juan, breathing down his irritation, 'it's very difficult to dislodge first impressions from the public's mind. There are still millions of Americans who believe that Saddam Hussein was responsible in some way for 9/11. Most of Seville will now believe that they have been the victim of an Islamic terrorist attack and we might not be able to come close to confirming the truth of the matter until we can get into the mosque, which could be days of demolition work away.'

'Perhaps we should look at the unique circumstances which led to this event,' said Falcón, 'and also look at the future, to see if there's anything that this bombing might be seeking to influence. From my own point of view, the reason I was very early on to the scene here was that I was at the Forensic Institute, discussing the autopsy of a body found on the main rubbish dump on the outskirts of Seville.'

Falcón gave the details of the unidentifiable corpse found yesterday.

'This could, of course, be an unconnected murder,' said Falcón. 'However, it is unique in the crime history of Seville and it does not appear to be the work of a single person, but rather a group of killers, who have gone to extreme lengths to prevent identification.'

'Have there been any other murders with similar attempts to prevent identification?' asked Juan.

'Not in Spain this year, according to the police computer,' said Falcón. 'We haven't checked with Interpol yet. Our investigation is still very new.'

'Are there any elections due?'

'The Andalucían parliamentary elections last took place in March 2004,' said Calderón. 'The Town Hall elections were in 2003 so they are due next March. The socialists are currently in office.'

Juan took a folded piece of paper out of his pocket.

'Before we left Madrid we had a call from the CGI, who had just been informed by the editor of the *ABC* that they had received a letter with a Seville stamp on the envelope. The letter consisted of a single sheet of paper and a printed text in Spanish. We have since discovered that this text comes from the work of Abdullah Azzam, a preacher best known as the leading ideologue of the Afghan resistance to the Russian invasion. It reads as follows:

'"This duty will not end with victory in Afghanistan; jihad will remain an individual obligation until all other lands that were Muslim are returned to us, so that Islam will reign again: before us lie Palestine, Bokhara, Lebanon, Chad, Eritrea, Somalia, the Philippines, Burma, Southern Yemen, Tashkent . . ."' he paused, looking around the room, '"and Andalucía."'

10

The meeting broke up with the news that another body had been found in the rubble. Calderón left immediately. The three CNI men spoke intently amongst themselves, while Falcón and Elvira discussed resources. Inspector Jefe Barros of the CGI stared into the floor, his jaw muscles working over some new humiliation. After ten minutes the CNI conferred with Elvira. Falcón and Barros were asked to leave the room. Barros paced the corridor, avoiding Falcón. Some moments later Elvira called Falcón back in and the CNI men moved towards the door, saying that they would conduct a detailed search of Imam Abdelkrim Benaboura's apartment.

'Is that information going to be shared?' asked Falcón.

'Of course,' said Juan, 'unless it compromises national security.'

'I'd like one of my officers to be present.'

'In the light of what's just been said, we have to do it now and you're all too busy.'

They left. Falcón turned to Elvira, hands open, questioning this state of affairs.

'They're determined not to make a mistake this time round,' said Elvira, '*and* they want all the credit for it, too. Futures are at stake here.'

'And to what extent do you have control over what they do?'

'Those words "national security" are the problem,' said Elvira. 'For instance, they want to talk to *you* on a matter of "national security", which means I'm told nothing other than it has to be private and at length.'

'That's not going to be easy today.'

'They'll make time for you – at night, whenever.'

'And "national security" is the only clue they've given?'

'They're interested in your Moroccan connections,' said Elvira, 'and have asked to interview you.'

'Interview me?' said Falcón. 'That sounds like it's for a job and I've already got one of those with plenty of work in it.'

'Where are you going now?'

'I'm tempted to be present at the search of the Imam's apartment,' said Falcón. 'But I think I'm going to follow up the Informáticalidad lead. That's a very strange way to use an apartment for three months.'

'So you're keeping an open mind on this, unlike our CNI friends,' said Elvira, nodding at the door.

'I thought Juan was very eloquent on the subject.'

'That's how they want everybody else to think, so that they've got all their bases covered,' said Elvira, 'but there's no doubt in my mind that they believe they've hit on the beginning of a major Islamic terrorist campaign.'

'To bring Andalucía back into the Islamic fold?'

'Why else would they want to talk to you about your "Moroccan connections"?'

'We don't know what *they* know.'

'I know that they're seeking redress and greater glory,' said Elvira, 'and that worries me.'

'And what was going on with Inspector Jefe Barros?' asked Falcón. 'He was present but nothing more, as if he'd been told he was allowed to attend but not to say a word.'

'There's a problem, which they will explain to you directly. All I have been told by the head of the CGI in Madrid is that, for the moment, the Seville antiterrorism unit cannot contribute to this investigation.'

Consuelo sat in her office in the restaurant in La Macarena. She had kicked off her shoes and was curled up foetally on her new expensive leather office chair, which rocked her gently backwards and forwards. She had a ball of tissue in her hands, which was crammed into her mouth. She bit against it when the physical pain became too much. Her throat tried to articulate the emotion, but it had no reference points. Her body felt like ruptured earth, spewing up sharp chunks of magma.

The television was on. She had not been able to bear the silence of the restaurant. The chefs weren't due to start preparing the lunch service until 11 a.m. She had tried to walk her extreme agitation out of herself, but her tour of the spotless kitchen, with its gleaming stainless steel surfaces, its knives and cleavers winking encouragement at her, had terrified rather than calmed. She'd walked the dining rooms and the patio, but none of the smells, the textures, not even the obsessive order of the table settings could fill this aching emptiness pressing against her ribs.

She had retreated to her office, locked herself in. The volume of the television was turned low so that she couldn't make out the words, but she took comfort from the human murmur. She looked out of the corner of her eye at the images of destruction playing on the screen. There was the sharp smell of vomit in the room as she'd just thrown up at the sight of the tiny bodies under their pinafores outside the pre-school. Tears tracked mascara down her cheeks. The mouth side of the ball of tissue was slimy with sharp saliva. Something had been levered open; the lid was no longer on whatever it was she had inside her, and she, who had always prided herself on her courage to face up to things, could not bear to take a look. She squeezed her eyes shut at a new rising of pain. The chair empathized with the shudder of her body. Her throat squealed as if there was something sharp lodged across it.

The destroyed apartment block flickered on the screen in the corner of her eye. She couldn't bear to switch off the TV and live with the only other occupant of the silence, even though the building's collapse was an appalling replication of her own mental state. Only a few hours ago she had been more or less whole. She had always imagined the gap between sanity and madness as a yawning chasm, but now found it was like a border in the desert: you didn't know whether you'd crossed it or not.

The TV pictures changed from the piles of rubble to a body bag being lifted into a cradle stretcher, to the wounded, staggering down pavements, to the jagged edges of shattered windows, to the trees stripped of all their leaves, to cars upside down in gardens, to a road sign speared into the earth. These TV news editors must be professionals in horror, every image was like a slap to the face, knocking a complacent public into the new reality.

Then calm returned. A presenter stood in front of the church of San Hermenegildo. He had a friendly face. Consuelo turned up the sound in the hope of good news. The camera zoomed in on the plaque and dropped back down to the presenter, who was now walking and giving a brief history of the church. The camera remained tight on the presenter's face. There was an inexplicable tension in the scene. Something was coming. The suspense transfixed Consuelo. The presenter's voice told them that this was the site of an old mosque and the camera cut to the apex of a classic Arabic arch. Its focus pulled wide to reveal the new horror. Written in red over the doors were the words: *AHORA ES NUESTRA*. Now it is ours.

The screen filled again with another montage of horror. Women screaming for no apparent reason. Blood on the pavements, in the gutter, thickening the dust. A body, with the terrible sag of lifelessness, being lifted out of the ruins.

She couldn't bear the sight of any more. These cameramen must be robots to handle this horror. She turned the TV off and sat in the silence of the office.

The images had jolted her. The lid seemed to have slipped back over the darkness welling inside her chest. Her hands trembled, but she no longer needed to bite on the ball of tissue. The shame of her first consultation with Alicia Aguado came back to her. Consuelo pressed her hands to her cheekbones as she remembered her words: 'blind bitch'. How could she have said such a thing? She picked up the phone.

Alicia Aguado was relieved to hear Consuelo's voice. Her concern raised emotion in Consuelo's throat. Nobody ever cared about her. She stumbled through an apology.

'I've been called worse than that,' said Aguado. 'Given that we're the most inventive insulters in the world, you can imagine the special reserves that are drawn on when it comes to psychologists.'

'It was unforgivable.'

'All will be forgiven as long as you come and see me again, Sra Jiménez.'

'Call me Consuelo. After what we've been through, all formality is out of the window,' she said. 'When can you see me?'

'I'd like to see you tonight, but it won't be possible before 9 p.m.'

'Tonight?'

'I'm very concerned about you. I wouldn't normally ask, but . . .'

'But what?'

'I think you've reached a very dangerous point.'

'Dangerous? Dangerous to whom?'

'You have to promise me something, Consuelo,' said Aguado. 'You have to come directly here to me after work, and when our consultation is over you must go straight home and have somebody – a relative or a friend – to be there with you.'

Silence from Consuelo.

'I could ask my sister, I suppose,' she said.

'It's very important,' said Aguado. 'I think you've realized the extreme vulnerability of your state, so I would recommend that you confine yourself to home, work and my consulting room.'

'Can you just explain that to me?'

'Not now over the phone, face to face this evening,' she said. 'Remember, come straight to me. You must resist all temptations to any diversion, however strong the urge.'

Manuela Falcón sat in Angel's big comfortable chair in front of the television. She was now incapable of movement, with not even the strength to reach for the remote and shut down the screen, which was transferring the horror images directly to her mind. The police were evacuating El Corte Inglés in the Plaza del Duque after four reports of suspicious packages on different floors of the department store. Two sniffer dogs and their handlers arrived to patrol the building. The image cut to a deserted crossroads in the heart of the city, with shoes scattered over the cobbles and people running towards the Plaza Nueva. Manuela felt pale, with just the minimum quantity of blood circulating around her head and face to maintain basic oxygenation and brain function. Her extremities were freezing, despite the open door to the terrace and the temperature outside steadily rising.

The telephone had rung once since Angel had left for the *ABC* offices where he hoped to put his finger to the thready pulse of a convulsing city. She'd had the strength then to answer it. Her lawyer had asked whether she'd seen the television and then told her that the Sevillana buyer had pulled out with an excuse about her 'black' money not being ready and that she would have to postpone the signing of the deed.

'That's not going to stop her from losing her deposit,' said Manuela, still able to raise some aggression.

'Have you been listening to what Canal Sur have been reporting?' said the lawyer. 'They've found a van with traces of a military explosive in the back. The editor of the *ABC* in Madrid was sent a letter from al-Qaeda saying that they would not rest until Andalucía was back in the Islamic fold. There's some security expert saying that this is the start of a major terrorist campaign and there'll be more attacks in the coming days.'

'Fucking hell,' said Manuela, jamming a cigarette into her mouth, lighting it.

'So that 20,000 deposit your buyer might lose is looking like a cheap way out for her.'

'What about the German's lawyer, has he called yet?'

'Not yet, but he's going to.'

Manuela had clicked off the phone and let it fall in her lap. She smoked on automatic with great fervour, and the nicotine surge enabled her to call Angel, whose mobile was off. They couldn't find him in the *ABC* offices, which sounded like the trading floor in the first minutes of a black day for the markets.

Her lawyer called again.

'The German has pulled out. I've called the notary's office and all deed signings have been cancelled for the day. There's been an announcement on the TV and radio, the Jefe Superior de la Policía and the chief of the emergency services have told us to only use mobile phones if absolutely necessary.'

The workshop was in a courtyard up an old alleyway with massive grey cobbles, off Calle Bustos Tavera. Marisa Moreno had rented it purely because of this alleyway. On bright sunny days, such as this one, the light in the courtyard was so intense that nothing could be discerned from within the darkness of the twenty-five-metre alleyway. The cobbles were like pewter ingots and drew her on. Her attraction to this alleyway was that it coincided with her vision of death. Its arched interior was not pretty, with crappy walls, a collection of fuse boxes and electric cables running over crumbling whitewashed plaster. But that was the point. It was a transference from this messy, material world to the cleansing white light beyond. There was, however, disappointment in the courtyard, to find that paradise was a broken down collection of shabby workshops and storage houses, with peeling paint, wrought-iron grilles and rusted axles.

It was only a five-minute walk from her apartment on Calle Hiniesta to her workshop, which was another reason she'd rented somewhere too big for her needs. She occupied the first floor, accessed via an iron staircase to the side. It had a huge window overlooking the courtyard, which gave light and great heat in the summer. Marisa liked to sweat; that was the Cuban in her. She often worked in bikini briefs and liked the way the wood chips from her carving stuck to her skin.

That morning she'd left her apartment and taken a coffee in one of the bars on Calle Vergara. The bar was unusually packed, with all heads turned to the television. She ordered her café con leche, drank it and left, refusing all attempts by the locals to involve her in any debate. She had no interest in politics, she didn't believe in the Catholic Church or any other organized religion, and, as far as she was concerned, terrorism only mattered if you happened to be in the wrong place at the wrong time.

In the studio she worked on staining two carvings and polishing another two, ready for delivery. By midday she had them rolled in bubblewrap and was down in the courtyard waiting for a taxi.

A young Mexican dealer, who had a gallery in the centre on Calle Zaragoza, had bought the two pieces. He was part Aztec, and Marisa had had an affair with him a few months before she'd met Esteban Calderón. He still bought every carving she made and paid cash on delivery every time. To see them greet each other you might have thought they were still seeing each other, but it was more of a blood understanding, his Aztec and her African.

Esteban Calderón knew nothing of this. He'd never seen her workshop. She didn't have any of her work in her apartment. He knew she carved wood, but she made it sound as if it was in the past. That was the way she wanted it. She hated listening to Westerners talking about art. They didn't seem to grasp that appreciation was the other way around: let the piece talk to you.

Marisa dropped off her two finished pieces and took her money. She went to a tobacconist and bought herself a Cuban cigar – a Churchill from the Romeo y Julieta brand. She walked past the Archivo de las Indias and the Alcázar. The tourists were not quite as numerous as usual, but still there, and seemingly oblivious to the bomb which had gone off on the other side of the city, proving her point that terrorism only mattered if it directly affected you.

She walked through the Barrio Santa Cruz and into

the Murillo Gardens to indulge in her after-sales ritual. She sat on a park bench, unscrewed the aluminium cap of the cylinder and let the cigar fall into her palm. She smoked it under the palm trees, imagining herself back in Havana.

Inés had pulled herself together after fifteen minutes weeping. Her stomach couldn't take it any more. The tensing of her abdominals was agony. She had crawled to the shower, pulled off her nightdress and slumped in the tray, keeping her burning scalp out from under the fine needles of water.

After another quarter of an hour she had been able to stand, although not straight because of the pain in her side. She dressed in a dark suit with a high-collared cream blouse and put on heavy make-up. There was no bruising to disguise but she needed a full mask to get through the morning. She found some aspirin, which took the edge off the pain so that she could walk without being creased over to one side. Normally she would walk to work, but that was out of the question this morning and she took a taxi. That was the first she knew of the bomb. The radio was full of it. The driver talked non-stop. She sat in the back, silent behind her dark glasses until the driver, unnerved by her lack of response, asked if she was ill. She told him she had a lot on her mind. That was enough. At least he knew she was hearing him. He went into a long soliloquy about terrorism, how the only cure for this disease was to get rid of the lot of them.

'Who?' asked Inés.

'Muslims, Africans, Arabs . . . the whole lot. Get shot

147

of them all. Spain should be for the Spanish,' he said. 'What we need now are the old Catholic kings. They understood the need to be pure. They knew what they had to do . . .'

'So you're including the Jews in this mass exile?' she asked.

'*No, no, no que no,* the Jews are all right. It's these Moroccans, Algerians and Tunisians. They're all fanatics. They can't control their religious fervour. What are they doing, blowing up an apartment block? What does that prove?'

'It proves how powerful indiscriminate terror can be,' she said, feeling her whole chest about to burst open. 'We're no longer safe in our own homes.'

The Palacio de Justícia was frantic as usual. She slowly went up to her office on the second floor, which she shared with two other fiscales, state prosecutors. She was determined not to show the pain each step unleashed in her side. Having wanted to wear the badge of his violence, she now wanted to disguise her agony.

The mask of her make-up got her through the first excited minutes with her colleagues, who were full of the latest rumour and theory, with hardly a fact between them. Nobody associated Inés with emotional wreckage so they glided over the surface and went back to their work unaware of her state.

There were cases to prepare and meetings to be attended and Inés got through it all until the early afternoon when she found herself with a spare half-hour. She decided to go for a walk in the Murillo Gardens, which were just across the avenue. The gardens would calm her down and she wouldn't have to listen to any more conjecture about the bomb. She had the little grenade attack in her relationship to consider. She knew a breather in the park wasn't going to help her sort it out, but at least she might be able to find something around which to start rebuilding her collapsed marriage.

Over the last four years when things had been going wrong for Inés in her marriage she played herself a film loop. It was the edited version of her life with Esteban. It never started with their meeting each other and the subsequent affair, because that would mean the film started with her infidelity, and she did not see herself as somebody who broke her marriage vows. In her movie she was unblemished. She had rewritten her private history and cut out all images that did not meet with her approval. This was not a conscious act. There was no facing up to unfortunate episodes or personal embarrassments, they were simply forgotten.

This movie would have been immensely dull to anyone who was not Inés. It was propaganda. No better than a dictator's glorious biopic. Inés was the courageous fiancée who had picked up her husband-to-be after the nasty little incident that they never talked about, given him the care and attention he needed to get his career back on track . . . and so it went on. And it worked. For her. After each of his discovered infidelities she'd played the movie and it had given her strength; or rather it had given her something to record over Esteban's previous aberration, so that she only suffered from one of his infidelities at a time, and not the whole history.

This time, as she sat on the park bench playing her

film, something went wrong. She couldn't hold the images. It was as if the film was jumping out of the sprockets and letting an alien image flood into her private theatre: someone with long coppery hair, dark skin and splayed legs. This visual interference was shorting out her internal comfort loop. Inés gathered the amnesiac forces of her considerable mind by pressing her hands to the sides of her head and blinkering her eyes. It was then that she realized that it was something on the outside, forcing its way in. Reality was intruding. The copper-haired, dark-skinned whore she'd seen only this morning, naked, on her husband's digital camera was sitting opposite her, smoking a cigar without a care in the world.

Marisa didn't like the way the woman sitting on the bench on the other side of the shaded pathway was looking at her. She had the intensity of a lunatic about her; not the raving-in-the-asylum type but a more dangerous version: too thin, too chic, too shallow. She'd come across them at the Mexican dealer's gallery openings, all on the verge of a nervous breakdown. They filled the air with high-pitched chatter to keep the real world from bursting through the levee, as if, by chanting their consumer mantras, the great nothing that was going on in their lives would be kept at bay. In the gallery she tolerated their presence as they might buy her work, but out in the open she was not going to have one of these *cabras ricas* ruining her expensive cigar.

'What you looking at?' said Marisa. 'You're ruining my cigar, you know that?'

It took a moment for Inés, fluttering her eyelids in

150

astonishment, to realize that this was directed at her. Then the adrenaline kicked into her prosecutorial system. Here was a confrontation. She was good at those.

'I'm looking at you. *La puta con el puro,*' said Inés. The whore with the cigar.

Marisa uncrossed her legs and leaned forward, with her elbows on her knees, to get a good look at her heavily made-up adversary. She didn't stop to think too long.

'Hey, look, you bony-assed bitch, I'm sorry if I'm on your patch, but I'm not working, I'm just enjoying a cigar.'

The insult slashed across Inés's face leaving it red with outrage. The blood dimmed Inés's vision at the edges and played havoc with her oral-cerebral linkage.

'I'm a fucking lawyer!' she roared, and the people in the park stopped to look.

'Lawyers are the biggest whores of them all,' said Marisa. 'Is that why you paint your face like that? To hide the pox?'

Inés leapt to her feet, forgetting her injuries. Even in her fury she felt that twinge in her side, the bumping of her bruised organs, and it was that which stopped her from a full physical onslaught. That, and the force field of Marisa's languid muscularity, and impassive vocal brutality.

'*You* are the whore,' she said, pointing a spindly white finger at Marisa's lustrous, mulatto sheen. 'You're the one fucking *my* husband.'

The shock that registered in Marisa's face encouraged Inés, who had misread it as consternation.

'How much is he paying you?' asked Inés. 'It doesn't

look as if it's much more than 15 Euros a night, and that's a disgrace. That's not even minimum wage. Or does he throw in the copper wig and buy you a fat cigar to keep you happy when he's not there?'

Marisa instantly recovered from the revelation that this was the pale, pathetic, stringy little wife that Esteban couldn't bear to go back to. She'd also seen that wince of pain as Inés had got to her feet and guessed at the hurt being disguised by the clownish panstick. She'd seen beaten women in the poverty of Havana and she could spot vulnerability at a hundred metres, *and* she had the ruthlessness to open it up and reveal it to its owner and the rest of the world.

'Just remember, Inés,' she said, 'that when he's beating you, it's because he's been fucking me so beautifully, all night, that he can't bear the sight of your disappointed little face in the morning.'

The sound of her name coming out of the mulatto's mouth made Inés catch her breath with a loud cluck. Thereafter the words sliced through her with the ferocity of blasted glass. The arrogance of her own anger disappeared. She felt the shame of being stripped naked in public with all eyes on her.

Marisa saw the fight go out of her and watched the sag in Inés's shoulders with some satisfaction. She felt no pity; she'd suffered much worse when she'd lived in America. In fact the thin white hand with which Inés now held her side, no longer able to disguise the pain, only made Marisa think of other possibilities. Fate had brought them together and now it was up to one to shape the destiny of the other.

11

A group of workmen had formed around the section of the building where Fernando had pinpointed his wife's position from the sound of her mobile phone. Fernando was on his haunches, with his hands clasped over the top of his head, trying to exert additional gravitational force, as if there was the possibility that more tragedy might carry him away like a child's lost helium-filled balloon.

The crane loomed over the scene with its wrist-thick steel cable, taut and creaking. There were workmen on ladders using motorized hand-held saws, capable of ripping through concrete and steel with a noise that went through Falcón taking shreds with it. They had inserted hydraulic props and thick scaffolding planks to keep the collapsed floors apart as they carved out a tunnel. Chunks of concrete were coughed from the hole within clouds of dust, and showers of sparks spewed out as the saws' teeth bit into steel. The goggled workmen, grey as ghosts, plunged further in until the unbearable sound stopped and there was a call for more props and planks. The sun beat down. The sweat tracked dark rivulets through the grey dust on the workmen's faces. Once the props and planks were inserted the saws started up again, making all humans aware of the savagery of their metal teeth. The workmen were off the ladders now, kneeling on pads strapped to their knees, staring into the tangled skeleton of the building, embraced by claws of steel rods jutting from the shattered concrete.

He knew he should move away, that the sight of the confused guts of the building was not good preparation for the task at hand, but Falcón was caught up in the drama and was feeding a profound sense of anger at the tragedy. Only Ramírez calling wrenched him out of his distraction.

'We're getting reports of a blue transit van that was parked outside the front of the building yesterday morning,' said Ramírez. 'There seems to be confusion about the numbers of people in it. Some say two, others three and still others, four. They brought in tool boxes, a plastic box of some sort of electrical supplies and insulation tubing, carried in rolls over their shoulders. Nobody remembers any company name on the side of the van.'

'And it all went into the mosque?'

'There's confusion there, too,' said Ramírez. 'Most of the people we're talking to don't live in the building, they were just passers-by. Some didn't know there was a mosque in the basement. We're getting snapshots of what happened. I've got Pérez working on the residents list. He's down at the hospital. Serrano and Baena are working the surrounding blocks and people in the street. Where's Cristina?'

'She should still be working those blocks on Calle

Los Romeros,' said Falcón. 'What we need to find is someone who was *inside* the mosque in the last forty-eight hours to corroborate what we're hearing about on the outside. What about that woman, Esperanza, who gave Comisario Elvira the list – didn't she leave a number? Call her and get some names and addresses. Those women must know.'

'Hasn't anybody from the Moroccan community approached the Comisario yet?'

'Somebody turned up with the Mayor,' said Falcón. 'You know what it's like. They've got to contain the media before they can give us any practical help.'

'You remember that mosque they wanted to build over in Los Bermejales?' said Ramírez. 'A huge place, big enough for seven hundred worshippers. There was a protest group organized by the locals called Los Vecinos de Los Bermejales.'

'That's right, they had a website, too, called www.mezquitanogracias.com. There were a lot of accusations about xenophobia, racism and anti-Muslim activity, especially after March 11th.'

'Maybe we should look up some of the personalities from that dispute,' said Ramírez. 'Or is that too obvious?'

'Keep working on what happened inside and outside the building in the last forty-eight hours,' said Falcón. 'In the end there are two possibilities: explosives were brought here by terrorists and accidentally exploded, or an anti-Muslim group has planted a bomb and set it off. There are a lot of complications within those scenarios, but those are the two basic concepts. Let's work with the information we find, rather than getting distracted by the possibilities.'

Falcón hung up. The saws had stopped. The workmen were shovelling out rubble by hand. Two more props, planks and lights were called for. Men ran up the ladders with the equipment. Props were passed in. Torches were trained into the hole. A single saw ripped into some steel and stopped. A length of metal rod was flung out followed by more rubble. Four paramedics leaned against their ambulance, waiting for their turn in the drama. Two cradle stretchers with straps were brought to the foot of the ladders by the rescue teams. Fernando was concentrating on his breathing, under orders from his trauma counsellor. There was a shout for a doctor. A Médico Forense stepped up the ladder with his bag and crawled down the tunnel. There was silence, apart from the rumble of the insulated diesel generators. The diggers had stopped work. The drivers were out of their cabs watching. There was a collective need to wring some hope out of this calamitous day.

Another shout, this time for a stretcher. The doctor backed out on all fours and came down the ladder, while two men from the rescue services dragged the stretcher up the other ladder. Fernando came off his haunches and in seconds was on the doctor, holding him by the sleeves of his shirt. The doctor grasped Fernando by the shoulders and spoke directly into his eyes. The tension in their strange embrace made them look like judoists, struggling for the upper hand. Fernando's hands fell to his sides. The doctor put his arm around him and beckoned the counsellor. Fernando leaned into him like a lost child. The doctor spoke to the trauma counsellor over Fernando's shoulder.

The doctor trotted over to the paramedics, who

radioed through to the hospital. He talked directly with the emergency room. The paramedics reversed the ambulance up to the ladders, opened the double doors, prepared the trolley with a head, neck and spine immobilizer, turned on the oxygen, charged the defibrillator.

The workmen, who'd plunged into the hole after the doctor had backed out, now called the rescue workers in with the stretcher. The Médico Forense joined Falcón, just as Calderón came round from the front of the building.

'Have we got a survivor in there?' asked Calderón.

'The woman is dead,' said the doctor, 'but her child is hanging on. She's breathing and there's a thready pulse. The mother seems to have fallen with her body protecting the child, as much as possible, from the debris falling on top of them. The problem is to get the girl out. The mother's back is facing the rescue workers, so they've got to lift the child up and over her body and there's no room in there. If the child has a spinal injury, just the movement could cause permanent paralysis, but if she stays there much longer she'll die.'

The workmen roared from the mouth of the hole and held their thumbs up. The rescue workers slid the steel cradle stretcher out, mounted it on the ladder's sliders and lowered it to the paramedics, who lifted the girl out, on the count, and fitted her into the immobilizer. Two television crews came running, pursued by local police. The Médico Forense made a full report to Calderón. The pneumatic drills, saws and diggers started up again as if galvanized by this thin slice of hope. Falcón got into the ambulance cab. The trolley was lifted into the back, followed by Fernando. A cameraman was pushed back roughly by one of the workmen. The door closed on a woman's microphone. The driver leapt into his seat and set the siren off. He drove slowly over the rough ground until he got back on to the tarmac. Photojournalists stormed the side and back of the ambulance, holding cameras up to the windows and flashing away. The lurid lights, hysterical siren and the sprinting journalists left pedestrians gaping and slack-faced.

The news of a survivor travelled faster than the ambulance and there was a media scrum, battling it out with a dozen local policemen and hospital orderlies, at the entrance to the hospital. The ambulance ramp was clear and they got the girl out and through the swing doors before the newsmen could get near her. Fernando was sucked in after her. The media rounded on Falcón, who they'd seen in the ambulance cab, and he steadied their hysteria by informing them that the girl had been removed from the destroyed building showing signs of life. A doctor would make a full statement once he'd completed his examination. Falcón held up his hand and pushed back the barrage of questions that followed.

Ten minutes later he'd picked up his car from the Forensic Institute and was easing his way out through a gaggle of journalists still desperate for his final words. He crossed the river and went into the old Expo ground. He found Informáticalidad in an office that fronted a large warehouse on Calle Albert Einstein. He showed his police ID to the woman in reception and told her he wanted an immediate interview with Pedro Plata in connection with a murder investigation. He gave her his stoniest policeman's stare and she phoned through. Sr Plata was in a board meeting but would make himself available in a few minutes. She took him through security to an office with glass walls on all sides. The receptionist was still the only visible person. There was a lack of movement in the building, as if business was slow, even dead.

Pedro Plata arrived with the receptionist, who set down two coffees and left. He had only been responsible for buying the property so could offer no help in explaining how it had been used.

'Any reason why you bought it rather than rented it?'

'Only if you assure me this is not going to get back to the tax authorities, or be used against this company in any way.'

'My job is finding murderers.'

'We had some black money to get rid of.'

'And its use wasn't discussed at a board meeting?'

'Not one I attended,' said Plata. 'It was Diego Torres's idea, he's the Human Resources Director, you'd best talk to him.'

More time leaked past. The chill of the air conditioning and his exposure in the glass office made him feel like an Arctic zoo animal. Diego Torres arrived and before he'd even sat down Falcón asked him how they'd used the apartment.

'We try to encourage our employees to think creatively, not just about our business but business in general,' said Torres. 'Where will the next opportunities come from? Is there another strand that we can attach to our core business? Is there another business out there that could improve our own, or help it to grow? Is there a totally different project that could be worth investing in? These sorts of things.'

'And you think you can achieve that by investing in a small apartment, in an anonymous block, in a poor neighbourhood of Seville?'

'That was a conscious decision,' said Torres. 'Our employees complained that they never had time to think creatively, they were always too busy with the work at hand. They came to us demanding "brainstorming time". A lot of companies offer this and it normally consists of sending employees away to an expensive country club, where they attend meetings and seminars, listen to gurus spouting common sense and charging a fortune, interspersed with tennis, swimming and staying up until five in the morning partying.'

'They must have been very disappointed by your solution,' said Falcón. 'How many employees did you lose?'

'None from that project, but there's always a certain amount of churn in the sales teams. It's hard work with demanding targets. We pay well, but we expect results. A lot of young guys think they can handle the pressure, but they burn out, or lose their drive. It's a young person's business. There are no sales reps over thirty.'

'You're telling me you didn't lose anybody when you showed them that apartment in El Cerezo?'

'We're not stupid, Inspector Jefe,' said Torres. 'We gave them a sweetener. The idea was that they should take the brainstorming seriously. We put them in a place outside their normal environment, with no distractions, not even a decent café to go to, so that they would concentrate on the task. They went in pairs and we swapped the people around. They were told it was a finite project, three months maximum, and they

160

wouldn't have to spend more than four hours at a time in the apartment. They were also told that they would be a part of any of their projects which received board approval.'

'Was that the sweetener?'

'We're not that tough on them,' said Torres. 'The sweetener was a fully paid break in a beach hotel, with golf and tennis, during the Feria – and they wouldn't have to do any work. We let them bring their girl-friends, too.'

'And boyfriends?'

Torres blinked, as if that little comment had short-circuited something in his brain. Falcón thought Torres might be inferring something 'inappropriate' from his remark until he remembered that only men had been seen going into the apartment.

'You *do* employ women, don't you, Sr Torres?'

'The receptionist who showed you in here is . . .'

'How do you recruit, Sr Torres?'

'We advertise at business schools and through recruitment agencies.'

'Give me some names and telephone numbers,' said Falcón, handing him his notebook. 'How many people have you fired in the last year?'

'None.'

'Two years?'

'None. We don't fire people. They leave.'

'It's cheaper that way,' said Falcón. 'I'd like a list of all the people who have left your employ in the last year, and I'd also like the names and addresses of all the *men* who frequented that apartment in Calle Los Romeros.'

'Why?'

'We have to know whether they saw anything while they were there, especially in the last week.'

'It might not be so easy for you to interview my sales reps.'

'You'll have to *make* it easy. We're looking for people who are responsible for the deaths of four children and five adults . . . so far. And the first forty-eight hours of an investigation are critical.'

'When would you like to start?'

'Two members of my squad will begin contacting your sales reps as soon as you've given me their names and phone numbers,' said Falcón. 'And why, by the way, did you insist on your employees being there in the hours of daylight?'

'Those are the hours they work anyway. They sell from nine in the morning until eight at night while businesses are open. Then there's the paperwork, team meetings, course studies, product information classes. Twelve-hour days are the short ones.'

'Let me have a list with addresses and phone numbers of all the board members, too.'

'Now?'

'Along with those other lists I asked for,' said Falcón. 'I *am* busy, too, Sr Torres. So if you could bring them to me in the next ten minutes it would be appreciated.'

Torres stood and went to shake Falcón's hand.

'I'd like you to bring me the lists, Sr Torres,' said Falcón. 'I'll have more questions by then.'

Torres left. Falcón went to the toilet; there was an electronic plaque above each urinal, which streamed quotes from the Bible and inspirational business maxims. Informáticalidad extracted the best out of its employees by embracing them in a culture not unlike a religious sect.

The receptionist was waiting for him outside the toilets. It looked as if she'd been sent to make sure he didn't roam too freely around the corridors, despite all the offices being controlled by security key pads. She took him back to Torres, who was waiting with the lists.

'Is Informáticalidad part of a holding company?' asked Falcón.

'We're in the high-technology division of a Spanish company based in Madrid called Horizonte. They are owned by a US investment company called I4IT.'

'Who are they?'

'Who knows?' said Torres. 'The I4 bit is Indianapolis Investment Interests Incorporated and IT is Information Technology. I think they started out investing only in Hi-Tech, but they're broader based than that now.'

Torres walked him back to reception.

'How many ideas and projects did your reps come up with while they were in Calle Los Romeros?'

'Fifteen ideas, which have already been incorporated into our working practices, and four projects which are still in the planning stage.'

'Have you ever heard of a website called www.vomit.org?'

'Never,' said Torres, and let the door slowly close.

Back in his car Falcón checked his mobiles for calls. Informáticalidad's building, a steel cage covered in tinted glass, reflected its surroundings. On top of the building were four banners with company logos: Informáticalidad, Quirúrgicalidad, Ecográficalidad and finally a slightly larger placard featuring a huge pair of spectacles with a horizon running through them and above, the word Optivisión. High technology, robotic surgical instruments, ultrasound machines and laser equipment for correcting visual defects. This company had access to the internal workings of the body. They could see inside you, remove and implant things and make sure you saw the world the way they saw it. It disturbed Falcón.

12

As Falcón pulled away, car rippling along the glass façade of the building, he put a call through to Mark Flowers, who was euphemistically known as a Communications Officer in the US Consulate in Seville. He was a CIA operative who, after 9/11, had been pulled out of retirement, posted to Madrid and transferred to Seville. Falcón had met him during an investigation back in 2002. They had stayed in touch, or rather Falcón had become one of Flowers' sources and, in return, received intelligence and a more direct and proactive line to the FBI.

'Returning your call, Mark,' said Falcón.

'We should talk.'

'Have you got anything for me?'

'Nothing. It came out of the blue. I'm working on stuff.'

'Can you get some information for me on a company called I4IT, that's Indianapolis Investment Interests Incorporated in Information Technology.'

'Sure,' said Flowers. 'When can we meet?'

'Tonight. Late. Our people want to "interview" me,'

said Falcón. 'If you come afterwards you might be able to give me some advice.'

Falcón hung up. The radio news gave its latest summary of events: a group called the Mártires Islámicos para la Liberación de Andalucía had called both TVE and RNE to claim responsibility for the attack. El Corte Inglés had been evacuated and there was a stampede in the Calle Tetuán because of a bomb scare. All roads out of Seville, especially the motorway south towards Jerez de la Frontera, were jammed with traffic.

Falcón had to resist the image of a vast dust cloud on the outskirts of Seville, thick with panicked cattle beneath.

As he drove back across the river his mobile vibrated; Ramírez wanting to know where he was.

'We've found somebody who's a regular at the mosque,' he said. 'He goes there every evening after work, for prayers. We'll see you in the pre-school.'

Falcón came into the barrio of El Cerezo from the north, to avoid any traffic around the hospital. In the pre-school he photocopied the lists of personnel from Informáticalidad and gave them to Ramírez with orders for two members of the squad to start interviewing the sales reps to see if they'd noticed anything. Ramírez introduced the Moroccan man, who was called Said Harrouch. He was a cook, born in 1958 in Larache in northern Morocco.

The demolition work was too loud for them to talk in any of the classrooms, none of which had any glass in the windows, so they moved to the man's apartment nearby. Harrouch's wife made them mint tea and they sat in a room facing away from the destroyed building.

'You're a cook for a manufacturing company in the Polígono Industrial Calonge,' said Ramírez. 'What hours do you work?'

'Seven in the morning until five in the afternoon,' he said. 'They let me go back home when they heard about the bomb.'

'Do you go to the mosque at a regular time?'

'I manage to get there some time between half past five and a quarter to six.'

'Every day?'

'On the weekends I go five times a day.'

'Do you just pray, or do you spend time there?'

'At the weekends there's tea and I'll sit around and talk.'

The man was calm. He sat back from the table with his hands clasped across his stomach. He blinked slowly with long lashes and no wariness of either policeman.

'How long have you lived in Seville?'

'Nearly sixteen years,' he said. 'I came over in 1990 to work on the Expo site. I never went back.'

'Do you like living here in this neighbourhood?'

'I preferred living in the old city,' he said. 'It was more like home.'

'How are the people here?'

'You mean the Spanish people?' he asked. 'They're all right, most of them. Some of them don't like so many of us Moroccans being here.'

'You don't have to be diplomatic,' said Ramírez. 'Tell us how it really is.'

'After the Madrid train bombings a lot of people are very suspicious of us,' said Harrouch. 'They might have been told that not every North African is a terrorist, but it doesn't help when there are so many of us about.

The Imam has done his best to explain to local people that terrorism is a problem with an extreme minority, and that he himself does not agree with their radical interpretations of Islam, and does not approve of it in his mosque. It hasn't helped. They are still suspicious. I tell them that even in Morocco you would struggle to find anyone who actively approves of what these few fanatics are doing, but they don't believe us. Of course, if you go to a teahouse in Tangier you will hear people getting angry about what the Americans and the Israelis are doing. You will see protests on the streets about the plight of the Palestinians. But that is just talk and demonstration. It doesn't mean we're all about to strap bombs to our chests and go out and kill. Our own people were killed in the suicide bombings in Casablanca in May 2003 and Muslims died on those trains in Madrid in 2004 and in London in 2005, but they don't remember that.'

'That's the nature of terror, isn't it, Sr Harrouch?' said Falcón. 'The terrorist wants people to know that this can happen in any place, at any time, to anybody – Christian, Muslim, Hindu or Buddhist. This seems to be the state we are in now, here in Seville. People can no longer feel safe in their homes. What we want to find out, as soon as possible, is: who wants us to be terrified or, if that's too difficult, why they want us to be terrified.'

'But, of course, everybody will assume it is us,' said Harrouch, putting his fingertips to his chest. 'As I left work this morning, I was insulted in the street by people who can only think in one way when they hear that a bomb has gone off.'

'On 11th March the government automatically thought it was ETA,' said Ramírez.

168

'We know that there are anti-Muslim groups,' said Falcón.

'We've all heard of VOMIT, for instance,' said Harrouch. Then, registering the policemen's surprise: 'We spend a lot of time on the internet. That's how we communicate with our families back in Morocco.'

'We only found out about it this morning,' said Falcón.

'But it isn't directed at you, is it?' said Harrouch. 'It's designed to show that Islam is a religion of hate, which is not true. We see VOMIT as just another way that the West has devised to set out to humiliate us.'

'But it isn't *the West* that has created that website,' said Ramírez. 'It's another fanatical minority within the West.'

'The fact is, Sr Harrouch, it's going to take time for us to reach the basement where the mosque was located,' said Falcón, drawing the discussion back to business. 'We're going to have to wait days for any forensic information from the site of the actual bomb. What we have to rely on, for the moment, is witness accounts. Who was seen going in and out of that building over the last seventy-two hours. So far we have had a sighting of two vehicles: a white Peugeot Partner with two Moroccan men, who were seen delivering cardboard boxes –'

'Of sugar,' said Harrouch, suddenly animated. 'I was there when they brought it in yesterday. It was sugar. It was clearly printed on the sides of the boxes. And they had plastic carrier bags of mint. It was for the tea.'

'Did you know those two men?' asked Ramírez. 'Had you seen them before?'

'No, I didn't know them,' he said. 'I'd never seen them before.'

'So who did know them? Who did they make contact with?'

'Imam Abdelkrim Benaboura.'

'What did they do with this sugar and mint?'

'They took it into the storeroom at the back of the mosque.'

'Were these men introduced to anybody?'

'No.'

'Do you know where they came from?' asked Falcón.

'Someone said they were from Madrid.'

'How long did they stay in the mosque talking to the Imam?'

'They were still there when I left at seven o'clock.'

'Could they have spent the night there?'

'It's possible. People have slept in the mosque before.'

'Do you remember when they arrived?' asked Ramírez.

'About ten minutes after I came in from work, so about a quarter to six.'

'Can you tell us exactly what they did?'

'They came in, each carrying a box with a carrier bag of mint on top. They asked for the Imam. He came out of his office and showed them the storeroom. They stowed the boxes and then went back outside and brought another two boxes in.'

'Then what?'

'They left.'

'Empty-handed?'

'I think so,' said Harrouch. 'But they came back a few minutes later. I think they went off to park their car. When they returned they went into the Imam's office and they hadn't come out again by the time I left.'

'Did you hear anything of their conversation?'

Harrouch shook his head. Falcón sensed the man's nausea at the endless questions about seemingly unimportant detail. Harrouch somehow felt he was compromising these two men, who he believed had just delivered sugar and nothing more. Falcón told him not to worry about the questions, they were asked only to see if they squared with other witness accounts.

'Did you hear any talk of other outsiders who'd turned up that morning?' asked Ramírez.

'Outsiders?'

'Workmen, delivery people . . . that sort of thing.'

'The electricians came at some stage. Something had gone wrong with the electrics on Saturday night. We were in the dark, with just candles, all Sunday and when I came in from work yesterday all the lights were back on. I don't know what happened or what work was done. You'll have to ask someone who was there in the morning.'

Ramírez asked him for some names and checked them off against the list of men given to Elvira by the Spanish woman, Esperanza. The first three names Harrouch gave him were on the list and therefore probably dead in the mosque. The fourth name lived in an apartment in a nearby street.

'How well do you know the Imam?'

'He's been with us nearly two years. He reads a lot. I've heard his apartment is full of books. But he still gives us as much of his time as he can,' said Harrouch. 'I told you he was not a radical. He never said anything that could be construed as extreme, and he even made his position clear on suicide bombing: that in his view the Koran did not regard it as permissible. And remember, there were Spanish

171

converts to Islam in the mosque, who would not tolerate anything extreme so . . .'

'If he was preaching radical Islam to younger people,' said Ramírez, 'do you think you would know about it?'

'In a neighbourhood like this it wouldn't be possible to keep it secret.'

'Apart from these two men who delivered the sugar and mint, have you ever seen the Imam with any other strangers? I mean people from out of town, or from abroad?'

'I saw him with Spanish people. He was very aware of the image of Islam in the light of what has been happening in the last few years. He made efforts to communicate with Catholic priests and spoke at their meetings to reassure them that not all North Africans were terrorists.'

'Do you know anything about his history?'

'He's Algerian originally. He arrived here from Tunis. He must have spent some time in Egypt, because he talked about it a lot and he's mentioned studying in Khartoum.'

'How did he learn Spanish?' asked Falcón. 'The countries you mention have either French, or English, as the alternative to Arabic.'

'He learnt it here. The converts taught him,' said Harrouch. 'He was a good linguist, he spoke quite a few –'

'What other languages?' asked Ramírez.

'German. He spoke German,' said Harrouch, who'd gone back on the defensive.

'Does that mean he'd spent time in Germany?' asked Ramírez.

'I suppose he did, but that doesn't have to mean anything,' said Harrouch. 'Just because the 9/11 bombers came from Hamburg, it doesn't mean that any Muslim who's been to Germany is also a radical. I hope you're not forgetting that it was the mosque that was bombed and there were more than ten people in it, and most of them were older men, with wives and children, and not young, radical, extreme bomb-makers. I would say that we were the *target* of an attack . . .'

'All right, Sr Harrouch,' said Falcón, calming him. 'You should know that we're looking at all the possibilities. You mentioned VOMIT. Are you aware of any other anti-Muslim groups who you think would go to such extremes?'

'There were some very unpleasant demonstrations against the building of our mosque in Los Bermejales,' said Harrouch. 'Maybe you don't remember – they slaughtered a pig on the proposed site of the mosque back in May last year. There's a very vociferous protest group.'

'We know about them,' said Ramírez. 'We'll be taking a close look at their activities.'

'Did you ever feel that you were being watched, or under some kind of surveillance?' asked Falcón. 'Has anybody joined the mosque recently, who you didn't know or who, in your opinion, behaved strangely?'

'People are suspicious of us, but I don't think anybody was watching us.'

Ramírez checked the descriptions of the two men from the Peugeot Partner with the men Harrouch had seen bringing boxes into the mosque. Harrouch answered with his mind elsewhere. They got up to leave.

'Now I remember, there was something else that

happened last week,' said Harrouch. 'Someone told me that the mosque had been inspected by the council. Because we're technically a public building, we have to conform to certain rules about fire and safety, and two men came round last week, without any warning, and went through everything – drains, plumbing, electrics – the lot.'

13

'What did you make of him?' Falcón asked Ramírez as they made their way back to the pre-school for a meeting with Comisario Elvira and Juez Calderón.

'The difficulty with these people is not disentangling the truth from the lies. I don't think Sr Harrouch is a liar. He's been an immigrant for sixteen years and he's developed the knack for telling you the story which will give him the least amount of trouble, and makes his people appear in the best possible light,' said Ramírez. 'He says the Imam has never preached a radical word in his life, but he faltered over the Imam's linguistic ability. Why wasn't he happy about revealing the languages the Imam could speak? Because it was German. Not only the Hamburg connection, but it also means he's moved around Europe. It's making the Imam look more suspicious.'

'He was straight about the two young guys turning up with their cardboard boxes.'

'Of *sugar*,' said Ramírez. 'He was very emphatic about that. He was reluctant to reveal anything more about them, though. He wanted to be able to say he knew them, but he couldn't. He wanted to be able to stand up for them in some way. But if they're just shifting sugar around, what's the problem? Why does he feel the need to protect them?'

'Loyalty to other Muslims,' said Falcón.

'Or repercussions?' said Ramírez.

'Even if they don't know each other, there's a sense of allegiance,' said Falcón. 'Sr Harrouch is a decent, hardworking man and he'd like us to think that all his people are the same. When something like this bombing happens they feel embattled, and the instinct is to put up the defences all around, even if he ends up defending the sort of people he may abhor.'

Elvira and Calderón had been joined by Gregorio from the CNI.

'There have been some developments in Madrid,' said Elvira. 'Gregorio will explain.'

'We've been working on the notes found in the margins of the copy of the Koran, from the Peugeot Partner,' said Gregorio. 'In the meantime, copies of the notes were faxed up to Madrid and they made comparisons with the handwriting of the van's owner, Mohammed Soumaya, and his nephew Trabelsi Amar. They don't match.'

'Do the notes reveal anything?' asked Calderón. 'Are there any extremist views?'

'Our expert on the Koran says that the owner of this book has made interesting, rather than radical, interpretations of the text,' said Gregorio.

'Have you found Trabelsi Amar yet?' asked Ramírez.

'He was still in Madrid,' said Gregorio, nodding. 'He was just keeping out of the way of his uncle until he got the van back, which was supposed to be this evening. When he heard about the bomb he went into hiding, which was obviously not part of the plan, because the best hiding place he could think of was a friend's house, not some prearranged safe house. The local police picked him up a couple of hours ago.'

'Has he identified the people he lent the van to?' asked Ramírez.

'Yes. He's very scared,' said Gregorio. 'The CGI's antiterrorist squad in Madrid say he hasn't been behaving like a terrorist at all. He's been happy to tell them the whole story.'

'Let's start with the names,' said Ramírez.

'The shaven-headed guy is Djamel Hammad, thirty-one years old, born in Tlemcen in Algeria. His friend is Smail Saoudi, thirty years old, born Tiaret in Algeria. Both were resident in Morocco and still should be.'

'What sort of records have they got?'

'Those are their original names. They've operated under a lot of pseudonyms. They were medium- to high-risk terror suspects, by which I mean they were not likely to actually carry out attacks, but they have been suspected of document forgery, recce and logistical work. They both have relatives who have been active in the GIA – the Armed Islamic Group.'

'And how did Trabelsi Amar get to know them?'

'They're all illegal immigrants. They came across the straits together, on the same shipment. Hammad and Saoudi made him their friend. They got him to Madrid and helped him with his documents. Then they called in the favour.'

'Didn't he find their slickness . . . suspicious?' asked Calderón.

'It was convenient for him not to,' said Gregorio. 'Trabelsi Amar is not very bright.'

'What's the story with the van?' asked Ramírez.

'Amar has been working for his uncle making deliveries. He also did a few things on the side, to make himself some extra cash. He ran errands, some of them were for Hammad and Saoudi. Then they asked to borrow the van; the first time for an afternoon, the second time for a whole day. It all happened gradually, so that when they asked to borrow the van to go to Seville for three days and said they'd give him €250, Trabelsi Amar just saw the money.'

'How did he explain that to his Uncle Mohammed?' asked Ramírez.

'He rented the van from him for €30 a day,' said Gregorio. 'He might not be bright, but he could still work out that he didn't have to do anything and he'd be €160 up on the deal.'

'So presumably he knows where Hammad and Saoudi live.'

'They're searching the apartment as we speak.'

'When exactly did Amar go into hiding?' asked Ramírez. 'When he heard about the bomb, or once it was reported that the Peugeot Partner had been found?'

'As soon as he heard about the bomb,' said Gregorio.

'So he'd probably worked out already that his new friends weren't just ordinary guys.'

'What about their relationship with the Imam Abdelkrim Benaboura,' asked Falcón, 'apart from the fact that they were all Algerians?'

'The only connection we can see at the moment was that Benaboura was born in Tlemcen, which doesn't mean much.'

'We've found out more about the Imam from a member of the mosque than we have from the CNI and the CGI put together,' said Falcón.

'We still don't have the authority to access any more information,' said Gregorio. 'And that includes Juan, who, as you've probably gathered, is a very senior officer.'

'The Imam is a player of some sort,' said Ramírez. 'I'm sure of it.'

'What about this group, the MILA, who, according to the television news, have claimed responsibility for the blast?' asked Falcón.

'It's not a group we've ever heard of having an active terrorist dimension,' said Gregorio. 'We've heard about their intention to "liberate" Andalucía, but we've never taken it seriously. With the current military set-up in this country it's just not possible for anyone but a major power to secure a region of Spain for themselves. The Basques haven't achieved it and they don't even have to invade.'

'And what did the CGI in Madrid know about Hammad and Saoudi being in Spain?' asked Calderón.

'They didn't,' said Gregorio. 'It's not as easy as it sounds to trace unknown radicals in a huge, constantly changing immigrant population, some of whom are legal and others who've been smuggled across the straits. We know, for instance, that some of these people come over, perform two or three tasks in this country and then move on, to be replaced by others from France, Germany or the Netherlands. Quite often they have no idea of the purpose of what they're doing. They deliver a package, drive a person somewhere, raise some money from stolen bank cards, travel on a train at certain times to report on passenger numbers and time spent at how many stations, or they're asked to look at a building and report on its security situation. Even if we catch them and extract their task from them, which is not easy, all we end up with is a little strip of footage that could be one of a hundred operations that might make up a major attack, or might just be something that ends up on the cutting-room floor.'

'Does anyone have any opinion about what Hammad and Saoudi might have been doing?' asked Falcón.

'We don't know enough. We hope to know more after we've searched their apartment,' said Gregorio.

'What about the hood and the Islamic sash?' said Ramírez. 'Isn't that what operatives wear when they videotape themselves before a suicide mission?'

'No comment from the CGI on that,' said Gregorio. 'Based on the interview with Trabelsi Amar, they think the guys were logistical and nothing more.'

Ramírez gave a report on the deliveries to the mosque, the council visit last week, the power cut on Saturday night and the electricians' repair work performed on Monday morning. Falcón held back on disclosing his findings from the interview with Diego Torres of Informáticalidad until they had more information from interviews with the sales reps.

'Do we know anything more about the explosive used?' asked Calderón.

'The bomb squad have given me this report,' said Elvira. 'Based on their preliminary investigation of the site, the distance from the epicentre to the furthest flung pieces of debris, and the extent of the destruction of the first three floors of the building, their conservative estimate is that three times the quantity of hexogen was exploded than was necessary, if the intention was to destroy the apartment block.'

'Do they deduce anything from that?' asked Calderón. 'Or is that left up to our, inexpert, assuming?'

'That's what they're prepared to put in writing at the moment,' said Elvira. 'Verbally, they tell me that to destroy a building of this size, with demolition knowledge easily found on the internet, they would need as little as twenty kilos of hexogen. They say that hexogen is commonly used in demolition work, but primarily to shear through solid steel girders. Twenty kilos expertly positioned in an ordinary reinforced concrete building would wreck the whole block, not just the section that was actually destroyed. They deduce from this that the explosive was located in one place in the basement of the building, more towards the back than the front, hence the damage done to the pre-school. They thought that it could have been as much as one hundred kilos of hexogen that exploded.'

'Well, that sounds like enough to start a serious bombing campaign in Seville,' said Calderón. 'And if this is a group with plans to liberate the whole of Andalucía . . .'

'You probably haven't seen the latest news,' said Elvira, 'but we're on red alert all over the region. They've evacuated the cathedral in Cordoba, and the Alhambra and Generalife in Granada. There are now special patrols going through the tourist resorts on the Costa del Sol, and there are more than twenty roadblocks along the N340. The Navy are off the coast and there are Air Force fighters on all major airstrips. More than forty helicopters are running up and down the main arterial routes through Andalucía. Zapatero is taking this threat very seriously indeed.'

'Well, he has the demise of his predecessor's political ambitions as an example,' said Calderón. 'And nobody wants to be the Prime Minister who lost Andalucía to the Muslims after more than five hundred years of Spanish rule.'

They weren't quite ready to laugh at Calderón's cynicism. The sense of all that activity described by Elvira was too powerful, and, as if to reinforce his words, a helicopter passed rapidly overhead, like the latest despatch to a new crisis point. Falcón broke the silence.

'The CGI antiterrorist squad in Madrid think that Hammad and Saoudi were providing logistical support for an unknown cell that was going to carry out an attack, or series of attacks. Clearly, a delivery of some sort was made on Monday 5th June. A single hood and sash were found in the delivery vehicle, possibly indicating that either Hammad or Saoudi might become operatives. It also might indicate that one of them was going to return the van to Madrid, so that Trabelsi Amar had his van back as arranged.

'What history can show us is that, prior to the March 11th attacks in Madrid, two cell members went up to Avilés to pick up explosives on the 28th and 29th February. They allowed themselves a full *ten* days to prepare for the attacks. In our scenario, here, we are being asked to believe that the hexogen in raw, powder form was delivered on Monday, and that on the same night they started preparing bombs so that they were all ready to go on Tuesday morning. Then at approximately 8.30 a.m. there was an accident and the explosion occurred. I realize that this is not impossible, and in the history of terrorism there probably exists an incidence of delivery, preparation and attack being carried out within twenty-four hours, but if you're a group planning the liberation of Andalucía this doesn't seem very likely.'

'What's the scenario you envisage?' asked Gregorio.

'I don't. I'm just picking holes. I was trying to find a line of logic, but there were too many breaks. I don't want our investigation to go down a single path within the first twelve hours of the incident,' said Falcón. 'We're probably going to have to wait two or three days to get forensic information from the mosque, and until that time I think we should keep both possibilities open: that there was an accident in the bomb-making procedure, or that this was an attack on the mosque.'

'Why would someone want to attack the mosque?' asked Calderón.

'Revenge, extreme xenophobia, political or business motivation, or perhaps a combination of all four,' said Falcón. 'Terror is just a tool to bring about change. Look at the havoc wreaked by this bomb. Terror focuses people's attention and creates opportunities for powerful people. The population of this city is already fleeing. With that sort of panic, unimaginable things become possible.'

'The only way to contain panic,' said Comisario Elvira, 'is to show people that we are in control.'

'Even if we aren't,' said Juez Calderón. 'Even if we don't have the first idea where to look.'

'Whoever is behind this, whether it's Islamic militants or "other forces", they've planned their media assault,' said Falcón. 'The *ABC* received the Abdullah

Azzam text in a letter with a Seville stamp. TVE tells us that the MILA have called to claim responsibility.'

'Would they be claiming responsibility for blowing up a mosque and killing their own people?' asked Calderón.

'That's an everyday occurrence in Baghdad,' said Elvira.

'If you send something like Azzam's text to the *ABC* then you're expecting to launch an attack imminently . . . not even within twenty-four hours,' said Gregorio. 'As far as I know, Islamic militants have never advertised their exact intentions; all the big ones have come out of the blue, with the intention of killing and maiming as many people as possible.'

Gregorio took a call on his mobile and asked to leave.

'We've had this preliminary report from the bomb squad about the explosion,' said Falcón, 'but what about the explosive? Where does it come from and what are all these different names for it?'

'Hexogen is the German name, cyclonite is American, RDX is British and I think the Italians call it T4,' said Elvira. 'They might each have signatures, which enables them to identify the origin, but they're not going to tell us.'

'We could use some shots of Hammad and Saoudi,' said Ramírez.

'If they're into document fraud there'll probably be a load of photographs in their apartment in Madrid,' said Falcón. 'Has there been an update on the demolition work outside yet?'

'They're still saying forty-eight hours minimum, and that's if they don't come across anything to slow them down.'

Juez Calderón took a call, announced the discovery of another body and left. Falcón made eye contact with Ramírez and he left the room.

'Still no news on the CGI?' asked Falcón 'I expected to be pooling resources and efforts with the antiterrorist unit, and the only person we've seen is Inspector Jefe Ramón Barros, who doesn't say very much and appears humiliated.'

'I'm told that their job is more to do with gathering data at this stage,' said Comisario Elvira.

'What about some lower level people to help with the interviewing?'

'Not possible.'

'This sounds like something you can't talk about . . .'

'All I'm going to say is that since March 11th one aspect of counterterrorism measures has been to check that our own organizations are clean,' said Elvira.

'Don't tell me,' said Falcón.

'The Seville branch is under investigation. Nobody is giving any detail, but as far as I can gather, the CNI ran a test on the Seville antiterrorism unit and did not get the right result. They believe they have been compromised in some way. There are some high-level discussions going on now as to whether they should be allowed to participate in this investigation or not. You're not going to get any active help from the Madrid CGI either. They're working flat-out on their own informer network, and they've got the whole Hammad and Saoudi mess to sort through.'

'Will we be getting informer feedback from the Seville CGI network?'

'Not for the moment,' said Elvira. 'I'm sorry to be so reticent, but the situation is delicate. I don't know what the members of the antiterrorism unit are being told to make them believe that they are not under suspicion, but the CNI are trying to play it both ways. They don't want the mole, if he exists, to know that they're on to him, but neither do they want him endangering the investigation without them knowing who he is. Ideally, they want to find him and then release the CGI into the investigation and give themselves the chance of using him.'

'That sounds like a risky manoeuvre.'

'That's why it's taking so long to decide. The politicians are involved now,' said Elvira.

Outside, the grind of machinery had become the acceptable ambient noise. Men moved like aliens in a grey lunar landscape over the stacked pancakes of the floors, with snakes of pneumatic hose trailing behind. They were followed by masked men with oxyacetylene torches and motorized saws. Swinging above them was the crane's writhing cable. The hammering, growling and howling, the clatter of falling rubble, the momentous gonging as sections of floor were dropped into the tippers, kept the curious crowds at bay. Only a few TV crews and photojournalists remained, with their cameras trained on the destruction in the hope of zooming in on a crushed body, a bloodied hand, a spike of bone.

Another helicopter stuttered overhead and wheeled away to fly over the nearby Andalucían Parliament. As he trotted down Calle Los Romeros, Falcón called Ramírez to get the name of the worshipper mentioned by Sr Harrouch, who used the mosque in the mornings. He was called Majid Merizak. Ramírez offered to join him but Falcón preferred to be alone for this one.

The reason that Majid Merizak was not one of the casualties in the mosque was that he was ill in bed. He was a widower who was looked after by one of his daughters. She hadn't been able to prevent her father from heading down the stairs to find out what had happened; only his partial collapse had done that. Now he was in a chair, head thrown back, wild-eyed and panting, with the television on full blast because he was nearly deaf.

The apartment stank of vomit and diarrhoea. He'd been up most of the night and was still weak. The daughter turned off the television and forced her father to wear his hearing aid. She told Falcón that her father's Spanish was poor and Falcón said that they could conduct the interview in Arabic. She explained this to her father, who looked confused and irritable, with too much happening around him. Once his daughter had checked that the hearing aid was functioning properly and had left the room, Majid Merizak sharpened up.

'You speak Arabic?' he asked.

'I'm still learning. Part of my family is Moroccan.'

He nodded and drank tea through Falcón's introduction and visibly relaxed on hearing Falcón's rough Arabic. It had been the right thing to do. Merizak was far less wary than Harrouch had been.

Falcón warmed him up with questions about when he attended the mosque – which was every morning, without fail, and he stayed there until the early afternoon. Then he asked about strangers.

'Last week?' asked Merizak, and Falcón nodded. 'Two young men came in on Tuesday morning, close to midday, and two older men came in on Friday morning at ten o'clock. That's all.'

'And you'd never seen them before?'

'No, but I did see them again yesterday.'

'Who?'

'The two young men who'd come in last Tuesday.'

Merizak's description fitted that of Hammad and Saoudi.

'And what did they do last Tuesday?'

'They went into the Imam's room and talked with him until about one thirty.'

'And what about yesterday morning?'

'They brought in two heavy sacks. It took two of them to carry one sack.'

'What time was this?'

'About ten thirty. The same time that the electricians arrived,' said Merizak. 'Yes, of course, there were the electricians, as well. I'd never seen them before, either.'

'Where did the two young men put these sacks?'

'In the storeroom next to the Imam's office.'

'Do you know what was in the sacks?'

'Couscous. That's what it said on the side.'

'Has anyone made a delivery like that before?'

'Not in those quantities. People have brought in bags of food to give to the Imam . . . you know, it's part of our duty to give to those less fortunate than ourselves.'

'When did they leave?'

'They stayed about an hour.'

'What about the men who came in on Friday?'

'They were inspectors from the council. They went all over the mosque. They discussed things with the Imam and then they left.'

'What about the power cut?'

'That was on Saturday night. I wasn't there. The

Imam was on his own. He said that there was a big bang and the lights went out. That's what he told us the following morning, when we had to pray in the dark.'

'And the electricians came in on Monday to fix it?'

'A man came on his own at eight thirty. Then three other men came two hours later to do the work.'

'Were they Spanish?'

'They were speaking Spanish.'

'What did they do?'

'The fuse box was burned out, so they put in a new one. Then they put in a power socket in the storeroom.'

'What sort of work was that?'

'They cut a channel in the brickwork from a socket in the Imam's office, through the wall and into the storeroom. They put in some grey flexible tubing, fed in the wire and then cemented it all up.'

Merizak had seen the blue transit van, which he described as battered, but he hadn't seen any markings or the registration number.

'How did the Imam pay for the work?'

'Cash.'

'Do you know where he got the phone number of this company?'

'No.'

'Would you recognize the electricians, council inspectors and two young men if you saw them again?'

'Yes, but I can't describe them to you very well.'

'You've been listening to the news?'

'They don't know what they're talking about,' said Merizak. 'It makes me very angry. A bomb explodes and it is automatically Islamic militants.'

189

'Have you ever heard of Los Mártires Islámicos para la Liberación de Andalucía?'

'The first time was on the news today. It's an invention of the media to discredit Islam.'

'Have you ever heard of the Imam preaching militant ideology in the mosque?'

'Quite the opposite.'

'I'm told that the Imam was a very capable linguist.'

'He learnt Spanish very quickly. They said his apartment was full of French and English books. He spoke German, too. He spoke on the telephone using languages I'd never heard before. He told me that one of them was Turkish. Some people came here in February and stayed with him for a week and that was another strange language. Somebody said it was Pashto, and that the men were from Afghanistan.'

14

The offices of the *ABC* newspaper, a glass cylinder on the Isla de la Cartuja, had been as close to bedlam as a hysterical business like journalism could get. Angel Zarrías watched from the edge of the newsroom as journalists roared down telephones, bawled at assistants and harangued each other.

Through the flickering computer screens, the phone lines stretched to snapping point and the triangles formed by hands slapped to foreheads, Angel was watching the open door of the editor's office. He was biding his time. This was the newshounds' moment. It was their job to find the stories, which the editor would knit together to construct the right image and tone, for the new history of a city in crisis.

On the way from Manuela's apartment to the *ABC* offices he'd asked the taxi to drop him off in a street near the Maestranza bullring where his friend Eduardo Rivero lived and which also housed the headquarters of his political party: Fuerza Andalucía. He'd been dining with Eduardo Rivero and the new sponsors of Fuerza Andalucía last night. A momentous decision had been made, which he hadn't been able to share with Manuela until it became official today. He had also not been able to tell her that he was now going to be working more for Fuerza Andalucía than the *ABC*. He had a lot more important things on his mind than grumbling about same-sex marriages in his daily political column.

Rivero's impressive house bore all the hallmarks of his traditional upbringing and thinking. Its façade was painted to a deep terracotta finish, the window surrounds were picked out in ochre and all caged in magnificent wrought-iron grilles. The main door was three metres high, built out of oak, varnished to the colour of chestnuts and studded with brass medallions. It opened on to a huge marble-flagged patio, in which Rivero had departed briefly from tradition by planting two squares of box hedge. In the centre of each was a statue; to the left was Apollo and to the right Dionysus, and in between was the massive bowl of a white marble fountain, whose restrained trickles of water held the house, despite these pagan idols, in a state of religious obeisance.

The front of the house was the party headquarters, with the administration below and the policy-making and political discussions going on above. Angel took the stairs just inside the main door, which led up to Rivero's office. They were waiting for him; Rivero and his second-in-command, the much younger Jesús Alarcón.

Unusually, he and Rivero were sitting together in the middle of the room, with the boss's wood and leather armchair empty behind his colossal English oak desk. They all shook hands. Rivero, the same age as Angel, seemed remarkably relaxed. He wasn't even wearing a tie, his jacket was hanging off the back of his chair. He was smiling beneath an ebullient white moustache. He did not look as if scandal had come anywhere near him.

'Like any good journalist, Angel, you've arrived at the crucial moment,' said Rivero. 'A decision has been made.'

'I don't believe it,' said Angel.

'Well, you'll have to believe it, because it's true,' said Rivero. 'I'd like you to meet the new leader of Fuerza Andalucía, Jesús Alarcón. Effective as from five minutes ago.'

'I think that's a bold and brilliant decision,' said Angel, shaking them both by the hand and embracing them. 'And one you've been keeping very quiet.'

'The committee voted on it last night before we met for dinner,' said Rivero. 'I didn't want to break the news until I had asked Jesús and he'd accepted. Something was going to have to happen before the 2007 campaign and, with this morning's explosion, that campaign will be starting today – and what better way to kick it off than with a new leader?'

Alarcón's expression was a mask of seriousness that bore all the weight and lines of the gravity that the situation demanded, but it could not hide what came shining out from within. His grey suit, dark tie and white shirt could not contain his sense of achievement. He was the schoolboy at the prize-giving, who'd already been told that he had won the top award.

Angel Zarrías had known Jesús Alarcón since the year 2000, when he'd been introduced to him by his old friend, Lucrecio Arenas the Chief Executive Officer of the Banco Omni in Madrid. In the last six years Angel had drawn Jesús into Eduardo Rivero's orbit and gradually eased him into positions of greater importance within the party. Angel had never had any doubt about Alarcón's brains, his political commitment or astuteness, but, as an old PR man, he had been worried by his lack of charisma. But the final wresting of the leadership from Rivero's trembling clutches had wrought an extraordinary change in the younger man. Physically he was the same, but his confidence had become dazzlingly palpable. Angel couldn't help himself. He embraced Jesús once again as the new leader of Fuerza Andalucía.

'As you know,' said Rivero, 'in the last three elections there has been steady growth in our share of the vote, but it has only grown to a maximum of 4.2 per cent and that is not enough for us to be the chosen partner of the Partido Popular. We need a new kind of energy at the top.'

'I have the business experience,' said Alarcón, breaking in with his new-found confidence, 'to raise our funding to unprecedented levels, but this is of limited significance in a torpid political atmosphere. What this morning's event has given us is a unique opportunity to focus voters' minds on the real and perceivable threat of radical Islam. It gives our immigration policy new bite where before, even after 11th March, it was dismissed as extreme and out of step with the ways in which contemporary societies were developing. If we spend the next eight months getting that message across to the population of Andalucía then we stand a chance of a substantial increase in our share of the vote, come 2007. So we have the right ideology for the time, and I can raise the money to make it heard across the region.'

'We don't think that it's a coincidence that the first call after the explosion in El Cerezo this morning should be from you, Angel,' said Rivero. 'You, more than anybody else, know what would make an enormous impression on the population of Andalucía tomorrow morning.'

Angel sat back in his chair, ran his fingers through his hair and hissed air out from between his clenched teeth. He knew what Rivero wanted and it was a tall order under the circumstances.

'Just think of the impact it would have,' said Rivero, nodding at Jesús, 'his face, his profile and his ideas in the pages of *ABC Sevilla* on the day after such a catastrophe as this. We would tread Izquierda Unida into the dust and make the Partido Andalucista writhe in their beds at night.'

'Are you ready for what I can do for you?' asked Angel.

'I'm more prepared for it than at any time in my life,' said Alarcón, and handed him his CV.

Angel had sat in the back of the cab on the way to the *ABC* offices, leafing through Alarcón's CV. Jesús Alarcón was born in Cordoba in 1965. He'd been accepted at Madrid University at the age of seventeen to study philosophy, political history and economics. As a staunch Catholic he despised the atheistic creed of communism and believed that the best way to break one's enemy was to know them. He went to Berlin University to study Russian and Russian political history. He was there – and a photograph existed to support this – when the Wall came down in 1989. It wasn't supposed to have happened like that and the crucial event had left him bereft of a cause.

At the same time his father's business collapsed and

he died soon after. His mother followed her husband into the grave six months later and Jesús applied to INSEAD in Paris to do an MBA. By Christmas 1991 he was working for McKinsey's in Boston, and in the following four years became one of their analysts and consultants in Central and South America. In 1995 he moved to Lehman Brothers, to join their mergers and acquisitions team. There he changed his sphere of operations to the European Union and built up a powerful list of investors looking to buy into the booming Spanish economy. In 1997 his life changed again when he met a beautiful Sevillana called Mónica Abellón, whose father had been one of Jesús's leading clients. Mónica's father effected an introduction to Lucrecio Arenas, who headhunted him for the secretive Banco Omni and he moved to Madrid, where Mónica was working as a model.

It was in the year 2000 that Angel, totally fed up with the Partido Popular, had taken on some PR work for Banco Omni clients. Lucrecio Arenas, convinced that he'd discovered a future leader of Spain in Jesús Alarcón, was eager for his new find to cut his teeth in regional politics, and had enlisted Angel's help. As soon as Angel introduced Alarcón to Eduardo Rivero and the other Fuerza Andalucía committee members, they welcomed him into the fold, recognizing one of their own. Jesús Alarcón was a traditionalist, a practising Catholic, a man who loathed communism and socialism, a believer in the power of business to do good in society and also a lover of the bulls. He was twenty years younger than any of them. He was good looking, if a little on the dull side, but he made up for it by having the beautiful Mónica Abellón as his wife, and two gorgeous children.

In the *ABC* offices Angel went to work on the dossier and archives. In an hour he'd put together a page, the editor was never going to look at more than that. The headline: THIS MAN HAS ANSWERS The main shot was part of a photograph he'd found of Jesús in a business magazine about Spain's future. Jesús was supposedly looking up to a sun, which was probably a photographer's lighting umbrella, and his face was shining with hope and belief in the future. He also had shots of Jesús with the stunning Mónica, and the couple with their children. There was a sub headline, which said: *The New Leader of Fuerza Andalucía Believes in Our Future.* The writing was in note form and described not just the radical immigration policy of Fuerza Andalucía, but also vital economic and agrarian reforms that were necessary to make Andalucía a force in the future. It included Jesús's employment profile, which showed that he was economically 'sensible', internationally connected and had the contacts in industry to make his ideas work.

There was a lull in activity just before lunch at around two o'clock. The traffic into the editor's office had calmed. Angel made his move

'We're probably going to have to cut your column for at least the next few days,' said the editor when he saw Angel crossing his threshold.

'Of course,' said Angel. 'Nobody wants political gossip at a time like this.'

'What do you want with me, then?' said the editor, interested now he knew that Angel hadn't come for a fight.

'Most of the stuff in tomorrow's newspaper is going to be hard news and a lot of it will be heart-rending, with reports on the destruction of the pre-school and the dead children. The only positive stories will be about the excellence of the emergency services, and I've heard that there's a survivor. You'll be writing a leader that captures the mood of the city, that reacts to the receipt of Abdullah Azzam's text, and that declares that we might not have moved so far forward since 11th March as everybody would like to think.'

'Well, Angel, now you've told me my job,' said the editor, 'you can get on with telling me what you're proposing.'

'A vision of hope,' he said, handing over the page he'd just created. 'In this time of crisis there's a young, energetic, capable man in the wings, who could make Andalucía a safe and prosperous place to live.'

The editor scanned the page, took it all in, nodded and grunted.

'So the rumours about Eduardo Rivero *are* true.'

'I'm not sure what you're referring to.'

'Come off it, Angel,' said the editor, flinging out a dismissive fist. 'He was caught with his pants down.'

'I don't think there's any truth in that.'

'With an under-age girl. There was talk of a DVD.'

'Nobody's seen it.'

'The rumblings have been very loud, and now this –' said the editor, waving the page in the air. 'If it wasn't for the bomb, I'd have someone digging in the dirt after your old friend.'

'Look, this has been in the pipeline for a long time,' said Angel. 'With this bomb going off he just feels that it's time to stand down and let somebody younger take the party to the next stage. He's going to be seventy at the end of this year.'

'So we have the first political casualty of the bomb.'

'That's not how we should be thinking about it,' said Angel. 'It's precipitated change and it's saying that change is what we have to do if we want to survive this challenge to our liberty.'

'You're serious, Angel. What's happened to the great deflator? The man with the sharpened nib who pops those hot-air egos?'

'Perhaps my cynicism is another casualty of the bomb.'

'Well, you're always complaining that nothing happens,' said the editor, 'and now . . . you believe in this guy and yet you've barely written a word about him before.'

'As you've just pointed out, my column was primarily for puncturing egos,' said Angel. 'Jesús Alarcón hasn't had time to develop an ego that needs to be punctured. He's quietly taken Fuerza Andalucía from being an organization with a small debt to one with regular contributions from members and businesses. He's done amazing, if uncharismatic, work.'

'So what makes you think he's got the personality for it?'

'I saw him this morning,' said Angel. 'He's learnt a lot . . .'

'But can you *learn* charisma?'

'Charisma is just an intense form of self-belief,' said Angel. 'Jesús Alarcón has always been confident. He's ambitious. He's dealt with serious personal setbacks, which, to me, are a far more powerful measure of the man than his ability to broker international finance deals. He has the inner steel and common sense that our last prime minister had. You know politics. It's like boxing. It's all very well to have the fast hands and fancy footwork, but even the greatest fighters get hit very hard and if you can't absorb punishment you're finished. Jesús Alarcón has all those qualities and, after the conferring of the leadership, I can now see emerging that indefinable quality that will make people want to follow him.'

'All right,' said the editor, thinking positively about it. 'A new face for a new era. Write me a profile. And, by the way, I agree with you about charisma, it *is* an intense form of self-belief. But there's something both blinding *and* blind about it, too. Its closest friend can quite quickly become corruption – the belief that you can do anything with impunity. I hope Jesús Alarcón does not have the makings of a tragic figure.'

'He's not a hollow man,' said Angel. 'He's suffered and come through it.'

'Get him to remember that suffering,' said the editor. 'Every politician should have the words of the president of the Terrorists' Victims' Association, Pilar Manjón, ringing in their ears: "They only think of themselves."'

The Madrid police and forensics had been working hard in the apartment used by Djamel Hammad and Smail Saoudi. Taped to the underside of a gas bottle they'd found a selection of stolen and forged IDs and passports, with pictures of the two men whose descriptions fitted those given by Trabelsi Amar and the Seville homicide squad. They'd also discovered € 5,875 in small-denomination notes in three separate packages hidden around the apartment. DNA was currently being generated from hairs, bristles and pubic hairs found in the bathroom. An empty pad on the kitchen table had revealed indentations, which proved to be complicated directions to a property southwest of Madrid, not far from a village called Valmojado. The isolated house near the Río Guadarrama was found to be empty, with no evidence of recent habitation. The police concluded that it was a staging post – a place to pick up and leave material – and nothing more. The property had been rented in the name of a Spaniard, whose ID was false. The owners had been paid six months in advance, which had made them reluctant to ask too many questions. The forensics were still conducting their search of the premises, but so far not a trace of explosive had been found. The Guardia Civil had questioned a number of locals, including shepherds, and reckoned that in the four months it had been rented it had been visited by a white van five times. Three of those visits corresponded roughly to the times Trabelsi Amar had lent the Peugeot Partner to Hammad and Saoudi.

There was a complication with this scenario, which was that the directions to the isolated house found in the Madrid apartment were freshly written in Hammad's handwriting, which would imply that their visit on Sunday at around midday was their first. This in turn implied that the other two times they'd borrowed Trabelsi Amar's van they'd lent it to others who had gone to the farmhouse. A clearer indication that the isolated farmhouse was being visited by people other than Hammad and Saoudi came from eyewitness reports that as many as six different people, including one woman, had been seen going there. This information had an adrenalizing effect on the CGI in Madrid, who concluded that Hammad and Saoudi were acting within a much larger network than at first thought. They contacted all the major intelligence agencies but none of them had picked up any 'chatter' about a planned attack in Spain. The fear now was that Hammad and Saoudi's logistical work was part of a wider effort.

The CGI, with the help of the Guardia Civil, were now trying to find Hammad and Saoudi's route from Madrid to the isolated house near Valmojado and then down to Seville. They wanted to know if they had made any other stopovers – anonymous-looking meetings in roadside bars, other visits to isolated houses or, worse, other deliveries to, for instance, a location in another major Andalucían city.

That was the primary content of a seven-page report, drafted by several senior officers of the counterterrorism unit and sent by the Madrid CGI to Comisario Elvira in the damaged pre-school in Seville. There was a conclusion attached, which had been written by the Director of the CNI and had also reached the hands of Prime Minister Zapatero:

On the basis of our own findings and the reports received so far from the offices of the CGI and, taken in conjunction with the preliminary reports from the bomb squad and the police on the ground at the site of the disaster, we can only conclude, at this point, that we have come across an Islamic terrorist network who were planning an attack, or, more likely, a series of attacks, with the intention of destabilizing the political and social fabric of the region of Andalucía. Whilst the investigating bodies have so far uncovered some anomalies to the usual modus operandi of radical Islamic groups, they

*have not brought to our attention any suspicious activity,
or even stated intention, of any other group that might
want to inflict damage on the Muslim population of
Andalucía. We therefore recommend that the government take the necessary steps to protect all major cities
in the region.*

The noise of demolition work reasserted itself in the
room after Comisario Elvira finished the reading of the
report. Inspector Jefe Falcón and Juez Calderón were
sitting on small children's desks, arms folded, ankles
crossed and staring into the ground, which had now
been swept clear of glass. Plastic sheeting, which had
been stretched across the empty window frames,
revealed an indistinct outside world that ballooned and
lurched with the hot breeze, blowing from the south.

'They seem to have made up their minds, don't they?'
said Calderón. 'Having told us not to disappear exclusively down one path, that's just what they've done
themselves. There's no mention of the VOMIT website
or of any other anti-Muslim groups.'

'Given all the stuff they've just found in the Madrid
apartment of Hammad and Saoudi, and the hexogen
deposit in the rear of the Peugeot Partner and the
Islamic paraphernalia in the front,' said Elvira, 'who
could blame them?'

'It doesn't look good for the Islamic radicals at the
moment,' said Falcón. 'But the bomb squad haven't got
to the epicentre of the explosion yet. There's still vital
forensic information to come. I've also spoken to the
forensics going over the Peugeot Partner and so far all
they've come up with is that a new tyre had been fitted
to the rear driver's side and the spare had a puncture.

'What they've found in the Madrid apartment and the existence of the isolated house could be interpreted as terrorist activity, or illegal immigrant activity. We've been told that Hammad and Saoudi have a track record of logistical involvement, but what does that mean? If they'd been caught with something, then we'd know about it. If they've been named by others, that's questionable information.'

'My reading of this document,' said Elvira, flapping the paper derisively in front of him, 'is that it's something that has been drafted for the politicians, so that they can appear knowledgeable and decisive on a day of crisis. The CNI and CGI have stuck to the known facts. They've mentioned "anomalies" but have given no detail. VOMIT and other groups aren't mentioned because there's nothing to support their involvement. The MILA doesn't appear either, despite its mention on the news. It's because they've got no intelligence to offer on any of them.'

'Are we allowed to talk about the CGI?' said Falcón, purposely disingenuous.

Calderón's secrecy radar was on to it in a flash. Elvira threw up his hands.

'Needless to say, this can't go out of this room,' said Elvira, 'but seeing as you're the instructing judge controlling this investigation you should know that there have been some concerns about the reliability of the Seville branch of the CGI. A decision from above has not yet been taken to allow them to fully enter the battle. Their agents have been in touch with their informer network and have drafted reports, but we haven't seen anything yet. They've been denied access to our reports and they know nothing about certain pieces of evidence, such as the heavily annotated copy of the Koran, which, as far as I know, has been kept out of the news.'

'That's a big blow to the investigation,' said Calderón. 'Shouldn't we have heard about this before now?'

'I don't have clearance to tell either of you,' said Elvira.

'So what is it about this heavily annotated copy of the Koran that's so important?' asked Calderón.

'I don't know, but it's received a very high level of interest from the CNI,' said Elvira. 'Anyway, that doesn't concern us right now. When was the last time you heard from your squad?'

'Recently enough to be able to say that we've got a pretty clear picture of what happened here in the last forty-eight hours, some of which is connected to occur-rences in the week before the explosion.'

Falcón now had at least two witnesses to each of the significant events that preceded the blast. Hammad and Saoudi had first been seen at the mosque on Tuesday 30th May at 12.00. They arrived on foot and stayed talking to the Imam until 1.30 p.m. The two other events of that week were the visit from council inspectors at 10 a.m. on Friday 2nd June and a power cut some time on Saturday 3rd June at night, when the Imam had been in the mosque alone.

This led to an electrician turning up at 8.30 a.m. on Monday 5th June to assess the damage and the work involved. He returned with two labourers at 10.30 a.m. to repair the blown fuse box and also install a power socket in the storeroom next to the Imam's office.

The second visit from the electrician coincided with Hammad and Saoudi's arrival in the Peugeot Partner and the unloading of two large polypropylene sacks, which were believed to contain couscous. They stayed about an hour. The electricians left just before lunch at about 2.30 p.m. Hammad and Saoudi returned at 5.45 p.m. with four heavy cardboard boxes believed to contain sugar and some carrier bags of mint, all of which went into the storeroom. They were still there at 7 p.m. and, so far, nobody had seen them leave the premises.

'And what are your areas of concern in all that?'

'We have witnesses to the arrivals and departures of all these people,' said Falcón. 'But we haven't been able to make contact with the electrician. In order to get this done as quickly as possible I've asked my squad, who are already overloaded with interview work, to co-ordinate with local police and get them to visit every electrician's outlet or workshop within a square kilometre of the explosion. So far we've come up with nothing. All we know is that three men arrived in a blue transit van with no markings and we have no witnesses for the registration number.'

'Do you want the media to make an announcement?' asked Elvira.

'Not yet. I want to do more footwork on this.'

'What else?'

'I have other members of my squad tied up interviewing the Informáticalidad sales reps. None of them has come back to me with anything significant, but I have yet to talk to them and find out what the story was there.'

'Is that it?'

'My greatest concern at the moment, apart from the

undiscovered electrician, is that the council have no record of sending any inspectors to the mosque, or any other part of this building, or even this barrio, on Friday 2nd June, or any day, for that matter, in the last three months.'

15

Before the three men left the bombsite for the night, Calderón gave an update on the deaths and injuries. Four children had died of head wounds and internal bleeding in the pre-school. Seven children had been seriously wounded – ranging from the loss of a leg below the knee to severe facial lacerations. Eighteen children had been lightly wounded, mainly cut by flying glass. Two men and a woman who had been passing by the building on Calle Los Romeros had been killed, either by flying debris or falling masonry. An elderly woman had died of a heart attack in an apartment across the road. There were thirty-two seriously injured people, who had been either inside, or around, buildings close to the stricken block and there were three hundred and forty-three lightly injured. From the rubble they had so far removed two men and two women who were dead and young Lourdes Alanis, who had survived. The list of missing in the mosque, including the Imam, numbered thirteen. Apart from them this gave a total so far of twelve dead, thirty-nine seriously injured and three hundred and sixty-one lightly injured.

The demolition crews were now removing the remaining slabs of concrete from what had been the fifth floor. The whole area was under floodlights as they prepared to work all night. An air-conditioned tent had been erected on some wasteground between the pre-school and another block of apartments to handle forensic evidence. Another tent was being erected to deal with the bodies and body parts, which would eventually be coming out of the crushed mosque. The judges, homicide squad, forensics and emergency services had worked out a duty roster, so that there would be someone on site all night from each group.

It was still light and very warm as Elvira, Falcón and Calderón left the pre-school just before 8 p.m. A group of people had gathered in a corner of the playground. Hundreds of candles flickered on the ground amidst bouquets of flowers. Banners and placards had been pinned up on the chain-link fencing – *No más muertes. Paz. Sólo los inocentes han caído. Por el derecho de vivir sin violencia* – No more death. Peace. Only the innocents have fallen. For the right to live without violence. But the largest banner of all was written in red against a white background – *ODIO ETERNO AL TERRORISMO* – Eternal Hate to Terrorism. In the bottom right-hand corner was written VOMIT. Falcón asked if anybody had seen the person who had unfurled this banner, but nobody had. It was this banner which had drawn people to that part of the playground and so it had become a natural place for the locals to pay tribute to the fallen.

They stood in the violet light of a sun that was beginning to set on this catastrophic day and, with the machinery inexorably clawing away at the piled rubble, their murmured prayers, guttering candles and the already wilting flowers were both pathetic and touching, as pitiful and moving as the futile deaths of all humans in the vast grotesqueness of war. As the lawmen backed away from the shrine, Elvira's mobile rang. He took the call and handed it to Falcón. It was Juan from the CNI, saying that they had to meet tonight. Falcón said he would be home in an hour.

The hospital was calm after the frenetic activity of the day. In the emergency room they were still picking glass out of people's faces and suturing lacerations. There were patients in the waiting room, but there was no longer the horror of the triage nurse wading through the victims, skidding on blood, looking into the wide, dark eyes of the injured, silently pleading. Falcón showed his police ID and asked for Lourdes Alanis, who was in the intensive care unit on the first floor.

Through the glass panels of the intensive care unit Fernando was visible at his daughter's bedside, holding her hand. She was hooked up to machines but seemed to be breathing on her own. The doctor in the ICU said she was making good progress. She had sustained a broken arm and a crushed leg, but no spinal injuries. Their main concern had been her head injuries. She was still in a coma, but a scan had revealed no evidence of brain damage or haemorrhaging. As they talked, Fernando left the ICU to go to the toilet. Falcón gave him a few minutes and went in after him. He was washing his hands and face.

'Who are you?' he asked, looking at Falcón via the mirror, suspicious, knowing he wasn't a doctor.

'We met earlier today by your apartment block. My name is Javier Falcón. I'm the Inspector Jefe of the homicide squad.'

Fernando frowned, shook his head; he didn't remember.

'Does this mean that you've caught the people who destroyed my family?'

'No, we're still working on that.'

'You won't have to look very far. That rat hole is crawling with them.'

'With who?'

'Fucking Moroccans,' he said. 'Those fucking bastards. We've been looking at them all this time, ever since 11th March, and we've been thinking . . . when's the next time going to be. We always knew that there was going to be a next time.'

'Who is "we"?'

'Alright, me. That's what *I've* been thinking,' said Fernando. 'But I know I'm not alone.'

'I didn't think the relations between the communities were so bad,' said Falcón.

'That's because you don't live in "the communities",' said Fernando. 'I've seen the news, full of nice, comfortable people telling you that everything is all right, that Muslims and Catholics are communicating, that there's some kind of "healing process" going on. I can tell you, it's all bullshit. We live in a state of suspicion and fear.'

'Even though you know that very few members of the Muslim population are terrorists?'

'That's what we're told, but we don't *know* it,' said Fernando. 'And what's more, we have no idea who *they* are. They could be standing next to me in the bar, drinking beer and eating *jamón*. Yes, you see, some of them even do that. Eat pig and drink alcohol. But it seems that they're just as likely to blow themselves up as the one who spends his life with his nose to the floor in the mosque.'

'I didn't come here to make you angry,' said Falcón. 'You've got enough to think about without that.'

'You didn't *make* me angry. I *am* angry. I've *been* angry a long time. Two years and three months I've been angry,' said Fernando. 'Gloria, my wife . . .'

He stopped. His face came apart. His mouth thickened with saliva. He had to support himself against the basin as the physical pain worked its way through. It took some minutes for him to pull himself together.

'Gloria was a good person. She believed in the good that exists in everyone. But her belief didn't protect her, it didn't protect our son. The people she spoke up for killed her, in the same way that they killed the ones they hate, and who hate them. Anyway, that's enough. I must get back to my daughter. I know you didn't have to come and find me here. You've got a lot on your plate. So I thank you for that . . . for your concern. And I wish you well in your investigation. I hope you find the killers before I do.'

'I want you to call me,' said Falcón, giving him his card, 'at any time, day or night, for whatever reason. If you're angry, depressed, violent, lonely or even hungry, I want you to call me.'

'I didn't think you people were supposed to get personally involved.'

'I also want you to tell me if you're ever contacted by a group who call themselves VOMIT, so it's important on two levels that we keep in touch.'

They left the toilet and shook hands outside, where,

on the other side of the glass, his daughter's life was readable in green on the screens. Fernando hesitated as he leaned against the door.

'Only one politician spoke to me today,' he said. 'I saw them all parading themselves before the cameras with the victims and their families. This was while they were operating on Lourdes' skull, so I had time to look at their ridiculous antics. Only one person found me.'

'Who was that?'

'Jesús Alarcón,' said Fernando. 'I'd never heard of him before. He's the new leader of Fuerza Andalucía.'

'What did he say to you?'

'He didn't say anything. He listened – and there wasn't a camera in sight.'

The sky darkened to purple over the old city like the discoloration around a recent wound that had begun to hurt in earnest. Falcón drove on automatic, his mind buried deep in intractable problems: a bomb explodes, killing, maiming and destroying. What is left after the dust clears and the bodies are taken away is a horrendous social and political confusion, where emotions rise to the surface and, like wind on the susceptible grass of the plain, influence can blow people's minds this way and that, turn them from beer-sippers into chest-thumpers.

The three CNI men were waiting for him outside his house on Calle Bailén. He parked his car in front of the oak doors. They all shook hands and followed him through to the patio, which was looking a little dishevelled these days. Encarnación, his housekeeper, wasn't as capable as she used to be and Falcón didn't have the money for the renovation required. And anyway, he'd grown to enjoy living in the encroaching shabbiness of his surroundings.

He dragged some chairs out around a marble-topped table on the patio and left the CNI men to listen to the water trickling in the fountain. He came back with cold beers, olives, capers, pickled garlic, crisps, bread, cheese and *jamón*. They ate and drank and talked about Spain's chances in the World Cup in Germany; always the same – a team full of genius and promise, which was never fulfilled.

'Do you have any idea why we want to talk to you?' asked Pablo, who was more relaxed now, less intensely observant.

'Something to do with my Moroccan connections, so I was told.'

'You're a very interesting man to us,' said Pablo. 'We don't want to hide the fact that we've been looking at you for some time now.'

'I'm not sure that I've got the right mentality for secret work any more. If you'd asked me five years ago, then you might have found the ideal candidate . . .'

'Who is the ideal candidate?' asked Juan.

'Someone who is already hiding a great deal from the world, from his family, from his wife, and from himself. A few state secrets on top wouldn't be such a burden.'

'We don't want you to be a spy,' said Juan.

'Do you want me to deceive?'

'No, we think deceiving would be a very bad idea under the circumstances.'

'You'll understand better what we want by answering a few questions,' said Pablo, wresting the interview back from his boss.

'Don't make them too difficult,' said Falcón. 'I've had a long day.'

'Tell us how you came to meet Yacoub Diouri.'

'That could take some time,' said Falcón.

'We're not in any hurry,' said Pablo.

And, as if at some prearranged signal, Juan and Gregorio sat back, took out cigarette packs and lit up. It was one of those occasions after a long day, with a little beer and food inside him, that made Falcón wish he was still a smoker.

'I think you probably know that just over five years ago, on 12th April 2001, I ran a murder investigation into the brutal killing of an entrepreneur turned restaurateur called Raúl Jiménez.'

'You've got a policeman's memory for dates,' said Juan.

'You'll find that date written in scar tissue on my heart when I'm dead,' said Falcón. 'It's got nothing to do with being a policeman.'

'It had a big impact on your life?' said Pablo.

Falcón took another fortifying gulp of Cruzcampo.

'The whole of Spain knows this story. It was all over the newspapers for weeks,' said Falcón, a little irritated with the knowingness with which the questions had started coming at him.

'We weren't in Spain at the time,' said Juan. 'We've read the files, but it's not the same as hearing it for real.'

'My investigation into Raúl Jiménez's past showed that he'd known my father, the artist Francisco Falcón. They'd started a smuggling business together in Tangier during and after the Second World War. It meant they could establish themselves and start families and

Francisco Falcón could begin the process of turning himself into an artist.'

'And what about Raúl Jiménez?' said Pablo. 'Didn't he meet his wife when she was very young?'

'Raúl Jiménez had an unhealthy obsession with young girls,' said Falcón, taking a deep breath, knowing what they were after. 'It wasn't *so* unusual in those days in Tangier or Andalucía for a girl to get married at thirteen, but in fact her parents made Raúl wait until she was seventeen. They had a couple of children, but they were difficult births and the doctor recommended that his wife didn't have any more.

'In the run-up to Moroccan independence in the 1950s, Raúl became involved with a businessman called Abdullah Diouri who had a young daughter. Raúl had sex with this girl and, I think, even got her pregnant. This would not have been a problem had he done the honourable thing and married the girl. In Muslim society he would have just taken a second wife and that would have been the end of it. As a Catholic, it was impossible. To complicate matters further, despite doctor's orders, his wife became pregnant with their third child.

'In the end Raúl took the coward's way out and fled with his family. Abdullah Diouri was incensed when he discovered this and wrote a letter to Francisco Falcón in which he told him of Raúl's betrayal and expressed his determination to be avenged, which he achieved five years later.

'The third child, a boy called Arturo, was kidnapped on his way back from school in southern Spain. Raúl Jiménez's way of dealing with this terrible loss was to deny the boy's existence. It devastated the family. His wife committed suicide and the children were damaged, one of them beyond repair.'

'Was it that sad story that made you decide to try to find Arturo thirty-seven years after he had disappeared?' asked Pablo.

'As you know, I met Raúl's second wife, Consuelo, while investigating his murder. About a year later we started a relationship and during that time we revealed to each other that the one thing that still haunted us about her husband's murder case, and all that surfaced with it, was the disappearance of Arturo. There was still a part of us that imagined the eternally lost six-year-old boy.'

'That was in July 2002,' said Pablo. 'When did you start looking for Arturo?'

'In September of that year,' said Falcón. 'Neither of us could believe that Abdullah Diouri would have killed the child. We thought he would have drawn him into his family in some way.'

'And what was driving you?' asked Juan. 'The lost boy . . . or something else?'

'I knew very well I was looking for a forty-three-year-old man.'

'Had something happened to your relationship with Consuelo Jiménez in the meantime?' asked Pablo.

'It finished almost as soon as it started, but I'm not going to discuss that with you.'

'Didn't Consuelo Jiménez break off the relationship?' asked Pablo.

'She broke it off,' said Falcón, throwing up his hands, realizing that the whole of the Jefatura knew what had happened. 'She didn't want to get involved.'

'And you were unhappy?'

'I was *very* unhappy about it.'

'So what was your motive in looking for Arturo?' asked Juan.

'Consuelo refused to see me or speak to me. She cut me out of her life.'

'Not unlike what Raúl had tried to do with Arturo,' said Juan.

'If you like.'

Juan took a pickled garlic and bit into it with a light crunch.

'I realized that the only way I'd be able to see her again under the right circumstances, rather than as a mad stalker, was to do something extraordinary. I knew that if I found Arturo she would have to see me again. It was the way we had connected in the first place and I knew it would stir something in her.'

'And did it work?' asked Juan, fascinated by Falcón's torment.

16

A warm breeze made a circuit of the patio and stirred up a large, dead and dried-out plant in a far dark corner of the cloister.

'I think it would be better to approach this chronologically,' said Pablo. 'Why don't you tell us how you found Arturo Jiménez?'

The rustle and rattle of the plant's dead leaves had drawn Falcón's gaze to its desiccated corner. He had to get rid of that plant.

'Because my search for Arturo was motivated by this hope for reconciliation with Consuelo, I imagined it as a sort of quest. It was a little more straightforward than that. I was lucky to have some help,' said Falcón. 'I went to Fès with a member of my new Moroccan family. He found a guide who took us to Abdullah Diouri's house deep in the medina. Apart from a magnificently carved door, the house looked like nothing from the outside. But the door opened into a paradise of patios, pools and miniature gardens, which had been allowed to decay from some greater former glory. There were tiles missing and cracked paving and the latticework

219

around the gallery was broken in places. The servant who let us in told us that Abdullah Diouri had died some twenty years ago but that his memory lived on, as he had been a great and kind man.

'We asked to speak to any of the sons, but he told us that only women lived in this house. The sons had dispersed throughout Morocco and the Middle East. So we asked if one of the women would be willing to speak to us about this delicate matter that had occurred some forty years ago. He took our names and left. He returned after quarter of an hour and told my Moroccan relative to stay at the door while he took me on a long trip through the house. We ended up on the first floor, with a view through some repaired latticework on to a garden below. He left me there and after a while I realized that there was somebody else in the room. A woman dressed in black, her face totally veiled, pointed me to a seat and I told her my story.

'Fortunately I'd talked to my Moroccan family about what I was intending to do, so I knew I had to be very careful about how I related this story. It had to be from the Moroccan perspective.'

'What did that entail?' asked Juan.

'That Raúl Jiménez had to be the villain of the piece and Abdullah Diouri the saviour of the family honour. If I sullied the name of the patriarch in any way, if I made him out to be a criminal, a kidnapper of children, I would get nowhere. It was good advice. The woman listened to me in silence, still as a statue under a black dustsheet. At the end of my story a gloved hand came out of her robe and dropped a card on to a low table between us. Then she got up and left. On the card was printed an address in Rabat with a telephone number and the name Yacoub Diouri. A few minutes later the servant came back and returned me to the front door.'

'Well, not quite the Holy Grail,' said Juan, 'but worthy of something.'

'Moroccans love mystery,' said Falcón. 'Abdullah Diouri was a very devout Muslim and Yacoub later told me that the Fès household was kept in that state in honour of the great man. None of the sons could stand the place, which was why it was so run down, and it had been given over exclusively to the women of the family.'

'So you had an address in Rabat . . .' said Pablo.

'I stayed the night in Meknes and called Yacoub from there. He already knew who I was and what I wanted, and we agreed to meet in his house in Rabat the next day. As you probably know, he lives in a huge modern place, built in the Arab style, in the embassy zone on the edge of the city. There must be two hectares of land with an orange grove, gardens, tennis courts, swimming pools – a small palace. He has liveried servants, rose petals in the fountains – that kind of thing. I was taken to a huge room overlooking one of the swimming pools, with cream leather sofas all around. I was given some mint tea and left to stew for half an hour until Yacoub turned up.'

'Did he look like Raúl?'

'I'd seen shots of Raúl when he was a younger man in Tangier and less battered by life. There were similarities, but Yacoub is a different animal altogether. Raúl's wealth never managed to get rid of the Andaluz peasant, whereas Yacoub is a very sophisticated individual, well-read in Spanish, French and English. He speaks German, too. His business demands it. He makes clothes for all the major manufacturers in Europe. He's got Dior and Adolfo Dominguez on his client list. Yacoub was a cheetah to Raúl's gnarled old lion.'

'So how did that first meeting go?' asked Pablo.

'We hit it off immediately, which doesn't happen to me very often,' said Falcón. 'These days I seem to find it hard to get on with people of my own class and background, while I seem to have a talent for engaging with misfits.'

'Why's that?' asked Juan.

'I suppose living with my own horrors has given me the ability to understand the complexities of others, or, at least, not to take things at face value,' said Falcón. 'Whatever, Yacoub and I became friends in that first meeting, and, although we don't see very much of each other, we still are. In fact, he called me last night to say he wanted to meet in Madrid at the weekend.'

'Did Yacoub know *your* story?'

'He'd read it in the press at the time of the Francisco Falcón scandal. It was big news over there that the famous Falcón nudes were actually painted by the Moroccan artist, Tariq Chefchaouni.'

'I'm surprised some journalist hadn't tried to track him down before,' said Pablo.

'They had,' said Falcón. 'But they didn't get any further than the outside of Abdullah Diouri's house in Fès.'

'You said Yacoub was a misfit,' said Gregorio. 'He doesn't sound like one. Successful businessman, married, two children, devout Muslim. He seems to fit in perfectly.'

'Well, that's how it looks from the outside, but from

the moment I first met him I knew he was restless,' said Falcón. 'He was happy with where he was and yet he felt he didn't belong there. He'd been torn away from his own family and yet Abdullah Diouri had made him a part of his and given him the family name. His real father had never come to search for him and yet he was treated no differently to Diouri's own sons. He told me once that he didn't just respect his kidnapper, Abdullah Diouri, he loved him as a father. But despite this acceptance from his new family, he never lost that terrible feeling of having been abandoned by his own. That's what I call a misfit.'

'You say he's married,' said Pablo. 'How many wives does he have?'

'Just the one.'

'Isn't that unusual for a man such as Yacoub Diouri?' asked Juan.

'Why don't you just ask your question to my face instead of wheedling –'

'Because we're interested in the extent of your relationship with Yacoub. If he's told you intimate details about himself, then that has meaning for us,' said Juan.

'Yacoub Diouri is homosexual,' said Falcón, wearily. 'His marriage is something that is expected of him by his society. It is part of his duty as a good Muslim to take a wife and have children, but his sexual interest is exclusively with men. And before you let your prurient interest get carried away, I mean men, not boys.'

'Why do you think that detail should be important to us?' asked Juan.

'You're spies, and I just wanted you to know that his homosexuality is not an area of vulnerability.'

'Why are we questioning you about Yacoub Diouri?' asked Juan.

'First *I'd* like to know how Yacoub came to tell you he was homosexual,' said Pablo.

'Sorry to disappoint you, Pablo, but he didn't make a pass at me,' said Falcón. 'How did *you* find out about him?'

'There's a lot of co-operation between the intelligence services these days,' said Juan. 'Prominent, devout and monied Muslims are . . . observed.'

'Yacoub and I were talking about marriage once and I told him that mine hadn't lasted very long, that my wife had left me for a prominent judge,' said Falcón. 'I told him about Consuelo. He told me that his own marriage was just for show and that he was gay and that the fashion industry suited him.'

'Why?'

'Because it was full of attractive men who weren't looking for a permanent relationship which he couldn't offer.'

Silence. Juan let it be known that it was time to move on.

'So what happened after you became friends with Yacoub?' asked Pablo.

'I saw him quite a lot at the beginning, several times over three or four months. I'd started learning Arabic and went down to see my Moroccan family in Tangier whenever I could. Yacoub would invite me over. We talked, he helped me with my Arabic.'

The CNI men drank their beers in unison.

'And what happened with Consuelo?' asked Juan, blowing smoke out into the night air.

'As I explained, I'd already told Yacoub about

Consuelo and my interest in her. He was quite happy to come to Seville and try to help me out. He liked the idea of being a go-between.'

'How long was this after you'd split up with Consuelo?'

'Nearly a year.'

'You took your time.'

'You can't rush these things.'

'How did you communicate,' asked Pablo, 'if she wouldn't speak to you?'

'I wrote her a letter and asked her if she'd like to meet Yacoub,' said Falcón. 'She wrote back and said she would very much like to meet him, but it would have to be alone.'

'You never even got to see Consuelo?' said Juan, amazed.

'Yacoub did his best for me. They liked each other. He asked her out to dinner on my behalf. She refused. He offered to play gooseberry. She turned him down. There were no explanations and that was the end of it,' said Falcón. 'Why don't we have another beer and you tell me the purpose of this intrusive and personal examination?'

In the kitchen Falcón caught sight of his transparent reflection in the darkened window. He hadn't revealed himself to that extent since being in the hands of Alicia Aguado more than four years ago. In fact, he hadn't been intimate with anyone other than Yacoub since then. It hadn't exactly been a relief to talk to strangers like that, but it had brought back a powerful resurgence of his feelings for Consuelo. He even saw himself in the reflection of the window unconsciously rubbing the arm that had brushed against her yesterday. He shook his head and opened another litre of beer.

'You're smiling, Javier,' said Juan, as Falcón came back. 'After an ordeal like that, I'm impressed.'

'I'm solitary, but not depressed,' said Falcón.

'That's not bad going for a middle-aged homicide detective,' said Pablo.

'Being a homicide detective isn't such a problem for me. There aren't that many murders in Seville and I crack most of them, so my work with the homicide squad actually gives me the illusion that problems are being resolved. And, as you know, an illusory state can contribute to sensations of well-being,' said Falcón. 'If I were trying to resolve something like global warming, or the oceans' dwindling fish stocks, then I'd probably be in much worse mental shape.'

'What about global terrorism?' asked Pablo. 'How do you think you'd cope with that?'

'That's not *my* job. I investigate the murder of people by terrorists,' said Falcón. 'I realize that it can be complicated. But at least we have a chance at resolution and tragedy brings out the best qualities in most people. I wouldn't want your job, which is to *foresee* and prevent terrorist attacks. If you succeed, you live as unsung heroes. If you fail, you live with the death of innocents, the scourge of the media and the admonishment of comfortable politicians. So, no thanks – if you were thinking of offering me a job.'

'Not a job exactly,' said Juan. 'We want to know if you'd be prepared to provide a connective piece or two for the intelligence jigsaw?'

'I've told you that I'm not really spy material any more.'

'In the first instance, we'd be asking you to recruit.'

'You want me to recruit Yacoub Diouri as an intelligence source?' asked Falcón.

The CNI men nodded, gulped beer, lit up cigarettes.

'First of all, I can't think what Yacoub could possibly tell you, and secondly, why me?' said Falcón. 'Surely you've got experienced recruiters who do this sort of thing all the time.'

'It's not what he can tell us now, it's what he could tell us if he was to make a certain move,' said Pablo. 'And you're right, we do have experienced people, but none of them have the special relationship that you do.'

'But my "special relationship" is based on friendship, intimacy and trust, and what will happen to that if one day I say: "Yacoub, will you spy for Spain?"'

'Well, it wouldn't be just for Spain,' said Gregorio. 'It would be for humanity as a whole.'

'Oh, would it really, Gregorio?' said Falcón. 'I'll remember to tell him that, when I ask him to deceive his family and friends and give information to someone he's only known for the last four years of his complicated life.'

'We're not pretending it's easy,' said Juan. 'And equally, we're not going to deny the value of such a contact, or that there are moral implications in what we're asking of you.'

'Thank you, that's put my mind at rest, Juan,' said Falcón. 'You said "in the first instance" – does that mean there's a second one as well? If so, you'd better tell me. I might as well try to digest that with the first lump of gristle you've just thrown me.'

The CNI men looked at each other and shrugged.

'We've just been told that they're going to release the antiterrorism unit of the Seville CGI into this investigation,' said Juan. 'We think there's a mole leaking information and we want to know who it is and who he's leaking it to. You're going to have to work closely with them. Your insight would be invaluable.'

'I don't know what makes you think I can do this work.'

'You've just scored very high points in your interview,' said Pablo.

'What was my score on moral certitude?'

The CNI men laughed as one. Not that they found it funny, it was just the relief at having got the ugliness over and done with.

'Do I get anything in return for all this?' asked Falcón.

'More money, if that's what you want,' said Juan, puzzled.

'I was thinking less in terms of euros and more along the lines of trust,' said Falcón.

'Like what?'

'You tell me things,' said Falcón. 'I'm not saying yes or no, you understand, but perhaps you could tell me what's so important about this annotated copy of the Koran that we found in the Peugeot Partner . . .'

'That's not going to be possible at this juncture,' said Pablo.

'We're beginning to think that what we've found here in Seville,' said Juan, overriding his junior officer, 'is the edge of a much larger terrorist plan.'

'Larger than the liberation of Andalucía?' asked Falcón.

'We're inclined to think that it's a sign of something

that's gone wrong in a plan that we know little about,' said Juan. 'What we think we have in our possession, in the form of this copy of the Koran, is a terrorist network's codebook.'

17

The restaurant was in the middle of the first service to the early tourists, before the main rush of locals at 10 p.m. Consuelo left her office to keep her second appointment with Alicia Aguado. She had been out only once, to her sister's house for lunch. They had talked exclusively about the bomb until the last minutes of the meal when Consuelo had asked her if she could be at her home in Santa Clara at around 10.30 p.m. Her sister had assumed that there was a problem with the nanny.

'No, no, she'll be there looking after the boys,' said Consuelo. 'It's just that I've been told I need someone who's close to me to be there when I get back.'

'Are you going to the gynaecologist?'

'No. The *psych*ologist.'

'You?' her sister had said, astonished.

'Yes, Ana, your sister, Consuelo, is going to see a shrink,' she said.

'But you're the most sane person I've ever known,' said Ana. 'If you're nuts, then what hope is there for the rest of us?'

230

'I'm not *nuts*,' she'd said, 'but I could be. I'm on a knife-edge at the moment. This woman I'm going to see will help me, but she says I need support when I get home. You are the support.'

The effect on her sister was shocking, not least because it had been an unsettling realization for both of them, that perhaps they weren't as close as they'd thought.

As she left the safety of her office, Consuelo felt something like panic forming in her stomach and, as if on cue, she remembered Alicia Aguado's words: 'Come straight to me from your work. Don't be distracted.' It started up some confusion in her, a voice asking: Why shouldn't I? And as she fastened her seat belt, her mind swerved away from its earlier objective and she thought about driving past the Plaza del Pumarejo, wondering if *he* would be there. Her heart raced and she hit the horn so hard and long that one of the waiters came running out into the street. She pulled away and drove straight through the Plaza del Pumarejo, eyes fixed ahead.

Fifteen minutes later she was in the lovers' seat in the cool blue room, her wrist exposed, waiting for Alicia Aguado's inquisitive fingers. They talked about the bomb first. Consuelo couldn't concentrate. She was busy trying to hold her fragmentary self together. Talk of the shattering effects of the bomb was not helping.

'You were a little late,' said Alicia, placing her fingers on the pulse. 'Did you come straight here?'

'I was delayed at work. I came as soon as I could get away.'

'No distractions?'

'None.'

'Try answering that question again, Consuelo.'

She stared at her wrist. Was her heartbeat so transparent? She swallowed hard. Why should this be so difficult? She'd had no problem all day. Her eyes filled. A tear slipped to the corner of her mouth.

'Why are you crying, Consuelo?'

'Aren't *you* going to tell *me*?'

'No,' said Aguado, 'it's the other way round. I'm just the guide.'

'I fought a momentary distraction,' said Consuelo.

'Were you reluctant to tell me because it was of a sexual nature?'

'Yes. I'm ashamed of it.'

'Of what exactly?'

No reply.

'Think about that before our next meeting and decide whether it's true,' said Aguado. 'Tell me about the distraction.'

Consuelo related the incident of the previous night, which had finally precipitated her call for help.

'You don't know this man?'

'No.'

'Have you seen him before, had some kind of casual contact?'

'He's one of those types that walks past women and mutters obscenities,' she said. 'I don't tolerate that sort of behaviour and I make a scene whenever it happens. I want to discourage them from doing it to other women.'

'Do you see that as a moral duty?'

'I do. Women should not be subjected to this random sexism. These men should not be encouraged to indulge in their gross fantasies. It has nothing to do with sex,

232

it's purely a power thing, an abuse of power. These men hate women. They want to verbalize their hate. It gives them pleasure to shock and humiliate. If there were women foolish enough to get involved with men like that, they would be physically abused by them. They are wife-beaters in the making.'

'So why are you fascinated by this man?' asked Aguado.

Tears again, which were combined with a strange sense of collapse, of things falling into each other and, just as the gravitational pull of all this inner crumpling seemed to be achieving a terminal velocity, she felt herself untethered, floating away from the person she thought herself to be. It seemed to be an extreme form of a phenomenon she referred to as an existential lurch: a sudden reflective moment, in which the question of what we are doing here on this planet spinning in the void seemed unanswerably huge. Normally it was over in a flash and she was back in the world, but this time it went on and she didn't know whether she was going to be able to get back. She leapt to her feet and held herself together in case she came apart.

'It's all right,' said Alicia, reaching out to her. 'It's all right, Consuelo. You're still here. Come and sit beside me again.'

The chair, the so-called lovers' chair, seemed more like a torturer's seat. A place where instruments would be inserted to reach unbearably painful clusters of nerves and tweak them to previously unexperienced levels of agony.

'I can't do this,' she heard herself saying. 'I can't do it.'

She fell into Alicia Aguado's arms. She needed the

human touch to bring her back. She cried, and the worst of it was that she had no idea what her suffering was about. Alicia got her back into the chair. They sat, fingers intertwined, as if they were now, indeed, lovers.

'I was falling apart,' said Consuelo. 'I lost sight . . . I lost my sense of who I was. I felt like an astronaut, floating away from the mother ship. I was on the brink of madness.'

'And what precipitated that sensation?'

'Your question. I don't remember what it was. Were you asking about a friend, or my father, perhaps?'

'Maybe we've talked enough about what's troubling you,' said Aguado. 'Let's try to end this on a positive note. Tell me something that makes you happy.'

'My children make me happy.'

'If you remember, our last consultation was terminated by a discussion about how your children made you feel. You said . . .'

'I love them so much it hurts,' finished Consuelo.

'Let's think about a state of happiness that's free from pain.'

'I don't feel pain all the time. It's only when I see them sleeping.'

'And how often do you watch them sleeping?'

Consuelo realized that it had become a nightly ritual, watching the boys in their careless sleep was the high point of every day. That pain right in her middle had become something she relished.

'All right,' said Consuelo, carefully, 'let's try to remember a moment of pain-free happiness. That shouldn't be too difficult, should it, Alicia? I mean, here we are in the most beautiful city in Spain. Didn't somebody say: "To whom God loves, He gives a house in Seville"? God's love must come with half a million euros these days. Let me see . . . Do you ask all your patients this question?'

'Not all of them.'

'How many have been able to give you an answer?' asked Consuelo. 'I imagine psychologists meet a lot of *un*happy people.'

'There's always something. People who love the country might think of the way the sunlight plays on water, or the wind in the grasses. City people might think of a painting they've seen, or a ballet, or just sitting in their favourite square.'

'I don't go to the country. I used to like art, but I lost . . .'

'Others remember a friendship, or an old flame.'

Their hands had come apart and Aguado's fingers were back on Consuelo's wrist.

'What are you thinking about now, for instance?' she asked.

'It's nothing,' said Consuelo.

'It's not *nothing*,' said Aguado. 'Whatever it is . . . hold on to it.'

Inés had been sitting in the apartment for over an hour. It was some time after 9.30 p.m. She had tried to call Esteban but, as usual, his mobile was turned off. She was quite calm, although inside her head there seemed to be a wire pulled taut to vibrating point. She had been to see her doctor but had left just before she was due to be called. The doctor would want to examine her and she didn't want to be looked at, pried into.

The incident in the park with the mulatto bitch-whore kept intruding on her internal movie, forcing the film out of the gate and jamming her head with other images: the lividness of Esteban's face as it appeared under the bed and the twitching of his bare feet on the cold kitchen floor.

The kitchen was not a place for her to be. The hard edges of its granite work surfaces, the chill of the marble floor, the distorting mirrors of all the chrome were reminders of the morning's brutality. She hated that fascist kitchen. It made her think of the Guardia Civil in jackboots and their hard, black, shiny hats. She couldn't see a child in that kitchen.

She sat in the bedroom, feeling tiny on the huge and empty marital bed. The TV was off. There was too much talk about the bomb, too many images of the site, too much blood, gore, and shattered glass and lives. She looked at herself in the mirror, over the ordered hairbrushes and cufflink collections. A question danced in her brain: What the fuck has happened to me?

By 9.45 p.m. she couldn't bear it any longer and went outside. She thought she was walking aimlessly, but found herself drawn to the young people already beginning to gather in the warm night under the massive trees of the Plaza del Museo. Then, unaccountably, she was in Calle Bailén and standing in front of her ex-husband's house. The sight of it brought up a spike of envy. She could have had this house, or at least half of it, if it hadn't been for that bitch of a lawyer Javier had hired. It was she who'd found out that Inés had been fucking Esteban Calderón for months and had asked (to her face!) if she'd wanted all that tawdry stuff dragged through the courts. And look at her now. What a great move she'd made. Married to an abuser

236

of women, who, when he wasn't sodomizing his wife, 'for purposes of contraception', was off with every unpaid whore who waggled her tits . . . Where had all this terrible language come from? Inés Conde de Tejada didn't use this sort of language. Why was her mind suddenly so full of filth?

But here she was, outside Javier's house. Her slim legs in her short skirt trembled. She carried on past the doors to the Hotel Colón and turned back. She had to see Javier. She had to tell him. Not that she'd been beaten. Not that she was sorry for what she had done. No, she didn't want to tell him anything. She just wanted to be near a man who had loved her, who had adored her.

As she hid in the darkness of the orange trees and prepared herself, the door opened and three men came out. They went to pick up a taxi outside the Hotel Colón. The door closed. Inés rang the bell. Falcón reopened the door and was stunned to see the oddly diminished figure of his ex-wife.

'Hola, Inés. Are you all right?'

'Hola, Javier.'

They kissed. He made way for her. They walked to the patio with Falcón thinking: She looks as small and thin as a child. He cleared away the remnants of the CNI party and returned with a bottle of manzanilla

'I should have thought after a day like today you'd be exhausted,' she said. 'And yet here you are having people round for drinks.'

'It's been a long day,' said Falcón, thinking: What is this all about? 'How's Esteban holding up?'

'I haven't seen him.'

'He's probably still at the site. They're working a

roster system through the night,' said Falcón. 'Are you all right, Inés?'

'You've asked me that already, Javier. Don't I look all right?'

'You're not worried about anything, are you?'

'Do I look worried?'

'No, just a little thin. Have you lost weight?'

'I keep myself in shape.'

It always bewildered Falcón, who was already running out of things to say to Inés, how he could ever have been obsessed by her. She struck him now as completely banal; an expert in chitchat, a beautiful presenter of received opinion, a snob and a bore. And yet before they married they'd had a passionate affair, with wild sexual encounters. The bronze boy in the fountain had fled from their excesses.

Her heels clicked on the marble flags of the patio. He had wanted to get rid of her as soon as he'd seen her, but there was something about her pitiful frailness, her lack of Sevillana *hauteur*, that made it hard for him to brush her off into the night.

'How's things?' he said, trying to nod something more interesting into his head, which was almost completely taken up with the decision he had to make within the next eight hours. 'How's life with Esteban?'

'You see more of him than I do,' she said.

'We haven't worked together for a while and, you know, he's always been ambitious, so . . .'

'Yes, he's always been ambitious,' she said, 'to fuck every woman that passes under his nose.'

Falcón's glass of manzanilla stopped on its way to his mouth, before continuing. He took a good inch off the top.

'I wouldn't know,' he said, avoiding a conversational line that had been common knowledge in the police and judiciary for years.

'Don't be so fucking ridiculous, Javier,' she said. 'The whole of fucking Seville knows he's been dipping his cock in every pussy that comes his way.'

Silence. Falcón wondered if he'd ever heard Inés use this sort of language before. It was as if some fishwife inside her was kicking down the barriers.

'I came across one of his whores today in the Murillo Gardens,' she said. 'I recognized her from a shot he'd taken of her with his digital camera. And she was sitting in front of me on a park bench, smoking a cigar, as if she was still thinking about sucking his –'

'Come on, Inés,' said Falcón. 'I'm not the person you should be talking to about this.'

'Why not?' she said. 'You know me. We've been intimate. You know him. You know what he's . . . that he's a . . . that I . . .'

She broke down. Falcón took the glass out of her hand, found some tissues. She blew her nose and thumped the tabletop with her fist and tried to dig her heel into the floor of the patio, which made her wince. She took a walk around the fountain and felt a sudden stabbing pain in her side and had to hold on to herself.

'Are you all right, Inés?'

'Stop asking me that question,' she said. 'It's nothing, just some kidney-stone trouble. The doctor says I don't drink enough water.'

He fetched her a glass of water and thought about how he was going to manage this situation, with Mark Flowers due any minute. His brain stalled on the ludicrous fact that *she* had come to see *him* to talk about her husband's incorrigible womanizing. What did that mean?

'I wanted to talk to you,' she said, 'because I have no one else I can talk to. My friends aren't capable of this level of intimacy. I'm sure some of them have become his conquests. My suffering would just be gossip to them, nothing more. I know you went through a very bad time a few years ago and that has given you the capacity to understand what I'm going through now.'

'I'm not sure my experiences are comparable,' said Falcón, frowning at her self-absorbed talk, the situation expanding out of his control by the moment.

'I know that when we split up you were still in love with me,' she said. 'I felt very sorry for you.'

He knew she'd felt nothing of the sort. She'd projected all her guilt on to him and taunted him with that horrific mantra about his heartlessness: *'Tú no tienes corazón, Javier Falcón.'*

'Are you thinking of leaving Esteban?' he asked, carefully, panicked by the notion that she might be thinking that he would have her back.

'No, no, no que no,' she said. 'It hasn't come to that. We're made for each other. We've been through so much. I'd never leave him. He needs me. It's just . . .'

It's just that there aren't enough clichés for the cheated wife to draw on, thought Falcón.

'It's just that . . . he needs help,' said Inés.

What was happening today? The CNI wanted him to persuade his new friend to become a spy. His ex-wife wanted him to encourage her husband, with whom he'd only ever had a professional relationship, to go and see a shrink.

'What do you think, Javier?'

'I think it's none of my business,' he said firmly.

'I still want to know what you think,' she said, her eyes huge in her head.

'You'll never persuade Esteban – or any man, for that matter – to go to a shrink or a marriage-guidance counsellor, unless he himself perceives that there is a problem,' said Falcón. 'And most men, in these situations, rarely see that the problem is theirs.'

'He's been whoring around in this marriage since . . . since *before* we got married,' she said. 'He must see that he needs to change.'

'The only thing that will change him is a major trauma in his life, which might make him reflect on his . . . insatiable needs,' said Falcón. 'Unfortunately, it might also mean that those close to him now will not remain so . . .'

'I stuck with him through his last crisis with the American bitch and I'll stick with him through this,' she said. 'I know he loves me.'

'That was my experience,' said Falcón, holding out his hands and realizing that he'd just told Inés why she wasn't a part of his life any more. 'My problem didn't happen to be womanizing, though.'

'No, it wasn't, was it? You were so *cold*, Javier,' she said.

That tone of false concern set his teeth on edge, but the doorbell rang, saving him from having to dig deeper into his reserves of patience. He walked her to the door.

'You're popular tonight,' said Inés.

'I don't know what people see in me,' said Falcón, braking hard on the irony.

'We don't see so much of each other these days,'

she said, kissing him before he opened the door. 'I'm sorry . . . if we don't see each other again . . .'

'Again?' said Falcón, and the doorbell rang once more.

'I'm sorry,' she said.

At 9.30 p.m. Calderón had arrived at Marisa's apartment. Twenty minutes later they lay naked and sex-smeared on the floor by the sofa. They were drinking Cuba Libres chock full of ice, and smoking their way through a packet of Marlboro Lights. She straddled him and brushed her hardened nipples against his lips, while lowering her pubis until it just tickled the tip of his exhausted penis. He filled his hands with her buttocks and bit her nipple a little too hard.

'Ai!' she yelped, pushing away from him. 'Haven't you eaten?'

'There hasn't been much time for eating,' he said.

'Why don't I make you some pasta?' she said, standing over him, still in her heels, legs astride, hands on hips, cigarette dangling from her plump lips.

I'm Helmut Newton, thought Calderón.

'Sounds good,' he said.

She put on a turquoise silk robe and went into the kitchen. Calderón sipped his drink, smoked, looked out into the dense, warm night, and thought: This is all right.

'Something strange happened to me today,' said Marisa, from the kitchen, knife working over some onion and garlic. 'I sold a couple of my pieces to one of my dealers. He pays cash and I like to treat myself to a nice cigar – a real one, made in Havana. I sit under the palm trees in the Murillo Gardens to smoke it, because it reminds me of home and it was really hot today, the first heat of the summer. And I'd just got myself into a really cool Cuban mood . . .'

Marisa could tell from the back of Calderón's head that he was barely listening to her.

'. . . when this woman sat down in front of me. A beautiful woman. Very slim, long dark hair, beautiful big eyes . . . Maybe a little too thin, now that I think about it. Her eyes were *so* big and she was staring at me in this *very* strange way.'

She had his attention now. His head was as still as rock.

'I like to smoke my cigars in peace. I don't like mad people looking at me. So I asked her what she was staring at. She told me she was looking at the whore with the cigar – *la puta con el puro*. Well, nobody calls me a whore, and nobody ruins a top-quality Havana cigar. So I gave her a piece of my mind – and you know what?'

Calderón took a viciously long drag of his cigarette.

'You know what she said to me?'

'What?' said Calderón, as if a long way off.

'She said: "You're the *whore* who's fucking my husband." She asked me how much you were paying me and said that it didn't look as if it was more than € 15 a night and that you'd probably thrown in the copper wig and the cigar to keep me happy. Can you tell me how the fuck Inés knows who I am?'

Calderón stood up. He was so angry he couldn't speak. His lips were pale and his genitals were shrivelled back into their pubic nest as if his rage had taken all available blood to keep it stoked. He was clenching and unclenching his fist and staring off into the night, with bone-snapping violence ricocheting around his head. Marisa had seen this trait in physically unimpressive men before. The big, muscly guys had nothing to prove, whereas the fat, the puny and the stupid had big lessons to hand out.

When she heard the shower running, Marisa stopped preparing the food. Calderón dressed in ominous silence. She asked him what he was doing, why he was leaving. He whipped his tie up into a tight choleric knot.

'Nobody talks to you like that,' he said, and left.

Inés stopped to look in a hand-painted tile shop on Calle Bailén. She felt better after seeing Javier. She'd persuaded herself, in the short walk after their brief encounter, that Javier still cared for her. How sweet of him to ask her if she was thinking of leaving Esteban. He still lived in hope after all these years. It was sad to have to disappoint him.

The darkness under the huge trees of the Plaza del Museo held the murmur of more young people, the chinking of beer bottles and the reek of marijuana. She walked through them feeling more cheerful. The light was on in the apartment, which elated her. Esteban was home. He had come back to her. They were going to repair the damage. She was sure, after what had happened this morning, that he would see reason and she could persuade him to make an appointment with a psychologist.

The stairs no longer inspired dread and although the pain in her side meant that she didn't exactly sprint up them, she reached the door with a lightness of heart. Her hair swung on her shoulders as she closed the door.

She instantly felt his looming presence. A smile was already spreading on her face when he sheafed her hair and turned it once around his wrist. She toppled backwards, falling to her knees, and he brought her face up close to the pallor of the pure hatred in his own.

18

Mark Flowers had already eaten. His American diges-
tive system had never got used to the Spanish custom
of not even thinking about dinner until 9.30 p.m. He
turned down Falcón's offers of beer and manzanilla
and opted for a single malt whisky. Falcón wolfed down
a quickly made sandwich in the kitchen and stuck with
the manzanilla. It was still very warm and they sat out
under the open sky of the patio.

'So what did "your own" people want to talk to you
about?' asked Flowers, always a man to get his questions in first.

'They're trying to persuade me to go into the recruitment business for them.'

'And will you do it?'

'I've got until 6 a.m. to decide.'

'Well, it was nice of them to wait until you had nothing
on your plate,' said Flowers, who was always determined
to show him that not all Americans had undergone an
irony bypass. 'I don't know who they want you to recruit,
but if he's a friend he might not stay a friend. That's the
way these things work, in my experience.'

'Why's that?'

'People react strangely to being asked to become a spy. It calls into question your prior relationship: Did he become my friend just to recruit me? It also implies moral duplicity. You, as the recruiter, have a singular purpose, which requires asking someone to lie and deceive on your behalf. It's an odd relationship.'

'Got any advice?'

'It's like going out on a date. It's all in the timing. You move in too early and the girl will accuse you of being too fresh. You come on too late and you might have bored her, shown her your uncertainty. It's a delicate process and, like dating, you only get better at it by doing it . . . a lot.'

'You've just filled me with confidence, Mark. I haven't been out on a date for more than a year.'

'Some people say it's like riding a bicycle,' said Flowers. 'But there's a big difference between an eighteen-year-old taking up cycling and a middle-aged man going back to it. I wish you'd change your whisky, Javier. This stuff is like drinking peat bog.'

'Maybe you'd like some Coca Cola to go with it?' said Falcón.

Flowers chuckled.

'Do your people know whether your Moroccan friend is "safe"?' he asked.

'Did I say that I was recruiting a friend, and that he was Moroccan?' asked Falcón.

Another chuckle from Flowers, followed by a big snort of whisky.

'You didn't say, but given our present circumstances it was a safe bet.'

'They seem to have researched him pretty well,' said Falcón, giving up quickly on the game.

'That's not how you find out if someone is "safe",' said Flowers. 'Research is like trying to learn how to succeed in business by reading a self-help book.'

'I know he's safe.'

'Well, you're a homicide cop, so you should know when someone is lying to you,' said Flowers. 'What sort of conversations have you had about terrorism, Iraq, the Palestinian question, that have led you to believe that your friend is "safe"?'

'None in which the outcome of the conversation has been crucial, if that's what you mean.'

'I can find thousands of Muslims in the tea houses of North Africa who would condemn the actions of these extremist groups and their indiscriminate violence, but I would struggle to find one who would give me information that might lead to the capture and possible death of a jihadi,' said Flowers. 'It's one of the strange contradictions of this kind of spying: it takes a profound moral certitude to behave immorally. So, how do you know he's "safe"?'

'I'm not sure what I can tell you that would help you believe, without sounding foolish,' said Falcón.

'Try me.'

'We recognized something in each other from the first moment we met.'

'What does that mean?'

'We've had comparable experiences, which have given us a level of automatic understanding.'

'Still not sure,' said Flowers, closing an eye over his raised glass.

'What happens when two people fall in love?'

'Take it easy, Javier.'

'How do two people sort out all that necessarily complicated communication that lets them know that they will be going to bed together that night?'

'You know the problem with that? Lovers cheat on each other all the time.'

'What you're saying, Mark, is that we can never know, we can only be as certain as possible.'

'The love analogy is right,' said Flowers. 'You've just got to be sure that he doesn't love someone more than you.'

'Thanks.'

'Who are we talking about, by the way?'

'You took your time.'

'Had I known you were going to be so coy, I'd have taken you out to dinner.'

'This isn't *my* business, it's CNI business.'

'Do you think you'll be able to get out of Casablanca airport without my guys spotting you?' asked Flowers.

'I'm surprised you haven't had me followed before.'

Silence. Flowers smiled.

'You knew all along,' said Falcón, throwing up his hands. 'Why do you play these games with me?'

'To remind you that, in my world, you're an amateur,' said Flowers. 'What are you hoping to get out of Yacoub Diouri?'

'I don't know. I'm not even sure whether I'm going to accept the task and, if I do, whether my superiors will allow me to do it.'

'What about the investigation here?'

'There's a lot still to be done, but at least we know

what went on inside and outside the mosque in the days leading up to the explosion.'

'Was that why you wanted me to research I4IT?'

'They're in the background . . . quite a long way in the background,' said Falcón, who filled him in on Horizonte and Informáticalidad.

'I4IT are not, in fact, based in Indianapolis,' said Flowers. 'The company headquarters is in Columbus, Ohio, due to its proximity to Westerville, Ohio, which was where the US temperance movement started, and from where National Prohibition took off back in the 1920s.'

'You're making this sound significant.'

'The corporation is owned and actively run by two born-again Christians, who discovered their faith through the excesses of their youth,' said Flowers. 'Cortland Fallenbach was a computer programmer who used to work for Microsoft until they "let him go" due to problems with alcohol and other substances. Morgan Havilland was a salesman for IBM, until his sex addiction got out of control and he had to be removed before the company ended up in court on the end of a sexual harassment suit.'

'Did these guys meet in therapy?'

'In Indianapolis,' said Flowers. 'And having both worked for the most powerful IT corporations in the world, they decided to set up a group to invest in hi-tech companies. Fallenbach was a software king and Havilland understood hardware. At first they just invested and took profit from their inside knowledge of the industry. Later they started buying companies outright, merging their strengths, and either selling them or setting them up in groups of their own. But there was, and is, one important stipulation if you want to be a part of I4IT . . .'

'You have to believe in God?' asked Falcón.

'You have to believe in the *right* god,' said Flowers. 'You have to be a Christian. That doesn't mean they don't buy companies owned by Hindus, Muslims, Buddhists or Shintoists – if that's what they're called – it just means that they don't become a part of I4IT. They either strip out what they want and, if they're still valuable, they sell them on; if they're not, they let them rot into the ground.'

'Ruthless Christians,' said Falcón.

'Crusaders might be a good word,' said Flowers. 'Very successful crusaders. I4IT has world-wide assets in excess of $12 billion. They showed a profit in the first quarter of this year of $375 million.'

'What about politics?'

'Fallenbach and Havilland are members of the Christian Right and therefore deeply Republican. Their ethos, though, is based on religion. As long as you practise the same religion they believe you can understand each other. If one is a Muslim and the other a Christian there will always be fundamental differences which will prevent perfect communication. Atheists are off the page, which means communists are unacceptable. Agnostics can still be "saved" . . .'

'Is this the level of discussion in board meetings before a take-over?'

'Sure. They take company culture very seriously and religion is the foundation of that culture,' said Flowers. 'Where they can get away with it, they don't employ women in the workplace, otherwise they keep to the bare legal minimum. They don't employ homosexuals. God hates fags . . . remember, Javier?'

'I don't remember that line from the Bible.'

'Their success and profitability is a manifestation of their righteousness.'

'How active are they outside their own corporation?'

'As far as we know, it's limited to *not* doing business with people whose principles they don't agree with. So they produce a lot of ultrasound equipment, for instance, and they won't sell to clinics known to perform abortions,' said Flowers. 'As far as any *active* anti-religious movement goes, we haven't heard of anything.'

'Do you think Informáticalidad using this apartment for brainstorming sessions is weird?'

'If you ask me what's weird, it's companies and governments spending billions of dollars and euros a year on management consultancies, who come in and give them the kind of common sense that my grandmother could have told them for free,' said Flowers. 'Informáticalidad sound like a company who haven't bought into the bullshit industry and have come up with a cheaper, and probably more productive, solution which leaves them with an asset at the end of it all. If you can place any of those Informáticalidad brainstormers in the mosque, now that's a different story . . .'

'Not so far,' said Falcón. 'Another thing: have you got any information on an organization called VOMIT?'

'VOMIT . . . yes, I've seen their website. We thought it stood for Victims of Muslim and Islamic Terror until one of our operators saw the Spanish. They can only be accused of not presenting the full picture, but that's just a matter of imbalance. It's not criminal. There's no incitement to take revenge, no bomb-making advice, weapons training or active recruitment to "a cause".'

'If it's just a few geeks with some phones and a computer, that's one thing,' said Falcón. 'If it's a multi-billion-dollar corporation with world-wide resources, wouldn't that be different?'

'First of all, I don't see that connection. Second, there'd have to be more of a perceived threat to get us to do any digging on VOMIT,' said Flowers. 'And anyway, Javier, why are you sniffing around the wacky fringes of this attack instead of getting stuck into the guts of it? I mean, VOMIT, I4IT . . .'

'The guts of the problem are under a few thousand tons of rubble at the moment,' said Falcón. 'Informáticalidad was an unignorable part of the scenario outside the mosque. VOMIT were introduced into the frame by the CNI. We have some suspicious occurrences in the mosque, which have not been adequately explained.'

'Like what?'

Falcón told him about the council inspectors, the blown fuse box and the electricians.

'I know what you're thinking,' said Flowers.

'No, you don't, because I haven't decided on a scenario yet myself. I'm keeping an open mind,' said Falcón. 'We know that two terror suspects – Djamel Hammad and Smail Saoudi – made deliveries to the mosque, which could be innocent or could have been bomb-making material. A deposit of hexogen – or cyclonite, as you call it – was found in the back of their van . . .'

'Fucking hell, Javier,' said Flowers, sitting up. 'And you don't call that damning evidence?'

'It looks bad,' said Falcón, 'but we're not talking about looks here. We've got to get beyond appearances.'

'Is there any more of this whisky? I'm getting the taste for this liquid-charcoal stuff.'

Falcón topped him up and gave himself another jolt of manzanilla. He sat back, feeling as he always did in his conversations with Flowers – stupid and flayed.

'You know, Mark, you still haven't told me anything I couldn't have found out for myself inside half an hour on the internet, whereas I've told you . . . everything. I know you like to keep your account with me in the black, but I'd appreciate some real help,' said Falcón. 'Why don't you tell me something about the MILA, or Imam Abdelkrim Benaboura?'

'There's a good reason why you don't get as much information from me as I do from you,' said Flowers, who let those names flash past him without a flicker. 'I'm running a station that covers southern Spain and its relations with Morocco, Algeria and Tunisia. I have no idea what is going on in Madrid, northern Spain or southern France. I only see a small corner of the whole picture. London, Paris, Rome and Berlin make their contributions, but I don't see any of it. Like you, I'm just a contributor.'

'You're making yourself sound very passive.'

'I'm getting information from all sorts of different sources, but I have to be very careful how I use it,' said Flowers. 'Spying is a game, but I never forget that it's being played with real people, who can get killed.

So *you* only get information that doesn't endanger you or any of my other sources. If I'm in any doubt, you won't be given it. Be glad that I'm not a risk-taking station head.'

'Thanks for that, Mark. Now why don't you tell me about Los Mártires Islámicos para la Liberación de Andalucía?'

'I first heard about them at the end of last year as El Movimiento rather than Los Mártires. My source in Algiers told me that they were a disaffected faction of the Algerian GIA, the Armed Islamic Group, who had crossed the border into Morocco and teamed up with a local group, whose goal at the time was the liberation of the Spanish enclaves in Morocco: Ceuta and Melilla. The Algerians brought with them a network, with operatives already installed in Madrid, Granada, Málaga and Valencia.'

'But not Seville?'

'I'm coming to that,' said Flowers. 'My source told me that what the Moroccans could supply was finance. They were cash rich from their connections in the hashish trade in the Rif mountains. What they didn't have was a network and a strategy. Both Ceuta and Melilla are small enclaves, well protected and well supplied by the Spanish mainland. The Algerians saw the money and told them to think big. Liberate Andalucía, cut off the Spanish supply line to Ceuta and Melilla, and this Western corner of the Islamic kingdom is whole once again.'

'You'd need an army and a navy to take Andalucía.'

'And there's the British in Gibraltar, who might have an opinion on the matter, too,' said Flowers. 'But that is not the point. The liberation of Andalucía is an inspiring *ideal* that fills the hearts of Islamic fanatics with a warm Allah-infused glow. It is the *dream* that will draw followers to the cause. My source also read the Algerians' intentions wrong. They didn't want access to the hashish trade because of finance, they wanted to tap into their smuggling routes to get people and material across to Spain.'

'Has that been happening?'

'Nobody's been caught,' said Flowers. 'Smuggling routes generally exist because they're allowed to. There's a constant stream of hashish from Morocco and cocaine from South America coming into the long, unpatrollable Iberian coastline, and there's plenty of money to keep the authorities happy and quiet.'

This talk made Falcón's sweat run cold. The money, organization and corruption were all in place to make a devastating campaign on Andalucía seem likely rather than crazy.

'What about Seville and the MILA?' asked Falcón.

'Some Afghans arrived in Morocco in January.'

'Where in Morocco? How do your sources get such information? Why aren't we getting it?'

'There's no base. There's no town hall with posters outside advertising "MILA Meeting Tonight". I have one source, at the wrong level, who is able to give me bits and pieces. You don't just walk into these groups off the street. You have to be vouched for. It's all to do with family and tribal ties. I believe my source's information, but I'm wary of sharing it because he's peripheral to the group's leading council.'

'Which means it could be invention?'

'You see, Javier, being given information doesn't necessarily make the picture any clearer.'

'Tell me about the Afghan connection.'

'Some Afghans arrived, offering the group a Seville connection. They said he was capable of giving recce and logistical support, but did not have the capacity to carry out an attack.'

'Name?'

'He couldn't give me one.'

'One of the worshippers in the mosque here told me that there had been a visit from a group of Afghans and that the Imam had spoken to them in Pashto.'

'I'd be careful about putting those two pieces of information together without more corroboration,' said Flowers.

'What's the news on Abdelkrim Benaboura?' asked Falcón. 'He doesn't seem to be high risk and yet there's a clearance problem with his history. What does that mean?'

'That they don't know who he is from a certain date, which is normally around the end of 2001 and the beginning of 2002 when the US went into Afghanistan and the Taliban regime broke up and dispersed. You have to remember, until 9/11 the US and European intelligence network in the Islamic world was negligible. We sorted out who was who on our own turf in the years that followed, but there were, and still are, very large gaps – as you'd expect from an introverted religion that stretches from Indonesia to Morocco and Northern Europe to South Africa. Factor in the difficulties of identification, given the clothes these people wear, the headgear and facial hair, and histories are not so easily matched to people.'

'You still haven't told me anything about Abdelkrim Benaboura.'

'Why do the CNI think it's so important for you to recruit Yacoub now, right at the moment when you're supposed to be heading the biggest murder enquiry of your career?'

'The CNI think they might have discovered something even bigger.'

'Like what?'

'They weren't prepared to say.'

'What have they got that's made them think that?'

'You don't miss much, Mark, do you?' said Falcón, but Flowers didn't answer. He was deep in distracted thought until he looked at his watch, knocked back his whisky and said he had to go. Falcón walked him to the door.

'Have you tried to recruit Yacoub Diouri yourself?' asked Falcón.

'Something worth remembering,' said Flowers, 'he doesn't like Americans. Now, who was that beautiful woman who left just as I arrived?'

'My ex-wife.'

'I've got two ex-wives,' said Flowers. 'It's funny how ex-wives are always more beautiful than wives. Think about that, Javier.'

'That's all you do, Mark, leave me with more to think about than when you arrived.'

'I'll give you something else to roll around your brain,' said Flowers. 'The CNI planted the story about the MILA in the press. How about that?'

'Why would they do that?'

'Welcome to my wonderful world, Javier,' said Flowers, walking off into the night.

He stopped at the end of the short avenue of orange trees and turned back to Javier, who was silhouetted in the doorway.

'One last piece of advice,' said Flowers. 'Don't try to understand the whole picture . . . there's nobody in the world who does.'

19

Manuela lay in bed alone, trying to ignore the faint click of Angel's fingers on the keys of his laptop in another room. She blinked in the dark, holding back the full contemplation of something very horrible: the sale of her villa in El Puerto de Santa María, an hour's drive south from Seville on the coast. The villa had been left to her by her father, and every room was packed with adolescent nostalgia. The fact that Francisco Falcón didn't much like the place and loathed all the neighbours, the so-called Seville high society, had been erased from Manuela's memory. She imagined her father's spirit writhing in agony at the proposed sale. It was, however, the only way that she could see of repairing her financial situation. The banks had already called her before close of business, asking where the funds were that she'd told them to expect. It was the only solution that had come to her, in the death and debt hour of four o'clock in the morning. The estate agent had told her the obvious: the Seville property market would be stalled until further notice. She had four possible buyers for her villa, who were constantly reminding her of their readiness to purchase. But could she let it go?

Angel had been calling her all day, trying to restrain the excitement in his voice. His conversation was full of the ramifications of Rivero's retirement and the great new hope of Fuerza Andalucía, Jesús Alarcón, who he'd been steering around all day, after interviewing him for the profile in the *ABC*. Angel's media manipulation had been brilliant. He'd kept Jesús off camera when he visited the hospital and got him to talk privately to the victims and their families. His greatest coup had been to get him through to Fernando Alanis in the intensive care unit. Jesús and Fernando had talked. No cameras. No reporters. And they'd hit it off. It couldn't have been better. Later, when the Mayor and a camera crew got through to intensive care, Fernando had mentioned Jesús Alarcón, on camera, as the only politician who hadn't sought to make any media capital out of the victims' misery. It was pure luck, but a total masterstroke for Angel's campaign. The Mayor had just managed to squeeze back the nervous smile that wanted to creep across his face.

Consuelo couldn't stop herself. Why should she? She couldn't sleep. What better way to remember carefree sleep than to watch the experts; the calm faces of the innocents, eyelids trembling, softly breathing, deep and dreamless in their beds. Ricardo was first, the fourteen-year-old, who'd reached the gawky age, where his face was stretching in odd directions, trying to find its adult mould. This wasn't such a peaceful age, with too many hormones shooting around the body and sexual yearning fighting with football in his mind. Matías was twelve and seemed to be growing up quicker than his elder brother; easier to walk in somebody else's footsteps than to tread out one's own, as Ricardo had done with no father to guide him.

Consuelo knew where this was heading, though. Ricardo and Matías took care of themselves. It was Darío, her youngest at eight years old, who drew her in. She loved his face, his blond hair, his amber-coloured eyes, his perfect little mouth. It was in his room that she sat down in the middle of the floor, half a metre from his bed, looking into his untroubled features and easing herself into the uneasy state she craved. It started in her mouth, with the lips that had kissed his baby head. She drank it down her throat and felt the twinge in her breasts. It settled in her stomach, high up around the diaphragm, an ache that transmitted its pain from her viscera to the tingling surface of her skin. She scoffed at Alicia Aguado's questioning. What was wrong with such a love as this?

Fernando Alanis sat in the intensive care unit of the Hospital de la Macarena. He watched his daughter's vital signs on the monitors. Grey numbers and green lines that told him good things, that she was capable of lighting up a machine, if not her father. His mind crashed and fell about like a hopeless drunk in a bin-filled narrow alleyway. One moment it was gasping at the catastrophic destruction of the apartment building, the next it was buckling at the sight of four covered bodies outside the pre-school. He still couldn't quite believe what he had lost. Was this a mechanism of the mind that suspended things too unbearable to comprehend, almost to the point of a barely remembered nightmare? He'd been told by people who'd survived bad falls from scaffolding that the rush of the ground coming to meet you was not so terrifying. The horror was in the eventual awakening. And with that he would lurch sickeningly forward to the bruised and battered face of his daughter, her oval mouth slack against the clear plastic concertina of tube. Everything inside him felt too big. His organs were jostled by the colossal inflation of hate and despair which had no direction, other than to make themselves as uncomfortable as possible. He went back to a time when his family and the building had been intact, but the thought of the third child he'd been proposing made him break down inside. He couldn't bear to take himself back to a state that would never exist again, he couldn't bear the notion of never seeing Gloria and Pedro again, he couldn't stomach the finality of that word 'never'.

He concentrated on his daughter's beating heart. The jumping line. Be-dum, be-dum, be-dum. The thready skip of the green fuse against the terminal blackness of the monitor made him rear back in his seat. It was all too fragile. Anything could happen in this life and did . . . and had. Perhaps the answer was to retreat into emptiness. Feel nothing. But that held its terror, too. The monstrous negativity of the black hole in space, sucking in all light. He breathed in. The air expanded his chest. He breathed out. His stomach wall relaxed. This, for the time being, was the only way to proceed.

Inés lay where she had fallen. She hadn't moved since he'd left. Her body was a miasma of pain from the pummelling it had sustained from his hard, white knuckles. Nausea humped in her stomach. He'd punched her through her flailing hands; one of her fingers had been bent back. In an escalation of his fury he'd torn off his belt and lashed her, with the buckle digging into her buttocks and thighs. With each stroke he'd told her through clenched teeth: 'Never . . . speak . . . to my girlfriend . . . like that . . . ever again. Do you hear me? Never . . . again.' She'd rolled to the corner of the room to get away from him. He'd stood over her, breathing heavily, not so different from when he was sexually aroused. Their eyes met. He pointed his finger at her as if he might shoot her. She didn't pick up what he said. She'd taken in the purity of his hatred from his blank, basilisk eyes, the colourless lips and his red, swollen neck.

No sooner had he left the apartment than she started to rebuild her illusion. His anger was understandable. The whore had told him some nonsense and set him against her. That was the way these things worked. He was just fucking the whore, but she wanted more now. She wanted to be in the wife's shoes, on the wife's side of the bed, but she was just the whore so she had to play her little games. Inés hated the whore. A line came into her head from an old conversation with Javier: 'Most people are killed by people they know, because it is only they who are capable of arousing the passionate emotions that can lead to uncontrollable violence.' Inés knew Esteban. My God, did she know Esteban Calderón. She'd seen him gilded with the laurel wreath, and cringing like the village cur. That was why she could arouse such emotions in him. Only she. That old cliché holds true. Love and hate have the same source. He would love her again once that black bitch stopped meddling with his mind.

She raised herself on to all fours. The pain made her gasp. Blood dripped from her mouth. She must have bitten her tongue. She crawled up the bed to stand on her feet. She unzipped her dress and let it fall. Unhooking her bra was a torture, bending to slip off her panties nearly made her faint. She stood in front of the mirror. A massive bruise spread across her torso where he'd hit her that morning. Her chest ached through to her spine. A criss-cross of weals covered her buttocks and upper thighs, broken by punctured skin where the buckle had dug in. She put a finger to one of these marks and pressed. The pain was exquisite. Esteban, in that passionate moment, really had given her his fullest attention.

Javier lay in the dark, with images from the late news still present in his mind: the demolished building under the surgical glare of the floodlights; the smashed plate-glass windows of a number of shops with Moroccan wares for sale; the fire brigade spraying a flaming apartment which had been fire-bombed by kids on the rampage; a cut, bruised and swollen-faced Moroccan boy, who'd been set upon by neo-Nazi thugs with clubs and chains; a butcher's selling halal meat with a car rammed through the metal blinds of the store front. Falcón shunted all the images out of his mind until all that was left was the ultimate remnant of terror – deep uncertainty.

He cast his mind back to before the bombing, looking for a clue amongst all those extraordinary emotions that might help him make sense of what was happening. His mind played tricks. Uncertainty had that effect. Human beings always believe that an event has been prefigured in some way. It's the necessary part of redis-covering the pattern. Mankind cannot bear too much chaos.

He had the illusion of the impenetrable darkness receding from him, like the endlessly expanding universe. This was the new certainty, the one that sent all the old narratives, with which we structured our lives, down into the black hole of human under-standing. We have to be even stronger now that science has told us that time is unreliable, and even light behaves differently if you turn your back. It was a terrible irony that, just as science was pushing back the limits of our comprehension, religion, the greatest and oldest of human narratives, was fighting back. Was it because of resentment at being found on the discard pile of modern European life that religion was making a stand? Falcón closed his eyes and concentrated on relaxing each part of his body until, finally, he drifted away from the unanswerable questions and into a deep sleep. He was a man who had made up his mind and had a car arriving early to take him to the airport.

The car, a black Mercedes with tinted windows, turned up at 6 a.m. with Pablo sitting in the back in a dark suit with an open-neck shirt.

'How did your talk with Yacoub go last night?' asked Pablo, as the car pulled away.

'Given that a bomb went off in Seville yesterday, he knows I'm not coming over on a social visit.'

'What did he say?'

'He was pleased that we were going to see each other, but he knows there's an ulterior motive.'

'He's going to be a natural at this business.'

'I'm not sure he'll take that as a compliment.'

'Because of your investigation this is time-critical, so we've arranged a private jet to take us down there. The flight to Casablanca will be less than an hour and a half as long as we get good air-traffic clearance. You've got diplomatic status so we'll get through any formalities quickly, and you'll be on the road to Rabat within two hours of take-off,' said Pablo. 'I presume you're meeting Yacoub in his home?'

'I'm a friend, not a business associate,' said Falcón. 'Although that might change after this meeting.'

'I'm sure Mark Flowers gave you some good tips.'

'How long have you known about Mark . . . and me?' asked Falcón, smiling.

'Since you first outwitted him back in July 2002 and he made you one of his sources,' said Pablo. 'We're not worried about Mark. He's a friend. After 9/11 the Americans said they were going to put someone in Andalucía and we asked for Mark. Juan has known him since they were in Tunis together, keeping an eye on Gaddafi. Did Mark give you any ideas on how to approach Yacoub Diouri?'

'I'm pretty sure he tried to recruit him and was rebuffed,' said Falcón. 'He said that Yacoub didn't like Americans.'

'That should make your task easier, if he's used to being approached.'

'I don't think Yacoub Diouri is someone you "approach". He's the sort of guy who would see you coming a long way off if you did. We'll just talk, as we always do, about everything. It will come out in the way it does. I'm not going to use any strategies on him. Like a lot of Arabs, he has a powerful belief in honour, which he learnt from the man who became his father. He is someone to whom you show respect, and not just as a gesture,' said Falcón. 'Perhaps you should tell me the sort of thing you want him to do, how you want him to operate, what contacts you're expecting him to make. Are you hoping to get information about the MILA from him?'

'MILA? Has Mark been talking to you about the MILA?'

'You're all the same, you intelligence people,' said Falcón. 'You can't take a question, you have to answer it with another. Do you exchange *any* information?'

'The MILA has nothing to do with what we want from Yacoub.'

'The TVE news said they were responsible for the bomb,' said Falcón. 'A text was posted from Seville to the Madrid office of the *ABC*, about Andalucía being brought back into the Muslim fold.'

'The MILA are only interested in money,' said Pablo. 'They've dressed their intentions up in jihadist rhetoric, but the reason they want to liberate Ceuta and Melilla is that they want the enclaves for themselves.'

'Tell me what we're trying to achieve,' said Falcón.

'For the purposes of this mission, what is crucial is not *who* destroyed that apartment building in Seville and *why*, but rather *what* the explosion has revealed to us,' said Pablo. 'Forget the MILA, they're not important. This is not about your investigation into yesterday's bomb. This is not about the past, but the future.'

'OK. Tell me,' said Falcón, thinking that Flowers may have been right about the CNI planting the MILA story.

'Last year the British held their parliamentary

elections. They didn't need the example of the Madrid bombings to know that these elections were going to be the target of a number of attempts by terrorists to change the way a population thinks.'

'And nothing happened,' said Falcón. 'Tony Blair, the "little Satan", got in with a reduced majority.'

'Exactly, and nobody knew that there were three separate cells with active plans, who were prevented from carrying out their attacks by MI5,' said Pablo. 'All those cells were sleepers, dormant until they received their instructions in January 2005. Every member of the cell was either a second- or third-generation immigrant, originally from Pakistan, Afghanistan or Morocco, but now British. They spoke perfect English with regional accents. They all had clean police records. They all had jobs and came from decent backgrounds. In other words, they were impossible to find in a country with millions of people of the same ethnicity. But they *were* found and their attacks *were* prevented because MI5 had a codebook to help them.

'When they were searching some suspects' properties after a series of arrests made in 2003 and early 2004 they came across identical editions of a text called the *Book of Proof* by a ninth-century Arab writer called al-Jahiz. Both editions had notes – all in English, because the accused didn't have a word of Arabic between them. Some of the notes in each copy were remarkably similar. MI5 photocopied the books, replaced the originals, released the accused and set their code-breakers to work.'

'And when did they share that information with the CNI?'

'October 2004.'

'So what happened with the London bombings of 7th and 21st July 2005?'

'The British think they stopped using the *Book of Proof* after the May 2005 elections.'

'And now you think you've discovered a new code-book,' said Falcón. 'What about the new copy of the Koran found on the front seat of the Peugeot Partner?'

'We think they were going to prepare another code-book to give to someone.'

'The Imam Abdelkrim Benaboura?'

'We haven't finished searching his apartment,' said Pablo, shrugging.

'That's taken some time.'

'The Imam lived in a two-bedroomed flat in El Cerezo and almost every room is full, floor to ceiling, of books.'

'I don't feel any closer to knowing why you want to recruit Yacoub Diouri.'

'The jihadis are in need of another big coup. Something on the scale of 9/11.'

'But not as "small scale" as a few hundred people killed on trains in Madrid and the underground in London,' said Falcón, not quite able to stomach this level of objectivity.

'I'm not diminishing those atrocities, I'm just saying that they were on a different scale. You'll learn about intelligence work as you do it, Javier; you're not in the trenches, seeing your friends getting killed. It has an effect on your vision,' said Pablo. 'Madrid was time-targeted, with a specific goal. It wasn't a big, bold state-ment. It was just saying: This is what we can do. There's no comparison to the operation that brought down the Twin Towers. No flight or hijack training. They just had to board trains and leave rucksacks. The most difficult aspect of the operation was to buy and deliver the explosives, and in that we now know they had considerable help from local petty criminals.'

'So what is the big coup?' asked Falcón, uneasy at this breezy talk of death and destruction. 'The World Cup in Germany?'

'No. For the same reason that the Olympics in Greece was untouched. It's just too difficult. The terrorists are competing with specialists who have been planning security at these events for years. Even the buildings are constructed with security in mind. The chances of discovery are increased enormously. Why waste resources?'

Silence, as the Mercedes tyres ripped over the tarmac towards the airport, which was smudged out by the early-morning haze.

'You don't know what it is, do you?' said Falcón. 'You just know it's coming, or maybe you "feel" it's coming.'

'We have no idea,' said Pablo, nodding. 'But we don't just "sense" their desperation, we know it, too. The design of the Twin Towers attack was to generate a fervour in Muslims all over the world, to get them to rise up against the decadent West, which they feel has humiliated them so much over the years, and to turn on their own dictatorial leaders and corrupt governments. It hasn't happened. The disgust level is rising in the Muslim world at what the fanatics are prepared to do – the kidnapping and beheading of people like the aid worker Margaret Hassan, the daily slaughter of Iraqis who just want to have a normal life – these things are not going down well. But the demographics of the Muslim world lean heavily on the side of youth, and a disenfranchised youth likes nothing better than a demonstration of rebel power. And that is what these radicals are in need of now: another symbol of their power, even if it's the last bang before they die out with a whimper.'

'So what has this bomb in Seville indicated to you?'

'The fact that hexogen was found is a cause for concern and, judging by the level of destruction, it was not a small quantity. Just the use of this material, which the jihadis have never used before, makes us think that the design was *not* to frighten the population of Seville, but something bigger,' said Pablo. 'The British have also revealed that local sources have heard talk about something "big" about to happen, but their intelligence network has picked up no changes in any of their communities. We have to remember that, since the July 7th London Underground bombings, those communities are more aware, too. This makes MI5 and MI6 think that it will be an attack launched from the outside, and Spain has proven to be a popular country for terrorists to gather and plan their campaigns.'

'So how are you expecting Yacoub Diouri to help you?' asked Falcón. 'He doesn't do much business in England. He goes to London for shopping and the two fashion weeks. He has friends, but they're all in the fashion industry. I'm assuming, by the way, that you want Yacoub to act for you because he's *not* involved in international terrorism, but that he might have contacts with people whose involvement in these activities he is unaware of.'

'We're not going to ask him to do anything unusual or out of character. He attends the right mosque and he already knows the people we want him to make contact with. He just has to take it a step further.'

'I didn't know he attended a radical mosque.'

'A mosque with radical elements, where it is possible, with a name like Diouri, to become "involved". As you know, Yacoub's "father", Abdullah, was active in the independence movement, Istiqlal, in the fifties; he was one of the prime movers against European decadence in Tangier. His name carries huge weight with the traditional Islamists. The radicals would love to have a Diouri on their side.'

'So you know who these radical elements are?'

'I go to church. I'm a moderate Catholic,' said Pablo. 'I don't have much time to get involved in church-related business or socialize with other members of the congregation. But even I know all the people who hold strong views, because they can't keep them in and they can't disguise their history.'

'But you can have powerful convictions and have enthusiasm for radical ideas without being a terrorist.'

'Exactly, which is why the only way to find out is to be involved and get to the next level,' said Pablo. 'What we're trying to find is a chain of command. Where do the orders come from to activate the dormant cells? Where do the ideas for terrorist attacks originate? Is there a planning division? Are there independent recce and logistical teams who move around, giving expert help to activated cells? Our picture of these terrorist networks is so incomplete that we're not even sure whether a network exists or not.'

'Where are the British in all this?' asked Falcón. 'They're expecting another major assault from the outside. They must know about Yacoub from his trips to London. Why haven't they tried to recruit him themselves?'

'They have. It didn't work,' said Pablo. 'The British are very sensitive to anything that happens in southern Spain and North Africa because they're in the middle, with their naval base in Gibraltar. They are aware of the potential for attacks, like the explosive dinghy launched at the USS *Cole* in Yemen in October 2000. They have sources in the ex-pat criminal communities operating between the Costa del Sol and that stretch of Moroccan coast between Melilla and Ceuta. The nature of the drug-smuggling business is that it is cash heavy and requires access to efficient money-laundering operations. Other criminal communities are inevitably involved. Information comes from all angles. When we told the British that hexogen had been used in the Seville bomb yesterday, it resonated with something they already knew, or rather something they'd heard.'

'Did they tell you what that was?'

'It needs to be corroborated,' said Pablo. 'The most important thing, at this stage, is to find out whether Yacoub is prepared to act for us. If he's already turned down the Americans and the British, it could be that he's not interested in that sort of life, because, believe me, it is very demanding. So let's see if he's a player and take it from there.'

The car had arrived at a private entrance to the airport, beyond the terminal buildings. The driver talked to the policeman at the gate and showed a pass. Pablo dropped the window and the policeman looked in with his clipboard. He nodded. The gate opened. The car drove into an X-ray bay and out again. They drove beyond the air cargo area until they arrived at a hangar where six small planes were parked. The car pulled up alongside a Lear jet. Pablo picked up a large plastic bag of that morning's newspapers from the floor of the Mercedes. They boarded the jet and took their seats. Pablo flicked through the newspapers, which were full of the bombings.

'How about that for a headline?' he said, and handed Falcón a British tabloid.

THE SECOND COMING? COUNT THE NUMBER
OF THE BEAST: 666
6 JUNE 2006

20

The plane touched down just after 8 a.m. Spanish time, two hours ahead of Moroccan time. They were met by a Mercedes, which contained a member of the Spanish embassy from Rabat, who took their passports. They were driven to a quiet end of the terminal building and after a few minutes they were through to the other side. The Mercedes drove to where the rental cars were parked. The man from the Spanish embassy handed over a set of keys and Falcón transferred to a Peugeot 206.

'We can't have an embassy vehicle turning up at his residence,' said Pablo.

The diplomat handed over some dirhams for the tolls. Falcón left the airport and joined the motorway from Casablanca to Rabat. The sun was well up and the heat haze was draining the colour from the dull, flat landscape. Falcón sat back with the window open and the moist sea air baffling over the glass. He overtook vastly overloaded trucks farting out black smoke, with boys sitting on top of sheet-wrapped bales, their legs hooked around the securing ropes. In the fields a man in a burnous sat on a bony white donkey, which he tapped and poked with a stick. Occasionally a BMW flashed past, leaving a flicker of Arabic lettering on the retina. The smell was of the sea, woodsmoke, manured earth and pollution.

The outskirts of Rabat loomed. He took the ring road and came into the city from the east. He remembered the turning after the Société Marocaine de Banques. The tarmac gave out immediately and he eased up the troughed and pitted track to the main gate of Yacoub Diouri's walled property. The gate man recognized him. He swung up the driveway, lined with Washingtonian palms, and stopped outside the front door. Two servants came out in blue livery with red piping, each wearing a fez. The hire car was driven away. Falcón was taken inside to the living room, which overlooked the pool where Yacoub swam his morning lengths. He sat down on one of the cream leather sofas, in front of a low wooden table inlaid with mother-of-pearl. The servant left. Birds fluttered in the garden. A boy dragged a hose out and began spraying the hibiscus.

Yacoub Diouri arrived, wearing a blue jellabah and white barbouches. A servant set down a brass tray with a pot of mint tea and two small glasses on the table and left. Yacoub's hair, which he'd allowed to grow long, was wet and he now had a close-cropped beard. They embraced with an enthusiastic Arabic greeting and held on to each other by the shoulders looking into each other's eyes and smiling; Falcón saw warmth and wariness in Yacoub's. He had no idea what was readable in his own.

'Would you prefer coffee, Javier?' asked Yacoub, releasing him.

'Tea is fine,' said Falcón, sitting on the other side of the table.

Falcón's question was humped up in his mind. He felt an unaccustomed nervousness between them. He knew for certain now that Spanish directness was not going to work; a more spiralling, philosophical dynamic was called for.

'The world has gone crazy once again,' said Diouri wearily, pouring the mint tea from a great height.

'Not that it was ever sane,' said Falcón. 'We've got no patience for the dullness of sanity.'

'But, strangely, there's an unending appetite for the dullness of decadence,' said Diouri, handing him a glass of tea.

'Only because clever people in the fashion industry have persuaded us that the next handbag decision is crucial,' said Falcón.

'*Touché*,' said Diouri, smiling and taking a seat on the sofa opposite. 'You're sharp this morning, Javier.'

'There's nothing like a bit of fear for honing the mind,' said Falcón, smiling.

'You don't look frightened,' said Diouri.

'But I am. Being in Seville is different to watching it on television.'

'At least fear provokes creativity,' said Diouri, veering away from Falcón's intended line, 'whereas terror either crushes it or makes us run around like headless chickens. Do you think the fear people experienced under the regime of Saddam Hussein made them creative?'

'What about the fear that comes with freedom? All those choices and responsibilities?'

'Or the fear from lack of security,' said Diouri, sipping

his tea, enjoying himself now that he knew Falcón was not going to be too European. 'Did we ever have that conversation about Iraq?'

'We've talked a lot about Iraq,' said Falcón. 'Moroccans love to talk to me about Iraq, while everybody north of Tangier hates to talk about it.'

'But *we*, you and I, have never had the *original* conversation about Iraq,' said Diouri. 'That question: Why did the Americans invade?'

Falcón sat back on the sofa with his tea. This was how it always was with Yacoub when he was in Morocco. It was how it was with Falcón's Moroccan family in Tangier; with all Moroccans, in fact. Tea and endless discussion. Falcón never talked like this in Europe. Any attempt would be greeted with derision. But this time it was going to provide the way in. They had to circle each other before the proposal could finally be made.

'Almost every Moroccan I've ever spoken to thinks that it was about oil.'

'You learn quickly,' said Diouri, acknowledging that Falcón had acquiesced to the Moroccan way. 'There must be more Moroccan in you than you think.'

'My Moroccan side is slowly filling up,' said Falcón, sipping the tea.

Diouri laughed, motioned to Javier for his glass, and poured two more measures of high-altitude tea.

'If the Americans wanted to get their hands on Iraqi oil, why spend $180 billion on an invasion when they could raise sanctions at the stroke of a pen?' said Diouri. 'No. That's the facile thinking of what the British like to call "the Arab street". The tea-house huffers and puffers think that people only do

279

things for immediate gain, they forget the urgency of it all. The invention of the Weapons of Mass Destruction pretext. Haranguing the UN for more resolutions. Rushing the troops to the borders. The hastiness of the planned invasion, which made no provision for the aftermath. What was all that about? Where was Iraqi oil going to go? Down the plug hole?'

'Wasn't it more about the *control* of oil in general?' said Falcón. 'We know a bit more about the emerging economies of China and India now.'

'But the Chinese weren't making a move,' said Diouri. 'Their economy won't be larger than America's until 2050. No, that doesn't make sense either, but at least you didn't say that word that I have to listen to now when I go to dinners in Rabat and Casablanca and find myself sitting next to American diplomats and businessmen. They tell me that they went into Iraq to give them democracy.'

'Well, they did have elections. There is an Iraqi assembly and a constitution, as a result of ordinary Iraqi people taking considerable risks to vote.'

'The terrorists made a political mistake there,' said Diouri. 'They forgot to offer the people a choice that didn't include violence. Instead they said: "Vote and we will kill you." But they had already been killing them anyway, when they were walking down the street to get some bread with their children.'

'That's why you have to swallow the word democracy at your dinners,' said Falcón. 'It was a victory for the "Occupation".'

'When I hear them use that word, I ask them – very quietly, I should add – "When are you going to invade

Morocco and get rid of our despotic king, and his corrupt government, and install democracy, freedom and equality in Morocco?"'

'I bet you didn't.'

'You see. You're right. I didn't. Why not?'

'Because of the state security system of informers left over from the King Hassan II days?' said Falcón. 'What *did* you say to them?'

'I did what most Arabs do, and said those things behind their backs.'

'Nobody likes to be called a hypocrite, especially the leaders of the modern world.'

'What I said to their faces were the words of Palmerston, a nineteenth-century British prime minister,' said Diouri. 'In talking about the British Empire he said: "We have no eternal allies and no perpetual enemies. What we have are eternal and perpetual *interests*."'

'How did the Americans react to that?'

'They thought it was Henry Kissinger who'd said it,' said Diouri.

'Didn't Julius Caesar say it before all of them?'

'We Arabs are often derided as impossible to deal with, probably because we have a powerful concept of honour. We cannot compromise when honour is at stake,' said Diouri. 'Westerners only have *interests*, and it's a lot easier to trade in those.'

'Maybe you need to develop some *interests* of your own.'

'Of course, some Arab countries have the most vital interest in the global economy – oil and gas,' said Diouri. 'Miraculously this does *not* translate into power for the Arab world. It's not only outsiders who find us impossible to deal with – we can't seem to deal with each other.'

'Which means you're always operating from a position of weakness.'

'Correct, Javier,' said Diouri. 'We behave no differently to anyone else in the world. We hold conflicting ideas in our heads, agreeing with all of them. We say one thing, think another and do something else. And in playing these games, which everybody else plays, we always forget the main point: to protect our interests. So a world power can condescend to us about "democracy" when their own foreign policy has been responsible for the murder of the democratically elected Patrice Lumumba and the installation of the dictator Mobutu in Zaire, and the assassination of the democratically elected Salvador Allende to make way for the brutality of Augusto Pinochet in Chile, because they have no honour and only interests. They always operate from a position of strength. Now, do you see where we are?'

'Not exactly.'

'That is another one of our problems. We are very emotional people. Look at the reaction to those cartoons which appeared in the Danish newspaper earlier this year. We get upset and angry and it takes us down interesting paths, but further and further away from the point,' said Diouri. 'But I must behave and get back to why the Americans invaded Iraq.'

'The half of my Moroccan family that doesn't think it was about oil,' said Falcón, 'thinks that it was done to protect the Israelis.'

'Ah, yes, another notion that seethes in the minds of the tea drinkers,' said Diouri. 'The Jews are running everything. Most of my work force thinks that 9/11 was a Mossad operation to turn world opinion against the Arabs, and that George Bush knew about it all along and let it happen. Even some of my senior executives believe that the Israelis demanded the invasion of Iraq, that Mossad supplied the false intelligence about weapons of mass destruction, and that Ariel Sharon was the commander-in-chief of the US forces on the ground. Where the Jews are concerned, we are the world's greatest conspiracy theorists.

'The problem is that it is their rage at the Israeli occupation of Palestine that blinds them to everything else. That fundamental injustice, that slap in the face for the Arab's sense of honour, brings up such powerful emotions in the Arab breast that they cannot think, they cannot see. They focus on the Jews and forget about their own corrupt leadership, their lack of lobbying power in Washington, the pusillanimity of almost all dictatorial, authoritarian Arab regimes ... Ach! I'm boring myself now.

'You see, Javier, we are incapable of change. The Arab mind is like his house and the medina where he lives. Everything looks inward. There are no views or vistas ... no visions of the future. We sit in these places and look for solutions in tradition, history and religion, while the world beyond our walls and shores grinds relentlessly forward, crushing our beliefs with their interests. People will look back on the twentieth century and gasp. How was it, they will say, that a race that held the world's most powerful resource, oil, the resource that made the whole system run, allowed most of its people to live in abject poverty, while its political, cultural and economic influence was negligible?

'You know the last people in the world who should be sent to talk to the Arabs are the Americans. We are polar opposites. In becoming an American, part of the pact is to walk away from your past, your history, and totally embrace the future, progress, and the American Way. Whereas, to an Arab, what happened in the seventh century or 1917 is still as vivid today as it was when it first occurred. They want us to embrace a new future, but we cannot forsake our history.'

'Why is it that, when you talk about the Arabs, sometimes you say "we" and sometimes "they"?'

'As you know, I have one foot in Europe and the other in North Africa, and my mind runs down the middle,' said Diouri. 'I perceive the injustice of the Palestinian situation, but I can't emotionally engage with their solutions: the intifada and suicide bombings. It's just a terrifying extension of throwing stones at tanks – an expression of weakness. An inability to draw together the necessary forces to bring about change.'

'Since Arafat has gone, things have been able to move forward.'

'Stagger forward . . . lurch from side to side,' said Yacoub. 'Sharon's stroke signified the end of the old guard. The vote for Hamas was a vote against the corruption of Fatah. We'll see if the rest of the world wants them to succeed.'

'But despite all these misgivings, *you* still have no desire to live in Spain.'

'That's my peculiar problem. I've been brought up

in a religious household and I've benefited from the daily discipline of religious observance. I love Ramadan. I always make sure I am here for Ramadan because for one month of the year the workings of the world drift into the background and the spiritual and religious life becomes more important. We are all joined together by it in communal fasting and feasting. It gives spiritual strength to the individual and the community. In Christian Europe you have Lent, but it has become something personal, almost selfish. You think: I'll give up chocolate or I won't drink beer for a month. It doesn't bind society like Ramadan does.'

'Is that the only reason you don't live in Spain?'

'You are one of the few Europeans I can talk to about these things, without having you laugh in my face,' said Diouri. 'But that is what I have learnt from my two fathers, the one who forsook me, and the one who taught me the right way to be. That is the difficulty for me in both Europe and America. You know, there's been a big change here recently. It was always the dream to get to America. Young Moroccans thought their culture was cool, their society much freer than racist-bound Old Europe, the attitude of Immigration and the universities more open. Now the kids have changed their minds. They were attracted to Europe, but now, after the riots in France last year and the disrespect shown in Denmark, their dreams are of coming home. For myself, when I'm alone in hotel rooms in the West and I try to relax by watching television, I gradually feel my whole being dissipating and I have to get down and pray.'

'And what's that about?'

'It's about the decadence of a society consumed by materialism,' said Diouri.

'To which you yourself make a considerable contribution, and from which you derive great benefit,' said Falcón.

'All I can say is, if I lived anywhere other than Morocco, I would be drained of will within a few weeks.'

'But then you rage against the lack of progress and the inability to change in the Arab world.'

'I rage against poverty, the lack of work for a young and growing population, the humiliation of a people by –'

'But if you give a young guy work, he'll make money and go out and buy a mobile phone, an iPod and a car,' said Falcón.

'He will, once he has made sure that his family is taken care of,' said Diouri. 'And that is fine, as long as the materialism doesn't become his new God. A lot of Americans are profoundly religious whilst being driven by materialism. They believe it goes hand in hand. They are wealthy because they are the chosen people.'

'Well, that's confused everything,' said Falcón.

'Only the extremist polarizes through simplification,' said Diouri, laughing. 'Extremists understand one thing about human nature: nobody wants to know about the complexity of the situation. The invasion of Iraq was about oil. No, it wasn't. It was all about democracy. The two extremes are a long way from the truth, but there's enough in both statements to make people believe. It *is* all about oil, but not Iraqi oil. And it is about democracy, but not the strange beast that will have to be cloned in order to hold Iraq together.'

'I think we've come full circle,' said Falcón. 'We must be close by now.'

'Oil, democracy and the Jews. There's truth in all of them. It was part of the brilliance of the plan,' said Diouri, 'to create such a colossal diversionary arena that the world would look nowhere else.'

'The problem with most conspiracy theories is that they always award phenomenal intelligence and foresight to people who've rarely exhibited those qualities,' said Falcón.

'This action didn't require huge intelligence or foresight, because it simplified all complexities down to a single perpetual interest. There's also a terrifying logic to it, which conspiracy theories always lack,' said Diouri. 'I told you that it was all about oil, democracy and protection, but none of it was to do with Iraq.

'For the Americans to maintain their world domination they need oil in a continuous supply at a competitive price. Democracy is a very fine thing, as long as the right person wins, and that means the person who will look after American interests most ably. Democracy in the Arab world is dangerous, because politics is always bound up with religion. It is only promoted in Iraq because the installation of another, more pliable, despot than Saddam Hussein would not be acceptable to the outside world.'

'At least it introduces the *concept* of democracy.'

'There have been attempts at democracy in the Arab world before now. It breaks down when it becomes clear that the winners in the elections would be the

Islamic candidates. Democracy puts power in the hands of the most numerous, and for them Islam will always come first. That doesn't offer much security to American interests, which is why the democratically elected Iraqi assembly and their constitution have had to be . . . wrestled into position.'

'Do you think that's the case?'

'It doesn't matter whether it is or not. It's the common perception in the Arab world.'

'So who are the Americans seeking to protect with all this activity in the region, if it isn't the Israelis?'

'The Israelis can take care of themselves as long as they have American support – which they are guaranteed, because they're so powerfully represented in Washington. No, the Americans have to protect the weak and the flabby, the decadent and the corrupt, who are the guardians of their greatest and most sacred interest: oil. I believe – and I'm not a mad, lone conspiracy theorist – that they invaded Iraq to offer protection to the Saudi royal family.'

'It's not as if Saddam Hussein had shown himself to be the most accommodating neighbour.'

'Exactly. So a perfect pretext was invented on the basis of past performance,' said Diouri. 'Anybody could see that after the first Gulf War in 1991 Saddam was a spent force, which was why Bush senior left him there, rather than create the unknown quantity of a power vacuum. Fortunately, Saddam still strutted about on his little stage with all the arrogance of a great Arab icon. He was cruel and genocidal: gassing the Kurds and massacring Shias. It was easy to create the image of an evil genius who was destabilizing the Middle East. I mean, they even managed to frame him for 9/11.'

'But he *was* cruel, violent and despotic,' said Falcón.

'So when are the coalition forces going to turn their attention to, say, Robert Mugabe in Zimbabwe?' said Diouri. 'But that's how the Americans play the game. They confuse the picture with elements of truth.'

'If Saddam was a spent force, why did the Saudis believe they needed protecting?'

'They were scared of the militancy that they themselves had created,' said Diouri. 'To maintain credibility as the guardians of the sacred sites of Islam, they bankrolled the medressas, the religious schools, which in turn became hotbeds of extremism. Like all decadent regimes, they are paranoid. They sensed the antipathy of the Arab world and its extremist factions. They couldn't invite the Americans in as they had done in 1991, but they could ask them to install themselves next door. The double reward for the Americans was that they not only secured their perpetual interest, the oil, but also drew the forces of terror away from the homeland by offering a target in the heart of Islam. Bush has repaid his corporate debts to the oil companies, the American population feels safer, and it can all be dressed up as the forces of Good crushing those of Evil.'

Silence, while Diouri lit his first cigarette of the morning and sipped some more tea. Falcón sucked on the sweet, viscous liquid in his own glass, his question crammed tight in his chest.

'Tea, cigarettes, food . . . they're all negotiating tools,' said Diouri, mysteriously.

Falcón studied Yacoub over the rim of his tea glass. Spies were necessarily complicated people, even those with a clear motive. The worrying and yet crucial aspect of their personality was their need, and therefore ability, to deceive. But why spy? Why did he himself provide information for Mark Flowers? It was because he had begun to find the illusion of life tiresome. The supposed reality of tussling politicians, beaming businessmen and fatuous pundits was exhausting to watch on TV when its veneer had been worn so thin. He spied, not because he wanted to exchange one facile illusion for a slightly more knowing one, but because he needed to remind himself that acceptance was passive, and he'd already discovered the dangers of denial and inaction in his own mind. But what he was asking his friend Yacoub to do was real spying, not just giving Mark Flowers some detail to fill in his little pictures. He was asking Yacoub to pass on information that could result in the capture, and perhaps death, of people that he might know.

'You're thinking, Javier,' said Diouri. 'Normally, at this stage, Europeans are writhing in their seats with ennui at having to talk about Iraq, the Palestinian question and all the rest of the insoluble horror. They have no appetite for polemic any more. In my world of fashion, all they want to talk about is Coldplay's new album or costume design in the latest Baz Luhrman movie. Even business people would rather talk about football, golf and tennis than world politics. It seems that we Arabs have created an interest that nobody wants. We've cornered the market in the most boring conversations in the world.'

'It's riveting to the Arabs because you haven't got what you want. The comfortable never want to talk about stuff that will make them feel uncomfortable.'

'I'm comfortable,' said Diouri.

'Are you?' said Falcón. 'You're wealthy, but do you have what you want? Do you know what you want?'

'I associate comfort with boredom,' said Diouri. 'It might be to do with my past, but I cannot bear contentment. I want change. I want a state of perpetual revolution. It's the only way I can be sure that I'm still alive.'

'Most Moroccans I've spoken to would like to be comfortable with a job, a house, a family and a stable society to live in.'

'If they want all that, they'll have to be prepared for change.'

'None of them wanted terrorism,' said Falcón, 'and none of them wanted a Taliban-type regime.'

'How many did you get to condemn acts of terrorism?'

'None of them approved . . .'

'I mean outright condemnation,' said Diouri firmly.

'Only the ones who had persuaded themselves that the terrorist acts had been committed by the Israelis.'

'You see, it's a complicated state, the Arab mind,' said Diouri, tapping his temple.

'At least they didn't find terrorism honourable.'

'You know when terrorism *is* honourable?' said Diouri, pointing at Falcón with the chalk stick of his French cigarette. 'Terrorism was considered honourable when the Jews fought the British for the right to establish their Zionist state. It was considered dishonourable when the Palestinians employed extreme tactics against the Jews in order to reclaim the land and property that had been stolen from them. Terrorists are acceptable once they've become strong enough to be perceived as freedom fighters. When they are weak and disenfranchised, they are just common bloody murderers.'

'But that's not what we're talking about here,' said Falcón, fighting back his frustration at how the conversation had spiralled off again.

'It will always be part of it,' said Diouri. 'That hard pip of injustice scores at the insides of every Arab. They know that what these mad fanatics are doing is wrong, but humiliation has a strange effect on the human mind. Humiliation breeds extremism. Look at Germany before the Second World War. The power of humiliation is that it is deeply personal. We all remember it from the first time it happened to us as a child. What extremists like bin Laden and Zarqawi realize is that humiliation becomes truly dangerous when it is collective, has risen to the surface and there's a clear purpose in venting it. That is what the terrorists want. That is the ultimate aim of all their attacks. They are saying: "Look, if we all do this together, we can be powerful."'

'And then what?' said Falcón. 'You'll be taken back to the glory days of the Middle Ages.'

'Forward to the past,' said Diouri, crushing out his cigarette in the silver shell of the ashtray. 'I'm not sure that's a price worth paying to have our humiliation assuaged.'

'Have you heard of an organization called VOMIT?' asked Falcón.

'That's the anti-Muslim website that people here get so enraged about,' said Diouri. 'I haven't seen it myself.'

'Apparently the site enumerates the victims of Muslim attacks on civilians, not just in the Western world but also Muslim-on-Muslim attacks such as the suicide bombings of Iraqi police recruits, women murdered in "honour" killings, and the gang-raping of women to inflict shame . . .'

'What's your angle, Javier?' asked Diouri, through narrowed eyes. 'Are you saying this organization has a point?'

'As far as I know, they are making no point other than keeping count.'

'What about the name of the website?'

'Well, "vomit" expresses disgust . . .'

'You know, Muslim life is regarded rather cheaply in the West. Think how valuable each of the 3,000 lives was in the Twin Towers, how much was invested in the 191 commuters in Madrid or the 50-odd people who died in the London bombings. And then look at the value of the 100,000 Iraqi civilians who lost their lives in the pre-invasion assault. Nothing. I'm not sure they even registered,' said Diouri. 'Was there a website that enumerated the victims of Serb slaughter in Bosnia? What about Hindu attacks on Muslims in India?'

'I don't know.'

'That's why VOMIT is anti-Muslim. It has singled out the acts of a fanatic few and made it the responsibility of an entire religion,' said Diouri. 'If you told me they were responsible for blowing up the mosque in Seville yesterday, it wouldn't surprise me.'

'They've established a presence,' said Falcón. 'Our intelligence agency, the CNI, are aware of them.'

'Who else are the CNI aware of?' said Diouri, uneasy.

'It's a very complicated situation,' said Falcón. 'And we're looking for intelligent, knowledgeable and well-connected people who are willing to help us.'

Falcón sipped his tea, grateful for the prop. He'd

finally got it out into the open. He almost couldn't believe he'd said it. Nor could Yacoub Diouri, who was sitting on the other side of the ornately decorated table, blinking.

'Have I understood you correctly, Javier,' said Diouri, his face suddenly solid as a plastic mask and his voice stripped of any warmth. 'You have presumed to come into my house to ask me to spy for your government?'

'You knew from the moment I called you last night that I wasn't coming here on a purely social visit,' said Falcón, holding firm.

'Spies are the most despised of all combatants,' said Diouri. 'Not the dogs of war, but the rats.'

'I would never have thought of asking you if for one moment I took you to be a man who was satisfied with what we are being asked to believe in this world,' said Falcón. 'That *was* the point of your discourse on Iraq, wasn't it? Not just to show me the Arab point of view, but also your appreciation of a greater truth.'

'But what has led you to believe that you could ask me such a question?'

'I ask it because, like me, you are pro-Muslim and pro-Arab and anti-terrorism. You also want there to be change and to make progress rather than a great regression. You are a man of integrity and honour . . .'

'I wouldn't normally associate those virtues with the amorality of spying,' said Diouri.

'Except that, knowing you, your purpose would not be financial reward or vanity, but rather a belief in bringing about change without pointless violence.'

'You and I are very similar people,' said Diouri, 'except that our roles have been reversed. We have both been wronged by monstrous fathers. You have suddenly discovered that you are half Moroccan, while I should have been brought up Spanish, but have *become* Moroccan. Perhaps we are the embodiment of two entwined cultures.'

'With messy histories,' said Falcón, nodding.

21

The radio promised the Sevillanos a day of towering heat, in excess of 40°C, with a light Saharan breeze to sting the eyeballs, dry the sweat and render the site of the destroyed building a serious health hazard. Consuelo was still groggy from the pill she'd taken at three in the morning, when she'd realized that watching Darío's fluttering eyelids was not going to help her sleep. As always, she had a busy day ahead, which would now be enclosed by the parentheses of sessions with Alicia Aguado. She did not think about them. She was removed from what was happening. She was more aware of the bone structure of her face and the snug mask of her skin, behind which she hoped to keep operating.

The mood of the radio presenter was sombre. His words of reflection did not penetrate, nor did his announcement of a minute's silence for the victims of the bombing, which had been called for midday. Her eyelids closed and opened as if she was expecting a new scene with every blink, rather than the same scene, minutely changed.

The sleeping pill dulled the adrenaline leak into her system. Had she been any sharper, the terrifying sense of coming apart that she'd experienced yesterday would have been too powerful a memory, and she would have glided past Aguado's consulting room and driven straight to work. As it was, she parked the car and let her legs carry her up the stairs. Her hand engaged with Alicia Aguado's white palm as her hips fitted between the arms of the lovers' chair. She bared her wrist. Words came to her from some way off and she didn't catch them.

'I'm sorry,' she said. 'I'm still a little tired. Can you repeat that?'

'Last night, did you think about what I told you to?'

'I'm not sure that I remember what I told . . . what you told me to think about.'

'Something that made you happy.'

'Oh, yes, I did that.'

'Have you been taking drugs, Consuelo? You're very slow this morning.'

'I took a sleeping pill at three this morning.'

'Why couldn't you sleep?'

'I was too happy.'

Aguado went to the kitchen and made a powerful café solo and gave it to Consuelo, who knocked it back.

'You have to be sharp for our meetings, or there's no point,' said Aguado. 'You have to be in touch with yourself.'

Aguado stood in front of Consuelo, tilted her face up, as if she were positioning a small child for a kiss, and pressed her thumbs into her forehead. Consuelo's vision brightened. Aguado sat back down.

'Why couldn't you sleep?'

'I was thinking too much.'

'About all those things that made you "too happy"?'

'Happiness is not my normal condition. I needed a respite.'

'What is your normal condition?'

'I don't know. I cover it too well.'

'Are you listening to yourself?'

'I can't help it. I have no resistance.'

'So you didn't do what I told you to do last night.'

'I told you. Happiness is not my normal condition. I'm not drawn to it.'

'What *did* you do?'

'I watched my children sleeping.'

'What does that tell you about the condition that you *are* drawn to?'

'It's uncomfortable.'

'Do you drive yourself hard in your work?'

'Of course, it's the only way to be successful.'

'Why is success important to you?'

'It's an easier measure . . .'

'Than what?'

Panic rose in Consuelo's constricting throat.

'It's easier to measure one's success in business than it is to measure, or rather to see . . . perceive . . . You know what I'm trying to say.'

'I want you to say it.'

Consuelo shifted in her half of the seat, took a deep breath.

'I balance my failures as a person by showing the world my brilliance in business.'

'So, what is your success to you?'

'It's my cover. People will admire me for that, whereas if they knew who I really was, what I had done, they would despise me.'

'Do your three children sleep in separate bedrooms?'

'Now they do, yes. The two older boys need their own space.'

'When you watch them sleeping, who do you spend most time with?'

'The youngest, Darío.'

'Why?'

'He is still very close to me.'

'Is there an age gap?'

'He's four years younger than Matías.'

'Do you love him more than the other two?'

'I know I shouldn't, but I do.'

'Does he look more like you or your late husband?'

'Like me.'

'Have you always looked at your children sleeping?'

'Yes,' she said, thinking about it. 'But it's only become . . . obsessive in the last five years, since my husband was murdered.'

'Did you look at them any differently, compared to now?'

'Before, I would look at them and think: these are my beautiful creations. Only after Raúl's death did I begin to sit amongst them – I put them all in the same room for a while – and, yes, it was then that the pain started. But it's not a bad pain.'

'What does that mean?'

'I don't know. Not all pain is bad. In the same way that not all sadness is terrible and not all happiness that great.'

'Talk me through that,' said Aguado. 'When is sadness not so terrible?'

'Melancholy can be a desirable state. I've had affairs with men which have satisfied me while they lasted and when they finished I was sad, but with the knowledge that it was for the best.'

'When can happiness not be so great?'

'I don't know,' said Consuelo, twirling her free hand. 'Maybe when a woman comes out of a courtroom saying that she's "happy" her son's killer was sentenced to life imprisonment. I wouldn't call that . . .'

'I'd like you to personalize that for me.'

'My sister thinks I'm happy. She sees me as a healthy, wealthy and successful woman with three children. When I told her about our sessions she was stunned. She said: "If you're nuts, what hope is there for the rest of us?"'

'But when do you see *your* happiness as not being so great?'

'That's what I mean,' said Consuelo. 'I should be happy now, but I'm not. I have everything anybody could wish for.'

'What about love?'

'My children give me all the love I need.'

'Do they?' asked Aguado. 'Don't you think that children *take* a lot of loving? You are their guiding light in the nurturing process, you teach them and give them confidence to face the world. They reward you with unconditional love because they are conditioned to do that, but they don't know what love is. Don't you think that children are essentially selfish?'

'You don't have children, Alicia.'

'We're not here to talk about me. And not every point of view that comes from me is my own,' said Aguado. 'Do you think life can be complete without adult love?'

'A lot of women have come to the conclusion that

it can be,' said Consuelo. 'Ask all those battered wives we have in Spain. They'll tell you that love can be the death of you.'

'You don't look like the battered type.'

'Not physically.'

'Have you suffered mental torment from a man?'

A tremor shuddered through Consuelo and Aguado's fingers jumped off her wrist. Consuelo thought that she'd kept the content of this session at a remove. What she'd been saying was in her head, of course, but it was confined there, fenced in. But now somehow it had broken out. It was as if the mad cows had realized the flimsiness of the barriers and crashed through to stampede around her body. She felt the wild terror of yesterday. The sense of coming apart – or was it the fear of something that had been contained getting loose?

'Keep calm, Consuelo,' said Aguado.

'I don't know where this fear comes from. I'm not even sure whether it's associated with what I've been saying, or if it's from some other source that's suddenly leaked into the mainstream.'

'Try to put it into words. That's all you can do.'

'I've become suspicious of myself. I'm beginning to think that a large chunk of my existence has been kept satisfied, or perhaps tied down, by some illusion that I've devised to keep myself going.'

'Most people prefer the illusory state. It's less complicated to live a life feeding off TV and magazines,' said Aguado. 'But it's not for you, Consuelo.'

'How do *you* know? Maybe it's too late to start breaking things down and rebuilding them.'

'I'm afraid it's too late for you to *stop*,' said Aguado. 'That's why you've ended up here. You're like someone who's walked down an alleyway and seen a naked foot sticking out of a rubbish bin. You want to forget about it. You don't want to get involved. But unfortunately you've seen the foot too clearly and you'll get no peace until the matter is resolved.'

'The reason I came here was because of the man in the Plaza del Pumarejo – my bizarre . . . attraction to him and its danger to me. Now we've talked about other things, unrelated to that, and I have the feeling that I've got nowhere to go. Nowhere in my head is safe. Only my work takes my mind elsewhere, and that's only temporary. Even my children have become potentially dangerous.'

'None of it is unrelated,' said Aguado. 'I'm teasing out the threads from the tangled knot. Eventually we'll find the source and, once you've seen it and understood it, you'll be able to move on to a happier life. This terror has its rewards.'

Inés woke up in a convulsion of fear. She blinked, taking in the room a piece at a time. Esteban wasn't there. His pillow was undented. She creaked up on an elbow and threw off the sheet. The pain made her whimper. She panted like a runner, summoning energy for the next lap, the next level of pain.

There didn't seem to be a pain-free position. She had to think her way around her body, trying to find new pathways to limbs and organs that didn't hurt. She got up on to all fours and gasped, hanging her head, staring down the tunnel of her falling hair. Tears blurred her vision. There was a circle of diluted red on her pillow. She got a foot down on to the floor and slid off the bed. She shuffled to the mirror and pushed her hair back. She could not believe it was her head on top of that body.

The contusions were gross. An abstract of purple, blue, black and yellow had spread out over her entire chest area and now joined the bruise on her torso, which reached down as far as her pubic hair. It was true, she did bruise easily. It wasn't as bad as it looked. The pain was more from stiffness than actual damage. A warm shower would help.

In the bathroom she caught sight of her back and buttocks. The welts looked angrier and uglier. She would have to disinfect the punctures left by the buckle. How easily this new regime came to her. She ran the water, held her hand – still puffy from where her finger had been bent back – underneath the flow. She stepped in and held on to the mixer tap, gasping at the pain of the water falling on her. She wouldn't be able to wear a bra this morning.

Tears came. She sank to the floor of the shower. The water seethed through her hair. What had happened to her? She couldn't even think of herself in the first person singular any more, she was so distant from the woman she used to be. She slapped the shower off and crawled out like a beaten dog.

She found reserves she didn't know she had. She took painkillers. She was going to work. It was impossible to stay in the hell of this apartment. She dried herself off, got dressed and made up. Nothing showed. She went out and caught a cab.

The driver talked about the bomb. He was angry. He hit his steering wheel. He called them bastards, without knowing who 'they' were. He said that the time had come to stop fucking about and teach these people a lesson. Inés didn't engage. She sat in the back, gnawing at the inside of her cheek, thinking how much she needed somebody to talk to. She went through all her friends. They were hopeless. Not one could she describe as intimate. Her colleagues? All good people, but not right for this. Family? She couldn't bear to reveal her failure. And it came to her out of the blue, a thought she'd never allowed herself before: her mother was a stupid person and her father a pompous ass who thought he was an intellectual.

The office was empty. She was relieved. Her schedule told her she had two meetings and then nothing. She'd made sure there was nothing because she had to prepare for a court appearance the next day. She headed for the door and one of her male colleagues blundered in with an armful of files. The pain of their collision detonated in her head. Fainting seemed like the only option to wipe clean the pain circuit. She dropped and held on to her foot as a distraction. Her colleague was all over her, saying he was sorry. She left without a word.

Meetings passed. Only at the end of the second one did the judge ask her if she was all right. She went to the lavatory and tried to ignore the trickle of blood she saw slowly dissipating in the water. Her period? She hadn't had one. It wasn't due. She didn't care. She took more painkillers.

She went across the avenue to the Murillo Gardens. She knew what she was after: she wanted to see the whore again. She wasn't sure why. One part of her wanted to show the whore what he'd done to her, the other part . . . What did the other part want?

The whore wasn't there. It was hot. The street signs

told her it was 39°C at 11.45. She walked through the Barrio Santa Cruz, amongst the ambling tourists. How was she going to find the whore? The painkillers were good. Her mind floated free of her body. Reality eased off a few notches. It hadn't occurred to her that painkillers killed all manner of pain.

Her lips tingled and did not feel like her own. Street sounds came to her muffled, her vision was soft focus. She was being drawn along by a great multitude of people who were crowding into the Avenida de la Constitución and heading for the Plaza Nueva. They carried banners, which she couldn't read because they were turned away from her. In the square there were hundreds of placards held up in the air, which said simply: *PAZ*. Peace. Yes, she would like some of that.

The clock struck midday and the crowd fell totally silent. She walked amongst them, wondering what had happened, looking into their faces for signs. They returned her gaze, stone-faced. The traffic noise had stopped, too. There was only the sound of birds. It was quite beautiful, she thought, that people should be gathering together to ask for peace. She wandered out of the square just as people returned to a state of animation and the murmur of humanity rose up behind her. She went down Calle Zaragoza thinking she would go to El Cairo for something to eat. They liked her in El Cairo. She thought they liked her in El Cairo. But everybody liked everybody else in bars in Seville.

It was then that she saw the whore. Not the whore herself, but a photograph. She stepped back into the street, confused. Could whores do that now? Advertise themselves in shop windows? They pipe porn into your living room after midnight now, but do they let whores

305

tout for business like this? She was surprised to find it was an art gallery.

A car gave her a light toot. She stepped back up to the window. She read the card next to the photograph: *Marisa*. Just that – Marisa. How old was she? The card didn't say. That's what everybody wants to know these days. How old are you? They want to see your beauty. They need to know your age. And if you're talented, that's a bonus, but the first two are crucial for the marketing.

Beyond the window display was a young woman at a desk. Inés went in. She heard her heels on the marble floor. She'd forgotten to look at the whore's work, but she was committed now.

'I love that Marisa,' she heard herself say. 'I just love her.'

The young woman was pleased. Inés was well dressed and seemed harebrained enough to pay the ridiculous prices. They veered off together to admire Marisa's work – two woodcarvings. Inés encouraged the woman to talk, and in a matter of minutes had found out where Marisa had her workshop.

Inés had no idea what she should do with this information. She went to El Cairo and ordered a stuffed piquillo pepper and a glass of water. She toyed with the bright red pepper, which looked obscene, like a pointed, inquisitive tongue looking for a moist aperture. She hacked it up and forked it into her cotton-wool mouth.

She went home, turned on the air conditioning and lay on the bed. She slept and woke up in the chill of the apartment, having dreamt and been left with an overwhelming sense of loneliness. She had never been as lonely as in that dream. It occurred to her that she would only be as lonely as that in death.

The painkillers had worn off and she was stiff with cold. She realized that she was talking to herself and was fascinated to know what she'd been saying.

It was 4.30 in the afternoon. She should go to the office and work on the case, but there didn't seem much point now. For some reason tomorrow had begun to seem unlikely.

She heard herself say: 'Don't be ridiculous.' She went to the kitchen and drank water and swallowed more painkillers. She came out of the apartment and into the street, which was thick with heat after the thin, chilled air inside. She caught a cab and heard her voice ask the cab driver to take her to Calle Bustos Tavera. Why had she asked to be taken there? There was nothing to be gained . . .

There was something jutting out of the gathered neck of her handbag, which she held on her lap. She didn't recognize what it was. She pulled open the bag and saw a steel button set flush in a black handle and a straight steel blade next to her hairbrush. She looked up at the driver, their eyes connected via the rear-view mirror.

'Have you seen that?' said the driver.

'What?' said Inés, in shock at the sight of the knife.

But he was pointing out of the window.

'People hanging hams outside their front doors,' he said. 'If they can't afford them, they're hanging pictures of hams. A ham manufacturer in Andalucía is distributing them. This guy on the radio was saying it's a passive form of protest. It goes back to the fifteenth century when the Moors were driven out of Andalucía and the Catholic Kings promoted the cooking and eating of pork to signify the end of Islamic domination. They're calling today *El Día de los Jamones*. What do you think of that?'

'I think . . . I don't know what I think,' said Inés, fingering the knife handle.

The driver switched the radio to another station. Flamenco music filled the cab.

'I can't listen to too much talk about the bomb,' he said. 'It makes me wonder who I've got in the back of my cab.'

22

Yesterday's emotionally charged workload, followed by
the three evening meetings, an uneven night's sleep,
the flight and the tension caused by the uncertainty of
his mission had left Falcón completely drained. He'd
briefly told Pablo that Yacoub had agreed to act for
them, but not without conditions, then he'd hit his
seat in the Lear jet and passed out instantly.

They landed at Seville airport just before 2.30 p.m.
and split up agreeing to meet later that night. Back at
home, Falcón showered and changed. His housekeeper
had left him a fish stew, which he ate with a glass of
cold red wine. He called Ramírez, who told him there
was to be another big meeting at 4.30 p.m. and gave
him a very thin update, of which the best news was
that Lourdes, the girl they'd pulled out of the wreckage
yesterday, had regained consciousness for a few minutes
just after midday. She was going to be all right. There
was no news on the electricians or the council inspectors, except that Elvira had arranged a press release
and there'd been announcements on TV and radio.
Nothing extraordinary had come out of the interviews

with the Informáticalidad sales reps. The one remarkable element in Ramírez's report was his praise for Juez Calderón, who had been handling a very aggressive media.

'You know I don't like him,' said Ramírez, 'but he's been doing a very good job. Since our big news yesterday the investigation has been completely stalled, but Calderón is making us look competent.'

'Realistically, what's the earliest we can expect to get to the epicentre of the bomb?' asked Falcón.

'Not before 9 a.m. tomorrow,' said Ramírez. 'Once they get down to the rubble directly over the mosque they're going to be working by hand, under bomb squad and forensic supervision. That's going to take time and the conditions are going to be horrible. In fact, they already are. The stink down there gets into you like a virus.'

'It's been confirmed with 99 per cent certainty that one of the dead in the mosque is a CGI source,' said Comisario Elvira, opening the 4.30 p.m. meeting. 'We won't have complete confirmation until the DNA samples are matched to those taken from his apartment.'

'And what was he doing in there?' asked Calderón.

'Inspector Jefe Barros has the report,' said Elvira.

'His name is Miguel Botín, he's Spanish, thirty-two years old and a resident of Seville,' said Barros.

'Esperanza – the woman who gave Comisario Elvira the list of men believed to be in the mosque – she had a partner who was in the destroyed building,' said Falcón. 'Was that Miguel Botín?'

'Yes,' said Barros. 'He converted to Islam eleven years

ago. His family came from Madrid and his brother lost a foot in the March 11th bombings. Miguel Botín was recruited by one of my agents in November 2004 and became active just over fourteen months ago, in April 2005.'

The only noise in the pre-school classroom was from the mobile air-conditioning units. Even the steady grinding of the machinery outside had receded as Barros began his report.

'For the first eight months Botín had very little to tell us. The members of the congregation, most of whom were of non-Spanish origin, were all good Muslims and none of them were in the slightest bit radical. They were all sympathetic to the story of his brother and they were all outraged by the London bombings, which occurred not long after Botín became active.

'It was in January this year that Botín first started to detect a change. There was an increase in outside visitors to the mosque. This had no noticeable effect on the congregation, but by March it seemed to be having a discernible effect on Imam Abdelkrim Benaboura. He was preoccupied and appeared under pressure. On 27th April my agent made a request to plant a microphone in the Imam's office. I had a discussion with the Juez Decano de Sevilla, who was issued with my agent's report. The evidence was deemed to be largely circumstantial and a bugging order was refused due to a lack of hard evidence.

'On my agent's request, Botín stepped up his activities and started following Imam Abdelkrim Benaboura outside the mosque. Between 2nd May and the date of this report, which was Wednesday, 31st May, Botín saw the Imam meet with three pairs of men, on ten separate occasions at ten different locations around Seville. He has no idea what was said at any of these meetings, but he did manage to take some photographs, only two of which show clearly visible people. On the basis of this report, with the photographic evidence, another bugging request was made last Thursday, 1st June. We did not receive a reply prior to the explosion yesterday morning.'

'How many men are visible in these two shots?' asked Falcón.

'Four,' said Barros, 'and since the CGI in Madrid have sent down a set of shots from the apartment they raided yesterday, we've been able to identify two of them as Djamal Hammad and Smail Saoudi. We have no idea yet who the other two men are, but the shots are currently in the hands of the CNI, MI6 and Interpol. Obviously I would like to have made this information available sooner, but . . .'

'What about these ten different locations?' said Calderón, cutting in on the self-pity. 'Is there anything exceptional about them? Are they near public buildings, addresses of prominent people? Do they appear to be part of a plan of attack?'

'There's a significant building within a hundred metres of each meeting place, but that's the nature of a big city,' said Barros. 'One of the meetings was in the Irish pub near the cathedral. Who knows if that was the perfect cover for three Muslims who didn't drink alcohol, or whether their meeting outside the only remaining structure of the twelfth-century Almohad mosque was significant.'

'When was the first request to bug the Imam's office turned down by the Juez Decano?' asked Falcón.

'On the same day it was applied for: 27th April.'

'And why wasn't the second bugging request authorized and acted on?'

'The Juez Decano was away in Madrid at the time. He didn't see the application until Monday afternoon – 5th June.'

'What was Miguel Botín's description of the Imam's state of mind during this month when he observed him more closely?' asked Falcón.

'Increasingly preoccupied. Not as engaged with his congregation as he had been the previous year. Botín became aware of him taking medication, but wasn't able to find out what it was.'

'We found Tenormin on his bedside table, which is a prescription for hypertension,' said Gregorio from the CNI. 'We also found an extensively stocked medicine cabinet. His doctor says that he has been treated for hypertension for the past eight years. He'd recently been complaining of heart rhythm problems and was on medication for a stomach ulcer.'

'When will we get access to the Imam's apartment and your findings?' asked Falcón.

'Don't worry, Inspector Jefe,' said Juan, 'we've been working with a forensics team since the moment we opened the apartment door.'

'We'd still like to get in there,' said Falcón.

'We're nearly finished,' said Gregorio.

'Does the CNI have an opinion about Botín's findings and the Imam's doctor?' asked Calderón.

'And has someone gained access to his mysterious history?' asked Falcón.

'We're still awaiting clearance on his history,' said Gregorio.

'The Imam was under a lot of pressure,' said Falcón, before Calderón could mount another attack on Juan. 'Hammad and Saoudi were known operators in the logistics of attacks. They met with the Imam. Were they asking the Imam to act in some way? Perhaps they were calling in a favour, or a promise made some time ago in his inaccessible history. Under those circumstances, what do you think would put a man like the Imam under severe stress?'

'That they were asking him to do something that would have very grave consequences,' said Calderón.

'But if he believed in "the cause" surely he would be happy?' said Falcón. 'It should be an honour for a radical fanatic to be asked to participate in a mission.'

'You think the pressure came from being a reluctant accomplice?' said Gregorio.

'Or the nature of what he was being asked to do,' said Falcón. 'There's a different pressure in storing an unknown product for a week or two, say, and being asked to actively participate in an attack.'

'We need more information on the Imam's activities,' said Elvira.

'It hasn't been confirmed yet, but we think it likely that Hammad and Saoudi were in the mosque when the building was destroyed,' said Falcón. 'Confirmation will come with DNA testing. The other two men photographed by Miguel Botín have to be identified and found if we want to know how the Imam was implicated.'

'That is in hand,' said Gregorio.

'I'd like to talk to the agent who ran Miguel Botín,' said Falcón.

Inspector Jefe Barros nodded. Comisario Elvira asked

for a résumé of the situation with the electricians and the council inspectors. Ramírez gave the same very thin update he'd just given to Falcón.

'We know the CGI antiterrorist squad did not have the mosque under surveillance,' said Falcón. 'We have two men posing as council inspectors, who were clearly intent on gaining access to the mosque. The electricians were responding to a blown fuse box. We have to look at the possibility of a link between the fake council inspectors and the electricians. I cannot believe that a legitimate electrician would not have come forward by now. The obvious advantage of being an electrician is that you can bring large quantities of equipment into a place, and witnesses have confirmed that this was the case.'

'You think that *they* planted the bomb?' asked Barros.

'It has to be considered,' said Falcón. 'We can't ignore it just because it doesn't fit with the discoveries we've made so far. It also does not exclude the possibility that there was already a cache of explosives in the mosque. We must talk to your agent. What state of mind is he in?'

'Not good. He's a young guy, only a little older than Miguel Botín. We've been recruiting in that age group because they can connect more easily with each other. His relationship with Botín was close. The two of them had a religious connection.'

'Were they both converts?'

'No, my agent was a Catholic. But they both took their religion seriously. They respected and liked each other.'

'We'd like to speak to him *now*,' said Falcón.

Barros left the room to call him.

'The forensics need to make contact with the wives

and families of the men who were in the mosque,' said Elvira. 'They have to start extracting DNA as soon as possible. The woman who represents them, Esperanza, says she will only talk to you.'

Elvira gave him the mobile number. The meeting ended. The men dispersed. Elvira hung on to Falcón.

'They're sending me some more people down from Madrid,' he said. 'No reflection on you or your squad, but we both know the demands that are being made. You need more foot soldiers and these are all experienced inspector jefes and inspectors.'

'Anything that's going to relieve pressure, I'm happy with,' said Falcón. 'As long as they don't complicate things.'

'They're under my jurisdiction. You don't have to deal with them. They'll be assigned where they're needed most.'

'Have the Guardia Civil been able to get more information on the route of Hammad and Saoudi from Madrid to Seville?'

'It's taking time.'

Barros pulled Falcón aside as he left the room.

'My agent's not back from lunch yet,' he said. 'They'll call me as soon as he gets in.'

'It's just gone 4.30 p.m.,' said Falcón, giving him his mobile number. 'He's running a bit late, isn't he?'

Barros shook his head, shrugged. Things were not going well for him.

'What's your agent's name?'

'Ricardo Gamero,' said Barros.

Falcón called Esperanza and they arranged to meet in some nearby gardens. He asked to bring a female police officer with him.

Cristina Ferrera was waiting for him outside the pre-school. He briefed her on the way. Esperanza recognized Falcón as he got out of the car. Introductions were made. They piled back in. Esperanza sat next to Falcón, Ferrera was behind, staring at Esperanza as if she recognized her.

'How are the women holding up?' asked Falcón. 'I imagine the circumstances are very difficult for them.'

'They oscillate between despair and fear,' she said. 'They're devastated by the loss of their loved ones and then they see the news – the assaults and damage to property. They feel a little more secure since your Comisario came on television and announced that violence against Muslims and vandalizing of their property would be dealt with severely.'

'You're their representative,' said Ferrera.

'They trust me. I'm not one of them, but they trust me.'

'You're not one of them?'

'I'm not a Muslim,' said Esperanza. 'My partner is a convert to Islam. I know them through him.'

'Your partner is Miguel Botín,' said Falcón.

'Yes,' she said. 'He wants me to convert to Islam so that we can get married. I'm a practising Catholic and I have some difficulties, as a European, with the treatment of women in Islam. Miguel introduced me to all the women in the mosque to help me understand, to help me get rid of some of my prejudices. But it's a big leap from Catholicism to Islam.'

'How did you meet Miguel?' asked Ferrera.

'Through an old school friend of mine,' said Esperanza. 'I ran into the two of them just over a year ago, and after that Miguel and I started seeing each other.'

'What's your friend's name?' asked Falcón.

'Ricardo Gamero,' she said. 'He does something in the police force – I don't know what. He says it's administrative.'

Seville was a village, thought Falcón. He told Esperanza what they needed from the women and said that Ferrera would accompany her to collect and mark up the DNA samples.

'We'll need a sample from Miguel Botín as well,' said Falcón. 'I'm sorry.'

Esperanza nodded, staring into space. She had a clear, unadorned face. Her only jewellery was a gold cross at her neck and two gold studs in her ear lobes, which were visible as her slightly crinkly black hair was scraped back. She had very straight eyebrows and it was these that first gave away her own emotional turmoil, and then the moisture flooding her dark brown eyes. She shook hands and got out of the car. Falcón quickly told Ferrera how Ricardo Gamero fitted in and asked her to find out if Esperanza knew what her partner had been doing.

'Don't worry, Inspector Jefe,' said the ex-nun. 'Esperanza and I recognize each other. We've been on the same path.'

The two women moved off. Falcón sat in the air-conditioned cool of the car and breathed the stress back down into its hole. He made himself believe that he had time on his side. The terrorist angle of the attack was not, at the moment, in his hands, nor was the Imam's history, but progress had been made. He had to concentrate his powers on finding a link to the fake council inspectors and the electricians. There had to be another witness, someone more reliable than Majid

Merizak, who'd seen the inspectors and the electricians. Falcón called Ferrera and asked her to find out from the women if there was anybody else who might have been in the mosque on the mornings of Friday 2nd June and Monday 5th June.

He went back to his notebook, too much occurring to him for his brain to have any chance of remembering detail. The first bugging request the CGI made to the Juez Decano was submitted and refused on April 27th. When did Informáticalidad buy the apartment? Three months ago. No date. He called the estate agency. The sale went through on the 22nd of February. What was he expecting? What was he looking for? He wanted to apply pressure on Informáticalidad. He was still suspicious of them, despite the performance by the sales reps in the police interviews. But he didn't want to apply pressure directly. It had to come from another source, other than the homicide squad. He wanted to see if they would react.

Maybe if he could find someone who'd been recently fired, or had "moved on"', from Informáticalidad they would still know people at the company, perhaps even some of the guys who'd used the apartment on Calle Los Romeros. He found the lists given to him by Diego Torres, the Human Resources Director. Names, addresses, home telephone numbers and the dates they left the company. How was he going to find these people at this time of day? He started with the employees who'd left the company most recently, reasoning that they might still be out of work until after the summer. He hit answer machine after answer machine, number no longer in use, and then, finally, a ringing tone that went on for some time. A female voice answered sleepily. Falcón asked for David Curado. She shouted and threw down the phone, which took a soft landing. Curado picked it up. He sounded just about alive. Falcón explained his predicament.

'Sure,' said Curado, waking up instantly. 'I'll talk to anybody about those wankers.'

Curado lived in a modern apartment block in Tabladilla. Falcón knew it. He'd been there years ago to observe a hostage situation across the street. Curado came to the door stripped to the waist, wearing a pair of white short trousers as seen on the tennis player Rafael Nadal. Like Nadal, he looked as if he went to the gym. Beads of sweat stood out on his forehead.

The apartment was hot. The girl who'd answered the phone was lying splayed across the bed in a pair of knickers and a tiny vest. Curado offered a drink. Falcón took some water. The girl groaned and rolled over. Her arms slapped against the mattress.

'She gets annoyed,' said Curado. 'When I'm not earning I don't turn on the air conditioning during the day.'

'Dav-i-i-id,' said the girl in a long whine.

'Now that you're here,' he said, rolling his eyes.

He got up and flipped the switch on the fuse box. A light mist appeared at the vents. The girl let out an orgasmic cry.

'How long did you work for Informáticalidad?' asked Falcón.

'Just over a year. Fifteen months, something like that.'

'How did you get the job?'

'I was head-hunted, but I did the research to make *sure* that I was head-hunted.'

'What was the research?'

'I went to church,' said Curado. 'The sales guys at Informáticalidad were the best paid in the business, and it wasn't all commission-based money. They paid a good basic salary of close to €1,400 a month and you could triple that if you worked hard. At the time I was working like a slave for €1,300 a month, all commission. So I started asking around and it was weird; nobody knew anything about how this company recruited. I called all the agencies, looked through the press and trade magazines, the internet. I even called Informáticalidad themselves and they wouldn't tell me how they recruited. I tried to get friendly with the Informáticalidad sales crew, but they brushed me off. I started looking at who they sold to, and it didn't matter what prices I offered, I could never make a sale. Once a company started buying from Informáticalidad, they bought exclusively. That's why they can offer the high basic salary. They don't have to compete. So, I began looking at the individuals in the companies they sold to and tried to get friendly with them. Nothing.

'I couldn't get anywhere until a buyer from one of these companies got fired. It was she who told me how it worked: you've got to go to church, and you mustn't be a woman. So I qualified on one score, but I hadn't been to church for fifteen years. There were three churches they used: Iglesia de la Magdalena, de Santa María La Blanca and San Marcos. I bought myself a black suit and went to church. Within a couple of months I'd been approached.'

'So you got the job, the money, the nice apartment,' said Falcón. 'What went wrong?'

'Almost immediately they started to cut in on my free time. We were sent on courses – sales training and product information. Normal stuff. Except that it was almost every weekend and there was a lot of repetitive company ethos shit *and* religion, and it wasn't always easy to differentiate between the two. They also did this other thing. They'd partner you off with a senior guy who'd been with the company for two or three years, and he would be your mentor. If you were unlucky and got one of the "serious" ones, they'd fill your head with even more shit. I saw people recruited at the same time as me who just disappeared.'

'Disappeared?'

'Lost their personality. They became an Informáticalidad man, with a glassy look in their eye and their brain tuned to one frequency. It gave me the creeps. That,' said Curado, leaning forward conspiratorially, 'and the total lack of women in the whole sales force. I mean, not one . . .'

'How did you get along with your mentor?'

'Marco? He was a good guy. I still talk to him occasionally, even though it's *forbidden* for Informáticalidad men to talk to ex-employees.'

'Why did you leave?'

'Apart from the lack of women and all the brainwashing shit,' said Curado, 'they wouldn't let me into where the big money was being made. Like I said, they sold to companies without having to compete, so you got the good basic salary. But if you wanted to make the big commissions, *that* was all in converting new prospects to the Informáticalidad way. Once they'd been converted, you got commission on everything that was sold to that company – *ever*.'

'And how did that work?'

'I never found out. I never got beyond the lowest tier of salesmen. I did not have the right mentality,' he said, tapping his forehead. 'In the end they forced me out through boredom. I was nothing more than a form-filler and a post boy. Taking orders, passing them on to "supply". It was the way they got rid of you at Informáticalidad.'

Falcón took a call from Inspector Jefe Barros.

'I'm on my way to an apartment on Calle Butrón,' said Barros. 'You'd better come along as well.'

'I'm in the middle of an interview,' said Falcón, annoyed.

'Ricardo Gamero *was* late coming back from lunch, so I sent another of my agents round to his apartment. There was no answer. The woman in the apartment below let him in. She said she'd seen Gamero going up, but hadn't seen him leave. The agent called back and I told him to get in there any way he could, which was when the woman started screaming. There's a central patio in the block. She'd opened the window to shout up the well. He was hanging out of his bedroom window.'

23

Marisa left her apartment. It was hot, easily over forty degrees, and the perfect time for her to work in her studio. Her tight mulatto skin yearned to sweat freely. Out in the street she walked in the sun and breathed in the desert air. The streets were empty. She stumbled on the cobbles of Calle Bustos Tavera until her eyes got used to the sudden shade. She turned up the alleyway to the courtyard. The light at the end was blinding. The sun had sucked out even the edges of the buildings beyond the arch. She shivered a little at the sensation she always had walking down this tunnel.

At the end, where the huge cobbles turned pewtery on the threshold, she stopped. The courtyard should have been empty at this hour. Instinct told her that someone was there. She saw Inés, halfway down the steps leading to the entrance of her studio.

Rage shuddered through her and bunched up behind her flat chest. This fatuous middle-class bitch now wanted to infect the sanctity of her work place with the received opinions of her bourgeois upbringing, with the soulless rant of her consumer needs, with her self-righteous smugness of 'being thin'. Marisa stepped back into the full darkness of the tunnel.

In turning back to go up the stairs to the studio, Inés revealed the lowest welts on the backs of her thighs. These people deserve each other, thought Marisa. They wander through life with total belief in their brilliant control of the reality around them, without ever seeing the iridescence of the illusory bubble in which they float. They might as well be dead.

Marisa suppressed the temptation to run up the steps, beat the wretched woman senseless, throw her down the stairs, break her skull open and discover the small-ness within. My God, she hated these people, grown from tradition, sporting their fancy names – Inés Conde de fucking Tejada – surname *and* title rolled into one.

Inés reached the top of the steps, put her handbag down, tugged open the neck and drew out a black-handled knife. Now this was interesting. Had the bitch come to kill her? Maybe the skinny-legged cow had some *cojones* after all. Inés scored something on the front door of the studio, stepped back and jutted her chin at her work. She put the knife back in the bag and walked down the steps. Marisa backed away, snarling, and retreated to her apartment for an hour. By the time she returned the courtyard was empty, the heat more intense. She ran up the stairs to see Inés's message. Scored into the door was the predictable word: *PUTA*. Whore.

It was time this was over, she thought. She couldn't have the bitch turning up at her place of work.

The news of Gamero's suicide had so disconcerted Falcón he'd left Curado with barely another word. Now, as he drove across town, ideas occurred to him and he called Curado on his mobile.

'Have you heard of someone called Ricardo Gamero?'

'Should I?' he asked. 'Was he at Informáticalidad?'

Maybe that had been too lurid an idea.

'I want you to do something for me, David,' said Falcón. 'I want you to call your old friend at Informáticalidad – Marco . . .?'

'Marco Barreda.'

'I want you to tell Marco Barreda that you had a visit from the Inspector Jefe del Grupo de Homicidios, Javier Falcón. The same cop who's investigating the Seville bombing. I want you to tell him what we discussed in a "thought you'd like to know" sort of way. Nothing sensational, just matter of fact. And tell him what my last question to you was.'

'About Ricardo Gamero?'

'Exactly.'

The Médico Forense was already up the ladder, carrying out his preliminary examination of Ricardo Gamero's body, as Falcón arrived on the crime scene. There was no doubt that he was dead. The CGI agent who'd found him, Paco Molero, had checked for a pulse. Even if Gamero had survived jumping off his window ledge with a rope tied around his neck, he would not have lived for long. On the floor were twelve empty trays of paracetamol. Even if they'd got him to hospital and pumped his stomach, he would probably have remained in a coma and died of liver failure within forty-eight hours. This was not attention seeking. This was an experienced policeman making sure. His apartment had been locked and chained. His bedroom door was also locked, with a chair tilted under the handle.

Falcón shook Inspector Jefe Barros's hand.

'I'm sorry, Ramón. I'm very sorry,' said Falcón, who'd never lost anybody from his squad, but knew that it would be terrible.

Two paramedics manoeuvred the body on to the ladder and pulled it up through the bedroom window. They laid him out on his living-room floor while the forensics went through the bedroom. Falcón asked the instructing judge for permission to search the body.

Gamero was wearing suit trousers and a shirt. He had a wallet in one pocket, loose change in another. As Falcón turned the body to check the back pockets, the head lolled with sickening flexibility. There was a ticket to the Archaeological Museum in the right-hand back pocket. Falcón showed it to Inspector Jefe Barros, who couldn't get rid of the dismay in his face. The ticket had today's date on it.

'He's a citizen of Seville,' said Falcón. 'He doesn't need to buy a ticket to get into this museum.'

'Maybe he didn't want to show his ID,' said Barros. 'Stay anonymous.'

'Was that where he met his informers?'

'They're taught not to follow a routine.'

'I'd like to talk to the agent who found him – Paco Molero?'

'Of course,' said Barros, nodding. 'They were good friends.'

Paco was sitting at the kitchen table with his face in his hands. Falcón touched him on the shoulder, introduced himself. Paco's eyes were red.

'Were you worried about Ricardo?'

'There's been no time for that,' said Paco. 'Obviously

he was upset, because he believed he'd lost one of his best sources in the mosque.'

'Did you know his source?'

'I've seen him, but I didn't know him,' said Molero. 'Ricardo asked me to come with him a few times, to check his back – just a routine precaution to make sure he wasn't being watched or followed.'

'Did he leave the office at all today, apart from going to lunch?'

'No. He went out at one thirty. He was due back two hours later. When he hadn't showed by four thirty, and his mobile was turned off, Inspector Jefe Barros sent me over here to find out what had happened.'

'What time did you find him?'

'I was here by ten to five, so maybe just gone five o'clock.'

'Tell me what happened yesterday . . . after the bombing.'

'We were all at work when it happened. We called our sources to arrange meetings. Ricardo couldn't get through to Botín. Then we were told not to leave the office, so we drafted up-to-date reports from what our sources had told us the last time we'd seen them. Lunch was brought in. We weren't released to go home until after 10 p.m.'

'Were you aware of any pressure on Ricardo, apart from the usual work stress?'

'Apart from the *unusual* work stress, you mean?'

'Why unusual?'

'We were being investigated, Inspector Jefe,' said Molero. 'We wouldn't be much of an antiterrorist outfit if we didn't know when our own department was being investigated.'

'How long have you known about this?'

'We reckon it probably started around the end of January.'

'What happened?'

'Nothing . . . just a change in attitude, or atmosphere . . .'

'Did you suspect each other?'

'No, we had total trust in each other and a belief in what we were doing,' said Molero. 'And I would say that, out of the four of us handling Islamic terrorist threats, Ricardo was the most committed.'

'Because he was religious?'

'You've had time to do some homework,' said Molero.

'I just met his source's partner, who happened to be an old school friend of Ricardo's.'

'Esperanza,' said Molero, nodding. 'They were at school and university together. She was going to become a nun before she met Ricardo.'

'Did they ever get together?'

'No. Ricardo was never interested in her.'

'Did he have a girlfriend?'

'Not that I know of.'

'Esperanza told me that the relationship Ricardo had with his source was based on a mutual respect for each other's religion.'

'Religion had something to do with it,' said Molero. 'But they were both against fanaticism, too. Ricardo had a special understanding of fanatics.'

'Why?'

'Because he'd been one himself,' said Molero and Falcón nodded him on. 'He believed that it came from a profound desire to be good, which interacted with a deep concern and constant worry about evil. That was where the hatred came from.'

'Hatred?'

'The fanatic, in his deep desire for goodness, is in constant fear of evil. He begins to see evil all around him. In what we think of as harmless decadence, the fanatic sees the insidious encroachment of evil. He begins to worry about everybody who is not pursuing good with the same zeal as himself. After a while he tires of the pathetic weakness of others and his perception shifts. He no longer sees them as misguided fools, but rather as ministers of the devil, which is when he starts to hate them. From that moment he becomes a dangerous person, because then he is someone receptive to extreme ideas.

'Ricardo had long conversations with Botín, who described a fundamental difference between Catholicism and Islam, which was The Book. The Koran is a direct transcription of the Word of God by the Prophet Mohammed. The word Koran means "recitation". It is not like our Bible, a series of narratives laid down by remarkable men. It is the actual Word of God as taken down by the prophet. Ricardo used to ask us to imagine what that would be like to a fanatic. The Book was not the inspired writing of gifted human beings, but the *Word of God*. In his desperation for goodness, and his fear of evil, the fanatic penetrates deeper and deeper into the Word. He seeks "better", more exactingly good interpretations of the Word. He works his way out, by degrees, to the extremes. That was Ricardo's strength. He'd been a fanatic himself, so he could give us an insight into the minds that we were up against.'

'But he wasn't a fanatic any more?' said Falcón.

'He said he'd once reached the point where he'd begun to look down on his fellow human beings and not just found them lacking but thought them subhuman in some way. It was a form of intense religious arrogance. He realized that once you've reached the point where you don't regard all humans as equals, then killing them becomes less of a problem.'

'And had he reached that point?'

'He'd been pulled back from it by a priest.'

'Do you know who this priest was?'

'He died of cancer last September.'

'That must have been a blow.'

'I suppose it must have been. He didn't talk to me about it. I think that was too personal for office consumption,' said Molero. 'He worked harder. He became a man with a mission.'

'And what was that mission?'

'To stop a terrorist attack *before* it happened, rather than helping to catch the perpetrators *after* a lot of people have been killed,' said Molero. 'In fact, last July was a bad time for Ricardo. The London bombings affected him very badly and then at the end of the month his priest was diagnosed with cancer. Six weeks later he was dead.'

'Why did the London bombings affect him like that?'

'He was disturbed by the bombers' profile: young, middle-class British citizens, some with small children, and all with family ties. They weren't loners. That was when he became focused on the nature of fanaticism. He developed his theories, bouncing ideas off one friend, the dying priest, and the other, the convert to Islam.'

'So, he would have taken this explosion as a personal failure.'

'That, and the fact that it also took the life of Miguel Botín, with whom he'd developed a very close relationship.'

'He'd just applied a second time for a bugging order.'

'We thought the refusal of the first was strange. Since the London bombings, we've been told to look for the slightest change of . . . inflexion in a community. And there was plenty going on in that mosque to justify a bug being placed there – according to Ricardo's source, anyway.'

'Do you think it had something to do with the department being under investigation?'

'Ricardo did. We didn't see the logic of it. We just thought he was angry at being turned down. You know how it is: your brain plays tricks and you see conspiracies wherever you look.'

'He had a ticket in his back pocket for the Archaeological Museum, which he must have visited in his lunch break today,' said Falcón. 'Any thoughts about that?'

'Apart from the fact that he didn't have to *buy* a ticket, no.'

'Would that be significant?' asked Falcón. 'Was he the sort of person who would leave something like that as a sign?'

'I think you're reading too much into it.'

'He met somebody in his lunch break and then killed himself,' said Falcón. 'His mind wasn't made up before the meeting; why would you bother to go if you were planning to kill yourself? So something happened *during* this meeting to tip him over the edge, to make him believe, perhaps with his mind in an emotional turmoil, that he was in some way responsible.'

'I can't think who that person could be, or what they could possibly have said to him,' said Molero.

'What church did his friend the priest belong to?'

'It's close. That's why he took this apartment,' said Molero. 'San Marcos.'

'Did he still attend that church, even after the priest's death?'

'I don't know,' said Molero. 'We didn't see much of each other outside the office. I only know about San Marcos because I offered to go with him to his priest's funeral Mass.'

To understand why Gamero had committed suicide they needed to talk to the person he'd met in the Archaeological Museum. Falcón asked Barros to find out from the rest of the antiterrorism squad if they'd seen Gamero with anybody they didn't recognize. He also wanted all names and telephone numbers from Gamero's office line, and in the meantime they'd check his mobile and the fixed line in his apartment. Barros gave him the mobile numbers of the other two officers in the anti-terrorism squad and left with Paco Molero. The instructing judge signed off the *levantamiento del cadáver* and Gamero's body was removed. Falcón and the two forensics, Felipe and Jorge, began a detailed search of the apartment.

'We know he committed suicide,' said Felipe. 'All the doors were locked from the inside and the prints on the water glass next to the paracetamol trays match the body's. So what are we looking for?'

'Anything that might give us a lead to the person he met in his lunch break,' said Falcón. 'A business card, a scribbled number or an address, a note of a meeting . . .'

Falcón sat at the table in the kitchen with Gamero's wallet and the museum ticket. The tendons of his hands rippled under the cloudy membrane of the latex gloves. He felt sure that there were connections to be made out there, which he was just missing. Every lead they were pursuing failed to unfold into the greater narrative of what was going on. There were movements, like seismic aftershocks, that brought about casualties such as Ricardo Gamero, a man dedicated to his work and admired by his colleagues, who'd seen . . . what? His responsibility, or was it just the recognition of his failure?

He teased out the contents of Gamero's wallet: money, credit cards, ID, receipts, restaurant cards, ATM extracts – the usual. Falcón called Serrano and asked him to get the name and number of the priest of the San Marcos church. He went back to the wallet, turning over the cards and receipts, thinking that Gamero was a man who was used to a high level of secrecy in his life. Vital phone numbers would not be written down or stored in his mobile but either memorized or encoded in some way. He wouldn't have, or couldn't have, made contact with the person he saw in the museum on the day of the bomb. His department was being watched and they were all being kept in the office. He could have called at night after they were released from work. He would probably have used a public phone. The only chance was that he might not have remembered an infrequently used mobile number. He turned over the last ATM extract in the wallet. Nothing. He thumped the table.

'Have you got anything out there?' asked Falcón.

'Nothing,' said Jorge. 'The guy's in the CGI, he's not

going to leave anything hanging around unless he wants us to find it.'

A call came through from Cristina Ferrera. She gave him the name and number of another Spanish convert, who would normally have been in the mosque at that time in the morning but had gone to Granada on the Monday evening. He was now back in Seville. His name was José Duran.

A few minutes later Serrano called with the name and number of the priest of the San Marcos church. Falcón told him to stop what he was doing and come to Calle Butrón, pick up Gamero's ID and take it to the Archaeological Museum, where he should ask the ticket sellers and security guards if they remembered seeing Gamero and anybody he might have met.

The priest couldn't see him until after evening Mass at about 9 p.m. It was already 6.30. Falcón couldn't believe the time; the day almost gone and no significant breakthrough. He called José Duran, who was in the city centre. They agreed to meet in the Café Alicantina Vilar, a big, crowded pastelería in the centre.

Serrano still hadn't showed up. Falcón left the ID with Felipe and decided it was quicker to walk to the pastelería than get stuck in evening traffic. As he walked he put a call through to Ramírez and gave him a quick report on Ricardo Gamero, and told him he'd stolen Serrano for a few hours.

'We're not getting anywhere with these fucking electricians,' said Ramírez. 'All this manpower to find something that doesn't exist.'

'They do exist, José Luis,' said Falcón. 'They just don't exist in the form we expect them to.'

'The whole world knows we're looking for them and

they haven't come forward. To me that means they're sinister.'

'Not everybody is a perfect citizen. They might be frightened. They probably don't want to get involved. They couldn't care less. They might be implicated,' said Falcón. 'So *we* have to find *them*, because they are the link from the mosque to the outside world. We have to find out how they fit into this scenario. There were three of them, for God's sake. Somebody, somewhere, knows something.'

'We need a breakthrough,' said Ramírez. 'Everybody's making breakthroughs except us.'

'You found the biggest breakthrough of all, José Luis – the Peugeot Partner and its contents. We have to keep up the pressure and then things will start to give way,' said Falcón. 'And what are all these other break-throughs?'

'Elvira's called a meeting for 8 a.m. tomorrow. He can't talk until then, but it's international. The web's spreading wider by the hour.'

'That's the way these things go now,' said Falcón. 'Remember London? They were rounding up suspects in Pakistan inside a week. But I tell you, José Luis, there's something homegrown about this, too. The intelligence services are equipped to deal with all that worldwide web of international terrorism. What we do is find out what happened on our patch. Have you read the file on the unidentified body found at the dump on Monday morning?'

'Fuck, no.'

'Pérez wrote a report on it and there's an autopsy in there, too. Read it tonight. We'll talk about it tomorrow.'

The waiter brought him a coffee and some sort of sticky pastry envelope with pus-coloured goo inside. He needed sugar. He had to wait half an hour for José Duran, in which time he took calls from Pablo of the CNI, Mark Flowers from the US Consulate, Manuela, Comisario Elvira and Cristina Ferrera. He turned his mobile off. Too many of them wanted to see him tonight and he had no more time to give.

José Duran was pale and emaciated, with hair plastered close to his head, round glasses and a fluffy beard. Deodorant was a stranger to his body and it was still 40°C outside. Falcón ordered him a camomile tea. Duran listened to Falcón's introduction and twizzled his beard into a point on his chin. He breathed on his glasses and wiped them clean with his shirt tail. He sipped his tea and gave Falcón his own introduction. He'd been to the mosque every day of last week. He'd seen Hammad and Saoudi talking to the Imam in his office on Tuesday, 30th May. He hadn't heard their conversation. He'd seen the council inspectors on Friday, 2nd June.

'They must have been from Health and Safety, because they looked at everything: water, drains, electricity. They even looked at the quality of the doors . . . something to do with fire,' said Duran. 'They told the Imam he was going to have to get a new fuse box, but he didn't have to do anything until they issued their report and then he had fifteen days to put it right.'

'And the fuse box blew on Saturday night?' said Falcón.

'That's what the Imam told us on Sunday morning.'

'Do you know when he called the electricians?'

'On the Sunday morning after prayers.'

'How do you know that?'

'I was in his office.'

'How did he find their number?'

'Miguel Botín gave it to him.'

'Miguel Botín *gave* the Imam the number of the electricians?'

'No. He reminded the Imam of the card he'd given him earlier. The Imam started to search the papers on his desk, and Miguel gave him another card and told him that there was a mobile number he could call any time.'

'And that was when the Imam called the electricians?'

'Isn't this sort of detail just a bit ludicrous in the light of . . .?'

'You've no idea how crucial this detail is, José. Just tell me.'

'The Imam called them on his mobile. They said they'd come round on Monday morning and take a look and tell him how much it was going to cost. I mean, that's what I assume from the questions the Imam was asking.'

'And you were there on Monday morning?'

'The guy turned up at eight thirty, took a look at the fuse box –'

'The guy was Spanish?'

'Yes.'

'Description?'

'There was nothing to describe,' said Duran, searching amongst the empty tables and chairs. 'He was an average guy, about 1.75 metres tall. Not heavy, but not thin either. Dark hair with a side parting. No facial hair. There was nothing particular about him. I'm sorry.'

'You don't have to try to tell me everything now, but think about it. Call me if anything occurs to you,' said Falcón, giving him his card. 'Did the guy say hello to Miguel Botín?'

Duran blinked. He had to think about that.

'I'm not sure that Miguel was there at that point.'

'And later, when he turned up with the other guys?'

'That's right, he needed help. The Imam wanted a socket in the storeroom and he had to cut a channel from the nearest junction box which was in the Imam's office,' said Duran. 'Miguel was with him in the office. I presume they said hello.'

'What about the other guys, the labourers – were they Spanish, too?'

'No. They spoke Spanish, but they weren't Spaniards. They were from those Eastern bloc countries. You know, Romania or Moldavia, one of those places.'

'Descriptions?'

'Don't ask me that,' said Duran, running his hands down his face in frustration.

'Think about them, José,' said Falcón. 'Call me. It's important. And have you got the Imam's mobile phone number?'

24

Falcón called Inspector Jefe Barros to see if anybody had searched Miguel Botín's apartment. Nobody from the CGI had been there. He called Ramírez, gave him Botín's address, told him to get round there and look for the electrician's card. He called Baena, gave him the Imam's mobile number and told him to get the phone records. He called Esperanza, Miguel's partner, she'd never heard of any friends of his who were electricians. By the time he'd made these calls he was at the doors of the Iglesia de San Marcos. It wasn't quite 9 p.m. He flicked through his messages to see if Serrano had called. He had. At the museum they'd remembered Ricardo Gamero at the ticket desk. Two security guards had seen him speeding through rooms taking no notice of the exhibits. A third security guard had seen Gamero talking to a man in his sixties for some twenty minutes. The guard was now at the Jefatura with a police artist working up a sketch of the older man.

Father Román was in his early forties. He was out of the robes of office and in an ordinary dark suit with the jacket folded over his arm. He was standing in the nave of the brick interior of the church, talking to two women dressed in black. On seeing Falcón he excused himself from the conversation, went over to shake hands, and led him up to his office.

'You look exhausted, Inspector Jefe,' he said, sitting at his desk.

'The first days after something like this are always the longest,' said Falcón.

'My congregations have doubled since Tuesday morning,' said Father Román. 'A surprising number of young people. They're confused. They don't know when this will end or *how* it can possibly end.'

'Not just young people,' said Falcón. 'But I'm sorry, Father, I must press on.'

'Of course you must,' said Father Román.

'You may know that one of your congregation committed suicide today – Ricardo Gamero. Did you know him?'

Father Román blinked at the swift devastation of this news. It left him dumb with shock.

'I'm sorry I wasn't able to break it to you more gently,' said Falcón. 'He took his life this afternoon. Obviously you knew him. I understand he was a very . . .'

'I met him when my predecessor was taken ill,' said Father Román. 'They were very close. My predecessor had helped him resolve a number of issues to do with his faith.'

'How well did *you* know Ricardo?'

'He didn't appear to be seeking the same sort of relationship with me as he'd had with my predecessor.'

'Did you know what these issues to do with his faith were?'

'That was between them. Ricardo hasn't spoken to me about them.'

'When was the last time you saw Ricardo?'

'He was here on Sunday for Mass, as always.'

'And you haven't seen him since?'

Silence from Father Román, who looked as if he was coping with a distressing nausea.

'Sorry,' he said, snapping out of it. 'I'm just trying to think of the last time we spoke . . . and if there was any indication that he was still troubled to the same extent as he had been in my predecessor's time.'

'You didn't happen to see him today, did you, Father?'

'No, no, not today,' he said, distracted.

'Have you heard of a company called Informáticalidad?' asked Falcón.

'Should I have done?' asked Father Román, frowning.

'They actively recruit personnel from amongst your congregation,' said Falcón. 'Is that without your knowledge?'

'Forgive me, Inspector Jefe, but I find it rather confusing the way this conversation has developed. I'm feeling the pressure of your suspicion, but I'm not sure about what?'

'It's better just to answer the questions rather than trying to understand what they're about. This has become a very complicated situation,' said Falcón. 'Have you ever met a man called Diego Torres?'

'It's not such an unusual name.'

'He happens to be the Human Resources Director at Informáticalidad.'

'I don't always know the profession of the members of my congregation.'

'But you have someone of that name who attends this church?'

'Yes,' said Father Román, squeezing it out like a splinter.

Falcón went through the list of board members of Informáticalidad. Four out of the ten were members of Father Román's congregation.

'Would you mind telling me what exactly is going on here?' said Falcón.

'Nothing is "going on here",' said Father Román. 'If, as you say, this company is using my church as an informal recruiting agency, what can I do? It is the nature of people that they will meet at a church and that there will be a social exchange. Quite possibly invitations are made and it's conceivable that jobs might be offered. Just because the Church seems to have less influence in society, doesn't mean that some churches don't perform in the way that they used to.'

Falcón nodded. He'd overreached himself in his excitement at finally realizing a connection, only to find it a little too loose.

'Did you know Ricardo Gamero's profession?'

'I knew from my predecessor that he was a member of the police force, but I have no idea what he does, or rather, did. Was he a member of your squad?'

'He was an agent with the CGI; specifically, the antiterrorism group,' said Falcón. 'Islamic terrorism.'

'I doubt that was something he talked to many people about,' said Father Román.

'Did you happen to notice if he mixed with any of the people I mentioned who worked for Informáticalidad?'

'I'm sure he would have done. When people leave church they go to the two cafés around the corner. They socialize.'

343

'Did you notice regular meetings?'

Father Román shook his head.

Falcón sat back. He needed more ammunition for this conversation. He was tired, too. The flight to Casablanca and back seemed to have been from a month ago. The fullness of every minute, with not only his own findings but the ramifications of concurrent investigations under the colossal concentration of manpower rolling out all over Spain, Europe and the world, made hours feel like days.

'Were you aware that Informáticalidad not only used your church but two others inside the old city for the same purpose?' said Falcón.

'Look, Inspector Jefe, it's quite possible that this company has an unspoken employment policy of only taking on practising Catholics. I don't know. These days, I believe, you're not allowed to ask a recruitment agency to discriminate on your behalf. What would *you* do?'

'They *do* have an unspoken employment policy,' said Falcón. 'They don't take on any women. I suppose that's not dissimilar to the Catholic Church.'

On the walk back to his car, Falcón called Ramírez, who was still searching Miguel Botín's apartment.

'We're not getting anywhere here,' said Ramírez. 'I don't know what it is about this place, but we're sure somebody's been around here before us. It's a bit tidy. We've turned the place upside down and we're going through his library now.'

'I have a witness who saw him give a card to the Imam.'

'Maybe they're still with him in his bag under the rubble.'

'What state was the bombsite in when you last saw it?'

'The heavy work is over. The crane has gone. They're working by hand now, with just a couple of tippers standing by. They've put scaffolding up and sheeted off the remaining rubble. About six teams of forensics are ready to go in. They reckon they'll get into the mosque itself by mid-morning tomorrow.'

'When you've finished at Botín's apartment, let everybody go home and get some sleep,' said Falcón. 'It's going to be another big day tomorrow. Have you seen Juez Calderón?'

'Only on television,' said Ramírez. 'He's been giving a press conference with Comisario Lobo and Comisario Elvira.'

'Anything we should know?'

'There's a job waiting for Juez Calderón as a chat-show host if he gets bored of being a judge.'

'So he's not telling them anything, but it looks as if he is.'

'Exactly,' said Ramírez. 'And given that we've come up with fuck-all today, he's making us sound like heroes.'

The drive back home was eerily quiet. At nearly 10 p.m. the streets should have been alive and the bars full of people. A lot of places were closed. There was so little traffic Falcón went through the centre of town. Only a few young people had gathered in the Plaza del Museo under the trees. The mood was sombre and the narrow streets tense with anxiety.

An investigation of his fridge revealed some cooked prawns and a fresh swordfish steak. He ate the prawns with mayonnaise while drinking a beer direct from the bottle. He fried up the fish, squeezed some lemon over it, poured himself a glass of white rioja and ate, his mind picking over the detail of the day. He went over the dialogue with Father Román. Had the priest been trying to avoid the sin of lying by omission, evasion and ducking the question? It felt like it. He poured himself another glass of white wine, pushed back his plate and folded his arms and had just started to contemplate the big event of the day – the suicide of Ricardo Gamero, when his first visitor arrived.

Pablo had come on business. He refused a beer and they went into the study.

'You mentioned Yacoub had some conditions before you fell asleep on the plane this morning,' said Pablo.

'The first condition is that he will only talk or deal with me,' said Falcón. 'He won't meet any other agents, or take phone calls from anyone but me.'

'That's quite normal except, of course, you'll be in different countries. I'll talk you through the communication procedure later, but it won't exactly be direct contact,' said Pablo. 'It puts *you* under a lot of pressure.'

'He also says he's not making a lifelong commitment,' said Falcón.

'That's understandable,' said Pablo. 'But you know, spying can have an addictive effect on certain personalities.'

'Like Juan,' said Falcón. 'He looks like a man with a few secrets. As if he's running two families that don't know about each other.'

'He does. He has his wife and two kids and the CNI,

and they don't know *anything* about each other. Keep going with the conditions.'

'Yacoub will not give us any information that could jeopardize the life of any of his family members,' said Falcón.

'That was to be expected,' said Pablo. 'But does he suspect any of his family members?'

'He says not. But they're all devout Muslims and they lead very different lives to him,' said Falcón. 'It could be that he finds out that they are closely involved or at some remove, but he will not be an instrument in their downfall if they are. These people have totally accepted him as one of their own and he won't give them up.'

'Anything else?' asked Pablo.

'My problem: Yacoub doesn't have any training for this work.'

'Most spies don't. They just happen to be in a position where information comes their way.'

'You make it sound easy.'

'It's only dangerous if you're careless.'

Falcón had to raise his concentration levels to take in Pablo's briefing about the method of communication with Yacoub. He got him to boil it down to the basics, which were: they would communicate via email, using a secure website run by the CNI. Both Falcón and Diouri would have to load their computers with different encryption software. The emails would go to the CNI website to be decrypted and passed on. The CNI would obviously see all emails and make their recommendations for action. All Falcón had to do this evening was to call Yacoub and tell him to go to the shop in Rabat and pick up a couple of books. These books would give Yacoub all the information he needed. Falcón made the call and kept it short, saying he was tired.

'We've got to get him working as soon as possible,' said Pablo. 'This whole thing is moving fast.'

'What whole thing?'

'The game, the plan, the operation,' said Pablo. 'We're not sure which. All we know is that, since the bomb went off yesterday, the level of encrypted emails on the web has gone up fivefold.'

'And how many of those encrypted emails can you read?'

'Not many.'

'So you haven't cracked the code from the Koran found in the Peugeot Partner?'

'Not yet. We've got the world's best mathematicians working on it, though.'

'What do the CNI make of Ricardo Gamero's suicide?' asked Falcón.

'Inevitably we're thinking that he was the mole,' said Pablo. 'But that's just a theory. We're trying to work up the logic around it.'

'If he was the mole, from what I know about him, I'd find it hard to believe he was passing information to an Islamic terrorist movement.'

'Right, but what about Miguel Botín? What do you know about him?'

'That his brother was maimed in the Madrid train bombings, giving him good reason to be operating *against* Islamic terrorism,' said Falcón. 'That his girl-friend was a school friend of Gamero who remains a devout Catholic, having so far been reluctant to convert to Islam. And it was Botín who followed the Imam and took shots of Hammad and Saoudi and these other two mystery men, which he handed over to the CGI. He was also prompting Gamero to get the Imam's office bugged. That's about it.'

'He doesn't sound like a promising candidate as a terrorist, does he?'

'Have you searched Botín's apartment?' asked Falcón.

Pablo cradled his knee, nodded.

'What did you find there?'

'I can't say.'

'But you found something that makes you think Botín was acting for the terrorists while working for Gamero?'

'This is what it's like, Javier,' said Pablo, shrugging. 'The Hall of Mirrors. We constantly have to revise what we're actually seeing.'

'You found another heavily annotated copy of the Koran, didn't you?' said Falcón, sitting back, dazed. 'What the hell does that mean?'

'It means you cannot say a word about this conversation to anybody,' said Pablo. 'It means we have to get our counterintelligence up and running as soon as possible.'

'But it also means that the terrorists, whoever *they* are, were letting Miguel Botín serve up information to the CGI that compromised the Imam, Hammad and Saoudi, along with whatever operation was being planned in the mosque.'

'We're still conducting our enquiries,' said Pablo.

'They were sacrificing them?' asked Falcón, nauseated by his inability to think his way around this new development.

'First of all, we live in an age of suicide bombing – there's sacrifice for you,' said Pablo. 'And secondly, intelligence services all over the world have always had to sacrifice agents for the greater good of the mission. It's nothing new.'

'So this electrician, whose card Miguel Botín handed over to the Imam, was the agent of their destruction? The electrician was sent by Botín's Islamic terrorist masters to bomb the building? That's just fantastic.'

'We don't know that,' said Pablo. 'But as you know, not all suicide bombers realize that they *are* suicide bombers. Some have just been told to deliver a car, or leave a rucksack on a train. Botín had just been told to give an electrician's card to the Imam. What we need to find out is *who* told him to do that.'

'Are we wasting our time here?' asked Falcón. 'Is this whole investigation just a show, for whichever terrorist group decided to abort their mission and blow up any possible leads back to their network?'

'We're still very interested to find out what's in the mosque,' said Pablo. 'And we're very keen to get Yacoub up and running.'

'And how do you know that Yacoub is approaching the right group, even?' asked Falcón, exhausted and close to rage from frustration.

'We have confidence in that because it has come from a reliable detainee and has also been verified by British agents on the ground in Rabat,' said Pablo.

'What group are we talking about?'

'The GICM, Groupe Islamique de Combattants Marocains, otherwise known as the Moroccan Islamic Combatant Group. They had links to the bombings in Casablanca, Madrid and London,' said Pablo. 'What

350

we're doing here is not something that was thought up yesterday as an idea worth trying, Javier. This represents months of intelligence work.'

Pablo left soon after. Falcón was almost depressed by their exchange. All the man-hours put in by his squad were beginning to look like a waste of energy, and yet there were unnerving gaps in what Pablo had told him. It was as if each group involved in the investigation put most trust in the information that they themselves uncovered. So the CNI believed in the annotated Koran as the codebook, because of the example of the *Book of Proof* uncovered by British intelligence, and that coloured everything they looked at. The fact that the witness in the mosque, José Duran, had described the electrician and his labourers as a Spaniard and two Eastern bloc natives, who did not sound anything like Islamic terrorist operatives, held little water for Pablo. But then again, it had been local Spanish petty criminals who'd supplied the Madrid bombers with explosives, and what does it take to leave a bomb? A little care and a psychotic mind.

After the press conference on TVE with Comisarios Lobo and Elvira, Juez Calderón had taken a taxi round to Canal Sur, where he was miked up and eased on to the set of a roundtable discussion about Islamic terrorism. He was the man of the hour and within moments the female chair of the programme had drawn him into the discussion. He controlled the rest of the programme with a combination of incisive and informed comment, humour, and a savage wit he reserved for so-called security specialists and terrorism pundits.

Afterwards he was taken out to dinner by some

executives from Canal Sur's current affairs department and the female chair of the programme. They fed and flattered him for an hour and a half until he found himself alone with the female chair, who let it be known that this could continue in more comfortable surroundings. For once Calderón demurred. He was tired. There was another long day ahead of him and – the main reason – he was sure that Marisa was a better lay.

Calderón sat in the middle seat in the back of the Canal Sur limousine. He felt like a hero. His mind was racing with endorphins after his TV performances. He had a sense of the world at his feet. Seville, as it flashed past in the night, began to feel small to him. He imagined what it must be like to be as high on success as this in a city like New York, where they really knew how to make a man feel important.

The limousine dropped him off outside the San Marcos church at 12.45 a.m. and, for once, rather than take his usual little deviation around the back, he strode past the bars on the other side, hoping that friends of Inés would be drinking there who would stop him and congratulate him. He really had been exceptionally brilliant. The bars, however, were already closed. Calderón, in his heightened state, had failed to notice how quiet the city was.

As he went up in the lift he knew that the only way he was going to sleep was after a strenuous, crazy fuck with Marisa, out on the balcony, in the hall, going down in the lift, out in the street. He felt so on top of the world he wanted everybody to see him performing.

Marisa had watched the TV programmes in a state of insensate boredom. She could tell that the press conference revolved around Esteban, as all the questions from journalists were for him. She could also see that he was controlling the roundtable discussion, and even that the female chair was dying to get into his trousers, but the drivel that was being talked had reduced her to a vegetative state. Why do Westerners have to get so exercised about things and talk them to death, as if it's going to be any help? Then it struck her. That was what irked her about Westerners. They always took things at face value, because that was what could be controlled, and what could be measured. They just served up their lies all round and then congratulated each other on 'their command of the situation'. That was why white people bored her. They had no interest beyond the surface. 'What are you doing, sitting there all day, Marisa?' had been the most frequently asked question she'd faced in America. And yet in Africa they'd never asked her that question – or any question, for that matter. Questioning existence didn't help you live it.

She looked down on Calderón's arrival from her balcony. She saw his jaunty steps, his little preparations. When he said his usual: 'It's me,' into her entry phone, she replied: 'My hero.'

He burst into her apartment like a showman, arms raised, waiting for the applause. He drew her to him and kissed her, pushing his tongue between the barrier of her teeth, which she did not like. Their kissing had only ever been lip deep.

It wasn't difficult to tell that he was still on the crest of the media wave. She let him drive her out on to the balcony, where they had sex. He looked up at the stars, holding on to her hips, imagining even greater glory. She participated by hanging on to the railings and making a suitable amount of noise.

As soon as he was finished, he was rendered mentally and physically drained, like someone coming off a coke high. She managed to steer him to the bed and get his shoes off before he fell into a deep sleep at 1.15 a.m. She stood over him, smoking a cigarette, wondering if she'd be able to wake him in a couple of hours' time.

She washed herself in the bidet, closing her right eye to the smoke rising from the cigarette. She lay on the sofa and let time do what it was good at. At 3 a.m. she started trying to rouse him, but he was completely inert. She held a lighter to his foot. He writhed and kicked out. It took time to get him to come round. He had no idea where he was. She explained that he had to go home, he had an early start, he had to get changed.

At 3.25 she called a taxi. She put his shoes on, got him standing, put his arms into his jacket and called the lift up to her floor. She stood outside with him, his head dropping and jerking off his chest and her shoulder. The taxi arrived just after 3.30. She put him in the back and instructed the driver to take him to Calle San Vicente. She said he was exhausted, that he was the leading judge in the Seville bombing, and that gave the driver a sense of mission. He waved away her € 10 note. For this man it was going to be free. The cab pulled away. Calderón had his head thrown back on the rear shelf. In the yellowish street lighting he looked as he would when dead. The whites of his eyes were just visible below the lids.

At that time of the morning, with Seville as silent as a ghost city, there was no traffic and the cab arrived at Calle San Vicente in just under ten minutes. After much cajoling, the cab driver had to reach in and physically haul Calderón out into the street. He walked him to the front door of the building and asked him for his keys. The driver got the door open and realized he was going to have to go all the way. They crammed themselves into the hall.

'Is there a light?' asked the driver.

Calderón slapped at the wall. Light burst into the hall and the ticking sound of a timer started up. The driver supported him up the stairs.

'This one here,' said Calderón, as they reached the first floor.

The driver opened the apartment door, which was double locked, and returned the keys to Calderón.

'Are you all right now?' he asked, looking into the judge's bleary eyes.

'Yeah, I'm fine now. I'll be OK, thanks,' he said.

'You're doing a great job,' said the driver. 'I saw you on the telly before I started my shift.'

Calderón clapped him on the shoulder. The driver went down the stairs and the light in the hall went out with a loud snap. The cab started up and pulled away. Calderón rolled over the doorjamb into the apartment. The light was on in the kitchen. He shut the door, leaned back on it. Even in his exhausted state, with his eyelids as heavy as lead, his teeth clenched with irritation.

25

Calderón came to with a start that thumped his head into the wall. His face was pressed against the wooden floor. The smell of polish was strong in his nose. His eyelids snapped open. He was instantly wide awake, as if danger was present and near. He was still dressed as he had been all day. He couldn't understand why he was lying in the corridor of his apartment. Had he been so exhausted that he'd slept where he fell? He checked his watch: just gone four o'clock. He'd only been out for ten minutes or so. He was mystified. He remembered coming into the apartment and the light being on in the kitchen. It was still on, but he was beyond it now, further into the flat, which appeared to be completely dark and cold from the air conditioning. He struggled to his feet, checked himself. He wasn't hurt, hadn't even banged his head. He must have slid down the wall.

'Inés?' he said out loud, puzzled by the kitchen light.

Calderón stretched his shoulders back. He was stiff. He stepped into the rhomboid of light on the corridor floor. He saw the blood first, a huge, burgeoning crimson pool on the white marble. The colour of it under the bright white light was truly alarming. He stepped back as if expecting an intruder still to be there. He lowered himself and saw her through the chair and table. He knew immediately that she was dead. Her eyes were wide open, with not a scintilla of light in them.

The blood had spread to the right side of the table and underneath it. It was viscous and seemed to be sucking at the chair and table legs. It was so horribly bright that it throbbed in his vision, as if there was still life in it. Calderón crawled on all fours round to the left of the table to where Inés's feet lay, slack and pointed outwards in front of the sink. Her nightie was rucked up. His eyes travelled from her white legs, over her white cotton panties, beyond the waistband – and that was where the bruising started. He hadn't seen it before. He'd had no idea his fists had accomplished such horrifically visible damage. And it was then that he thought he might have seen this before after all, because his whole body was suddenly consumed with a remembered panic that seemed to constrict his throat and cut off the blood supply to his brain. He reared back on his knees and held his head.

He crawled back out of the kitchen and got to his feet in the corridor. He went swiftly out of the apartment, which required him to unlock the door. He hit the stair light, looked around and went back in. The light was still on in the kitchen. Inés was still lying there. The blood was now one floor tile's width from the wooden floor of the corridor. He pressed the balls of his palms into his eye sockets and ripped them away, but it made no difference to the horror of what lay before him. He dropped to all fours again.

'You fucking bitch, you stupid fucking bitch,' he said. 'Look what the fuck you've gone and done now.'

The noisily bright blood resounded in the hard kitchen. It was also moving, consuming the white marble, reaching towards him. He went back around the table. The ghastly purple of the contusions seemed to have deepened in colour in the interim, or his constant toing and froing in and out of the light was playing tricks. Between her splayed thighs he now saw the welts from his belt lashing. He sank to his knees again, pressed his fists into his eyes and started sobbing. This was it. This was the end. He was finished, finished, finished. Even the most incompetent state judge couldn't fail to make a watertight case against him. A wife-beater who'd gone a step too far. A wife-beater who'd just come back from fucking his mistress, had another confrontation and this time . . . Oh, yes, it might have been an accident. Was it an accident? It probably was. But this time he'd overdone it and she'd smashed her stupid head open. He pounded the table.

It cleared as suddenly as it had arrived. Calderón sank back on his heels and realized that the terrible panic had gone. His mind was back on track. At least, he felt it was back on track. What he hadn't realized was the nature of the damage done by the panic, the way it had opened up electronic pathways to the flaws in his character. As far as Calderón was concerned, his mind was back to the steel-trap clarity of the leading judge in Seville, and it came to him that, with no chest freezer, the only solution was to get her out of the apartment, and he had to do it now. There was just over an hour before dawn.

Weight was not the problem. Inés was currently 48

kilos. Her height at 1.72m was more of a difficulty. He stormed around the table and into the spare room, where the luggage was kept. He pulled out the biggest suitcase he could find, a huge grey Samsonite with four wheels. He grabbed two white towels from the cupboard.

One of the towels he laid across the kitchen doorway to stop the blood from seeping into the corridor. The other he wrapped around Inés's head. It nearly made him sick. The back of her head was a flat mush and the blood soaked gratefully into the towel, consuming the whiteness with its incarnadine stain. He found a bin liner and pulled it over her head, securing it with cooking string. He washed his hands. He put the case on the table, picked Inés up and laid her in it. She was far too big. Even foetally she didn't fit. He couldn't cram her feet in and, even if he could, her shoulders were too broad for the case to shut. He looked down on her with his considerable intellect surging forward, but fatally, in the wrong direction.

'I'll have to cut her up,' he said to himself. 'Take her feet off and break her collar bones.'

No. That was not going to work. He'd seen films and read novels where they cut up bodies and it never seemed to work, even in fiction where everything can be made to bloody work. He was squeamish, too. Couldn't even watch *Extreme Makeover* on TV without writhing on the sofa. Think again. He walked around the apartment looking at everyday objects in a completely new light. He stopped in the living room and stared at the carpet, as if willing it not to be the cliché of all clichés.

'You can't wrap her up in the carpet. It'll come

straight back to you. Same with the luggage. Think again.'

The river was only three hundred metres from Calle San Vicente. All he had to do was get her in the car, drive fifty metres, turn right on Calle Alfonso XII, go straight up to the traffic lights, cross Calle Nuevo Torneo and there was a road he remembered as quite dark, which ran down to the river and veered left behind the huge bus station of Plaza de Armas. From there it was a matter of metres to the water's edge, but it was a stretch used by early-morning runners, so he would have to act quickly and decisively.

The decorators. The memory of his irritation at them leaving their sheet up the stairs a few days ago juddered into his brain. He ran out of the apartment again, slashed on the stairwell light and stopped himself. He put the apartment door on the latch. That would be too much to bear: locked out of his apartment with his dead wife on the kitchen floor. He leapt down the stairs three at a time and there it all was, under the stairs. There were even full cans of paint to weigh down the body. He pulled out a length of paint-spattered hessian sheeting. He sprinted back up the stairs and laid it out on the clean half of the kitchen floor. He lifted her out of the suitcase, where she'd been lying like a prop in an illusionist's trick, and laid her on the sheet. He folded the edges over. He gasped at the momentary peak of horror at what he was doing. Inés's beautiful face reduced to a scarecrow's stuffed bin liner.

The blood had reached the towel across the doorway and he had to leap over it. He crashed with the deranged heaviness of a toppled wardrobe into the corridor, cracking his head and shoulder a glancing blow on the wall. He shrugged off the pain. He went into his study, tore open the drawers, found the roll of packing tape. He kissed it. On the way back he steadied himself and hopped more carefully over the blood-soaked towel.

He wrapped the tape around her ankles, knees, waist, chest, neck and head. He pocketed the cooking string and tape. He didn't bother to admire his mummified wife, but ran out of the apartment, grabbing his keys and the garage remote as he left. He took the door off the latch. Slapped the fucking light on again – tick, tick, tick, tick, tick – and rumbled down the stairs. He sprinted down Calle San Vicente to the garage, which was just around the corner. He hit the button of the remote as he rounded the bend and the garage door opened, but so slowly he was jumping up and down in towering frustration, swearing and punching at the air. He rolled underneath the quarter-open door and hurtled down the ramp, pressing another button on the remote for the light. He found his car. He hadn't driven the damn thing for weeks. Who needs a car in Seville? Thank *fuck* I've got a car.

No mistakes. He reversed out calmly, as if suddenly on beta-blockers. He eased up the ramp. The garage door was only just fully open. The car hopped out on to the street, which was deadly quiet. The red digits on the dashboard told him it was 4.37. He pulled up outside the apartment, clicked the button to open the boot. He sprinted upstairs, in the dark this time, fell and cracked his shin such a blow on the top stair that the pain ricocheted up his skeleton to the inside of his skull. He didn't even stop. He unlocked the door, slowed down at the kitchen and stepped over the bloody towel.

Inés. No, not Inés any more. He picked her up. She

was absurdly heavy for someone who was less than fifty kilos and had lost at least three kilos of blood. He got her into the corridor, but she was too heavy to cradle-carry her. He hoisted her over his shoulder and closed the apartment door. He stepped carefully down the stairs in the dark again. That fucking tick, tick, tick of the light just too unbearably stressful at this stage. He stuck his head out into the street.

Empty.

Two steps. In the boot. Shut the boot. Close the apartment building door. Wait. Slow down. Think. The tins of paint to weigh down the body. Open the boot. Back under the stairs. Pick up the two cans of paint. As heavy as Inés. Heave them into the boot. Close the boot. In the car. Rear-view mirror. No headlights. Calm. Nice and slow. You're nearly there. This *is* going to work.

Calderón's car was alone at the traffic lights by the Plaza de Armas, which were showing red. The lights from the dash glowed in his face. He checked the rear-view again, saw his eyes. They were pitiful. The lights changed to green. He eased across the six empty lanes and took the ramp down to the river. It was first light. It wasn't quite as dark as he would have liked down by the river. He would have preferred something subterranean, as black as antimatter, as utterly lightless as a collapsed star.

There was still plenty to do. He had to get the body out, attach the cans of paint, and push it into the river. He had a good, long look around until he couldn't believe that everything wasn't moving. He shook the paranoia out of his mind, opened the boot. He lifted the body out and laid it down on the pavement close to the car for cover. He heaved out the cans of paint

362

with superhuman strength. Sweat cascaded. His shirt was stuck to him. His mind closed off. This was the home stretch. Get it done.

He didn't see the man at the back of the bus station, was not aware of him making his fatal call to the police. He worked with savage haste while the man muttered what he was seeing into his mobile phone, along with Calderón's registration number.

With no traffic it took less than a minute for a patrol car to arrive. It had been cruising down by the river less than a kilometre away when the two officers were notified by the communications centre in the Jefatura. The car rolled down the ramp towards the river with its headlights and engine switched off. Only Calderón's car was visible. He was kneeling behind it, taping the second can of paint to Inés's neck. His sweat was dripping on to the hessian sheet. He was finished. All he had to do now was hump close to 100 kilos about a metre across the pavement and then up over a low wall and into the water. He summoned his last reserves of strength. With the two paint cans attached, the body had become incredibly unwieldy. He jammed his hands underneath, not caring about the skin he tore from his fingers and knuckles. He drove forward with his thighs and, with his chest and pelvis close to the floor, he looked like an enormous lizard with some unmanageable prey. Inés's body shifted and thumped into the low wall. He was panting and sobbing. Tears streamed down his face. The pain from his stubbed fingers and torn nails didn't register, but when the headlights of the patrol car finally came on and he found himself encased in light, like an exhibit in the reptile house, he stiffened as if he'd just been shot.

The policemen got out of the patrol car with their weapons drawn. Calderón had yanked his arms out from under the body, rolled over, and was now lying on his back. His stomach convulsed with each racking sob. A lot of the emotion he was coughing up was relief. It was all over. He'd been caught. All that hideous desperation had flowed out of him and now he could relax into infamy and shame.

While one patrolman stood over the sobbing Calderón, the other ran a torch over the taped-up hessian sheet. He put on some latex gloves and squeezed Inés's shoulder just to confirm what he already knew, that this was a body. He went back to the patrol car and radioed the Jefatura.

'This is Alpha-2-0, we're down by the river now, just off the Torneo at the back of the bus station in Plaza de Armas. I can confirm that we have a male in his early forties attempting to dispose of an unidentified body. You'd better get the Inspector Jefe de Homicidios down here.'

'Give me the car registration number.'

'SE 4738 HT.'

'Fuck me.'

'What?'

'That's the same number given to me by the guy who reported the incident. I don't fucking believe this.'

'Who's the owner of the vehicle?'

'Don't you recognize him?'

The patrolman called out to his colleague, who passed a torch over Calderón's face. He was barely recognizable as human, let alone a specific person. His face bore the contortions of a particularly agonized flamenco singer. The patrolman shrugged.

'No idea,' the patrolman said, into the radio.

'How about Juez Esteban Calderón?' said the operator.

'Fuck!' said the patrolman and dropped the mouthpiece.

He shone his own torch in the man's face, grabbed him by the chin to hold him still. Calderón's agony slackened off with surprise. The patrolman let a sly grin spread across his face before he went back to the car.

Falcón had to claw his way out of sleep like an abandoned potholer, desperately trying to reach a star of light in a firmament of blackness. He came to with a jerk and grunt of disgust, as if he'd been spewed up by his own bed. The bedside light hurt him. The green digits on his clock told him it was 5.03. He grappled with the phone and sank back into his pillow with it clasped to his ear.

The voice was of the duty officer in the communications centre of the Jefatura. He was babbling. He was speaking so fast and with such a heavy Andaluz accent that Falcón only picked up the first syllable of every other word. He stopped him, got him to start again from the top.

'We have a situation down by the bus station at the Plaza de Armas. Behind the bus station, down by the river near the Puente de Chapina, a man has been apprehended attempting to dispose of a body. We have a positive identification of the owner of the vehicle used to bring the body to that point, and we have a positive ID of the man who was attempting to dispose of the body. And the man's name, Inspector Jefe, is . . . Esteban Calderón.'

Falcón's leg spasmed as if some high voltage had shot up it. In one movement he was out of bed and pacing the floor.

'Esteban Calderón, the judge? Are you positive?'

'We are now. The patrolman at the scene has checked the ID and read the number back to me. That and the car's registration confirm the man as Esteban Calderón.'

'Have you spoken to anyone about this?'

'Not yet, Inspector Jefe.'

'Have you called the Juez de Guardia?'

'No, you're the first person. I should have —'

'How was the incident reported?'

'An anonymous phone call from a guy who said he was walking his dog down by the river.'

'What time?'

'It was timed at 4.52 a.m.'

'Is that when people walk their dogs?'

'Old people who can't sleep do, especially in this heat.'

'How did he report it?'

'He called in on his mobile, told me what he was seeing, gave me the registration number and hung up.'

'Name and address?'

'Didn't have time to ask him.'

'Don't talk to anyone about this,' said Falcón. 'Call the patrolmen and tell them there is to be radio silence on this matter until I've spoken to Comisario Elvira.'

The bedroom seemed to fill up with the catastrophe of scandal. Falcón went out on to the gallery overlooking the patio. The morning was warm. He felt sick. He called Elvira, gave him some seconds to wake up and then told him the news in the most measured tone he could muster. Falcón broke the ensuing silence himself, by telling Elvira how many people, at this point, knew what had taken place.

'We have to get him, the body and the car off the street as soon as possible, whatever happens,' said Elvira. 'And we need a judge and a Médico Forense to do that.'

'Juez Romero is reliable and neither a friend, nor enemy, of Esteban Calderón.'

'This mustn't look like a cover-up,' said Elvira, almost to himself.

'This isn't something that can be covered up,' said Falcón.

'We have to do things absolutely by the book. The investigation might have to be taken off your hands, given Esteban Calderón's status.'

'I think it better for me to initiate the proceedings,' said Falcón.

'Let's go for normal procedure, but nobody, absolutely nobody, is to talk about this. We must have no leaks until we can get a press statement together. I'll speak to Comisario Lobo. Tell the communications officer to make the usual calls but not, under any circumstances, to inform the press. If it gets out before we're ready there'll be hell to pay.'

'The only person we can't control is the anonymous caller who reported the incident,' said Falcón.

'Well, *he* shouldn't know who it was he was reporting, should he?' said Elvira.

This was too big a scandal to contain. Elvira was asking too much. This was going to come sweating out of the Jefatura walls. Falcón called the communications centre, gave the instructions and asked the officer to call Felipe and Jorge to the crime scene. He showered, standing under the drilling water, trying to think of any plausible, innocent explanation for Calderón being discovered down by the river with a dead body.

It was 5.30 and the dawn was well advanced by the time he walked across the Plaza de Armas to the incident. The traffic on the Torneo was still very light. A patrol car had parked at the top of the ramp and some cones had been put out to stop any traffic from turning down the road. The duty judge was already at the scene, as was a police photographer, who was taking some shots. Jorge and Felipe arrived and were allowed down the ramp.

There was no sign of Calderón. Two patrolmen were making sure no early-morning joggers came past the scene along the riverbank. The duty judge told Falcón that Calderón was sitting in the back of the patrol car with one of the policemen who'd first come across the incident.

'We're just waiting for a Médico Forense to arrive and inspect the body.'

A set of tyres squeaked at the top of the ramp and a car rolled down and parked up. The Médico Forense got out with his bag. He was already dressed in a white hooded boiler suit and had a mask hanging from his neck. He shook hands, put on gloves, and they proceeded to the body. An ambulance arrived with no siren or flashing lights.

The Médico Forense used a scalpel to cut the tape wrapped around the body. He worked from the feet up to the head. He laid open the hessian sheet. The head wrapped in the black bin liner looked sinister, as if the body had been the subject of some sexual deviancy. Falcón started to feel dizzy. The Médico Forense murmured into his dictaphone about the heavy bruising on the torso. He put his scalpel through the cooking string at the neck of the body and eased away the bin liner. A darkening at the edges of his vision made Falcón clutch at the duty judge's sleeve.

'Are you all right, Inspector Jefe?' he asked.

Under the bin liner the head was wrapped in a towel. The front was white, with blood smears over it. The Médico Forense lifted up one corner of the towel and folded it back. The outline of the face was visible, as under a shroud. He pulled away the other corner of the towel and Falcón dropped unconscious to the floor, with the features of his ex-wife imprinted on his retina.

Falcón came to on the ground. The duty judge had managed to catch him and break his fall. The paramedics from the ambulance were over him. He heard the duty judge above their heads.

'He's in shock. This is his ex-wife. He shouldn't really be here.'

The paramedics helped him up. The Médico Forense continued to murmur into his dictaphone. He checked the thermometer, made a calculation and muttered the time of death.

Tears welled up as Falcón looked down once more on Inés's inert body. This was a scene from her life that he'd never imagined – her death. Over the years he'd done a lot of thinking and talking about Inés. He'd relived their life together ten times over, until he'd nearly driven Alicia Aguado insane. He'd only been able to get rid of her permanent occupation of his mind by finally seeing her for what she was, and realizing how badly she'd behaved and treated him. But this was not how it should have ended. No amount of selfishness deserved this.

The paramedics moved him away from the body and got him sitting on the low wall by the river, away from where the Médico Forense was working. Falcón breathed deeply. The duty judge came over.

'You can't handle this case,' he said.

'I'll call Comisario Elvira,' said Falcón, nodding. 'He'll appoint somebody from the outside. My entire squad is an interested party.'

Elvira was speechless until he finally managed to come up with his condolences. The catastrophe was so much worse than he'd imagined and, as he spoke, first to Falcón and then the duty judge, the hideousness of the morning press conference began to spread like a malignancy through his innards.

The duty judge finished the call and handed the mobile back to Falcón. They shook hands. Falcón took one last look at the body. Her face was perfect and undamaged. He shook his head in disbelief and had an image from years ago, when he'd come across Inés in the street. She'd been laughing; laughing so hard that she was doubled up with her hair flung forward, staggering backwards on her high heels.

He turned away and left the scene. He walked past the patrol car where Calderón was being held. The door was open. The radio squawked. Calderón's wrists were cuffed, his torn and bleeding hands lay in his lap. He stared straight ahead and his vision did not deviate even when Falcón leaned in.

'Esteban,' said Falcón.

Calderón turned to him, and said the sentence that Falcón had heard more times from the mouths of murderers than any other.

'I didn't do it.'

26

The classroom in the pre-school had been reglazed and new blinds put up. The air conditioners were already working full blast, which was the only way to keep the sulphurous stink of the corrupted bodies still in the destroyed apartment building at a bearable level. It was already past eight o'clock and still Comisario Elvira had not arrived. Everybody was tired, but there was a buzz of expectation in the room.

'Something's happened,' said Ramírez, 'and I've got the feeling it's something big. What do you think, Javier?'

Falcón couldn't speak.

'Where's Juez Calderón?' said Ramírez. 'That's what makes me think it's big. He's the man for the press conference.'

Falcón nodded, appalled to silence by what he'd seen down by the river. The door opened and Elvira came in and made his way to the blackboard at the far end of the room, followed by three men. Already present at the meeting were Pablo and Gregorio from the CNI, Inspector Jefe Ramón Barros and one of his senior officers from the antiterrorist squad of the CGI, and Falcón and Ramírez from the homicide squad. Elvira turned. His face was grim.

'There's no easy way to put this,' he said, 'so I'm just going to give you the facts. At around six o'clock this morning Juez Esteban Calderón was placed under arrest on suspicion of murdering his wife. Two patrolmen found him earlier this morning, attempting to dispose of his wife's body in the Guadalquivir. Given these circumstances, he will no longer be acting as the Juez de Instrucción in our investigation. It will also be impossible for our own homicide squad to conduct the murder enquiry, which will be carried out by these three officers from Madrid, led by Inspector Jefe Luis Zorrita. Thank you.'

The three homicide officers from Madrid nodded and filed out of the room, stopping briefly to introduce themselves and shake hands with Falcón and Ramírez. The door closed. Elvira resumed the meeting. Ramírez stared at Falcón in a state of shock.

'We have decided to appoint a Juez de Instrucción from outside Seville,' said Elvira, 'and Juez Sergio del Rey is on his way down from Madrid now. On his arrival an announcement will be made to the press at a conference to be held in the Andalucian Parliament building and until that time I would ask you to keep this information to yourselves.

'Following the suicide yesterday of Ricardo Gamero of the CGI, there have been some major developments and the CNI will now explain these to us.'

Something had been sucked out of Elvira's face overnight. The staggering import of his announcements had left him haggard. He sat back in the teacher's chair, inanimate, with his chin resting on his fist, as if his head needed that sort of support to keep it in place. Pablo made his way to the front.

'Just prior to the suicide of the CGI agent, Ricardo Gamero, we had received information from British intelligence that they had successfully identified the other two men photographed by Gamero's source, Miguel Botín. These two men are of Afghan nationality, living in Rome. They were known to MI5 because they were arrested in London two weeks after the failed 21st July bombings and held for questioning under the Terrorism Act. They were released without being charged. The British were not able to establish what these men were doing in London at the time, other than that they were visiting family. The known addresses of these two men in Rome were raided by the Italian police last night and found to be empty. Their current whereabouts is unknown. What concerns us about these suspects is that they are believed to have connections to the high command of al-Qaeda in Afghanistan, and are believed by the British to have forged links with the GICM in Morocco. In the last year they are known to have visited the UK, Belgium, France, Italy, Spain and Morocco. All these countries are believed to have GICM sleeper cells. There is considerable intelligence work still to be done to ascertain Miguel Botín's role, Imam Abdelkrim Benaboura's relationship to these two men, and their involvement with what has happened here in Seville.

'After Ricardo Gamero's suicide we conducted a search of Miguel Botín's apartment and discovered a heavily annotated copy of the Koran which matches the edition found in the Peugeot Partner driven by

Hammad and Saoudi. Large chunks of the notes are exact transcripts and we believe that this is a codebook. It is now thought that as each sleeper cell is activated they are issued with a new codebook, which they use until their mission is complete.

'The significance of finding this copy of the Koran in Miguel Botín's apartment is that it *could* mean that Ricardo Gamero's source was a double: working with the CGI and operating for a terrorist cell. This throws considerable confusion into the current investigation, because it would mean that the only intelligence Botín was communicating to Gamero was what his commanders *wanted* us to know. This would mean that Hammad and Saoudi, the two Afghans, and the Imam were all expendable.

'There is one final confusing detail about Botín's actions in this scenario. As you know, a great deal of manpower has been spent trying to find the fake council inspectors and the electricians. Inspector Jefe Falcón has found a witness who was in the mosque on the Sunday morning, after the fuse box blew on the Saturday night. This witness saw Botín give the electrician's card to the Imam, and he watched as the Imam called the number and made the appointment. Inspector Jefe Barros has informed us that this was not something sanctioned by him or anyone in his department. The CGI was still waiting for authorization to bug the mosque.

'We now have to examine the possibility that the council inspectors and the electricians were members of, or in the pay of, a terrorist cell. It could be – and we might only have a chance of verifying this when the forensics have reached the mosque – that the council inspectors laid a device to blow the fuse box and that the electricians were brought in to set a bomb that would wipe out the Imam, Hammad and Saoudi, and Botín himself.'

'There seems to be a break in the logic chain of that scenario,' said Barros. 'It might just be believable that Botín was the unwitting agent of their destruction, but I don't see any terrorist commander allowing that quantity of hexogen, brought into this country at what one imagines was considerable risk and expense, to be destroyed.'

'The electricians and council inspectors would constitute a type of terrorist cell we've never come across before, too,' said Falcón. 'The witness said they were a Spaniard and two Eastern Europeans.'

'And how does Ricardo Gamero's suicide fit into this scenario?' asked Barros.

'A profound sense of failure at his inability to prevent this atrocity,' said Pablo. 'We understand that he took his work very seriously.'

Silence, while everybody wrestled with the CNI's possible scenario. Falcón snapped out of his shocked state and burned with his theory that too much weight was being attached to the copy of the Koran as a codebook. But it was impossible to understand how two identical copies could have ended up in the Peugeot Partner and Botín's apartment.

'Why do you think this cell self-destructed?' asked Barros.

'We can only think that it was a spectacular diversionary tactic, to occupy our domestic investigating teams and all European intelligence services while they plan and carry out an attack elsewhere,' said Pablo. 'If

Botín was a double agent, his terrorist masters would have known that the mosque was under suspicion. They fed that suspicion further by bringing in the hexogen and Hammad and Saoudi, two known logistics men. They then blew it up. They don't mind. They're all going to paradise, whether as successful bombers or magnificent decoys.'

'What about the Afghans?' asked Barros. 'They've been identified, but not exactly sacrificed.'

'Perhaps Botín intended the shot of the two Afghans to be interpreted by us as an indication of an attack planned for Italy. Botín supplied those photographs when he was a trusted CGI source.'

'So, another diversionary tactic?'

'The Italians, Danish and Belgians are all on red alert, as they were after the London bombings.'

'So this letter sent to the *ABC* with the Abdullah Azzam text and all the media references to MILA – was that all part of this grand diversion?' asked Barros, nearly enjoying himself at being able to finally needle the CNI, who had so humiliated him and his department.

'What we're working on now is the real target,' said Pablo. 'The Abdullah Azzam text and the idea of MILA are powerful tools of terror. They inspire fear in a population. We see this as part of the escalation of this particular brand of terrorism. We are fighting the equivalent of a mutating virus. No sooner do we find one cure than it adapts to it with renewed lethal strength. There is no model. Only after we have sustained attacks do we become aware of a modus operandi. The intelligence gathered from the hundreds of people interviewed after the Madrid and London bombings is no help to us now. We are not talking about an integrated organization with a defined structure, but more of a satellite organization with a fluid structure and total flexibility.'

'Are you sure you're not reading too much into the diversionary tactic?' said Elvira. 'After the Madrid bombings –'

'We're pretty sure that ETA provided the diversion which led to the devastating success of the Madrid bombings. We don't think it was a coincidence that, 120 kilometres southeast of Madrid, the Guardia Civil stopped a van driven by two ETA incompetents, and loaded with 536 kilos of titadine for delivery to Madrid; and on the same day, 500 kilometres away in Avilés, three Moroccan terrorists were taking delivery of the 100 kilos of Goma 2 Eco used on the Madrid trains,' said Pablo. 'British security forces and intelligence were focused on an attack on the G8 Summit in Edinburgh when suicide bombers blew themselves up on the London Underground.'

'All right, so there is a history of diversion,' said Elvira.

'And a diversion that is prepared to sacrifice 536 kilos of titadine,' said Pablo, looking pointedly at Barros.

'The reality,' said Elvira, 'is that we have no idea who we are dealing with most of the time. We call them al-Qaeda because it helps us to sleep at night, but we seem to have come up against a very pure form of terrorism whose "goal" is to attack our way of life and "decadent values" at whatever cost. There even seems to be competition between these disparate groups to think up and carry out the most devastating attack possible.'

'This is what we're concerned about here,' said Pablo, enthused by Elvira seeing his point of view. 'Are we experiencing a series of diversionary jabs prior to the main attack – something on the scale of the World Trade Center in New York?'

'What *we* need to know,' said Ramírez, tiring of all the conjecture, 'is where our investigation here, in Seville, should be heading.'

'There is no Juez de Instrucción until Sergio del Rey arrives from Madrid,' said Elvira. 'The Madrid CGI have been pulling in all contacts of Hammad and Saoudi for interviews, but so far they appear to have been operating alone. The Guardia Civil have successfully plotted the route taken by the Peugeot Partner from Madrid to the safe house near Valmojado, where it is believed they were keeping the hexogen. They are having difficulties plotting the route taken by the vehicle from Valmojado down to Seville. There are concerns that it diverted on its route.'

'Where was the last sighting of the Peugeot Partner?' asked Falcón.

'Heading south on the NIV/E5. It stopped at a service station near Valdepeñas. The concern is that ninety kilometres later the road forks. The NIV continues to Cordoba and Seville, while the N323/E902 goes to Jaen and Granada. They are looking at both routes, but it's not easy to track a particular white van amongst the thousands on the roads. Their only chance is if the vehicle stopped and the two men got out so that someone could identify them, as happened at the service station near Valdepeñas.'

'Which means there's a distinct possibility that there's more hexogen elsewhere,' said Pablo. 'Our job at the moment is to find out what connections Botín made, and we'll be speaking to his partner, Esperanza, this morning.'

'That's great,' said Ramírez. 'But what are *we* supposed to do? Keep searching for the non-existent electricians and council inspectors? We're looking like incompetents at the moment. Juez Calderón was doing a good job of protecting us from too much media attention. Now he's in a police cell. A CGI antiterrorist agent has committed suicide and *his* source *could* be a double agent. We're at crisis point here. Our squad can't just carry on as we were.'

'Until we receive forensic information from inside the mosque, there's not a lot else we can do,' said Falcón. 'We can go back to the congregation of the mosque and interview them about Miguel Botín, see what that throws up. But I believe we *should* keep hammering away at the electricians and council inspectors – who *do* exist. They *have* been seen. And if I understand the CNI correctly, the council inspectors created a pretext so that the electricians could plant a bomb. They are the perpetrators of this atrocity. We *have* to find them and the people who sent them. *That*, as the Grupo de Homicidios, is our goal.'

'But possibly one that you can only achieve through quality intelligence,' said Elvira. 'Are they part of an Islamic terrorist cell or not? Perhaps the answer lies somewhere in the history of Miguel Botín, who gave their card to the Imam.'

'And what *about* the Imam?' said Ramírez, not wanting to be thwarted. 'Where is he in all this? Has the CNI search of his apartment been completed? Can we have their findings? Has access to his history finally been granted to someone who's allowed to tell us?'

'We can't access it because we do not hold it,' said Pablo.

'Who does hold it?'

'The Americans.'

'Did you find a heavily annotated copy of that edition of the Koran in the Imam's apartment?' asked Falcón.

'No.'

'So you don't think he was in the loop?' said Ramírez.

'We don't know enough to be able to answer that question.'

The meeting broke up soon after that exchange. The CNI and CGI men left the pre-school together. Elvira asked Falcón to attend the press conference in the Andalucian Parliament building when the new judge arrived, to show a united front. Ramírez was waiting outside the classroom.

'I'm sorry for your loss, Javier,' he said, holding him by the shoulder and shaking his hand. 'I know you and Inés had grown apart, but . . . it's a terrible thing. I hope you didn't go to the crime scene.'

'I did,' said Falcón. 'I don't know what I was thinking. They told me over the phone that he'd been identified as Juez Calderón and that he'd been trying to dispose of a body. I don't know why . . . I just didn't think it would be Inés.'

'Did he do it?'

'I went to talk to him in the patrol car. All he said was: "I didn't do it."'

Ramírez shook his head. Denial was a very common psychological state for husbands when they murdered their wives.

'There's going to be a feeding frenzy,' said Ramírez. 'A lot of people have been waiting for this moment.'

'You know, José Luis, the worst thing . . .' said Falcón, struggling, 'was that she was very badly bruised over her torso, down her left side . . . and it was old bruising.'

'He'd been *beating* her?'

'Her face was completely clear.'

'You'd better take the riot squad with you into that press conference,' said Ramírez. 'They're going to go mad if they hear about that.'

'Inés came round to my house the other night,' said Falcón. 'She was behaving very strangely. I thought for a moment she wanted to get back with me, but now I think she was trying to tell me what was happening to her.'

'Did she seem in pain at all?' asked Ramírez, preferring to stick to the facts.

'She was swearing like I'd never heard her swear before and, yes, she did hold on to her side at one point,' said Falcón. 'She was furious with him for all his . . .'

'Yes, we know,' said Ramírez, who hadn't banked on this level of intimacy.

Falcón's eyes filled, his mind taking its grief in gulps. Ramírez squeezed his shoulder with his huge mahogany hand.

'We'd better start thinking about today,' said Falcón. 'Did you manage to read that file about the unidentified body found at the dump on Monday?'

'Not yet.'

'We don't get that many dead bodies in Seville,' said Falcón. 'And in my career I have never come across such a disfigured corpse, and poisoned with cyanide, too. And all this happens days before a bomb goes off in the city.'

'There doesn't *have* to be a connection,' said Ramírez, wary of letting himself in for more fruitless work.

'But before we get a ton of forensic information from the mosque, I'd like to see if there is one,' said Falcón. 'At least I'd like to identify the victim. It might open up another pathway into this situation.'

'Any pointers before I start reading?'

'The Médico Forense thought he was mid forties, long-haired, desk bound but tanned and didn't wear shoes very much. He had traces of hashish in his blood. There was also tattoo ink in the lymph nodes, which is the reason his hands were severed: they had tattoos on them, small ones, but presumably distinctive.'

'Sounds like a university type to me,' said Ramírez, who was suspicious of anybody with too much education. 'Post-graduate?'

'Or maybe a professor trying to recapture his youth?'

'Spanish?'

'Olive-skinned,' said Falcón. 'He'd had a hernia op. The Médico Forense removed the mesh. See if you can get a match for it, find the company that supplied it and to which hospital. Of course, he might have had it done abroad . . .'

'Do you want me to do this on my own?'

'Take Ferrera with you. She's done some work on this already,' said Falcón. 'Pérez, Serrano and Baena can tour the construction sites of Seville, especially any with immigrant labour. Tell them they *have* to find the electricians.'

'Didn't I hear someone say that you were having a

model made of this guy's head – the one from the dump?'

'The sculptor's a friend of the Médico Forense,' said Falcón. 'I'll follow that up.'

'You missed your session last night,' said Alicia Aguado.

'Something cropped up,' said Consuelo. 'Something very upsetting.'

'That's why we're here.'

'You told me to make sure I had a family member to look after me when I came home after my session on Tuesday evening,' said Consuelo. 'I asked my sister. She was there, but couldn't stay for long. We talked about the session. She could see that I was calm and so she left. Then yesterday afternoon she called me to check that I was still OK, and we chatted and she remembered something she'd meant to ask me about the night before. My new pool man.'

'Pool man?'

'He looks after the pool. He checks the pH levels, hoovers the bottom, skims the surface, cleans the . . .' said Consuelo, getting carried away on the detail.

'OK, Consuelo, I'm not going into the pool-cleaning business,' said Aguado.

'The point is, I don't *have* a new pool man,' said Consuelo. 'The same guy has been coming round every Thursday afternoon since I bought the house. I inherited him from the previous owners.'

'And what?'

Consuelo tried to swallow, but couldn't.

'My sister described him, and it was the same disgusting *chulo* from the Plaza del Pumarejo.'

'Very upsetting,' said Aguado. 'It unnerved you, I'm

384

sure. So you called the police and stayed with your children. I can understand that.'

Silence. Consuelo was slumped to one side of the chair, as if she'd lost some stuffing.

'All right,' said Aguado. 'Tell me what you did, or did not do.'

'I didn't call the police.'

'Why not?'

'I was too embarrassed,' she said. 'I'd have to explain everything.'

'You could have just told them that an undesirable person was snooping around your home.'

'You probably don't know very much about the police,' said Consuelo. 'I was a murder suspect for a couple of weeks five years ago. What they put you through is not so different to what you're doing to me here. You start talking and they smell things. They know when people are hiding the shit in their lives. They see it every day. They'd ask a question like: "Do you think it possible that you know this person?" and what would happen? Especially in my fragile mental state.'

'I know you might find this difficult to believe, but to me this is a positive development,' said Aguado.

'It makes *me* feel like a failure,' said Consuelo. 'I don't know whether this person could be a danger to my children, and just because of my own shame I'm prepared to put them at risk.'

'But at least now I know that he's real,' said Aguado.

Silence from Consuelo, who hadn't considered this alarming possibility.

'Our minds have ways of correcting imbalances,' said Aguado. 'So, for instance, a powerful chief executive who controls thousands of people's lives may redress the balance by dreaming of being at school and the teacher telling him what to do. This is a very benign form of balancing things out. More aggressive forms exist. It's not unusual to find successful businessmen who visit a dominatrix in order to be tied up, rendered powerless and punished. A New York psychologist told me he had clients who went to nurseries where they could wear nappies and sit in oversized playpens. The danger comes with the uncertainty between the fantastic, the real and the illusory. The mind becomes confused and cannot differentiate, and then a breakdown can ensue, with possible lasting damage.'

'What you mean is, I've had the fantasy and I may take the next step and seek out the reality.'

'But at least you weren't describing an illusion to me,' said Aguado. 'Before your sister confirmed his existence, I wasn't sure how advanced you were. I told you not to allow yourself to be distracted on your way here because, if he was real, then the reality you were seeking was very dangerous for you . . . personally. This man has no idea of the nature of your problems. He has sensed some vulnerability and is probably just a predator.'

'He knows my name and that my husband is dead,' said Consuelo. 'Those two details came out when he accosted me on Monday night.'

'Then you really should talk to the police about it,' said Aguado. 'If they think you're strange, refer them to me.'

'Then they'll know I'm a lunatic and take no notice,' said Consuelo. 'There's been a bomb in

Seville, and a rich bitch is worried about a *chulo* in her garden.'

'Try talking to them,' said Aguado. 'This man might assault or rape you.'

Silence.

'What are you doing now, Consuelo?'

'I'm looking at you.'

'And you're thinking . . .?'

'That I trust you more than I've trusted anyone in my life.'

'Anyone? Even your parents?'

'I loved my parents, but they knew nothing about me,' said Consuelo.

'So who have you trusted in your life?'

'I trusted an art dealer in Madrid for a bit, until he moved down here,' said Consuelo.

'Who else?' asked Aguado. 'What about Raúl?'

'No, he didn't love me,' said Consuelo, 'and he lived in a closed-off world, trapped by his own misery. He didn't talk to me about his problems and I didn't reveal my own.'

'Was there anything between you and the art dealer?'

'No, our attraction was nothing remotely sexual or romantic.'

'What was it then?'

'We recognized that we were complicated people, with secrets we couldn't talk about. But he did once tell me that he'd killed a man.'

'That's not an easy thing to do,' said Aguado, sensing that they might be closer to the heart of the tangled knot than Consuelo suspected.

'We were drinking brandy in a bar on the Gran Via. I was depressed. I'd just told him everything about my abortions. He traded this secret of his, but he said it was an accident when, in fact, it was much more shameful than that.'

'More shameful than appearing in a pornographic movie to pay for an abortion?'

'Of course it was. He'd killed somebody for –'

Consuelo stopped as if she'd been knifed in the throat. The next word wouldn't come out. She could only cough up a croak as if there was a blade across her windpipe. A powerful shudder of emotion rippled through her. Aguado released her wrist, grabbed her by the arm to steady her. A strange sound came from Consuelo as she slid to the floor. It was something like an orgasmic cry, and, in fact, it was a release, but not one of pleasure. It was a cry of acute pain.

Aguado had not expected to reach this point so quickly in the treatment, but then the mind was an unpredictable organ. It threw things up all the time, vomited horrors into the consciousness and, this was the strange thing, sometimes the conscious mind could hurdle these terrible revelations, side-step them, leap across the sudden chasm. Other times it was scythed to the ground. Consuelo had just experienced the equivalent of being hit by a half-ton bull from behind. She ended up in the foetal position on the Afghan rug, squeaking, as if something enormous was trying to get out.

27

The pressroom in the Andalucian Parliament building was filled to capacity, and there were more people outside in the corridors. The double doors had been left open. It was inconceivable to Falcón that something hadn't leaked. The heaving level of interest in a routine press conference could not be so vast.

The gravity of the revelations had brought Comisario Lobo to the conference and his glowering presence was a comfort. Lobo commanded respect. He induced fear. Nobody took his huge frame and coarse cumin complexion lightly. He was the most senior policeman in Seville and yet he seemed to be a man just managing to keep the lid on an extremely violent temperament.

On the raised platform were six chairs set behind two tables, on which had been placed six microphones. The six stars of the press conference – Comisarios Lobo and Elvira, Juez del Rey, the Magistrado Juez Decano de Sevilla Spinola, Inspectors Jefe Barros and Falcón – were standing in the wings, occupying themselves with the folded lengths of card on which their names were printed. Del Rey had arrived only five minutes earlier, having taken a cab straight from the Estación Santa Justa. He looked remarkably calm for a man who'd been woken up at 6.15 in the morning and told to catch the next AVE train to Seville and take control of the largest criminal investigation Andalucía had ever seen.

At exactly 9.30 Lobo led them out, like a cadre of gladiators being presented to the public. There was a clatter of shutters and flickering of flashes from the photojournalists. Lobo sat in the middle, held up a large finger and surveyed his audience, who instantly battened down to total silence.

'The prime objective of this press conference is to introduce the new team who will be conducting the investigation into the Seville bombing, now referred to as 6th June.'

He presented each member of the team, explaining their role. There was a human tremor at the introduction of Sergio del Rey as the new judge directing the investigation, which meant that Falcón's role was lost in the aftershock.

'Where's Juez Calderón?' shouted a voice from the back of the room.

Lobo's huge finger was raised once again, this time with a slightly admonishing edge to it. Silence fell.

'The Magistrado Juez Decano de Sevilla will now explain the reason behind the change in our Juez de Instrucción.'

Spinola stood up and gave a similar, terse and factual description of the events of the early morning down by the Guadalquivir river as Elvira had done an hour earlier. When he'd finished there was a missed beat and then a roar, as of a crowd in an enclosed basketball arena who'd just witnessed a heinous foul. Their hands came out waving pens, notebooks, and dictaphones. When their shouting failed to penetrate they started screaming, like maddened traders in the bear pit of a crashing *bourse*. It was impossible to hear any questions. Lobo stood. The Colossus of the Jefatura made no impact. The scandal was just too vast, and the herd too demented, to care about his immense authority. The journalists rushed the platform. Falcón was grateful for the barrier of the table. Lobo was decisive. The six men left the stage just managing not to break into a run for the door at the back. Barros was the last man out and he had to wrest his arm from the clutches of a woman's blood-red nails. The door was shut and locked by security. The journalists hammered from the other side. The double doors seemed to swell, as if they might be about to burst open.

'There's no talking to them,' said Lobo. 'And, anyway, there's nothing to be said beyond that statement. We'll hold another press conference later and ask them to present their questions beforehand.'

They left the building and all except Lobo, Elvira and Spinola were driven back to the pre-school. Juez del Rey still hadn't completed his reading of the case file, which was already huge. He said he'd need until midday to complete it and then he would like a meeting with the investigating team.

Falcón called Dr Pintado, the Médico Forense who'd handled the unidentified corpse from the dump, and asked for Miguel Covo's number, saying he had to see anything that the sculptor had been able to accomplish as soon as possible. Pintado said that Covo would call if he had anything to show.

A call came through on his personal mobile. It was Angel. He should have turned the damn thing off.

'I was there,' said Angel. 'I've never seen anything like that in my life.'

'I thought we were going to have to fire tear gas at you lot,' said Falcón, trying to keep it light.

'This is a disaster for your investigation.'

'Juez del Rey is a very capable man.'

'You're talking to me, Javier – Angel Zarrías: public relations expert. What you've got on your hands is . . .'

'We know, but what can we do? We can't turn the clock back and bring Inés back to life.'

'I'm sorry,' he said, her name reminding him to be solicitous. 'I'm really sorry, Javier. I just got carried away with the madness in there. It must have been hard for you. Not even your experience could have prepared you for that.'

The saliva thickened in Falcón's mouth as the bitterness of his grief hit him again in another unexpected wave. He was surprised. He'd thought he'd rid himself of all emotional entanglements with Inés and yet here were these odd residues. He'd loved her, or at least he thought he'd loved her, and he was amazed at how that seemed to have stood the test of her cruelty and selfishness.

'What can I do for you, Angel?' he said, businesslike.

'Look, Javier, I'm not a fool. I know you can't talk about anything even if you did know what had happened,' he said. 'I just want you to know that the *ABC* is on your side. I've spoken to the editor. If Comisario Elvira needs help we're prepared to give our full support.'

'I'll tell him, Angel,' said Falcón. 'I've got to go now, I've got another call.'

Falcón closed down that mobile and opened the other. It was the sculptor, Miguel Covo. He had something to show him. He gave Falcón directions to his workshop. Falcón said he could be there in ten minutes. He called Elvira on the way and mentioned the conversation with Angel Zarrías.

'Nothing comes for free in this world,' said Elvira, 'but we *are* going to need all the help we can get. I've just read the autopsy report and . . . I'm sorry, Javier, I shouldn't have mentioned that.'

'I saw her,' said Falcón, his stomach lurching.

But he didn't want to hear it. He'd read autopsies before of battered wives and girlfriends and been stunned at the body's capacity to absorb punishment and still keep going. He tuned himself out from Elvira's voice. He really didn't want to know what Inés had suffered.

'. . . a civilized man, a respected and brilliant legal mind, a cultured person. We used to bump into each other at the opera. There's no telling, Javier. It's a terrifying thought that even these certainties cannot be trusted.'

'Perhaps I shouldn't have told you about Angel Zarrías's offer.'

'I don't follow you.'

'That's Angel Zarrías's talent. He has a genius for the manipulation of image.'

'The suspicion is going to be that we knew about Calderón's behaviour and condoned it with our silence because of his exceptional ability,' said Elvira, who seemed more panicked by the power of the media now that he'd lost Calderón, his brilliant front man. 'Things are going to come out once Inspector Jefe Zorrita starts

digging. And then there'll be all the women he was . . .
you know . . .'

'Fucking?'

'That wasn't the word I was after, but, yes, I understand it wasn't just one or two,' said Elvira. 'Less scrupulous newspapers than the *ABC* might get hold of them and there'll be more stories stretching back over the years . . . We'll all look complete idiots, or worse, for not having spotted the flaws in his character beforehand.'

'None of us *did* know about it,' said Falcón. 'So we shouldn't feel guilty about presenting our case. And it's the way of the world that these things have to be conducted through the media. But at least some good will come out of it.'

'How's that?'

'It will change people's perceptions. They'll now know that anyone can be an abuser of women. It's not the preserve of uneducated brutes with no self-control, but possibly civilized, cultured, intelligent men who can be moved to tears by *Tosca*.'

They hung up. Covo's workshop was near the Plaza de Pelicano, an ugly, modern square of 1970s apartment blocks, whose central sitting area had become a place where dog owners brought their pets to shit. Falcón parked outside Covo's studio in an adjacent compound of small workshops and took a digital camera out of the glove compartment.

'I used to keep it all in the house,' said Covo, as he led Falcón through a steel-caged door into a room that was completely bare of any decoration and had only a table and two chairs. 'But my wife started to complain when I worked my way into other rooms.'

Covo made some strong coffee and broke the filter off a Ducado and lit it. His head was shaved to a fine white bristle all over. He wore half-moon glasses with gold rims, so that he looked like an accountant from the neck up. He was slim with a nut-brown body, and his arms and legs were all sinew and wiry muscle. This was all visible because he wore a black string vest, a pair of running shorts and sandals.

'The only problem with this place is that it gets very hot in the summer,' he said.

They drank coffee. Covo didn't volunteer any more information. He studied Falcón's face, eyes flicking up and down, side to side. He nodded, smoked, drank his coffee. Falcón did not feel uneasy. He was glad to have a respite from the madness of the world outside in the company of this strange individual.

'We're all unique,' said Covo, after some minutes, 'and yet remarkably the same.'

'There are types,' said Falcón. 'I've noticed that.'

'The only problem is that we live in a part of Europe where there has been a lot of genetic exchange. So that, for instance, you will find the Berber genetic marker e3b both in North Africa and on the Iberian peninsula,' said Covo. 'Much as we'd like to, we're not going to be able to tell you where exactly your corpse comes from, other than that he is either Spanish or North African.'

'That's already something,' said Falcón. 'How did you find the genetic marker?'

'Dr Pintado has been calling in some favours from the labs,' said Covo. 'Your corpse has good teeth. You already know that he's had corrective work to make them straight; expensive and unusual for someone of his generation. The work was not done in Spain.'

'You've been very thorough.'

'I presumed that this man's death has something to do with the bomb, so I have been working hard and fast,' said Covo. 'The important thing is to work out how this affects the shape of the face and the overall effect of good teeth is impressive. Hair is also important, head and facial.'

'You think he was bearded?'

'The job they did with the acid was not as thorough as it could have been. I'm certain he was bearded, but that presents other problems. How did he keep it? All I can say is that it wasn't long and shaggy. The teeth perhaps indicate a man who cared about his appearance.'

'And he kept his hair long.'

'Yes, and he had high cheekbones,' said Covo. 'A prominent nose – part of the septum was still intact. I think we're talking about a rather striking individual, which was why they probably went to such lengths to destroy his features.'

'I'm surprised they didn't smash up his teeth.'

'They would have had to extract each one to make sure. It was probably too time-consuming,' said Covo. 'Let me show you what I've done.'

Covo stubbed out his Ducado after a last long drag and they went into the studio. Lights came on in certain areas. In the centre of the room was a block of stone from which a number of faces were emerging. They all gave the impression of struggle, as if they were inside the rock and nosing out into the world, desperate to be free from the stultifying substance. Around the walls, in the gloom, were the spectators. Hundreds of heads, some in clay, others frighteningly real in wax.

'I don't let many people in here,' said Covo. 'They get spooked.'

'By the silence, I imagine,' said Falcón. 'One would expect so many faces to be expressing themselves.'

'It reminds people too much of death,' said Covo. 'My talent is not artistic. I am a craftsman. I can recreate a face, but I cannot give it life. They are inanimate, without the motivation of soul. I embalm people in wax and clay.'

'The faces coming out of the rock seem animated to me,' said Falcón.

'I think I've started to feel the restraint of my own mortality,' said Covo. 'Let me show you our friend.'

To the right of the block of stone was a table with what looked like four heads under a sheet.

'I made up four copies of his faceless head,' said Covo. 'Then I made a series of sketches of how I thought he looked. Finally, I started to build.'

He lifted the sheet off the first head. It had no nose, mouth or ears.

'Here I'm trying to get the feeling for how much skin and fat would cover the bones,' said Covo. 'I've looked at the whole body and estimated the extent of his covering.'

He lifted the sheet off the next two heads.

'Here I've been working with the features, trying to fit the nose, mouth, ears and eyes together on the face,' said Covo. 'The third one, as you've probably noticed, is more decisive. Once I've reached this stage I do more sketches, working with hair and colour. This fourth figure I made last night. I painted him and attached the hair just this morning. It's my best guess.'

The sheet slipped off to reveal a head with brown

eyes, long lashes, aquiline nose, sharp cheekbones, but with the cheeks themselves slightly sunken. The beard was clipped close to the skin, the hair long, dark and flowing and the teeth white and perfect.

'I'm only worried that I may have got carried away,' said Covo, 'and made him too dashing.'

Falcón took photographs, while Covo made a selection from the sketches of other possible looks. By 11 a.m. Falcón was heading back across the river to the Jefatura. He had the sketches scanned and the image of the victim transferred to the computer. He called Pintado and asked him to email the dental X-rays. He put together a page with the corpse's approximate age, height and weight, the information about the hernia op, tattoos and skull fracture. He called Pablo, who gave him the email address of the right man in the CNI in Madrid who would distribute it to all other intelligence agencies, the FBI and Interpol.

Ramírez called just as he was leaving.

'I've spoken to the vascular surgeon at the hospital,' he said. 'He's identified the hernia mesh taken from the body as one known by the trade name SURUMESH, made by Suru International Ltd of Mumbai in India.'

'Does he use them?'

'For inguinal hernias he uses a German make called TiMESH.'

'You're learning stuff, José Luis.'

'I'm completely fascinated,' said Ramírez, drily. 'He tells me Suru International would probably supply hospitals through medical supplies wholesalers.'

'I'll speak to Pablo. The CNI can get a list from Suru International.'

'Then they've got to contact the hospitals supplied

by those wholesalers. It's quite possible that a hospital takes meshes made by a number of different manufacturers. Then there are the specialist hernia clinics. This is going to take time.'

'We're moving on a lot of fronts,' said Falcón. 'I have a face to work with now. We have dental X-rays. I'm thinking more about America. He had orthodontic work done –'

'Most inguinal hernias occur over the age of forty,' said Ramírez. 'Dr Pintado estimates the guy's hernia op as three years old. So we're only looking at, say, the last four, maximum five years of hernia operations. Maybe two and a half million ops worldwide.'

'Keep thinking positively, José Luis.'

'I'll see you next year.'

Falcón told him about the meeting with Juez del Rey at midday and hung up. He sent another email about Suru International to his contact in the CNI. He got up to leave again. His personal mobile vibrated, no name came up on the screen. He took the call anyway.

'*Diga*,' he said.

'It's me, Consuelo.'

He sat down slowly, thinking, my God. His stomach leapt, his blood came alive. His heart beat loudly in his head.

'It's been a long time,' he said.

'I saw the news about Inés,' she said. 'I wanted to tell you how sorry I am and to let you know that I'm thinking of you. I know you must be very busy . . . so I won't keep you.'

'Thank you, Consuelo,' he said, willing something else to come to mind. 'It's good to hear your voice again. When I saw you in the street . . .'

'I'm sorry for that, too,' she said. 'It couldn't be helped.'

He didn't know what that meant. He needed something to keep her on the phone. Nothing seemed relevant. His mind was too full of the corpse, hernia meshes and two and a half million ops world-wide.

'I should let you go,' she said. 'You must be under a lot of pressure.'

'It was good of you to call.'

'It was the least I could do,' she said.

'I'd like to hear from you again, you know.'

'I'm thinking of you, Javier,' she said, and it was all over.

He sat back, looking at the phone as if her voice was still inside it. She'd kept his number for four years. She was thinking of him. Do these things have meaning? Was that just social convention? It didn't feel like it. He saved her number.

The car park at the back of the Jefatura was brutally hot, the car windscreens blinded by the sun in the clear sky. Falcón sat in the car with the air conditioning blasting into his face. Those few sentences, the sound of her voice, had opened up a whole chapter of memory which he'd closed off for years. He shook his head and pulled out of the Jefatura car park. He headed for El Cerezo the back way, via the Expo ground, crossing the river at the Puente del Alamillo. He arrived at the bombsite at the same time as Ramírez.

'Any news about the electricians?' asked Falcón.

'Pérez called. They've been through seventeen building sites. Nothing.'

'What's Ferrera doing?'

'She's chasing down witnesses who might have seen

our friend with the hernia being dumped in the bin on Calle Boteros.'

They went into the pre-school. Juez del Rey was alone, waiting for them in the classroom. They sat down on the edges of the school desks. Del Rey folded his arms and stared into the floor. He gave them a perfect recap of the major findings of the investigation so far. He didn't use notes. He got all the names of the Moroccan witnesses correct. He had the whole timetable of what had happened in and around the mosque, in his head. He'd decided to make an impression on the two detectives and it worked. Falcón felt Ramírez relax. Calderón's replacement was no fool.

'The two most significant recent developments in the investigation concern me the most,' said del Rey 'Ricardo Gamero's suicide and the belief that his source was working as a double agent.'

'We had a sighting of Gamero by a security guard in the Archaeological Museum in the Parque María Luisa,' said Falcón. 'We've got a police artist working on some sketches of the older man he was seen talking to.'

'I'll call Serrano,' said Ramírez, 'see how that's going.'

'I'm not convinced that a sense of failure at preventing this bomb attack from taking place was enough to drive a man like Gamero to suicide,' said del Rey. 'There's something more. Failure is too general. Feeling personally responsible is what drives people to kill themselves.'

'The police artist didn't have much luck with the security guard last night,' said Ramírez, coming back from his call. 'He's been with him again this morning. They should have something by lunchtime.'

'I'm not convinced by Miguel Botín as a double, either,' said del Rey. 'His brother was maimed by an Islamic terrorist bomb, for God's sake. Can you see someone like that being turned?'

'He was a convert,' said Falcón. 'He took his religion very seriously. It's difficult to know what sort of impression a charismatic radical preacher could make on someone like that. We have the example of Mohammed Sidique Khan, one of the London bombers, who was transformed from a special needs teacher into a radical militant.'

'We don't know what the relationship between Miguel Botín and his injured brother was like, either,' said Ramírez.

'I'm also uncomfortable about the electricians and the fake council inspectors. I don't buy the CNI line that they were a terrorist cell. The CNI seem to me to be trying to cram square information into a round hole.'

There was a knock at the door. A policeman put his head round.

'The forensics have been working their way through the rubble above the storeroom in the mosque,' he said. 'They've found a fireproof, shock-proof metal box. It's been taken to the forensic tent and they thought you might like to be there when they open it.'

28

Outside the pre-school everybody was wearing masks against the stench and Falcón, Ramírez and del Rey walked with their hands clasped over their mouths and noses. There was an anteroom to the main body of the forensics' tent, where they all dressed in white hooded boiler suits and put on masks. The interior of the tent was air conditioned down to 22°C. Five forensic teams were currently working at the site. All of them had stopped for the opening of the box. Something within the human psyche making it impossible, even for forensics, to resist the mystery of a closed, secure container.

A dictaphone was tested and set in the middle of the table. The leader of the forensic team nodded to the judge and detectives as they gathered around. His hands, in latex gloves, were spread on either side of a red metal box. Next to him was a shallow cardboard evidence box, dated and with the address of the Imam's apartment on the lid. Inside were three small plastic bags containing keys. A white-suited figure nudged into Falcón. It was Gregorio.

'This could be interesting if those keys open that box,' he said. 'Two sets came from the desk and one from the kitchen of the Imam's apartment.'

'Are we ready?' asked the forensics team leader. 'Here we are on Thursday, 8th June 2006 at 12.24 hours. We have a sealed metal box, which has sustained some blast damage to the lid, although the lock still appears to be sound. We are going to attempt to open this box, using keys taken from the Imam's apartment during a search of those premises on Wednesday, 7th June 2006.'

He rejected the first sachet of keys but selected the next one and poured the two keys into his hand. He fitted one of the identical keys into the lock, turned it, and the lid sprang open.

'The box has been successfully opened by a key found in the kitchen drawer of the Imam's apartment.'

He opened the lid and lifted out three coloured plastic folders, thick with folded paper. This emptied the box, which was removed to another table. He opened up the first green folder.

'Here we have one sheet of writing in Arabic script, which has been paper-clipped to what appears to be a set of architect's drawings.'

He opened out the drawings, which proved to be a detailed plan of a secondary school in San Bernardo. The other two folders followed the same pattern. The second set of drawings featured the plan of a primary school in Triana, and the third, the biology faculty on Avenida de la Reina Mercedes.

Silence, while the men and women of the forensic teams contemplated their find. Falcón could feel the minds in the room working their way towards more and more uneasy conclusions. Each Islamic terrorist atrocity had released new viral strains of horror into the body of the West. No sooner had the West become reconciled to men as bombs, than they had to accept women as bombs, and even children as bombs. It seemed sickeningly obvious now that car bombs would transmute to boats as bombs, and then planes as bombs. Finally the atrocities would no longer remain at a distance in the Middle East, Far East or America, but come to Madrid and London. Then there was the unimaginable. The stuff that would make a horror novelist tremble at night: executions beamed around the world of men and women being beheaded with kitchen knives. And finally Beslan: children held hostage, given no food or water, explosives hung over their heads. How is an ordinary mind supposed to work under these conditions of easy contagion?

'Were they going to blow these places up?' asked a voice.

'Take hostages,' said a woman. 'Look, they're after kids from five years old up to twenty-five years old.'

'Bastards.'

'Is there nothing these people won't do? Are there no fucking boundaries?'

'I think,' said Juez del Rey, quick to put a lid on the mounting hysteria, 'that we should wait until we have translations of the Arabic script in our hands before we jump to conclusions.'

It was not the voice of reason that people wanted to hear. Not just yet, anyway. They'd been waiting a long time to get their hands on solid evidence and now they'd found something spectacular they wanted to vent some of their anger. Del Rey sensed this. He moved things along once more.

'As a precaution, these three buildings should be searched. If there was a plan to seize them it's possible that weaponry has been stored there.'

Everybody nodded, glad to see that even the man from Madrid suffered the same paranoia, the same corrupted brain circuit as themselves.

'Let's get these drawings and the Arabic texts through the forensic process as soon as possible. We need those translations fast,' he said.

'There's something else,' said the forensics team leader. 'The bomb disposal people have come across something interesting on the explosives front.'

An army officer in white overalls with a green armband pushed his way through to the table.

'So far we've only had full access to the area above the storeroom, because there's no evidence of bodies or human tissue. We still believe that the main destructive explosion was caused by a large quantity of hexogen being detonated, but we have also found trace evidence of Goma 2 Eco, which is the mining explosive that was used in the Madrid bombings.'

'Did one set off the other?'

'It's certainly possible, but we have no way of proving it.'

'Is there any reason why two types of explosive would be used?'

'Goma 2 Eco is industrial quality, whereas hexogen is military. If you have a large quantity of hexogen, which has greater brisance than Goma 2 Eco, I don't see why you'd use a lower grade explosive, unless your intention was to cause other distracting explosions, or to hold people in a state of fear.'

'You estimated the hexogen stored in the building to be in the region of 100 kilos,' said del Rey.

'Conservative estimate.'

'What sort of damage would 100 kilos do to these schools and the university faculty on these drawings?'

'A real expert, who understood the architecture of the buildings, could probably raze them to the ground,' said the army officer. 'But it would be a demolition job. They would have to drill into the reinforced skeleton of the building and wire the charges together for a simultaneous explosion.'

'And what about people?'

'If everyone was herded into one or two rooms of each building, with 30 kilos of hexogen there would be no, or only very few, survivors.'

'Is it possible for you to tell how much Goma 2 Eco exploded in the storeroom of the mosque?'

'Personally, I would say 25 kilos or less, but I wouldn't be able to stand up in court and say that, because the hexogen trace is too dominant.'

'Is hexogen manufactured in Spain?'

'No. The UK, Italy, Germany, USA and Russia,' he said. 'They probably make it in China, too, but they're not telling us if they are.'

'Why go to the trouble of importing it?'

'Its availability,' said the army officer. 'Wherever there's conflict in the world, there's ordnance, and hexogen can easily be extracted from it. You end up with low-volume high explosive which is untraceable, easy to transport, hide and disguise. Domestic gunpowder magazines are more tightly controlled since 11th March, although there have been thefts – for instance in Portugal last year. I would also say that the chances of hexogen being spotted in an open European transport system are slim. Whereas mounting a robbery of a gunpowder magazine in this country would get you lower grade explosive, and draw the immediate attention of the authorities.'

'What about the home-made variety, used in the London bombings?' asked del Rey. 'Wouldn't it be easier to mix up easily available ingredients than go to the trouble and risk of bringing in hexogen, or stealing Goma 2 Eco?'

'You're right, triaceton triperoxide can be made quite easily, but I wouldn't like to be around someone dealing with it, unless he had a chemistry post-graduate degree and we were operating in temperature-controlled laboratory conditions. It's volatile,' he said. 'Also it depends on what sort of atrocity you want to commit. TATP is fine if you're intent on killing people, but if you want a spectacular explosion, with serious destruction and loss of life, then hexogen is much more capable of doing that. Hexogen is also stable and not temperature sensitive, something that's important at this time of year in a place like Seville, where daytime temperatures can vary by as much as twenty degrees.'

The work rate was increasing. Material was coming in at a constant rate from the bombsite. Bits of credit card, scraps of ID, driving licences, strips of clothing, shoes. The more macabre findings, such as body parts, were taken to the tented morgue next door. While del Rey watched the forensic work, Falcón briefed Elvira, who'd just arrived from a meeting in the town hall with the Mayor, Comisario Lobo and Magistrado Juez

Decano Spinola. Elvira ordered searches of the three buildings immediately. Evacuation would be carried out by the local police and searches conducted by the bomb squad in case of booby traps. Elvira was concerned that other terrorist cells might have become active, preparing to take over the buildings. The CGI had to be alerted. Gregorio of the CNI was already in touch with Pablo, who was asking for the translations to be sent to him by secure email as soon as they were ready.

Falcón, Ramírez and del Rey stripped off their boiler suits in the forensic tent's anteroom and went back to the pre-school to resume their meeting.

'What do you make of *that* development, Inspector Jefe?' asked del Rey.

'We were asked to keep an open mind in this investigation, especially by the senior CNI man,' said Falcón. 'And yet, since we found the Peugeot Partner and its contents, almost all subsequent findings have directed us towards the belief that an Islamic terrorist campaign was being planned in this mosque.'

'*Almost* all subsequent findings?'

'We cannot satisfactorily explain the fake council inspectors and the electricians, and yet we are very suspicious of their involvement,' said Falcón. 'They seem to be an intrinsic part of the actual explosion. Now that we've spoken to the bomb squad officer it seems clear that a smaller device was planted, which set off the stored hexogen. We have a link between Miguel Botín and the electricians. He was seen handing over the card to the Imam. But who was he working for?'

'You don't buy the CNI line either?'

'I would if there was any proof for it, but there's none.'

'What about those keys from the Imam's apartment opening the box?' said Ramírez. 'Where does that place the Imam now?'

'As part of the plot,' said del Rey.

'Except that the keys were found in a kitchen drawer,' said Falcón. 'I find that strange when all the other keys were kept in his desk. And the two keys were identical. Would you keep them together?'

'If we are to believe that Botín was a double agent and that he was serving up the Imam to the CGI on behalf of another terrorist commander, as the CNI seem to think, then what are we to make of the drawings in the metal box?' asked del Rey.

'The Imam's keys opened the box, therefore whatever is in that box is an expendable operation,' said Falcón. 'The CNI would be forced to admit it was another part of the diversion.'

'And what do you think, Inspector Jefe?'

'I don't have enough information to think anything,' said Falcón.

'You said you were keeping an open mind, Inspector Jefe. What does that mean exactly? That you've been conducting other enquiries?'

Falcón told him about Informáticalidad, giving the background on Horizonte and I4IT. He gave their reasons for buying the property and how the sales reps used it. He also told him about Informáticalidad's recruiting procedure.

'Well, all that sounds strange, but I can't see anything in particular that's pointing to their involvement in this scenario.'

'I've never heard anything like it,' said Ramírez.

'So far, the only illegal thing I can find is that they used black money to buy the apartment,' said Falcón. 'I've been trying to find something that links them to what was going on in the mosque.'

'And you haven't found it.'

'The only connection is that one of the churches used in recruiting employees for Informáticalidad was the same one used by the CGI antiterrorist agent Ricardo Gamero – San Marcos.'

'But you have no proof that Gamero met anyone from Informáticalidad?'

'None. I spoke to the priest from San Marcos and I would describe some of his responses as extremely guarded, but that's all.'

'Are you hoping that the police artist's drawing of the man Gamero met in the museum is going to provide that link to Informáticalidad?'

'That's a tricky process: to extract a likeness from a museum security guard's view of a person he wasn't particularly interested in,' said Falcón. 'They're looking for troublemakers, not two adults having a conversation.'

'Which is why, after five hours, we still have nothing,' said Ramírez

'We're also pushing forward with an enquiry we started the day before the bomb,' said Falcón, and described the circumstances of the mutilated corpse.

'And because of the timing, you think that there might be a link to the bombing?' asked del Rey.

'Not just that; after this particularly brutal treatment to hide the victim's identity, the body had been sewn into a shroud. That struck me as respectful and religiously motivated. The corpse also had what is known as a Berber genetic marker, which means that he was either from the Iberian peninsula or North African.'

'You said he was poisoned.'

'He ingested it,' said Falcón, 'which could imply that he didn't know he was being "executed". Then they removed his identity but treated him with respect.'

'And how will this help us to identify the fake council inspectors and the electricians?'

'I won't know that until I identify the murdered man,' said Falcón. 'I'm hoping that can be done now that an image of the victim's face and a full set of dental X-rays have been sent out to intelligence services worldwide, including Interpol and the FBI.'

Del Rey nodded, scribbled notes.

'We're not getting anywhere looking for these electricians through conventional channels,' said Ramírez.

'While the bomb squad officer was talking, it occurred to me that an explosives expert would have to know about electronics and therefore probably electrics in general,' said Falcón. 'Goma 2 Eco is a mining explosive, so perhaps we should sit our witnesses down in front of photo IDs for all licensed explosive handlers in Spain.'

'Have your witnesses been able to describe the electricians?'

'The most reliable one is a Spanish convert called José Duran, but he couldn't describe them very well. There didn't seem to be anything particular about them.'

'Witnesses plural, you said.'

'There's an old Moroccan guy, but he didn't even spot that the two labourers weren't Spanish.'

'Maybe we should send an artist along to see José Duran while he looks at the licensed explosive handlers,' said Ramírez. 'I'll get on to it.'

Falcón gave him his mobile to extract Duran's number. Ramírez left the room.

'I'm concerned that the CNI are either not seeing things straight, or they're not telling us everything we should know,' said del Rey. 'I don't know why they haven't let you into the Imam's apartment yet.'

'They're not concerned about what happened here any more,' said Falcón. 'This explosion was either a mistake or a decoy, and either way there's no point in expending energy to find out very little when there's possibly another, more devastating attack being planned elsewhere.'

'But you don't agree with the CNI's point of view?'

'I think there are two forces at play here,' said Falcón. 'One force is an Islamic terrorist group, who appeared to be planning an attack using hexogen, brought here in the Peugeot Partner and stored in the mosque . . .'

'An attack on those schools and the biology faculty?'

'Let's see what forensic information we get, if any, from the drawings and the texts,' said Falcón. 'And also the content of the translations.'

'And the other force?'

'I don't know.'

'But how does this force manifest itself?'

'By a breakdown of logic in the scenario,' said Falcón. 'We can't fit the council inspectors and the electricians into our scenario, nor can we explain the Goma 2 Eco.'

'But who do you think this force is?'

'What are these Islamic terrorist groups fighting for,

or who do you think they're fighting against?' asked Falcón.

'It's difficult to say. There doesn't seem to be any coherent agenda or strategy. They just seem to be meting out a series of punishments. London and Madrid were supposedly because of Iraq. Nairobi, the USS *Cole* and the Twin Towers because they believe that America is an evil empire. Bali because of Australian action in East Timor against the Islamic nation of Indonesia. Casablanca was supposedly against Spanish and Jewish targets. Karachi . . . I don't know; it was the Sheraton, wasn't it?'

'And that's our problem here,' said Falcón. 'We have no idea who their enemy is. Perhaps this other force is just a group of people who've had enough and decided they don't want to be passively terrorized any more. They want to fight back. They want to preserve their way of life – whether it's considered decadent or not. They could be the people behind the VOMIT website. They could be an unknown local Andalucian group who've heard about the MILA and perceived it as a threat to them and their families. Maybe it's a religious group who want to maintain the sanctity of the Catholic faith in Spain and drive Islam back into North Africa. Or perhaps we are even more decadent than we know and this is pure power play. Somebody has seen the political or economic potential in terrifying the population. When those planes hit the Twin Towers everything changed. People see things differently now – both good and bad people. Once a new chapter in the human history of horror has been opened, all sorts of people start applying their creative powers to the writing of its next paragraphs.'

29

'Did you manage to talk to your ex-mentor, Marco Barreda, at Informáticalidad?' asked Falcón.

'I did better than that,' said David Curado. 'I went to see him.'

'How did that go?'

'Well, I called him and started to tell him what you and I talked about, and he stopped me, said it was a pity we hadn't seen each other since I'd left the company and why didn't we meet for a beer and a tapa?'

'Has that happened before?'

'No way, we've only ever talked on the phone,' said Curado. 'I was surprised; you're not even supposed to talk to ex-employees, let alone meet them for a beer.'

'Was it just the two of you?'

'Yes, and it was odd,' said Curado. 'He'd been all enthusiastic on the phone, but when we met it was almost as if he'd changed his mind about the whole thing. He seemed distracted, but I could tell it was an act.'

'How?'

415

'I told him about our conversation and he barely took any notice,' said Curado. 'But then I asked the question about Ricardo Gamero and he was stunned. I asked him who this Ricardo Gamero was, and he said he was a member of his church who'd committed suicide that afternoon. As you know, I used to go to San Marcos myself and I'd never come across Ricardo Gamero, so I asked him if he'd killed himself because the cops were after him and Marco said that the guy *was* a cop.'

'How do you think he'd taken the news of Ricardo Gamero's suicide?'

'He was sick about it, I could tell. Very upset, he was.'

'Were they friends?'

'I assume so, but he didn't say.'

Falcón knew he had to speak to Marco Barreda directly. Curado gave him his number. They hung up. Falcón sat back in his car, tapping the steering wheel with his mobile. Had Gamero's suicide made Marco Barreda vulnerable? And if that was a weakness and Falcón could get some leverage, would it reveal enough, would it, in fact, reveal anything?

He had no idea what he was getting into. He had spoken to Juez del Rey about these two forces – Islamic terrorism and another, as yet unknown – both of whom had demonstrated a ruthlessness in their operations, but he knew nothing about their structures, nor their aims, other than a preparedness to kill. Had the one movement learnt from the other: declare no coherent agenda, operate a loose command structure, create self-contained, unconnected cells who, having been remotely activated, carry out their destructive mission?

Talking this through to himself produced a moment of clarity. *That* was one cultural difference between Islam and the West: whenever an Islamic attack occurred, the West always looked for the 'mastermind'. There had to be an evil genius at the core, because that was the order that the Western mind demanded: a hierarchy, a plan with an achievable goal. What was the chain?

He worked back from the electrician who'd planted the bomb. He'd been brought in by a call from the Imam, who in turn had been given the electrician's card by Miguel Botín. The card was the connection between the mission and the hierarchy who'd ordered it. Neither the electricians, nor the council inspectors for that matter, had been in the building at the time of the explosion, and both sets of people were as much a part of the plan as the card. This would not be how an Islamic terrorist cell would operate. That would mean, logically, that the only other person who could have activated Miguel Botín was Ricardo Gamero. Why had Gamero committed suicide? Because, in activating Miguel Botín with the electrician's card, Gamero did not realize that he was making him the agent of destruction of the building and all the people inside.

That would be reason enough to take your own life.

On the day of the bombing, the CGI antiterrorist squad couldn't move because of the possibility of a mole in their ranks. Only on day two could Ricardo Gamero have got out and demanded to see someone senior – the older man in the Archaeological Museum – from whom he demanded an explanation. That explanation had not been good enough to prevent his suicide. Falcón called Ramírez.

'Has that police artist come up with a sketch of the man Gamero met in the museum yet?'

'We've just scanned it and sent it to the CNI and CGI.'

'Send a copy to the computer in the pre-school,' said Falcón.

'The witness José Duran is due here any moment. We'll show him the shots of the licensed explosive handlers, but I'm not holding out much hope,' said Ramírez. 'The bomb could have been made up by somebody else and left in the mosque, or he could have been an assistant to an explosives expert and learnt everything necessary.'

'Keep at it, José Luis,' said Falcón. 'If you want a really impossible task, try looking for the fake council inspectors.'

'I'll add that to the list of two and a half million hernia ops I've still got to go through,' said Ramírez.

'Another thought,' said Falcón. 'Contact all the Hermandades associated with the three churches: San Marcos, Santa María La Blanca and La Magdalena.'

'How's that going to help?'

'Whatever's happening here has some religious motivation. Informáticalidad recruits from church congregations. Ricardo Gamero was a devout Catholic attending San Marcos. The Abdullah Azzam text was sent to the *ABC*, the main Catholic newspaper, and it included a direct threat to the Catholic faith in Andalucía.'

'And what do you think the Brotherhoods in these churches could have to do with it?'

'Maybe nothing. You'd be too exposed as a known Brotherhood but, you never know, they may have heard of a secret one, or seen strange things going on in the churches that might give us some leverage with the priests. We have to try everything.'

'This could get ugly,' said Ramírez.

'Even uglier than it is already?'

'The media are all over us again. I've just heard that Comisario Lobo and the Magistrado Juez Decano de Sevilla are going to give another press conference to explain the situation following Juez Calderón's dismissal,' said Ramírez. 'I heard the one at the Parliament building earlier today was a disaster. And now the television and the radio are full of arseholes telling us that since Calderón's arrest on suspicion of murder and wife abuse, our investigation has completely lost credibility.'

'How has all this got out?'

'The journalists have been all over the Palacio de Justicia, talking to Inés's friends and colleagues. Now they're not just talking about the evident physical violence, but also a prolonged campaign of mental torture and public humiliation.'

'This is just what Elvira was frightened of.'

'A lot of people have been waiting a long time to get Esteban Calderón down on the ground and, now they've got him there, they're going to kick him to death, even if it means our investigation is effectively destroyed.'

'And what do Lobo and Spinola hope to achieve in this press conference?' asked Falcón. 'They can't talk about a murder investigation that's in progress.'

'Damage control,' said Ramírez. 'And they're going to talk up del Rey. He's due to come on afterwards, with Comisario Elvira, to give a recap of the case so far.'

'No wonder he was so word perfect with us,' said Falcón. 'Maybe it wouldn't be such a good idea for him to talk about what we're working on now.'

'You're right about that,' said Ramírez. 'You'd better call him.'

Del Rey had switched his mobile off. Maybe he was already in the studio. Falcón called Elvira and asked him to give a rather cryptic message to del Rey. There was no time to explain the detail. Falcón picked up the sketch from the computer operator in the pre-school. At least it looked like a drawing of a real person. A man in his sixties, possibly early seventies, in a suit and tie, some hair on top with a side parting, no beard or moustache. The artist had included the man's height and weight as given by the security guard, he was on the small side at 1.65m and 75 kilos. But did it look like the man they wanted to find?

Back in the car he took a look at the lists given to him by Diego Torres, the Human Resources Director at Informáticalidad. Marco Barreda was not one of the employees who'd spent time in the apartment on Calle Los Romeros. Maybe he was too senior for that. He called the mobile number David Curado had given him and introduced himself with his full title.

'I think we should talk face to face,' said Falcón.

'I'm busy.'

'It'll take fifteen minutes of your time.'

'I'm still busy.'

'I'm investigating an act of terrorism, multiple murder and a suicide,' said Falcón. 'You have to make time for me.'

'I'm not sure how I can help. I'm neither a terrorist, nor a murderer, and I don't know anybody who is.'

'But you did know the suicide, Ricardo Gamero,' said Falcón. 'Where are you now?'

'I'm in the office. I'm just on my way out.'

'Name a place.'

Deep breath from Barreda. He knew he couldn't brush him off forever. He named a bar in Triana.

Falcón called Ramírez again.

'Have you got the printout of all calls made on Ricardo Gamero's mobiles?'

Ramírez crashed around the office for a minute and came back. Falcón gave him Barreda's number.

'Interesting,' said Ramírez. 'That was the last call he made on his personal mobile.'

'While I think about it,' said Falcón, 'we need the list of calls the Imam made on his mobile. Especially the one he made in front of José Duran on Sunday morning, because that is the electricians' mobile number.'

The bar was half full of people. Everybody was looking at the television, ignoring their drinks. The news had just finished and now it was Lobo and Spinola. But Ramírez had been wrong, it wasn't a press conference; they were being interviewed. Falcón walked through the bar, looking for a lone young man. Nobody nodded to him. He sat down at a table for two.

The interviewer, a woman, was attacking Spinola. She could not believe that he hadn't known about the campaign of terror conducted by Calderón against his wife. The Magistrado Juez Decano de Sevilla, an old-school pachyderm with saurian eyes and an easy, but

421

quite alarming, smile, was not uncomfortable with his moment in the hot seat.

Falcón tuned out of the pointless argument. Spinola was not going to be drawn. The female interviewer had lost herself in the emotional aspect of the case. She should have been hitting Spinola on Calderón's ability to perform and his integrity as a judge in the investigation. Instead she was looking for some riveting personal revelation and she had gone to precisely the wrong man for it.

A young guy in a suit caught Falcón's eye. They introduced themselves and sat down. Falcón ordered a couple of coffees and some water.

'You people are having a hard time,' said Barreda, tilting his head at the TV.

'We're used to it,' said Falcón.

'So how many times has it happened that a Juez de Instrucción has been found trying to dispose of his wife's dead body during a major international terrorism investigation?'

'About as many times as a valued member of an antiterrorist squad has committed suicide during a major international terrorism investigation,' said Falcón. 'How long have you known Ricardo Gamero?'

'A couple of years,' said Barreda, subdued by Falcón's swift response.

'Was he a friend?'

'Yes.'

'So you didn't just see him at Mass on Sundays?'

'We met occasionally during the week. We both like classical music. We used to go to concerts together. Informáticalidad had season tickets.'

'When did you last see him?'

'On Sunday.'

'I understand that Informáticalidad use San Marcos and other churches to recruit employees. Did anybody else from the company know Ricardo Gamero?'

'Of course. We'd go for coffee after Mass and I'd introduce him around. That's normal, isn't it? Just because he's a cop doesn't mean he can't talk to people.'

'So you knew he was in the antiterrorist squad of the CGI.'

Barreda stiffened slightly as he realized he'd been caught out.

'I've known him two years. It came out eventually.'

'Do you remember when?'

'After about six months. I was trying to recruit him to Informáticalidad, making him better and better offers, until finally he told me. He said it was like a vocation and he wasn't going to change his career.'

'A vocation?'

'That was the word he used,' said Barreda. 'He was very serious about his work.'

'*And* his religion,' said Falcón. 'Did he feel the two were bound up together?'

Barreda stared at Falcón, trying to see inside.

'You were a friend he met at church, after all,' said Falcón. 'I would have thought you were bound to talk about the Islamic threat. And then once it came out . . . the nature of his work, I mean. It would seem a natural progression to at least discuss the connection.'

Barreda sat back with an intake of breath and looked around the room, as if for inspiration.

'Did you ever meet Paco Molero?' asked Falcón.

Two blinks. He had.

'Well, Paco,' continued Falcón, 'said that Ricardo, by

his own admission, had been a fanatic, that he'd only just managed to transform himself from being an extremist to being merely devout. And that he'd managed to achieve this through a fruitful relationship with a priest, who died recently of cancer. Where would you describe yourself as being on that integral scale between say, lapsed and fanatical?'

'I've always been very devout,' said Barreda. 'There's been a priest in every generation of my family.'

'Including your own?'

'Except mine.'

'Is that something you feel . . . disappointed by?'

'Yes, it is.'

'Was that one of the attractions of the culture at Informáticalidad?' said Falcón. 'It sounds a bit like a seminary, but with a capitalist aim.'

'They've always been very good to me there.'

'Do you think there's a danger that people with like minds and with the same intensity of faith might become, in the absence of a balancing outside influence, drawn towards an extreme position?'

'I've heard of that happening in cults,' said Barreda.

'How would you describe a cult?'

'An organization with a charismatic leader, that uses questionable psychological techniques to control its followers.'

Falcón left that hanging, sipped his coffee and took the top off his water. He glanced up at the television to see that Lobo and Spinola had now been replaced by Elvira and del Rey.

'The apartment which Informáticalidad bought on Calle Los Romeros near the mosque – did you ever go there?'

'Before it was bought they asked me to look at it to see if it was suitable.'

'Suitable for what?' asked Falcón. 'Diego Torres told me . . .'

'You're right. There wasn't much to look at. It was entirely suitable.'

'How upset were you by Ricardo's death?' asked Falcón. 'That's a terrible thing for a devout Catholic to do: to kill himself. No last rites. No final absolution. Do you know *why* people commit suicide?'

A frown had started up on Marco's forehead. A trembling frown. He was staring into his coffee, biting the inside of his cheek, trying to control emotion.

'Some people kill themselves because they feel responsible for a catastrophe. Other people suddenly lose the impetus for carrying on. We all have something that glues us into place – a lover, friends, family, work, home, but there are other extraordinary people who are glued into place by much bigger ideals. Ricardo was one of those people: a remarkable man with great religious faith *and* a vocation. Is that what he suddenly lost when that bomb exploded on 6th June?'

Barreda sipped his coffee, licked the bitter foam from his lips and replaced the cup with a rattle in its saucer.

'I was very upset by his death,' said Barreda, just to stop the barrage of words from Falcón. 'I have no idea why he committed suicide.'

'But you recognize what it means for a man of his faith to do that?'

Barreda nodded.

'You know who Ricardo's other great friend was?' asked Falcón. 'Miguel Botín. Did you know him?'

No reaction from Barreda. He knew him. Falcón piled on the pressure.

'Miguel was Ricardo's source in the mosque. A Spanish convert to Islam. They were very close. They had great respect for each other's faith. I have a feeling that it was as much Miguel Botín as Ricardo's old priest, that pulled him back from the brink of fanaticism to something more reasonable. What do you think?'

Barreda had his elbows up on the table, his fingertips pressed into his forehead and his thumbs pushing into his cheekbones, hard enough for the skin to turn white.

Falcón had Barreda right there on the brink, but he couldn't get him to move that last centimetre. His mind seemed locked in a state of great uncertainty and doubt. Falcón still had his ace up his sleeve, but what about the drawing? If he showed it to him and the man was unrecognizable he would lose his present advantage, but if it was a close likeness it could blow the whole thing open. He decided to play the ace.

'The last time you saw Ricardo was on Sunday,' said Falcón. 'But it wasn't the last time you spoke to him, was it? Do you know who was the last person on earth that Ricardo spoke to before he hanged himself out of his bedroom window? The last number on the list of mobile calls he made?'

Silence, apart from the television burble at the far end of the café.

'What did he say to you, Marco?' asked Falcón. 'Were you able to give him absolution for his sins?'

The whole bar suddenly erupted. All the men were on their feet, hurling insults at the television. A couple of empty plastic bottles were thrown, which glanced off the TV, whose screen was full of del Rey's face.

'What did he say?' Falcón asked the man nearest to him, who was shouting: '*Cabrón! Cabrón!*' in time with the rest of the men in the bar.

'He's trying to tell us that it might not have been Islamic terrorists after all,' said the man, his tremendous belly quivering with rage. 'He's trying to tell us that it could have been our own people who've done this. Our own people, who want to blow up an apartment block and schools, and kill innocent men, women and children? Go back to Madrid, you fucking wanker.'

Falcón turned back to Marco Barreda, who looked stunned by the reaction around him.

'Fuck off back to Madrid, *cabrón*'!

The bar owner stepped in and changed the channel before someone put a glass bottle through the screen. The men settled back into their chairs. The fat guy nudged Falcón.

'The other judge, he beat his wife, but at least he knew what he was talking about.'

The television showed another current affairs programme. The interviewer introduced her two guests. The first was Fernando Alanis, whose introduction was lost in applause from the bar. They knew him. He was the one who'd lost his wife and son, and whose daughter had miraculously survived and was now fighting for her life in hospital. Falcón realized that this was the man they were all going to believe. It didn't matter what he said, his tragedy had conferred on him a legitimacy that Juez del Rey's vast experience and command of the facts totally lacked. In the other chair was Jesús Alarcón, the new leader of Fuerza Andalucía. The bar was silent, listening intently. These were the people who were going to tell them the truth.

427

Barreda excused himself to go to the toilet. Falcón sat back from the table in a state of shock. He'd lost all the leverage he'd just created. Why hadn't Elvira given del Rey the message that he shouldn't mention the other angle of the investigation? Now that the mistake had been made, it was clear that, even as an enquiry, let alone a possible truth, it was totally unacceptable to the local populace.

The topic of the TV discussion was immigration. The interviewer's first question was irrelevant, as Fernando had come to the cameras well primed. There wasn't a sound in the bar as he started to talk.

'I'm not a politician. I'm sorry to say this in front of Sr Alarcón, who is a man I've grown to respect over the days since the explosion, but I don't like politicians and I don't believe a word they say, and I know I'm not alone. I am here today to tell you how it is. I'm not an opinion-maker. I am a labourer who works on a building site, and I used to have a family,' said Fernando, who had to stop momentarily as his Adam's apple jumped in his throat. 'I lived in the apartment block in El Cerezo which was blown up on Tuesday. I know from the media people I've met over the last few days that they would like to believe, and they would like the world to believe, that we live in a harmonious and tolerant modern society here in Spain. In talking to these people I realized why this is the case. They are all intelligent people, far more intelligent than a mere labourer, but the truth of the matter is that they do not live the life that I do. They are well off, they live in nice houses, in good areas, they take regular holidays, their children go to good schools. And it is from this point of view that they look at their country.

They want it to continue in the way that it appears to them.

'I live . . . I mean, I lived in a horrible apartment in a nasty block, surrounded by lots of other ugly blocks. Not many of us have cars. Not many of us take holidays. Not many of us have enough money to last the month. And *we* are the people living with the Moroccans and the other North Africans. I am a tolerant person. I have to be. I work on building sites where there is a lot of cheap immigrant labour. I have a respect for people's rights to believe in whichever god they want to, and to attend whichever church or mosque they want to. But since 11th March 2004 I have become suspicious. Since that day, when 191 people died in those trains, I have wondered where the next attack is coming from. I am not a racist and I know that the terrorists are very few out of a large population, but the problem is that . . . I don't know who *they* are. They live with me, they live in my society, they enjoy its prosperity, until one day they decided to put a bomb under my apartment block and kill my wife and son. And there are many of us who have lived in suspicion and fear since 11th March until last Tuesday, 6th June. And now it is we who are angry.'

Barreda came back from the toilet. He had to go. Falcón followed him out into the heat and fierce light of the street. All his advantage and initiative had gone. They stood under the awning of the bar and shook hands. Barreda was back to normal. He'd recomposed himself in the toilet and perhaps been strengthened by listening to Fernando Alanis's speech on his way back.

'You didn't tell me what Ricardo said to you in that final phone call,' said Falcón.

429

'I'm embarrassed to have to talk about it after . . . what we've said about him.'

'Embarrassed?'

'I didn't realize how he felt about me,' said Barreda. 'But then . . . I'm not gay.'

30

'So why weren't all these other lines of enquiry written up in a report?' asked Comisario Elvira, looking from del Rey back to Falcón.

'As you know, I've been helping the CNI with one of their missions,' said Falcón. 'I've had to maintain the enquiry into this murder which happened prior to the bombing, and I've since acquired a suicide to investigate. However, all these enquiries, I believe, are linked and should be moved forward together. At no point have I deviated from my initial intention, which was to find out what happened in the destroyed building. You have to agree that there has been a breakdown of logic in the scenario, and it's my job to create different lines of enquiry to find the necessary logic to resolve it. I didn't hear what happened on television, but it has now been explained to me that it was the interviewer who interrupted Juez del Rey and said: "So you believe it was one of our own people that committed this atrocity?" It was *that* question which caused this public relations problem.'

431

'Problem? Public relations catastrophe,' said Elvira. 'Another one, on top of this morning's debacle.'

'Did you talk to Angel Zarrías of the *ABC*?' asked Falcón.

'We're a bit shy of the media right now,' said Elvira. 'Comisario Lobo and I are having a strategy meeting after this to see how we can repair the damage.'

'Juez del Rey has done a great job bringing himself up to speed on a very complicated and sensitive investigation,' said Falcón. 'We can't allow the thrust of our enquiry to be dictated by the media, who have seen an opportunity to manipulate a nervous population by playing games with us on television.'

'What we're playing with here is the truth,' said Elvira. 'The presentable truth and the acceptable truth. And it's all a question –'

'What about the *actual* truth?' said Falcón.

'And it's all a question,' said Elvira, nodding at his little slip, 'of timing. Which truth is released when.'

'Have the translations of the Arabic script attached to the drawings been completed?' asked Falcón.

'So you didn't see the news *before* we went on,' said Elvira. 'And nor did we, which was why the wretched interviewer seized on what Juez del Rey was saying. Only afterwards did we find out that the evacuations of the two schools and biology faculty had been filmed, *and* a translation of one of the Arabic texts was aired with it.

'Each text gave full instructions on how to close off each building, where to hold the hostages and where to place the explosives in order to ensure maximum loss of life, should special forces storm the building,' said del Rey. 'There was a final instruction in each text,

432

which was that one hostage – starting with the youngest child in the case of the schools – was to be released every hour and, as they made their way to freedom, they were to be shot, in full view of the media. This process was to continue until the Spanish government recognized Andalucía as an Islamic state under Sharia law.'

'Well, that explains why there was nearly a riot in the bar I was in,' said Falcón. 'How did the media get hold of the text?'

'It was delivered by motorbike to Canal Sur's reception in a brown padded envelope, addressed to the producer of current affairs,' said del Rey.

'An enquiry is underway,' said Elvira. 'What were you doing in this bar?'

'I was interviewing the last man to speak to Ricardo Gamero before he killed himself,' said Falcón. 'He's a sales manager at Informáticalidad.'

'This isn't the old guy who was seen talking to Gamero in the Archaeological Museum?' said del Rey.

'No. This was the last call Gamero made on his personal mobile,' said Falcón. 'I presume that all members of the CGI's antiterrorist squad would be vetted, Comisario, including their sexuality?'

'Of course,' said Elvira. 'Anybody with access to classified information is vetted to make sure they're not vulnerable.'

'So it would be known if Gamero was homosexual?'

'Absolutely . . . unless he was, you know, not practising . . . so to speak.'

'The guy I was talking to, Marco Barreda, was at cracking point when the bar went crazy. He knows something. I think he feels that whatever it is that *he* or *they* have got involved in, it has spiralled out of control. He's sick about Gamero's death, for a start. That was not part of the script.'

'And what script is that?' asked Elvira, who was desperate for one.

'I don't know,' said Falcón. 'But it's something that explains what happened in that mosque on Tuesday. If we had the manpower, I'd have the whole of Informáticalidad down at the Jefatura and interview them until they broke down.'

'So what did Marco Barreda say were Gamero's last words?' asked Elvira.

'That Gamero was in love with him,' said Falcón. 'He'd been reluctant to say anything because he was embarrassed about it. I thought it was significant that he'd been to the toilet. I'm sure he called someone and was given advice about what to say. He was at cracking point and then suddenly he seemed to be back on the rails.'

'So what have we got on Informáticalidad?'

'Nothing, apart from the fact that the apartment was bought with black money.'

'And what do you think this apartment was used for?'

'Surveillance of the mosque.'

'With what purpose?'

'With the purpose of attacking it, or enabling others to attack it.'

'For any particular reason?'

'Other than that they are an organization recruited from the Catholic Church and therefore representative of the religious Right and opposed to the influence of Islam in Spain, I'm not entirely sure. There might be a political or financial angle that I don't, as yet, know about.'

'You haven't got enough,' said Elvira. 'You've interviewed all the sales reps and you've tried to capitalize on Marco Barreda's vulnerability without success. All you have is an unsubstantiated theory to go on. How could you apply any more pressure? If you brought them down here, they'd come with lawyers attached. Then there'd be the media to contend with. You're going to need something much more solid than your instinct to break open Informáticalidad.'

'I'm also concerned that that was *all* they did,' said Falcón, nodding. 'Provide surveillance information and nothing more. In which case we could interview them for days and get no further than that. I need another link. I want the old guy seen talking to Gamero in the museum.'

'Did you show the drawing to Marco Barreda?' asked del Rey.

'No. I was concerned that it might not be a close enough likeness and I wanted to apply pressure to his vulnerable point, which was Ricardo Gamero.'

'What's your next move?'

'I'm going to take a look at all the board directors of Informáticalidad and the other companies in their group, including the holding company, Horizonte, and see if I can find a likeness to the sketch,' said Falcón. 'What are the CNI and CGI doing?'

'They're concerned with the future now,' said Elvira. 'Juan has gone back to Madrid. The others are using the names from this investigation to try to get leads to other cells or networks.'

'So we're on our own with this investigation here?'

'They'll only come back to us if we find, from the DNA sampling, that the Imam, or Hammad and Saoudi, weren't in the mosque at the time of the explosion,' said Elvira. 'As far as they're concerned, there's nothing more for them to extract from this situation and they're more worried about future attacks.'

Back in his office, Falcón ran an internet search for Informáticalidad and Horizonte and extracted photographs of the directors of all the individual companies, their groups and the holding company. As he scrolled through the search engine's results for Horizonte he came across a web page dedicated to the celebration of their fortieth anniversary in 2001. As he'd hoped, the page showed a banquet with more than twenty-five shots of the great and the good at their tables.

The memory is a strange organ. It seems to be random and yet it can be jogged into patterns by other senses. Falcón knew if he hadn't just seen him on television he would never have picked him out from all the other faces at the Horizonte candlelit, floral dinner. He stopped, scrolled back. It was unmistakably Jesús Alarcón, with his beautiful wife sitting three places to his right. He looked at the caption, which said nothing, other than this was a table belonging to Horizonte's bankers – Banco Omni. Well, that figured. Alarcón had been a banker in Madrid before he came to Seville. He printed out the page with all its photographs and left the Jefatura, Serrano having given him the name of the security guard at the Archaeological Museum.

The security guard was called to the ticket desk and Falcón showed him the photographs, which he flipped through quickly, shaking his head. He ran his finger over the fortieth anniversary banquet shots. Nothing jumped out at him.

It was too hot even for a quick snack under the purple flowers of the jacarandas in the park, and Falcón drove back into town with too much on his mind. Pablo from the CNI called and they agreed to meet in a bar on Calle Leon XII near the destroyed apartment building.

Falcón was there first. It was a downtrodden place. The staff hadn't bothered to clear away the ankle-deep fag butts, sugar sachets and paper napkins after the coffee-break rush. He ordered a gazpacho, which was a little fizzy, and a piece of tuna, which had less flavour than the plate it was served on, and the chips were soggy with oil. Things were going well. Pablo arrived and ordered a coffee.

'First thing,' he said, sitting down. 'Yacoub has made contact and we've given him his instructions on your behalf. He knows what to do now.'

'And what is that?'

'Yacoub belongs to two mosques. The first is in Rabat: the Grand Mosque Ahl-Fès, which is attended by the powerful and wealthy. It's not known for any radical Islamic stance. But he also belongs to a mosque in Salé, near his work, which is a different kind of place altogether, and Yacoub knows it. All he has to do is step over to the other side and start getting involved. He knows the people . . .'

'How does he know the people?'

'Javier,' said Pablo, with an admonishing look, 'don't ask. You don't have to know.'

'How dangerous is this going to be for him?' asked Falcón. 'I mean, radical Islam isn't known for its

437

forgiving nature, and I imagine they're especially unforgiving when it comes to betrayal.'

'As long as he maintains his role there's no danger. He communicates with us at a distance. There's no face to face, which is where things normally come unstuck. If he needs to see anybody then he can organize a business trip to Madrid.'

'What happens if they take him over and start feeding us emails of disinformation?'

'There's a phrase he has to use in his correspondence with us. If that phrase isn't employed then we know it isn't him writing and we react accordingly.'

'How quickly will they come to trust him?' said Falcón. 'You've always been of the opinion that this bomb was a mistake, or a diversion. Maybe you're expecting an information return too quickly if you think that he can help you with attacks which have already been planned.'

'They'll recognize his value immediately . . .'

'Has he been approached by the GICM before?' asked Falcón, these things only just occurring to him.

'He's in a unique position because of his business,' said Pablo, pointedly ignoring Falcón's question. 'He can travel freely and is widely known, respected and trusted by his business partners. He will arouse no suspicion from the Moroccan authorities looking for radicals, or European authorities looking for terrorists or their planners. He's the perfect person for a terrorist organization to make use of.'

'But they'll test him first, surely?' said Falcón. 'I don't know how it works, but they might give him some valuable information and see what he does with it. See, for instance, if it appears elsewhere. Just like the CNI did with the CGI here in Seville, come to think of it.'

'That's *our* job, Javier. We know what we can use from him and what we can't. If we have information that could only possibly have come from him, then we know to be careful,' said Pablo. 'If he tells us that there's a GICM cell operating from an address in Barcelona, we don't just storm the building.'

'What's the other thing?'

'We want you to communicate with Yacoub tonight. There's nothing to be said, but we want him to know you're here and in touch with him.'

'Is that it?'

'Not quite. The CIA have come back to us with the identity of your mystery man with no hands or face.'

'That was quick.'

'They've developed quite a system over there for tracing people of Arabic origin, even when they've become American citizens,' said Pablo. 'Your model man did a good job with the face, and his identity was corroborated by the hernia op, tattoos and dental X-rays.'

'What were the tattoos?'

'On the webbing between thumb and forefinger he had four dots configured in a square on his right hand, and five dots on his left hand.'

'Any reason?'

'It helped him count,' said Pablo.

'Up to nine?'

'Apparently women never failed to comment on them.'

'*That* is on his *file*?' said Falcón, amazed.

'You'll see why when I tell you he was a professor in Arabic Studies at Columbia University until March last year, when he was fired after being found in bed with one of his students,' said Pablo. 'And you know how they found out? He was shopped by one of his other students who he was bedding at the same time.

'You don't do that sort of thing at an American university and get caught. The police were brought in. The girls' parents threatened to sue the university and then him personally. It was the end of his career – and it cost him, too. He managed to settle out of court on advice from his lawyers, who knew he would lose and that they wouldn't get paid. He had to sell his mid-town apartment, which had been left to him by his parents. The only job he could get after the case blew over was teaching maths privately in Columbus, Ohio. He lasted three months of a Mid West winter and then flew to Madrid in April last year.

'After that, our information gets a little sparse. We've a record of him taking a trip to Morocco for three weeks at the end of April. He took the ferry from Algeciras to Tangier on 24th April and he came back on 12th May. That's it.'

'Does he have a name?'

'His real name is Tateb Hassani,' said Pablo. 'When he became an American citizen in 1984 – which was also the year both his parents died, one in a car crash and the other of cancer – he changed his name to Jack Hansen. It's not so unusual for immigrants to anglicize their names. He was born in Fès in 1961 and his parents left Morocco in 1972. His father was a businessman who went back and forth frequently. Tateb only went back to Morocco twice in thirty years. He didn't like it. His parents forced him to maintain an Arabic education and his mother spoke to him only in French. He wrote and spoke Arabic fluently. He graduated in mathematics, but couldn't get a place as a post-graduate, so he switched to Arabic Studies and wrote a thesis on Arab mathematicians. He came out of Princeton with a doctorate in 1986. He spent time in the universities of Madison, Minnesota and San Francisco before ending up in New York. He had a good life: a university salary, with the rent from his parents' apartment coming in. Then, when he landed the professorship at Columbia, he took over the apartment and had the perfect existence, until he started sleeping with his students.'

'What about his religion?'

'He's down as a Muslim, but, as you might have gathered from his history, he'd let that lapse.'

'Was he known for any opinions about radical Islam?'

'You can read the file sent over by the CIA,' said Pablo, taking it out of his briefcase, laying it on the table. It looked to be about ten pages long.

'Are there any samples of his handwriting in here?' asked Falcón.

'Not that I've seen.'

'Can the CIA send some across to us?' asked Falcón, flicking through the pages. 'In both Arabic script and English.'

'I'll get them on to it.'

'Any other languages, apart from French, English and Arabic?'

'He spoke and wrote Spanish, too,' said Pablo. 'He used to give a maths course every summer over here at Granada University.'

'Comisario Elvira told me that you're not much interested in our investigation any more and that Juan has gone back to Madrid,' said Falcón. 'Does that mean you've cracked the code in the annotated versions of the Koran?'

'Juan's been called back to Madrid because there have been reports of other cells, not connected with Hammad and Saoudi, which are now on the move,' said Pablo. 'We're still interested in your investigation, but not in the way you are. And, no, we haven't cracked the code.'

'How's the diversion theory going?'

'Madrid have hit dead ends with the Hammad and Saoudi connections,' said Pablo. 'Arrests have been made, but it's the usual thing. They only knew what *they* were doing. They received encrypted emails and did what they were told to do. So far we've only picked up a few "associates" of Hammad and Saoudi, which hardly constitutes unravelling the whole network – if there was one to unravel. We're hoping Yacoub can help us there.'

'What about the MILA?'

'A story invented by the media based on some truth – that this group does, in fact, exist – but they weren't involved in any way,' said Pablo. 'It was a neat follow-on from the Abdullah Azzam text sent to the *ABC*. Something to capture the public's imagination, but, in the end, bogus. If you ask me, it's irresponsible journalism.'

'And VOMIT?' asked Falcón. 'Did you break them down, too?'

'That's not a priority for us,' said Pablo, riding over Falcón's irony. 'We're more concerned about future attacks on European countries which emanate from Spain rather than an enumeration of the past.'

'So nothing has changed?' said Falcón. 'You still

believe that Miguel Botín was a double, and he was instructed to give the electrician's card to the Imam by someone in his radical Islamic network?'

'I know you don't have any faith in it,' said Pablo, 'but we have more information than you do.'

'And you're not going to give it to me?'

'Ask your old friend, Mark Flowers,' said Pablo. 'I've got to go now.'

'You know, it was a set of keys from the Imam's kitchen drawer that opened the fireproof box recovered from the storeroom of the mosque,' said Falcón. 'Gregorio was with me when they opened it and he was very interested by that, although, as usual, he didn't say why the CNI was so fascinated.'

'This is just the way we have to be, Javier,' said Pablo. 'It's nothing personal, it's just the nature of our work and the work of others in our business.'

'Make sure you call me when the handwriting comes through from the CIA,' said Falcón.

'What do you want us to do with it?'

'You've got a handwriting expert back in Madrid, haven't you?'

'Sure.'

Falcón bowed his head and started flicking through Tateb Hassani's file. He knew it was childish, but he wanted to show that two could play at the withholding information game.

'Gregorio and I will come by your house tonight.'

He nodded, waited for Pablo to leave. He closed the file, sat back and let his mind wander. The television was on and the four o'clock news showed the evacuations of the schools and the biology faculty while the bomb squad went in with their dogs. Gradually, a palimpsest of the Arabic script found with the architect's drawings appeared over the action images with a voice-over of their translations. Cut to a journalist outside the school, trying to make something out of the fact that nothing, as yet, had been found on the premises.

The chair recently vacated by Pablo slid into Falcón's vision. He went back to the photographs of Horizonte's fortieth anniversary and the shot of Banco Omni's table. That's what he'd noticed: an empty chair next to Jesús Alarcón's wife, Mónica. A closer look showed that the chair had just been vacated by a man in a dark suit who was walking away. Against the dark background, only a cuff of shirt, a hand and his collar with some grey hair above it was visible.

The pre-school was empty, apart from a policewoman at the door and another on the computer in one of the classrooms. The stink from the bombsite did not make it a popular location to hang out. Falcón logged on to the internet and entered: *Horizonte: fortieth anniversary*. He clicked on the first article, which was from the business pages of the *ABC*. The byline jumped out at him because it was A. Zarrías. He read through the article just looking for a mention of Banco Omni. It was there, but no names. The photograph was of the Horizonte board at the dinner. He went for another article, which had been published in a business magazine. Again the byline was for A. Zarrías. Falcón clicked on five other articles, of which three had been placed by Angel. He must have been doing the PR for Horizonte's fortieth anniversary. Interesting. He entered Banco Omni and Horizonte into the search engine.

There were thousands of hits. He scrolled down

through the pages of hits until he got to articles written in 2001. He clicked on the articles, not reading them but checking who placed them. Angel Zarrías had written 80 per cent of them. So, when Angel had quit politics he'd gone into journalism, but he'd also picked up a lucrative sideline in PR with Banco Omni, who presumably put him in touch with Horizonte. He entered 'Banco Omni board of directors' into the search engine. He went back through the years, pulling up articles on to the screen. There were names, but never any photographs. In fact, the only photograph he could find of any employees of Banco Omni was from the table shot taken at Horizonte's fortieth anniversary banquet.

31

'It's taken me hours to get to speak to this person,' said Ferrera, 'but I think it's been worth it. I've got a . . . reliable witness to the dumping of the body which was later found on the rubbish dump outside Seville.'

'We now have a name for that body. He's called Tateb Hassani,' said Falcón. 'You didn't sound very sure of that word "reliable".'

'He drinks, which is never a good thing for a court to hear, and I'm not sure we could ever get him to court anyway.'

'Tell me what the guy saw and we'll worry about his credentials if it gets us anywhere.'

'He lives in an apartment at the end of a cul-de-sac just off Calle Boteros. His daughter owns the third and fourth floors of this building. She lives on the third and her father lives above. Both apartments have the perfect view of those bins on the corner of Calle Boteros.'

'I'm sure that's why the daughter bought them,' said Falcón. 'And what's this guy doing awake at three in the morning, looking out of his window?'

446

'He's an insomniac, or rather he can't sleep at night, only during the day,' she said. 'He sleeps from eight until four. The daughter wouldn't let me disturb him until she'd given him lunch. She knows that if she breaks his routine it'll be hell for her for a week.'

'He goes straight into lunch?' said Falcón. 'She doesn't give him breakfast?'

'He likes to drink wine, so she gives him something substantial to eat with it.'

'So, what's his problem exactly?'

'Quite unusual for a Sevillano: he's agoraphobic. He can't go outside and he can't bear more than two people in a room.'

'I see the problem with the court appearance now,' said Falcón. 'Anyway, he was awake at three in the morning, but not so drunk that he couldn't see what was going on by the bins.'

'He was drunk, but he says it doesn't affect his vision,' said Ferrera. 'Just after three o'clock on Sunday morning, he saw a large, dark estate car pull into the cul-de-sac and reverse back towards the bins. The driver and passenger got out of the front, both male, and a third man got out of the back. The driver stood in the middle of Calle Boteros, and looked up and down. The other men opened the boot. They checked the bins, which were empty at that time of night, tipped one of them on its side and leaned it against the rear of the car. They reached into the back and dragged something into the bin. They manoeuvred the bin, which now appeared heavy, back up to the pavement and returned to the rear of the car. They removed two black bin liners, which the witness described as bulky but light, and swung them into the bin on top of whatever they'd just put in there. They closed the bin. The driver slammed the boot shut. They got back into the car, reversed into Calle Boteros and headed off in the direction of the Alfalfa.'

'Could he give you anything on the three men?'

'He thought, from the way they moved, that the two guys who did the work were young – by that he meant around thirty. The driver was older, thicker around the waist. They were all dressed in dark clothes, but seemed to be wearing what looked like white gloves. I assume he means latex gloves. The driver and one of the younger men had dark hair and the third was either bald or had had his head shaved.'

'Not bad for an old drunk in an attic,' said Falcón.

'There's some street lighting on that corner,' said Ferrera. 'But, still . . . not bad for someone who his daughter says will drink until he falls over.'

'Just don't include that in his witness statement,' said Falcón. 'What about these two "bulky but light" bin liners they threw on top of the body?'

'He thought they probably contained something like gardening detritus – hedge clippings, that sort of thing.'

'Why?'

'He's seen that sort of stuff thrown in there before, but at the end of the afternoon, not at three in the morning.'

'Have you found any large houses in that area which might have that quantity of gardening detritus?' asked Falcón. 'It's mostly apartments around the Alfalfa.'

'They could have picked up a couple of bin liners of stuff from anywhere,' said Ferrera.

'If they'd done that, those bin liners would have

come out first, whereas, according to your friend, they dealt with "something heavy" first.'

'I'll see what I can find.'

'Come to think of it, Felipe and Jorge said they had a bin liner of clippings that they'd picked up near the body on the rubbish dump,' said Falcón. 'I'll see if they've had time to have a look at it, yet.'

Ramírez called as Falcón was on his way out to the forensics' tent.

'The Imam's mobile phone records,' said Ramírez. 'The CNI have got them and they won't release them to me. Or rather, Pablo said he would look into it, but now he doesn't take or return my calls.'

'I'll see what I can do,' said Falcón.

The forensic tent was filled with more than twenty masked and boiler-suited individuals who were impossible to differentiate. Falcón called Felipe and told him to come outside. Felipe remembered the gardening detritus, which he'd also had a chance to look at.

'It was all from the same type of hedge,' he said. 'The kind they use in ornamental gardens. Box hedge. Small, shiny, dark green leaves.'

'How fresh was it?'

'It had been cut that weekend. Friday afternoon or Saturday.'

'Any idea how much hedge we'd be looking at?'

'Remember, that might have been just part of the clippings,' said Felipe. 'And I live in an apartment. Hedges are not my speciality.'

Calderón was lying on the fold-down bed in his police cell. His head was resting on his hands, while his eyes stared at four squares of white sunlight high on the wall above the door. When he closed his eyes the four squares burned red on the inside of his eyelids. If he looked into the darkness of the cell they smouldered greenly. He was calm enough for this. He had been calm since the moment he'd been caught trying to get rid of Inés. Get rid of Inés? How had that phrase broken its way into his lexicon?

They'd brought him down to the Jefatura in the early-morning summer light. He was shirtless because the forensics had bagged that horrifically blood-stained garment. The cops had the air conditioning on even at that hour and his nipples were hard and he was shivering. As they crossed the river, two rowing eights, out for early training, slipped under the bridge and he had the sensation of an enormous weight coming off his shoulders. The relaxing of the muscles in his neck and between his scapulae was almost erotic. It was a powerful post-fear drug that his body chemistry had concocted, and it had the awkward result of arousing him.

He had gone through the process of incarceration dumbly, like an animal for slaughter, moving from transport, to pen, to holding cell with no idea of the implications. A DNA swab had been taken from the inside of his cheek, he'd been photographed and given an orange short-sleeve shirt. The relief of finally being left alone, with no possessions, his belt removed, and just a pack of cigarettes, was immense. His tiredness drew him to the bed. He kicked off his loafers and sank back on the hard bunk and fell into a dreamless sleep, until he was woken at three in the afternoon for lunch. He'd eaten and applied his ferocious intellect to what he was going to say in his interview with the detective before falling into this dazed state of looking at the squares of light on the wall. It was unexpectedly pleasant to be released from the oppression of time. At five o'clock the guard came to tell him that Inspector Jefe Luis Zorrita was ready to interview him.

'You are, of course, allowed to have your lawyer present,' said Zorrita, coming into the interview room.

'I *am* a lawyer,' said Calderón, still with all his pre-crime arrogance. 'Let's get on with it.'

Zorrita made the introductions to the tape and asked Calderón to confirm that he'd been given the opportunity to have a lawyer present, and had declined.

'I didn't want to talk to you until I'd had the full autopsy report from the Médico Forense,' said Zorrita. 'Now I've got that and had the opportunity to conduct my preliminary enquiries . . .'

'What sort of preliminary enquiries?' asked Calderón, just to show that he wasn't going to be passive.

'I've more or less established what you and your wife had been doing over the last twenty-four hours before her murder.'

'More or less?'

'There are still some details to fill in on what your wife was doing yesterday afternoon. That's all,' said Zorrita. 'So what I'd like you to do, Sr Calderón, is to tell me, in your own words, what happened last night.'

'From what time?'

'Well, let's start from the moment you left the Canal Sur studios and arrived at your lover's apartment,' said Zorrita. 'The time before that is well accounted for.'

'My lover?'

'That was the word Marisa Moreno used to describe your relationship,' said Zorrita, looking through his notes. 'She was firm about not wanting to be called your mistress.'

That admission from Marisa made him feel quite sentimental. How ridiculous it was that a police enquiry had drawn that from her. Having not thought about her very much since being arrested, he suddenly missed her.

'Is that a fair description?' asked Zorrita. 'From your point of view?'

'Yes, I would say that we were lovers. We'd known each other for nine months or so.'

'It would explain why she was doing her best to protect you.'

'Protect me?'

'She was trying to make out that you'd left her apartment later than you had, which would have made it more difficult for you to have murdered your wife . . .'

'I did *not* kill my wife,' said Calderón, summoning the full severity of his professional voice.

'. . . but she "forgot" that she'd called a taxi for you and that we can access all the phone records, as well as the cab company logs, and talk to the driver himself, of course. So her attempts to help you were, I'm afraid, quite futile.'

The interview was not following the pattern that Calderón had outlined to himself in his lawyer's mind while lying on his bunk. He'd witnessed only a few police interrogations in his time as a judge and so had little idea of the way in which they moved. It was for this reason that, barely a minute into his interview with Zorrita, he was in a quandary. Warmed by the thought that Marisa had called him her lover, but chilled by the idea that she believed he needed her help, which

452

had ugly implications. The effect of these two extremes of temperature alive in his body was to undermine his equilibrium. His thoughts would not line up in their usual orderly fashion, but seemed to mill around, like shoals of children careering around the school playground.

'So, Sr Calderón, please tell me when you arrived at your lover's apartment.'

'It must have been about 12.45.'

'And what did you do?'

'We went out on to the balcony and made love.'

'Made love?' said Zorrita, deadpan. 'You didn't indulge in anal sex, by any chance?'

'Certainly not.'

'You seem very firm about that,' said Zorrita. 'And I only ask you such a personal question because the autopsy revealed that your wife seemed to be accustomed to being penetrated in this fashion.'

Panic rose in Calderón's chest. He had lost control of the interview in a matter of a few exchanges. His arrogance had cost him dear. His assumption that he could trounce Zorrita in any mind or word game had proved to be wide of the mark. This was a man who was used to the wiliness of criminals, and had come to the interview with a clear strategy, which made Calderón's analytical brain seem worthless.

'We made love,' said Calderón, unable to add anything more without making it sound like some biological transaction.

'Would you say that these two relationships generally worked in this fashion?' asked Zorrita. 'You treated your lover with respect and admiration, while abusing your wife as if she was some cheap whore.'

Outrage was the first emotion that leapt into Calderón's throat, but he was learning. He saw Zorrita's two interrogating weapons: emotional stabs, followed by logical bludgeon.

'I did not treat my wife like a cheap whore.'

'You're right, of course, because not even a cheap whore allows herself to be beaten up *and* sodomized for no money at all.'

Silence. Calderón gripped the edge of the table so hard his nails whitened with the pressure. Zorrita was unconcerned.

'At least you don't have the temerity to deny that you treated your wife in such shameful fashion,' said Zorrita. 'I presume your lover didn't know these two sides to your personality?'

'Who the fuck do you think you are, to presume to know anything about my relationship with my wife, or my lover?' said Calderón through lips gone blood-less with rage. 'Some fucking Inspector Jefe, come down from Madrid . . .'

'Now I can see why your wife would be terrified of you, Sr Calderón,' said Zorrita. 'Underneath that brilliant legal mind, you're a very angry man.'

'I am not fucking angry,' said Calderón, pounding the table hard enough to jog a hank of his hair loose. '*You* are *goading* me, Inspector Jefe.'

'If I'm goading you, I'm not doing it by shouting at you or insulting you. I'm only doing it by asking you questions based on proven fact. The autopsy has revealed that you sodomized your wife and that you beat her up so badly that some of her vital organs were damaged. There's also a history of humiliation, which even extended to pursuing an affair with another woman on the same day that you announced your engagement to your wife.'

'Who've you been talking to?' asked Calderón, still unable to control his fury.

'As you know, I've only had today to work on this case, but I've managed to talk to your lover, which was a very interesting conversation, and a number of your colleagues and your wife's colleagues. I've also spoken to some of the secretaries in the Edificio de los Juzgados and the Palacio de Justicia, and the security guards, of course, who see everything. Of the twenty-odd interviews I've conducted so far, not one person has been prepared to defend your behaviour. The least emotional description of your activities was "an incorrigible womanizer".'

'What was so interesting about your conversation with Marisa?' asked Calderón, unable to resist the bait of that remark.

'She was telling me about a conversation you had about marriage. Do you remember that?' asked Zorrita.

Calderón blinked against the rush of memory; too much had happened in too short a time.

'The reason you married Inés . . . Maddy Krugman? How Inés represented stability after that . . . catastrophic affair?'

'What are you trying to do here, Inspector Jefe?'

'Jog your memory, Sr Calderón. You were there, I wasn't. I've only spoken to Marisa. You talked about "the bourgeois institution of marriage" and how she, Marisa, wasn't interested in it. You agreed with her, didn't you?'

'What do you mean?' asked Calderón.

'You weren't happy in your marriage, but you didn't want to get divorced. Why was that?' asked Zorrita.

Calderón couldn't believe it. He was in the elephant pit again. He pulled himself together this time.

'I believe that once you've made a commitment before God, in church, you should adhere to it,' he said.

'But that wasn't what you said to your lover, was it?'

'What did I say to her?'

'You said: "It's not so easy." What did you mean by that, Sr Calderón? It's not as if we're living in fear of excommunication any more. Breaking your vows wasn't your concern. So what were you worried about?'

Even Calderón's giant brain couldn't compute the numerous possible answers to this question in less than half a minute. Zorrita sat back and watched the judge agonize over everything except the truth of the matter.

'It's not that difficult a question,' said Zorrita, after a full minute's silence. 'Everybody knows what the repercussions of divorce are. If you want to extricate yourself from a legal commitment, you're going to lose out. What were you afraid of losing, Sr Calderón?'

Put like that, it didn't seem so bad. Yes, it *was* a common fear for men facing divorce. And he was no different.

'The usual things,' he said, finally. 'I was worried about my financial situation and my apartment. It was never a serious possibility. Inés was the only woman I'd ever . . .'

'Were you concerned, as well, that it might affect your social status, and perhaps your job?' asked Zorrita. 'I understand your wife had been very supportive of you after the Maddy Krugman debacle. Your colleagues said she helped you to get your career back on track.'

His colleagues had said that?

'There was never any serious threat to my career,' said Calderón. 'There was no question that I would be appointed as the Juez de Instrucción for something as important as the Seville bombing, for instance.'

'Your lover offered you a solution to the problem, though, didn't she?' said Zorrita.

'What problem?' said Calderón, confused. 'I just said there was no problem with my career, and Marisa –'

'The awkward problem of the divorce.'

Silence. Calderón's memory baffled around his head, like a moth seeking the light.

'"The bourgeois solution to the bourgeois problem",' said Zorrita.

'Oh, you mean that I could kill her,' said Calderón, snorting with derisive laughter. 'That was just a silly joke.'

'Yes, on *her* part,' said Zorrita. 'But how did it affect your mind? That's the question.'

'It was ridiculous. An absurdity. We *both* laughed at it.'

'That's what Marisa said, but how did it affect *your* mind?'

Silence.

'It never, for one moment, entered my mind to kill my wife,' said Calderón. 'And I *didn't* kill her.'

'When did you first beat your wife, Sr Calderón?'

This interview was like a steeplechase, with the fences getting higher as he progressed around the course. Zorrita watched the internal struggle that he'd seen so many times before: the unacceptable truth, followed by the necessary delusion, and the attempt to construct a lie from those two unreliable sources.

'Had you beaten her before the beginning of this week?' asked Zorrita.

'No,' he said firmly, but instantly realized that it implied some admission of guilt.

'That's cleared something up,' said Zorrita, making a note. 'It was difficult for the Médico Forense to establish the occurrence of the first beating you gave her because, well, as I understand it, old bruising isn't as easy to measure as say . . . body temperature. Dating old bruising is a difficult business . . . as is organ rupture and internal bleeding.'

'Look,' said Calderón, inwardly gasping at these shocking revelations, 'I know what you're trying to do.'

'I'd really like to establish a specific time when you first beat Inés. Was it Sunday night or Monday morning?'

'They weren't beatings, they were accidents,' said Calderón, aghast that he'd used the plural now. 'And, whatever the case, it does not mean that I murdered my wife . . . I didn't.'

'But did the first beating occur on Sunday or Monday?' asked Zorrita. 'Or was it Tuesday? Of course, you used the plural. So it was probably Sunday, Monday, Tuesday and then, finally and tragically, Wednesday, and we'll never be able to attribute what bruise to which day. What time did you get back on Tuesday morning, having spent the night with Marisa?'

'It was around 6.30 a.m.'

'Well, that squares with what Marisa said. And was Inés asleep?'

'I thought she was.'

'But she wasn't,' said Zorrita. 'She woke up, didn't she? And what did she do?'

'All right, she found my digital camera and started downloading the images I had on it. They included two shots of Marisa.'

'You must have been *very* angry when you found out. When you came across her in the act, caught her red-handed,' said Zorrita, not quite able to ease back on his relish. 'She was very fragile, your wife, wasn't she? The Médico Forense estimates her weight before the catastrophic blood loss as 47 kilos.'

'Look, we were in the kitchen, I just brushed her aside,' said Calderón. 'I didn't realize my own strength or her fragility. She fell awkwardly against the kitchen counter. It's made out of granite.'

'But that doesn't explain the fist mark on her abdomen, or the toe mark over her left kidney, or the amount of her hair we've found distributed around your apartment.'

Calderón sat back. His hands fell from the edge of the table. He was not a career criminal and he was finding resistance very hard work. The only time he could remember having to trump up such a quantity of lies was when he'd been a small boy.

'As I swept her aside I must have tapped her diaphragm. She hit the counter and came down on my foot.'

'The autopsy found a ruptured spleen and a bleeding kidney,' said Zorrita. 'I think it was less of a tap and more of a punch, wasn't it, Sr Calderón? The Médico Forense thinks from the shape of the bruise around her loin area and the darker red imprint of a toenail, that it was more of a kick with a bare foot than someone "falling" on to a foot, which would, of course, be flat on the floor.'

459

Silence.

'And all that took place on Tuesday morning?'

'Yes,' said Calderón.

'How long was that after your lover's little joke about solving the problem of your divorce?'

'Her joke had nothing to do with that.'

'All right, when was the next time you beat your wife?' asked Zorrita. 'Was it after you found out that your wife and lover had accidentally met in the Murillo Gardens?'

'How the fuck do you know that?' asked Calderón.

'I asked Marisa if she'd ever met your wife,' said Zorrita, 'and she started off by lying to me. Why did she do that, do you think?'

'I don't know.'

'She said she hadn't, but you know, I've been interviewing liars more than half my working life and after a while it's like dealing with children; you become so practised at reading the signs that their attempts become laughable. So why do you think she lied on your behalf?'

'On *my* behalf?' asked Calderón. 'She didn't do anything on my behalf.'

'Why didn't she want me to know that she had had this . . . vocal confrontation with your late wife?'

'I've no idea.'

'Because *she* was still angry about it, Sr Calderón, that's why,' said Zorrita. 'And if she was angry about being insulted by your wife, about being called a whore, in public, by your wife . . . I'm wondering how she made you feel about it . . . Well, she told me.'

'She *told* you?'

'Oh, she tried to protect you again, Sr Calderón. She

460

tried to make it sound like nothing. She kept repeating: "Esteban's not a violent man," that you were just "annoyed", but I think she also realized just how very, very angry you were. What did you do on the night that Marisa told you Inés had called her a whore?'

More silence from Calderón. He'd never found it so difficult to articulate. He was too stoked up with emotion to find the right reply.

'Was that the night you came home and pummelled your wife's breasts and whipped her with your belt so that the buckle cut into her buttocks and thighs?'

He'd come into this interview with a sense of resistance as dense and powerful as a reinforced concrete dam, and within half an hour of questioning all that was left were some cracked and frayed bean canes. And then they caved in. He saw himself in front of a state prosecutor, facing these same questions, and he realized the hopelessness of his situation.

'Yes,' he said, on automatic, unable to find even the schoolboy creativity to invent the ridiculous lie to obscure his brutality. There was nothing ambiguous about the welt of a belt and the gouge of its buckle.

'Why don't you talk me through what happened on the last night of your wife's life,' said Zorrita. 'Earlier we'd reached the moment when you'd just made love to Marisa on the balcony.'

Calderón's eyes found a point midway between himself and Zorrita, which he examined with the unnerving intensity of a man spiralling down to the darker regions of himself. He'd never had these things said to him before. He'd never had these things revealed to him under such emotional circumstances. He was stunned by his brutality and he couldn't understand

461

where, in all his urbanity, it came from. He even tried to imagine himself dealing out these beatings to Inés, but they wouldn't come to him. He did not see himself like that. He did not see Esteban Calderón's fists raining down on his fine-boned wife. It *had* been him, there was no doubt about that. He saw himself before and after the act. He remembered the anger building up to the beatings and it subsiding afterwards. It struck him that he had been in the grip of a blind savagery, a violence so intense that it had no place in his civilized frame. A terrifying doubt began to crowd his chest and affect the motor reflex of his breathing, so that he had to concentrate: in, out, in, out. And it was there, in the lowest and darkest circle of his spiralling thoughts, the completely lightless zone of his soul, that he realized that he *could* have murdered her. Javier Falcón had told him once that there was no greater denial than that of a man who had murdered his wife. The thought terrified him into a state of profound concentration. He'd never looked with such microscopic detail into his mind before. He began to talk, but as if he was describing a film, scene by horrible scene.

'He was exhausted. He had been completely drained by the experiences of the day. He stumbled into the bedroom, collapsed on to the bed and passed out immediately. He was aware only of pain. He lashed out wildly with his foot. He woke up with no idea where he was. She told him he had to get up. It was past three o'clock. He had to go home. He couldn't wear the same clothes as he had yesterday and appear on television. She called a taxi. She took him down in the lift. He wanted to sleep on her shoulder in the street. The cab arrived and she spoke to the driver. He fell into the back seat and his head rolled back. He was only vaguely aware of movement and of light flashing behind his eyelids. The door opened. Hands pulled at him. He gave the driver his house keys. The driver opened the door to the building. He slapped on the light. They walked up the stairs together. The driver opened the apartment door. Two turns of the lock. The driver went back down the stairs. The hall light went out. He went into the apartment and saw light coming from the kitchen. He was annoyed. He didn't want to see her. He didn't want to have to explain . . . again. He moved towards the light . . .'

Calderón paused, because he was suddenly unsure of what he was going to see.

'His foot crossed the edge of the shadow and stepped into the light. He turned into the frame.'

Calderón was blinking at the tears in his eyes. He was so relieved to see her standing there at the sink in her nightdress. She turned when she heard his footfall. He was going to skirt the table and pull her to him and squeeze his love into her, but he couldn't move because when she turned she didn't open her arms to him, she didn't smile, her dark eyes did not glisten with joy . . . they opened wide with abject terror.

'And what happened?' asked Zorrita.

'What?' asked Calderón, as if coming to.

'You turned into the kitchen doorway and what did you do?' asked Zorrita.

'I don't know,' said Calderón, surprised to find his cheeks wet. He wiped them with the flat of his palms and brushed them down his trousers.

'It's not unusual for people to have blank moments about terrible things that they have done,' said Zorrita.

'Tell me what you saw when you turned into the doorway of the kitchen.'

'She was standing at the kitchen sink,' he said. 'I was so happy to see her.'

'Happy?' said Zorrita. 'I thought you were annoyed.'

'No,' he said, holding his head in his hands. 'No, it was . . . I was lying on the floor.'

'*You* were lying on the floor?'

'Yes. I woke up on the floor in the corridor and I went back to the kitchen light and it was then that I saw Inés lying on the floor,' he said. 'There was a terrible quantity of blood and it was very, very red.'

'But *how* did she end up lying on the floor?' asked Zorrita. 'One moment she was standing and the next she's lying on the floor in a pool of blood. What did you do to her?'

'I don't know that she *was* standing,' said Calderón, searching his mind for that image to see if it really existed.

'Let me tell you a few facts about your wife's murder, Sr Calderón. As you said, the cab driver opened the door of the apartment for you, with two turns of the key in the lock. That means the door had been double locked from the inside. Your wife was the only person in the apartment.'

'Ye-e-e-s,' said Calderón, concentrating on Zorrita's every syllable, hoping they would give him the vital clue that would unlock his memory.

'When the Médico Forense took your wife's body temperature down by the river it was 36.1°C. She was still warm. The ambient temperature last night was 29°C. That means your wife had just been killed. The autopsy revealed that your wife's skull had been smashed at the back, that there had been a devastating cerebral haemorrhage and two neck vertebrae had been shattered. Examination of the crime scene has revealed blood and hair on the black granite work surface and a further large quantity of blood on the floor next to your wife's head which also contained bone fragments and cerebral matter. The DNA samples taken from your apartment belong only to you and to your wife. The shirt that was taken from you down by the river was covered in your wife's blood. Your wife's body showed indications of your DNA on her face, neck and lower limbs. The scene in the kitchen of your apartment was consistent with someone who had picked Inés up by the shoulders or neck and thrown her down on the granite work surface. Is that what you did, Sr Calderón?'

'I only wanted to embrace her,' said Calderón, whose face had broken up into the ugliness of his inner turmoil. 'I just wanted to hold her close.'

32

Seville – Thursday, 8th June 2006, 18.30 hrs

The Taberna Coloniales was at the end of the Plaza Cristo de Burgos. There was something colonial about its green windows, long wooden bar and stone floor. It was well known for the excellence of its tapas and it was popular for its traditional interior and the seating outside on the pavement of the plaza. This was Angel and Manuela's local. Falcón didn't want Angel's journalistic nose anywhere near the police work around the destroyed apartment block, nor did he want to have to discuss anything sensitive in the glass cylinder of the *ABC* offices on the Isla de la Cartuja. Most important of all, he needed to be close to Angel's home so that there would be the least trouble possible for him to give Falcón what he wanted. This was why he was sitting outside the Taberna Coloniales under a calico umbrella, sipping a beer and biting into the chilled flesh of a fat green olive, waiting for Angel to appear.

He took a call from Pablo.

'The Americans have sent over the handwriting samples you asked for – the Arabic and English script belonging to Jack Hansen.'

'He looks more like a Tateb Hassani to me than a Jack Hansen,' said Falcón.

'What do you want us to do with the samples?'

'Ask your handwriting experts to make a comparison between Tateb Hassani's Arabic script and the notes attached to the drawings found in the fireproof box in the mosque. And compare the English script to the handwritten notes in the copies of the Koran found in the Peugeot Partner and Miguel Botín's apartment.'

'You think he was one of them?' asked Pablo. 'I don't get it.'

'Let's make the comparison first and the deductions afterwards,' said Falcón. 'And, by the way, the Imam's mobile phone records – we need to have a look at them. One of those numbers he called on Sunday morning belongs to the electrician.'

'I've spoken to Juan about that,' said Pablo. 'Gregorio's checked out all the numbers the Imam called on Sunday morning. The only one he couldn't account for was made to a phone registered in the name of a seventy-four-year-old woman living in Seville Este who has never been an electrician.'

'I'd like access to those records,' said Falcón.

'That's something else for you to talk to your old friend Flowers about,' said Pablo, and hung up.

Falcón sipped his beer and tried to persuade himself that he was calm, and that the present strategy was the right one. He'd taken Serrano and Baena away from their task of touring the building sites looking for the electricians, and had directed them to help Ferrera locate the hedge whose clippings had been dumped with the body. Ramírez and Pérez had photographs of Tateb Hassani and were walking the streets around the

Alfalfa trying to find anybody who recognized him. This meant that no one from the homicide squad was now working on anything directly linked to the Seville bombing. He wasn't worried about Elvira for the moment. The Comisario had his hands too full of public relations problems to be worried about the gamble Falcón was taking.

'For a man who's supposed to be running the largest criminal investigation in Seville's history, you're looking remarkably relaxed, Javier,' said Angel, taking a seat, ordering a beer.

'We have to present a calm exterior to a nervous population who need to believe that somebody has everything under control,' said Falcón.

'Does that mean that it isn't under control?' asked Angel.

'Comisario Elvira is doing a good job.'

'He might be, from the policeman's point of view,' said Angel. 'But he doesn't imbue the general public with confidence in his ability. He's a public relations disaster, Javier. What was he thinking of, asking that poor bastard . . . the judge . . .'

'Sergio del Rey.'

'Yes – him. Putting him on national television when the guy could barely have had time to read the files, let alone comprehend the emotional aspect of the case,' said Angel. 'The Comisario must know by now that television is not about the truth. Is he the kind of guy who watches reality TV and thinks that it *is* reality?'

'Don't be too hard on him, Angel. He's got a lot of excellent qualities that just don't happen to suit the televisual age.'

'Well, unfortunately, that's the age we're in now,'

said Angel. 'Now, Calderón, he was *the* man. He gave the TV what it craves: drama, humour, emotion and brilliant surface. He was a huge loss to your effort.'

'You said it: "brilliant surface". It wasn't so pretty underneath.'

'And how do you think you look now?' asked Angel. 'Remember the London bombings? What was the story that kept rolling out in the days after those attacks? The story that maintained the emotional pitch and focused the emotions? Not the victims. Not the terrorists. Not the bombs and the disruption. That was all part of it, but the big story was the mistaken shooting by plainclothes special policemen of that Brazilian guy, Jean Charles de Menezes.'

'And what's our big story?'

'That's your problem. It's the arrest, under suspicion of his wife's murder, of the Juez de Instrucción of the whole investigation. Have you seen the stuff coming out of the television about Calderón? Just listen . . .'

The tables around them had filled up and a crowd had gathered outside the open doors of the bar. They were all talking about Esteban Calderón. Did he do it? Didn't he do it?

'Not your investigation. Not the terrorist cells that might be active in Seville at the moment. Not even the little girl who survived the collapse of the building,' said Angel. 'It's all about Esteban Calderón. Tell Comisario Elvira that.'

'I have to say, Angel, that for a man who loves Seville more than almost anyone I know, you seem . . . buoyant.'

'It's terrible, isn't it? I am. I haven't felt as energized

in years. Manuela's infuriated. I think she preferred me when I was dying of boredom.'

'How is she?'

'Depressed. She thinks she's got to sell the house in El Puerto de Santa María. In fact she *is* selling it,' said Angel. 'She's lost her nerve. This whole idea of the Islamic "liberation" of Andalucía has taken hold in her mind. So now she's selling the gold mine to save the tin and copper mines.'

'There's no talking to her when she's like that,' said Falcón. 'So, why are you so buoyant, Angel?'

'If you're not watching the news very much you probably don't know that my little hobby is doing rather well.'

'You mean Fuerza Andalucía?' said Falcón. 'I saw Jesús Alarcón with Fernando Alanis on television a few hours ago.'

'Did you see the whole thing? It was sensational. After that programme Fuerza Andalucía picked up 14 per cent in the polls. Wildly inaccurate, I know. It's all emotional reaction, but that's 10 per cent more than we've ever polled before, and the Left are floundering.'

'When did you first meet Jesús Alarcón?' asked Falcón, genuinely curious.

'Years ago,' said Angel, 'and I didn't much care for him. He was a bit of a boring banker type and I was dismayed when he said he wanted to go into politics. I didn't think anybody would vote for him. He was a stiff in a suit. And as you know, these days it's not about your policies or your grasp of regional politics, it's all about how you come across. But I've got to know him better since he came down here and, I tell you, this relationship he's developed with Fernando

Alanis . . . it's gold dust. As a PR man, you just dream of something like that.'

'Was that the first time you met him – when you were doing PR work?'

'When I left politics I did a PR commission for Banco Omni.'

'That must have been nice work to walk into,' said Falcón.

'We Catholics stick together,' said Angel, winking. 'Actually, the Chief Executive Officer and I are old friends. We went to school, university, did our national service together. When I finished with those wankers in the Partido Popular, he knew that I wouldn't be able to just "retire", so he commissioned me and it led to other things. They were the bankers for a group in Barcelona and I did their fortieth anniversary PR for them; then there was an insurance group in Madrid, and a property company on the Costa del Sol. There was a business for me if I could have been bothered with it. But, you know, Javier, corporate PR, it's so . . . small. You're not going to change the world doing that shit.'

'You didn't change it in politics.'

'To tell you the truth, the PP was no different. It *was* like working for a huge corporation: play safe, toe the party line, everything happening by millimetres, no striding out to new horizons and changing the way people think and live.'

'Who wants change?' said Falcón. 'Most people hate change so much that we have to have wars and revolutions to bring it about.'

'But look at us now, Javier, talking like this in a bar,' said Angel. 'Why? Because we're in crisis. Our way of life is being threatened.'

'You said it yourself, Angel. Most people can't cope with it, so what *do* they talk about?'

'You're right. It's Esteban Calderón on everybody's lips,' said Angel. 'But at least it's not the usual trivia. It's tragedy. It's hubris bringing down the great man.'

'So what would you tell Comisario Elvira to do now?' asked Falcón.

'Aha! Is this what it's all about, Javier?' said Angel, smirking. 'You've brought me down here to get some free advice for your boss.'

'I want the PR man's take on the world.'

'You have to focus, and you have to focus on certainty. Because of the nature of the attack it's been difficult for you, but now you've finally got into the mosque it's time for you to reveal more and be specific. The evacuations of the schools and university buildings, what's that all about? People need a bone to chew on; uncertainty creates rumour, which does nothing to quell panic. Juez del Rey's mistake was that he hadn't taken the pulse of the city, so when he started spreading uncertainty again . . .'

'It was the interviewer's question that spread uncertainty,' said Falcón.

'That wasn't the way the viewers saw it.'

'Del Rey only found out afterwards that someone had leaked the Arabic script.'

'Del Rey should never have presented the truth of the situation: that there is still considerable confusion about what went on in that mosque. He should have pressed home the certainties. If, in the end, the truth happens to be something else, you just change your story. Your investigation lost a lot of its credibility when your spokesman was arrested for murder. The only chance of regaining that credibility lies in confirming the public's suspicions. The interviewer *knew* that the public would be in no mood to be told that there *might* be a homegrown element to this terrorist plot.'

'Elvira has trouble deciding when to use what kind of truth so that his investigation can get on with the business of finding out what actually happened,' said Falcón.

'Politics is great preparation for that,' said Angel.

'So you think Jesús Alarcón has got what it takes?'

'He's made a good start, but it's too early to say. It's what's going to happen six or seven months from now that's important,' said Angel. 'He's riding a big wave of public emotion now, but even the biggest waves end up as ripples on the beach.'

'He could always go back to the Banco Omni if it didn't work out.'

'They wouldn't have him,' said Angel. 'You don't *leave* the Banco Omni. Once they've given you a job, they take you into their confidence. If you leave them and become an outsider, that's where you remain.'

'So, Jesús is taking some risks.'

'Not really. He had a good introduction from my friend, who thinks very highly of him. He'll find him something else to do if it all comes to nothing.'

'Have I met this mysterious friend of yours?'

'Lucrecio Arenas? I don't know. Manuela's met him. He's not so mysterious now that he's retired.'

'You mean he was mysterious before?'

'Banco Omni is a private bank. It runs a hefty percentage of the Catholic Church's finances. It's a secretive organization. You won't even see any photographs of Banco Omni executives. I did a specific PR job for them, but I only got that job because of Lucrecio. I found out nothing about the organization, other than what I needed to know in order to perform my task,' said Angel. 'Why *are* we talking about Banco Omni?'

'Because Jesús Alarcón is the man of the moment,' said Falcón. 'After Esteban Calderón.'

'Ah, yes. You still haven't told me what you want to see me about,' said Angel.

'I'm sounding you out, Angel,' said Falcón, shrugging. 'I told Elvira about our conversation earlier today when you offered to help us, but he's wary. I want to be able to go back to him and make him feel better about employing your talents. He just needs to be pushed, that's all.'

'I'm prepared to help in a crisis,' said Angel. 'But I'm not looking for permanent work.'

'Elvira's problem is that he sees you as a journalist, and therefore the enemy,' said Falcón. 'If I can talk to him about your PR activity and the sort of clients you've represented, that will give him a different perspective.'

'I'll give advice but I won't be employed,' said Angel. 'Some might think there was a conflict of interest.'

'Just give me some other company names that you've worked for,' said Falcón. 'Who was it you represented for their fortieth anniversary?'

'Horizonte. The property company was called Mejorvista and the insurance group was Vigilancia,' said Angel. 'Don't promote me too much, Javier. I've got my work cut out steering Fuerza Andalucía through the media maze.'

'The only thing is that PR is a difficult concept to sell. Other people's press cuttings are meaningless. If I could show Elvira the quality of the people you've worked for, that might help. Have you got shots of the people at Horizonte, or Banco Omni, or something from the Horizonte fortieth anniversary celebrations? You know, pictures of Angel Zarrías with senior executives. Elvira likes tangible things.'

'Of course, Javier, anything for you. Just don't over-sell me.'

'We're in crisis,' said Falcón. '*Both* our instructing judges have been discredited. We *have* to rebuild our image before it's too late. Elvira is a good policeman, and I don't want to see him fail just because he doesn't know how to play the media game.'

They went up to the apartment. Manuela wasn't there. It was a huge, four-bedroomed place, with two of the bedrooms used as offices. Angel walked to the wall of his study and pointed at a shot in the middle.

'That's the one you want,' he said, tapping a framed photograph in the centre of the wall. 'That's a rare shot of all the executives of Horizonte and Banco Omni in the same place. It was taken for the fortieth anniversary event. I've got a copy of it somewhere.'

Angel sat at his desk, opened a drawer and went through a stack of photographs. Falcón searched the shot for a likeness of the police artist's drawing of the man seen with Ricardo Gamero.

'Which one is Lucrecio Arenas?' asked Falcón. 'I don't see anybody I recognize here. If I'd met him, where would that have been?'

'He has a house in Seville, although he doesn't live in it for half the year. His wife can't stand the heat so they go and live in some palatial villa, built for them by Mejorvista, down in Marbella,' said Angel. 'You remember that big dinner I had in the Restaurante La Juderia last October? He was there.'

'I was away teaching a course at the police academy.'

Angel gave him the shot and pointed out Lucrecio Arenas, who was in the centre, while Angel was on the very edge of the two rows of men. Arenas had similarities to the police artist's drawing in that he was the right age, but there was no revelatory moment.

'Thanks for this,' said Falcón.

'Don't lose it,' said Angel, who put it in an envelope for him.

'What about this shot of you and King Juan Carlos,' said Falcón. 'Have you got a copy of that?'

They both laughed.

'The King doesn't need me to do his PR for him,' said Angel. 'He's a natural.'

'Are you getting anywhere, José Luis?' asked Falcón.

'I can't believe it, but we've drawn a total blank,' said Ramírez. 'If Tateb Hassani *was* staying with someone in this area, he didn't go for a coffee, he didn't eat a tapa, drink a beer, buy bread, go to the supermarket, get a newspaper – nothing. Nobody has seen this guy before, and he's got a face you don't forget.'

'Any news from Cristina and Emilio?'

'They've seen most of the big houses in the area and there are no box hedges. They've all got internal patios rather than gardens. There's the Convento de San Leandro and the Casa Pilatos, but that doesn't help us much.'

'I want you to find and check out another house. I don't have the address, but it belongs to someone called Lucrecio Arenas,' said Falcón. 'And I spoke to the CNI

476

about the Imam's phone records. They've checked out the electrician's number already. It was a dead end.'

'Can we have a look at those records ourselves?'

'They've become classified documents,' said Falcón, and hung up.

He was on his way to see the security guard who'd finished his shift at the Archaeological Museum and gone home. It was a long drive out to his apartment in the northeast of the city. He took a call from Pablo.

'You're going to be pleased about this,' the CNI man said. 'Our handwriting expert has matched the Arabic script to the notes attached to the architect's drawings of the schools and the biology faculty. He's also matched Tateb Hassani's English script to the annotations in both copies of the Koran. What does this mean, Javier?'

'I'm not absolutely sure of its greater significance, but I'm confident you can tell your code breakers to stop looking for a key to crack the non-existent cipher in those copies of the Koran,' said Falcón. 'I think they were planted in the Peugeot Partner *and* Miguel Botín's apartment, specifically to confuse us.'

'And that's all you can say for the moment?'

'I'll be seeing you later at my house,' said Falcón. 'I'm hoping it will all be clearer by then.'

The lift to the security guard's apartment on the sixth floor was not working. Falcón was sweating as he rang the doorbell. The wife and kids were despatched to bedrooms and Falcón laid the photograph down on the dining-room table. His heart was beating tight and fast, willing the guard to find Lucrecio Arenas.

'Do you see the older man in this photograph?'

There were two rows of men, about thirty in all. The security guard had done this before. He took two pieces of paper and isolated each face from the rest of the shot and took a good look at it. He started on the left and worked his way across. He studied them carefully. Falcón couldn't bear the tension and looked out of the window. It took the guard some time. He knew it must be important for an Inspector Jefe to come all the way out to his apartment to show him this shot.

'That's him,' said the guard. 'I'm absolutely sure of it.'

Falcón's heart was thundering as he looked down. But the guard wasn't pointing at Lucrecio Arenas in the centre of the shot. He was tapping the face at the extreme right of the second row – and that face belonged to Angel Zarrías.

33

The sun was setting on the third day since the explosion. As Falcón drove back into the city his mind reached a static but profound level of concentration focused entirely on Angel Zarrías.

Back in the security guard's apartment he'd become quite angry. He'd torn the police sketch out of his pocket, smoothed it out on the dining-room table and asked the poor guy to show him the similarities. Falcón had been forced to admit a few things: that all old people looked the same, or invisible, to younger people; that Angel was 1.65m and only a little heavier than 75 kilos; that Angel had no facial hair and he did have a side parting and, even if he was a bit thin on top, he used all available hair to make it look as if he was still hanging on to it. Only when the security guard had talked him through the jaw line and nose did Falcón see Angel in the sketch, as an adult finally sees the outline of a face in a cloud, as pointed out by a frustrated child.

Ramírez met him in the car park outside the preschool.

479

'We found Lucrecio Arenas's house,' said Ramírez. 'It was in the Plaza Mercenarias. I sent Cristina over there to take a look and it was all closed up. The neighbours say they don't spend much time there in the summer and there's no garden, only an internal patio. They didn't recognize Tateb Hassani either.'

They went into the classroom at the back where Juez del Rey and Comisario Elvira were waiting. Eight hours' sleep in three days was ruining Elvira. They sat down. They were all exhausted. Even del Rey, who should have been fresh, looked rumpled, as if he'd been jostled by a disgruntled crowd.

'Good news or bad?' asked Elvira.

'Both,' said Falcón. 'The good news is that I've identified the man seen speaking to Ricardo Gamero in the Archaeological Museum in the hours before he killed himself.'

'Name?'

'Angel Zarrías.'

Silence, as if they'd all seen someone sustain an ugly blow.

'He's your sister's partner, isn't he?' said Ramírez.

'How did you identify him?' asked Elvira.

Falcón briefed them on his conversation outside the Taberna Coloniales and how he'd extracted the Horizonte/Banco Omni executive photograph from Angel.

'But that's only part of the bad news,' said Falcón. 'The other part is that I'm not sure whether this gets us any further down the chain.'

'Meaning?'

'What have we found out that will help us apply pressure on Zarrías to reveal more?' said Ramírez.

'Exactly,' said Falcón. 'He was the last person to speak to Ricardo Gamero, but so what? He knew Gamero from church and that's the end of it. Why did he go to Zarrías and not his priest? His priest is dead. What did they talk about? Gamero was very upset. What about? Maybe Zarrías will give the same answer that Marco Barreda gave me. Perhaps Zarrías told Barreda to *tell* me that Gamero had been a closet gay. We don't know enough to be able to crack him open.'

'I can't believe that Ricardo Gamero would go to Angel Zarrías at that particular moment to discuss emotional problems,' said del Rey.

'You could show Zarrías the shot of Tateb Hassani and see what reaction you get,' said Elvira.

Neither Elvira nor del Rey had heard from Pablo, so Falcón told them about Tateb Hassani and how his handwriting matched that of the documents found in the fireproof box from the mosque and the notes found in the two copies of the Koran.

'And why did you ask for that comparison to be made in the first place?' asked Elvira.

'It went back to a question I asked my officers when we first discovered the dead body on the rubbish dump: Why kill a man and take such drastic steps to destroy his identity? You would only do that because knowledge of the victim's identity would lead investigators to people known to the victim, or because knowledge of his expertise might jeopardize a future operation. Tateb Hassani's identity revealed a number of things. His expertise, as a professor of Arabic Studies, meant that he could write Arabic and would have a sound knowledge of the Koran. He had also given maths classes in Granada during the summer months and

481

therefore spoke and wrote Spanish. His profile was not that of an Islamic militant – he was an apostate, a sexual predator and a drinker of alcohol. Once he lost his job at Columbia University, which had cost him his New York apartment, he became so desperate for money that he'd taught maths privately in Columbus, Ohio, which was the home of I4IT, who own Horizonte, who in turn own Informáticalidad. Finally, I was not comfortable with the fact that the keys found in the Imam's apartment, which successfully opened the fireproof box from the mosque, had been discovered in the kitchen drawer and not in the Imam's desk with his other keys. This struck me as a plant by someone who had access to the Imam's apartment, but not his study when he wasn't there.'

'Who would have planted the keys?'

'Botín, under instructions from Gamero?' said Ramírez.

'At the beginning of this investigation Juan was telling us to keep an open mind and not to look at this attack historically, because there is no pattern in the way Islamic terrorists work. That's true. That's their style. Each attack comes out of the blue and there's always some new twist that teases greater terror into the mind of the West. Just think about the virtuosity of the attacks experienced so far.

'When I was driving back from the security guard's apartment, something that struck me about the Seville bombing was its *lack* of originality. Of course, that wasn't my first thought. My first thought was: these terrorists are prepared to attack residential property. But now I'm beginning to see that the Seville bomb refers back to some element in those previous attacks. The collapse of the apartment building reminded us of the Moscow apartment blocks coming down in 1999. The discovery of the Islamic sash, the hood and the Koran in the Peugeot Partner reminded us of the Koran tapes and detonators found in the Renault Kangoo outside the station at Alcalá de Henares. The use of Goma 2 Eco in the device planted in the mosque reminded us of the explosive used on 11th March. The threat to the two schools and the biology faculty was reminiscent of Beslan. It was as if the person who planned this operation was drawing inspiration from something in those previous attacks.'

'VOMIT,' said Ramírez. 'If there's anybody who knows everything there is to know about Islamic terrorist attacks, it's the author of that website.'

'And now that the security guard has pointed the finger at Angel Zarrías there's a logic to it. He's a journalist, but he's also a PR man. He knows how things work in the human mind,' said Falcón. 'I'm now asking myself: who leaked the Arabic script found in the fireproof box to Canal Sur? Or rather, who didn't have to leak it, because it was already in their possession? And who planted the stories about the MILA? Who sent the Abdullah Azzam text to the *ABC* in Madrid from Seville?'

'How far do you think this goes?' said Elvira. 'If they planted the Korans, the hood and the sash, was it because they knew about the hexogen?'

'I don't think so,' said Falcón. 'I think the idea was conceived as just an attack against the mosque and the people in it. They were getting information from Miguel Botín, via Ricardo Gamero, that something was happening. The CGI had been frustrated in their first attempt to get a bugging order. Gamero found another way, or rather, another way was revealed to him by Zarrías, which was that the mosque could be put under surveillance by Informáticalidad's sales reps. Once it appeared that Hammad and Saoudi were making sinister preparations they decided to kill them, and anybody else unfortunate enough to be in the mosque at the time, before they could carry out the attack they were planning.

'The decision was made. The surveillance terminated. The apartment on Calle Los Romeros rented out again. Meanwhile the fake council inspectors went into the mosque, laid a small device that would blow the fuse box, which would give the electricians access. Miguel Botín was given the electrician's card and told to make it available to the Imam. It's quite possible that Botín wasn't part of the conspiracy and that he was told by Gamero that they had now been granted a bugging order and these electricians were going to position the microphone so that the CGI could carry out their surveillance. Botín was there to ensure that the Imam made the call to the right electricians. The Goma 2 Eco bomb was planted, along with the fireproof box. The design of the attack was to make it look like a bomb had gone off in the preparatory stage. Everybody would be killed and the ultimate, atrocious aim of the plot that was supposedly being planned would be found in the fireproof box.

'They knew that Hammad and Saoudi were up to no good, but what I don't believe they realized was just how powerful the explosive was that they were storing in the mosque. The detonation of 100 kilos of hexogen and the complete destruction of the apartment building and the damage to the pre-school were not part of the plan. And that was why Ricardo Gamero killed himself. Not just because his friend and source had been killed, but also because he felt responsible for all the deaths.'

'Well, that returns the logic to the scenario,' said Elvira. 'But first of all, I can't see Angel Zarrías as the sole perpetrator and mastermind of this conspiracy. And secondly, I don't know how the hell you set about proving any of it so that it can stand up in a court of law.'

'The problem is that, if this scenario is the correct one, I cannot go to Angel Zarrías and reveal my hand, because the only cards I've got are the fact that I know he was the last person to speak to Gamero, face to face, and the shock value of having identified Tateb Hassani.'

'You have to find the next link in the chain *after* Angel Zarrías,' said del Rey. 'He's a journalist and a PR man. What are his PR connections?'

'That's how I got to him in the first place,' said Falcón. 'I was sure that the people from Informáticalidad couldn't be operating on their own. I assumed they would be getting orders from their parent company. I looked at Horizonte, and that's where I came across their bankers: Banco Omni. And . . .'

'And?'

'Jesús Alarcón used to work for Banco Omni,' said Falcón, more things occurring to him. 'He was put forward as a political candidate by Angel Zarrías's old friend, the Chief Executive of Banco Omni, Lucrecio Arenas.'

'Political candidate for what?' asked del Rey.

'He's the new leader of Fuerza Andalucía.'

'But Fuerza Andalucía are nowhere in regional politics,' said Elvira. 'They poll 4 per cent of the vote, if they're lucky.'

'After Jesús Alarcón appeared with Fernando Alanis on television today they polled 14 per cent,' said Falcón. 'Zarrías was very excited about it. He calls the PR work he does for Fuerza Andalucía his hobby, but I think it's bigger than that. He's looking for a share of power with the Partido Popular because, for once in his political life, he wants to have the strength to change things. I think he's trying to manoeuvre Jesús Alarcón into a position where he can challenge for the leadership of the Partido Popular. I don't think I'm exaggerating when I say that he is to Jesús Alarcón what Karl Rove was to George Bush.'

'So who is the next link in the chain?' asked del Rey.

'Tateb Hassani was staying somewhere while he was being put to work and it was there that he was probably killed,' said Falcón. 'I had assumed it would be in a house near where he was dumped. The bins were in a cul-de-sac on a quiet street, and that implied knowledge. That knowledge, I realize, came from Zarrías, who lives nearby, on the Plaza Cristo de Burgos. I'm now thinking that the house where Tateb Hassani was probably staying was the headquarters of Fuerza Andalucía, which belongs to Eduardo Rivero on Calle Castelar.'

'Does it have a garden?' asked Ramírez. 'With a hedge?'

'There is some sort of formal garden between the front of the house, where Rivero has the office, and the back part, which is the family home. I went there once with Angel and Manuela for a party, but it was in the dark and I wasn't looking at hedges. What we need now is a sighting of Tateb Hassani going into that house, which will give us our next link in the chain.'

'What about Angel Zarrías?' asked Ramírez. 'Do you think it's worth putting him under twenty-four-hour surveillance?'

'I think it would be, especially as it might not be for long,' said Falcón. 'But there is something else which bothers me about all this, and that is the killing.'

'Tateb Hassani was poisoned with cyanide,' said Ramírez. 'It's not like stabbing, shooting, or strangling.'

'First of all, how did they get hold of cyanide?' asked Falcón. 'And then there was the disfigurement. The clean amputation of the hands. I'm thinking there must be a doctor or surgeon involved in all this.'

'And what about the bomb?' said Ramírez. 'It takes real criminal ruthlessness to do something like that.'

Falcón called Angel Zarrías to arrange a meeting with Comisario Elvira to talk about reviving the image of the investigative team. They'd agreed to profess an interest in Zarrías's PR talents. It would also bring Zarrías to them so that Serrano and Baena could start the first shift of the surveillance.

It was too risky for Falcón to be seen in Calle Castelar near Eduardo Rivero's house where he might be recognized. The work of placing Tateb Hassani in Rivero's household fell to Ferrera, Pérez and Ramírez.

Elvira, del Rey and Falcón waited in the pre-school for Angel to turn up.

'You're not happy, Javier,' said Elvira. 'Are you concerned about how this will affect your relationship with your sister?'

'No. That *does* concern me, but it's not that,' said Falcón. 'What I'm thinking about now is that, if my scenario proves to be the correct one, it still doesn't explain why Hammad and Saoudi brought 100 kilos of hexogen to Seville.'

'That's the CNI's job, not yours,' said Elvira.

'What scares me is that if you *did* want to bring Andalucía back into the Islamic fold, without an army or navy, then your best chance of achieving that would be with a Beslan-type siege,' said Falcón. 'I thought at the time that the Russian special forces probably started that firefight because Putin could see how impossible the situation was becoming. He had to act before the global media circus made it an intense, emotional focal point. Once that happened he could only see himself making concessions. Putin's reputation is built on strength and toughness. He couldn't allow a bunch of terrorists to make him look weak. So he met their ruthlessness with his own and more than three hundred people died. If a similar situation happened here, with children taken hostage just at the moment when they should be going on holiday, can you imagine the reaction in Spain, Europe and the world? Putin-style ruthlessness would not be acceptable.'

'Steps have been taken,' said Elvira. 'We can't go through all the schools in Andalucía in the same way that we've gone through the three buildings here in Seville, but we've told them to search their premises and we've got the local police involved, too.'

'You've also told us that you believe the idea of MILA involvement to be a media invention of Zarrías,' said del Rey. 'So we have no real idea what the Islamic terrorists' original intention was.'

'But why bring powerful explosive to Seville, the capital of Andalucía?' said Falcón. 'There's an unnerving brilliance to the idea of the MILA launching a ruthless attempt to bring Andalucía back into the Islamic fold. It's as if the fiction and the truth could easily meet. Have we had any results from the DNA sampling? Are we certain that Hammad and Saoudi died in the mosque? Do we know yet whether they deviated from their route between the safe house in Valmojado and Seville?'

'The forensics have been told to contact me as soon as they've had confirmation, but I doubt that will be today,' said Elvira. 'We haven't heard anything more from the Guardia Civil about the route of the Peugeot Partner. Don't try to overthink this situation, Javier. Just concentrate on *your* task.'

Angel Zarrías arrived at 9 p.m. Falcón made the introductions and left them to it. He went over to the forensics tent. They were working under lights on the bombsite, which was almost flat. The crane had gone, as had the diggers. Only one tipper was waiting to remove any further rubble. Falcón changed into a boiler suit and went into the tent, which was bright with halogen light. He found the chief of the forensics hovering over a vast array of rags, bits of shoe, plastic, strips of leather. He introduced himself again.

'I'm looking for anything that could be construed as an instruction for making and placing bombs,' said Falcón.

'Something more than what we've already found in the fireproof box?'

'Detail about the bomb making is what I'm after,' said Falcón. 'It might have been sewn into a jacket lining or in a wallet.'

'We've still got plenty of work to do to get into the mosque. We got to the fireproof box early, because it happened to have been blown upwards in the blast,' he said. 'We're working our way downwards now, but it's piece-by-piece work, with everything having to be documented as we go. Tomorrow morning will be the earliest that we'll get into the main body of the mosque.'

'I just wanted you to know that we're still looking for another piece in the jigsaw,' said Falcón. 'It could be in code, numbers or Arabic script.'

There were ten people working outside under the lights. It was similar to an archaeological dig, with a plan of the mosque under a reference grid on a table where each find was logged. The forensics were barely thirty centimetres below ground level. The stink of putrefaction was still heavy in the warm air. They worked in silence and low murmurs. It was hard, gruesome work. Falcón put a call through to Mark Flowers and asked for a meeting.

'Sure, where are you?'

'I'm at the bombsite now but I was thinking a good place to meet would be the apartment of Imam Abdelkrim Benaboura,' said Falcón. 'You know where that is, don't you, Mark?'

Flowers didn't respond to the sarcasm. Falcón walked to the Imam's apartment, which was in a block nearby, similar to the one that had been destroyed. There was a permanent police guard on the door. Falcón showed his ID and the guard said that he did not have the authority to allow him to enter.

'You know who I am?' said Falcón.

'Yes, Inspector Jefe, but you're not on my list.'

'Can I see your list?'

'Sorry, sir. That's classified.'

The guard's mobile rang and he took the call, listening intently.

'He's already here,' he said, and hung up.

He unlocked the door and let Falcón in.

The CNI men had not been exaggerating about the quantity of books in the apartment. The living and dining rooms were lined with books, and the bedroom floors were stacked with them. They covered all areas of human knowledge and were mostly in French and English, although there was a whole room given over to Arabic texts. The back room should have been the master bedroom but was the Imam's study, with just a single bed at one end and his desk at the other. The walls were covered in books. Falcón sat at the desk in a wooden swivel chair. He looked through the drawers, which were empty. He swivelled in the chair and reached for a book on the nearest shelf. It was called *Riemann's Zeta Function*. He put it back without troubling to open it.

'He'd read them all,' said Flowers, standing at the door. 'Pretty amazing to think of all this knowledge in one guy's head. We had a few people in Langley with this kind of reading behind them, but not many.'

'How long had you known him?' said Falcón. 'Assuming that he's dead.'

'I'm sure he's dead,' said Flowers. 'We met in Afghanistan in 1982. He was a kid then, but he was one of the few mujahedeen who spoke English, because, although he was born in Algeria, he went to school in Egypt. We were supplying them with weapons and tactics to fight the Russians. He appreciated what we did for them; helping to keep those atheistic communists out of the land of Allah. As you know, not many of the others did. Isn't there a saying about helping people being the quickest road to resentment?'

'And you kept in touch all this time?'

'There have been breaks, as you'd expect. I lost track of him in the 1990s and then we resumed contact in 2002. I dug him out on one of my foraging trips to Tunis. He never bought into the Taliban and all that Wahhabi stuff. As you probably gathered, he was a bright guy and he couldn't find an interpretation of any line of the Koran that approved of suicide bombing. He was one of them, but he saw things very clearly.'

'And you didn't think to tell one of your new spies, who was investigating –'

'Hey, look, Javier, you had the information from day one. Juan told you he didn't have clearance for his history and that the Americans had vouched for him on his visa application. What more do you want? His CV? Don't expect to be spoon-fed in this game,' said Flowers. 'I can't have it released into the public domain that I was running an Imam as a spy in a local mosque in Seville.'

'And that's why we didn't get in here,' said Falcón, 'and why we didn't get access to his phone records?'

'I had to make sure the place was clear of anything that might implicate him in CIA work. That meant going through all these books,' said Flowers. 'And I'm not irresponsible. I made sure the CNI checked out the electrician's number.'

'All right, I accept that. I should have been a bit more . . . aware,' said Falcón. 'Did Benaboura tell you about Hammad and Saoudi?'

'No, he didn't.'

'That must have hurt.'

'You don't understand the pressure on these people,' said Flowers. 'He gave me plenty of useful information, names, movements, all sorts of stuff, but he didn't tell me about Hammad and Saoudi because he couldn't.'

'You mean he couldn't risk telling you about them, and you then acting on the information, with the result that all fingers would be pointing at Abdelkrim Benaboura?'

'You're learning, Javier.'

'Did he know about Miguel Botín?'

'Benaboura was an experienced guy.'

'I see,' said Falcón, thinking that through. 'So he decided that Miguel Botín was an acceptable route for the information about Hammad and Saoudi to come out, which was why he used the electricians Botín put forward.'

'He read that situation very clearly. He understood why the fake council inspectors came in, he appreciated the fuse box blowing and the "right" electrician being put in his hand,' said Flowers. 'What he didn't expect was for the electricians to plant a bomb, as well as a microphone.'

'There was a microphone?'

'Of course, he had to find out where it was so that he could have his conversations there,' said Flowers. 'They put it in the plug socket in his office.'

'I wonder if that was in use and who was listening to it?' said Falcón. 'What did the CNI have to say about it?'

'It was supposed to be the CGI who planted it,' said Flowers. 'Botín was working for Gamero, who was with the CGI, and I never spoke to them about it because

I was told that there was a security problem in their ranks.'

'What about the extra socket Benaboura had installed in the storeroom?'

'That was probably a request from Hammad and Saoudi,' said Flowers. 'He never spoke to me about it.'

'So you didn't know about the hexogen either?'

'It would have all come out when Benaboura was ready for it to come out.'

'Did he pick up on the surveillance?'

'In the apartment across the street?' said Flowers. 'He was so amazed at how unprofessional it was he'd begun to think it wasn't surveillance.'

'Did you talk to somebody about that on his behalf?'

'I asked Juan and he said it wasn't anything to do with them and he nosed around the CGI for me and said they weren't involved either. I had a look in the apartment myself one evening and it was empty. No equipment. I didn't bother with it any more after that.'

'You're uncharacteristically allowing me to ask a lot of questions.'

'It's all old news.'

'You don't seem bothered by the fact that Botín's electricians put a bomb in the mosque.'

'Oh, I'm bothered, Javier. I'm very bothered by that. I've lost one of my best agents.'

'Do you buy the CNI's story?'

'That Botín was a double?' said Flowers. 'That the Islamic terrorists he was working for knew about Benaboura and wanted to get rid of him?'

'And Hammad and Saoudi.'

'That's bullshit,' said Flowers, bitterly. 'But I'm not

thinking about that now. It's *your* job to rummage in the past.'

'Now you're thinking: what were Hammad and Saoudi going to do with 100 kilos of hexogen in Seville?'

'The GICM are not interested in returning Andalucía to the Islamic fold,' said Flowers. 'Their priority is to make Morocco an Islamic state, under Sharia law, but they do hold the same feelings about the West as those people we call al-Qaeda.'

'Is it certain that Hammad and Saoudi were GICM?'

'They've worked for them before.'

'So what was the hexogen going to be used for?'

'And was there more of it elsewhere?' asked Flowers. 'Those are the big unanswerable questions. It was probably still in its raw form when it exploded. We can only hope for more clues when we get into the mosque.'

'What would have had to be done to it to make it usable?'

'Normally they'd have mixed it with some plastique so that it could be moulded. The best clue would be to find what they were going to pack it into. The hardware.'

'But if you wanted to destroy a building, you could just stick it all in a suitcase, put it in the boot of a car and drive it through the entrance?'

'That's correct.'

'Do you know what the CNI are working on?' asked Falcón, realizing now that his conversation with Flowers was no longer evolving.

'You'd have to ask them,' said Flowers. 'But my advice to you is to do what you're paid to do, Javier. Stick to the past.'

Falcón's mobile vibrated. It was Ramírez. He took the call in the kitchen, well away from Flowers.

'We can confirm a sighting of Tateb Hassani in Rivero's house,' said Ramírez. 'We weren't having any luck on the outside, but Cristina spotted a woman coming out of the house who happened to be the maid looking after Hassani's room. She first saw him on 29th May and last saw him on 2nd June. She didn't work weekends, none of the maids in the main house do. She's not absolutely certain, but she doesn't think he left the house the entire time he was there. He worked in the Fuerza Andalucía offices at the front of the building and took most of his meals over there.'

'What news about Angel Zarrías?'

'That's why I'm calling. He's just arrived at Rivero's house about five minutes after Jesús Alarcón turned up. They're all here. It must be a Fuerza Andalucía strategy meeting.'

'Tell Cristina she has to find someone who was working at Rivero's house on Saturday evening. There must have been some kind of dinner for Tateb Hassani, which means cooks, serving staff, those kinds of people.'

34

'I think we should get Eduardo Rivero on his own,' said Falcón, 'without any sense of support from Jesús Alarcón and Angel Zarrías. Tateb Hassani was in *his* house, as *his* guest, and he was murdered there in *his* offices. If we can break him first, I'm sure he'll give us the rest.'

'What about the transport?' said Elvira. 'Can we get our hands on the car that took the body from Rivero's house to dump it in those bins on Calle Boteros?'

'The only sighting we've had of that car has been by an elderly alcoholic who was looking down from a height of about ten metres at night. All we've got from him is that it was a dark estate,' said Falcón. 'Ramírez is round there now, with Pérez, trying to find a more reliable witness. We're also checking all the cars in Rivero's name, and his wife's, to see if any match the basic description.'

'And who's watching Rivero's house?'

'Serrano and Baena are keeping Angel Zarrías under twenty-four-hour surveillance. They won't leave until

497

he does,' said Falcón. 'What about a search warrant for Rivero's house?'

'I'm worried about that, Javier,' said Elvira. 'Rivero might not be the leader of an important party, but he is a huge figure in Seville society. He knows everybody. He has important friends in all walks of life, including the judiciary. The trump card you hold at the moment is surprise. He doesn't realize that you've identified Tateb Hassani and located him at his house in the days before his murder. If I apply for a search warrant I have to make the case and reveal everything to the judge. The vital advantage you have has more opportunities to leak.'

'You'd rather I tried to break him first?'

'There are risks either way.'

'They're having a meeting now and they'll probably have dinner afterwards,' said Falcón. 'Let's see what the next hours bring us and we'll confer before we make the final move.'

Falcón went back to his house to have something to eat and to think about the best way to get Eduardo Rivero to talk. Inspector Jefe Luis Zorrita called, wanting to talk to him about Inés's murder. Falcón told him that now was the only moment he could spare.

Encarnación had left him some fresh pork fillet. He made a salad and sliced up some potatoes and the meat. He smashed up some cloves of garlic, threw them into the frying pan with the pork fillet and chips. He dashed some cheap whisky on top and let it catch fire from the gas flame. He ate without thinking about the food and drank a glass of red rioja to loosen up his mind. Instead of thinking about

Rivero, he found his mind full of Inés again, and it was playing tricks on him. He couldn't quite believe that she was dead, despite having seen her lying by the river. She'd been here only . . . last night, or was it the night before?

It was stuffy in the kitchen and he took his glass of wine and sat on the rim of the fountain in the patio, under the heat, which was still sinking down the walls like a giant, invisible press. They'd made love in this fountain, he and Inés. Those were wild, exhilarating days: just the two of them in this colossal house, running naked around the gallery, down the steps, in and out of the cloisters. She had been so beautiful then, in that time when youth was still running riot. He, on the other hand, was already carrying his ball and chain, he just didn't know it, couldn't see it. It occurred to him that he'd probably driven her into the arms of Esteban Calderón, the man who would eventually kill her.

The doorbell rang. He let Zorrita in and sat him down in the patio with a beer. Falcón had just finished describing his marriage to Inés, her affair with Calderón, their separation and divorce when his mobile vibrated. He took it in his study, closed the patio door.

'We've had some luck with the car,' said Ramírez. 'There's a bar on Calle Boteros called Garlochi. Strange place. All decked out with pictures and effigies of the Virgin. The bar has a canopy over it like a float from Semana Santa. It's lit with candles, they burn incense and the house cocktail comes in a glass chalice and it's called "Sangre de Cristo".'

'Suitably decadent.'

'It's always been shut when we've checked the area before. The owner tells me he was closing up on Saturday night, or rather, early Sunday morning, when he saw the car turn into the cul-de-sac and reverse up to the bins. He described it just as Cristina's witness had, except that he got a good view of it when the car reversed out of the cul-de-sac. He recognized it as a Mercedes E500 because he wanted to buy one himself but couldn't afford it. He also looked for the registration because he thought the three guys were behaving suspiciously, but that was nearly a week ago. All he could remember was that it was a new type of number which began with 82 and he thought that the last letter was an M.'

'Does that help you?'

'Baena just called me to say that three other cars have now turned up at Rivero's house,' said Ramírez. 'We've checked the plates and they're owned by Lucrecio Arenas, César Benito and Agustín Cárdenas. We're running a search on those people . . .'

'Lucrecio Arenas introduced Jesús Alarcón to Fuerza Andalucía through Angel Zarrías,' said Falcón. 'I don't know anything about the other two.'

'Listen. Agustín Cárdenas's car is a black Mercedes Estate E500 and the registration is 8247 BHM.'

'That's our man,' said Falcón.

'I'll get back to you when I know more.'

Falcón went back to Zorrita, apologized. Zorrita waved it away. Falcón told him about the last time he'd seen Inés. How she'd unexpectedly turned up at his house on Tuesday night, swearing about her husband and his endless affairs.

'Did you like Esteban Calderón?' asked Zorrita.

'I used to. People were surprised. I only found out much later that he and Inés had been having an affair for the last part of our short married life,' said Falcón. 'I thought he was an intelligent, well-informed, cultured person and he probably still is. But he's also arrogant, ambitious, narcissistic, and a lot of other adjectives that I can't retrieve from my brain at the moment.'

'Interesting,' said Zorrita, 'because he asked me if you'd go and see him.'

'What for?' asked Falcón. 'He knows I can't talk about his case.'

'He said he wants to explain something to you.'

'I'm not sure that's a good idea.'

'It's up to you,' said Zorrita. 'It won't bother me.'

'Off the record,' said Falcón. 'Did he break down and confess?'

'Nearly,' said Zorrita. 'There was a breakdown, but not in the usual way. Rather than his conscience forcing out the truth, it was more as if he suddenly doubted himself. To start with he was all arrogance and determined resistance. He refused a lawyer, which meant I could be quite brutal with him about the way he'd abused his wife. I think he was unaware of the intensity of his rage, the savagery it unleashed and the damage he'd done to her. He was shocked by the autopsy details and that's when his certainty really wavered and he began to believe that he *could* have done it.

'He described arriving at his apartment as if he was telling me about a movie and there was some confusion about how the script played out. At first he said that he'd seen Inés standing by the sink, but then he

501

changed his mind. In the end, I think there were two Calderóns. The judge and this other person, who was locked up most of the time but would come out and take over.'

'Inés said he needed psychological help,' said Falcón, 'but I don't think she had something as serious as schizophrenia in mind.'

'Not clinical schizophrenia,' said Zorrita. 'There's a beast inside most of us, it just never gets to see the light of day. For whatever reason, Calderón's beast got out of the cage.'

'You're convinced he did it?'

'I'm certain there was nobody else involved, so the only question is whether it was premeditated or accidental,' said Zorrita. 'I don't think his lover stood to gain anything out of Inés's death. She didn't want to marry him. She's not the marrying kind. She admitted that they'd had a "joke" about "the bourgeois solution to a bourgeois institution" being murder, but I don't think it was her intention that he should go off and kill his wife. He'll try to make out it was accidental, although no court is going to like the sound of how he abused her beforehand.'

Zorrita finished his beer. Falcón walked him to the door. Ramírez called again. Zorrita walked off into the night with a wave.

'OK, César Benito is the Chief Executive of a construction company called Construcciones PLM S.A. He is on the board of directors of Horizonte, in charge of their property services division, which includes companies like Mejorvista and Playadoro. The other guy, Agustín Cárdenas, is a bit more interesting. He's a qualified surgeon who runs his own cosmetic surgery clinics in

Madrid, Barcelona and Seville. He is also on the board of Horizonte, in charge of their medical services division, which runs Quirúrgicalidad, Ecográficalidad and Optivisión.'

'It looks like a gathering of the conspiracy to plan their next move now that the first phase has been successfully completed,' said Falcón.

'But I'm not convinced that we've got the full picture,' said Ramírez. 'I can see Rivero, Zarrías, Alarcón and Cárdenas poisoning Hassani, and probably Cárdenas did the work on the corpse, but none of these guys fits the descriptions of any of the men in the Mercedes E500 who dumped the body.'

'And who planted the bomb, or gave orders for it to be planted?'

'There's a missing element,' said Ramírez. 'I can see the money and the power and a certain amount of ruthlessness to deal with Tateb Hassani. But how could you get somebody to do the work in the mosque and rely on them to keep their mouths shut?'

'The only way to find that out is to put them under pressure in the Jefatura,' said Falcón, hearing the doorbell. 'Give Elvira an update. I've got a meeting with the CNI here. And tell Cristina she *has* to get a sighting of Tateb Hassani, as late on Saturday evening as possible. It's important that we have that before we talk to Rivero.'

Pablo and Gregorio went straight to the computer. Gregorio set to work, booting up the computer and getting access to the CNI's encrypted site, through which they would 'chat' to Yacoub Diouri.

'We've arranged for you to talk to Yacoub at 23.00 hours every night, unless you agree not to beforehand.

That's 23.00 Spanish time, which is 21.00 Moroccan time,' said Pablo. 'Obviously you have to be on your own to do this, nobody even in the house with you. The way in which you recognize each other is that each time you make contact you will start with a paragraph of incidental chat in which you will include a phrase from this book –'

Pablo handed him a copy of *Tomorrow in the Battle Think on Me* by Javier Marías.

'On the first day he will choose a phrase from the opening paragraph of page one, and you will respond with a phrase from the closing paragraph of page one,' said Pablo. 'Once you've recognized each other you can talk freely.'

'What if he doesn't use the phrase?'

'The most important thing is that you do not remind him and you don't respond with any classified information. You include your introductory phrase in your opening paragraph and if he still doesn't rectify the situation you log off. You must then not communicate with him until we've checked out his status,' said Pablo. 'The other thing is: no printouts. We will have a record on our website, which you will not be able to access unless we are here with you.'

'I still don't understand how you know that Yacoub will be accepted so easily into the GICM,' said Falcón.

'We didn't say that,' said Pablo. 'We said that he would be accepted into the radical element of the mosque in Salé. You have to remember Yacoub's history; what his real father, Raúl Jiménez, did and how his surrogate father, Abdullah Diouri, retaliated. That did not happen in a bubble. The whole family knew about it. That is the source of a certain amount of sympathy with some of the more radical elements of Islam. Don't ask any more . . . let's just see whether Yacoub has made contact with the radical element in the mosque and, if he has, how quickly he'll be put in touch with the high command of the GICM.'

'So what is the purpose of my conversation with him?'

'At this stage, to let him know that you're here,' said Pablo. 'Ultimately, we want to find out what was supposed to happen here in Seville and whether they still have the capability to make it happen, but we might have to be satisfied with confirmation of the history at this stage.'

The communication started at 23.03. They made their introductions and Falcón asked his first question.

'How's your first day been back at school?'

'It's more like the first day as a new member of a club. Everybody's sizing me up, some are friendly, others suspicious and a few are unfriendly. It's like in any organization, I've come in at a certain level and been welcomed by my equals, but I'm despised as a usurper by those who thought they were becoming important. There's a hierarchy here. There has to be. It's an organization with a military wing. The striking difference is that the commander-in-chief is not a man, but Allah. No action by this group, or any of the others that they read about, is referred to without mention of the ultimate source of the commands. We're constantly reminded that we're involved in a Holy War. It is powerful and inspirational and I've come back feeling dazed. Home seems strange, or rather, extremely banal after a day spent with people so certain of their place and destiny in the will of Allah. I can see how powerfully this would work on a young mind. They're also clever at depersonalizing the enemy, who are rarely specific people – unless you count Tony Blair and George Bush – but rather the decadence and godlessness that has engulfed the West. I suppose it's easier to bomb decadence and godlessness than it is men, women and children.'

'Any talk about what happened in Seville on 6th June?'

'They talk about nothing else. The Spanish satellite news is avidly watched for more information, but it's not so easy to work out the extent of their involvement.'

'Any talk about Djamel Hammad and Smail Saoudi and what they were doing bringing 100 kilos of hexogen to Seville?'

'I'm not sure how much is speculation and how much is hard fact. You must understand that these people are not the GICM themselves. They support the actions of the GICM, and some members have been involved in their activities, but mainly on the home front. Don't think that I've walked off the street into a tent full of mujahedeen with AK-47s. At this stage, I can only tell you what has happened rather than what *will* happen, as that is only known by the GICM commanders, who, as far as I know, are not here.

'My friends tell me that Hammad and Saoudi have worked for a number of groups, not just the GICM. They fund themselves through cash-machine fraud. They were only involved in recce, logistics and documents. They were not bomb makers. The hexogen came from Iraq. It was extracted from an American ammunitions cache captured at the beginning of 2005. It went via Syria into Turkey, where it was repackaged as cheap washing powder and sent to Germany in containers, for sale to the immigrant Turkish community there. Nobody knows how it got to Spain. The total quantity sent to Germany in the washing powder consignment is believed to be around 300 kilos.'

'Any speculation about how they intended to use it?' asked Falcón.

'No. All they say is that everything in the Spanish press and news is total fabrication: Abdullah Azzam's text, the MILA, the intention to attack schools and the biology faculty and the idea of bringing Andalucía back into the Islamic fold. They want to bring Andalucía back into Islam, but not yet. Making Morocco an Islamic state with Sharia law is the priority and we talked about that, which is of no interest to you. The current strategy, as far as foreign operations are concerned, is not specific, although they are still very angry with the Danish and think they should be punished. They want to weaken the European Union economically by forcing huge expenditure on antiterrorist measures. They plan to attack financial centres in Northern Europe, namely London, Frankfurt, Paris and Milan, while conducting smaller campaigns in the tourist areas of the Mediterranean.'

'Ambitious.'

'There's a lot of big talk. As to their capability . . . who knows?'

'The hexogen in Seville doesn't seem to fit with their general strategy.'

'They say the hexogen exploding was nothing to do with them.'

'And how do they know that?'

'Because the "hardware" for making the bombs had not arrived,' wrote Yacoub. 'Given that Hammad and Saoudi were recce and logistics, I assume there were others who were due to arrive with the "hardware" – the containers, plastique, detonators and timers – from some other source.'

'How much of this do you believe?' asked Falcón.

'There is definitely something going on. There's a tension and uncertainty in the air. I can't be more specific than that. This is information that has come to me. I am not enquiring as yet. I haven't asked about operational cells in Spain, for instance. I can only gather from the way people talk that there are operators in the field doing something.'

Falcón's mobile vibrated on the desktop. He took the call from Ramírez while Pablo and Gregorio talked over his head.

'Cristina has found a domestic who saw Tateb Hassani on Saturday evening, before dinner. His name is Mario Gómez. He says that the dinner wasn't served but laid out as a buffet, but he saw Tateb Hassani, Eduardo Rivero and Angel Zarrías going up to the Fuerza Andalucía offices just before he left, which was around 9.45.'

'He didn't see anybody else?'

'He said no cars had arrived by the time he left.'

'I think that's going to be good enough,' said Falcón and hung up.

'Ask him if he's heard any names, anything that will

508

give us a clue as to a network operating over here,' said Pablo.

Falcón typed out the question.

'They don't use names. Their knowledge of foreign operations is vague. They are more informative about the present state of Morocco than anything abroad.'

'Any foreigners?' asked Pablo. 'Afghans, Pakistanis, Saudis . . .?'

Falcón tapped it out.

'One mention of some Afghans who came over earlier this year, nothing else.'

'Context?'

'I couldn't say.'

'Where does the group meet?'

'It's in a private house in the medina in Rabat, but I was brought here and I'm not sure I could find it again.'

'Look for clues in your surroundings. Documents. Books. Anything that might indicate research.'

'There's a library which I've been shown, but I haven't spent any time there.'

'Get access and tell us what books they have.'

'I have been told/warned that there will be an initiation rite, which is designed to show my allegiance to the group. Everybody has to go through this, whatever your connections to the senior members may be. They have assured me that it will not require violence.'

'Do they know about your friendship with me?' asked Falcón.

'Of course they do, and that worries me. I know how their minds work. They will make me show allegiance to them by forcing me to betray the confidence of someone close to me.'

The 'chat' was over. Falcón sat back from the computer, a little shattered by the last exchange. The CNI men looked at him to see how he'd taken this new level of involvement.

'In case you're wondering,' said Falcón, 'I didn't like the sound of that.'

'We can't expect just to *receive* information in this game,' said Gregorio.

'I'm a senior policeman,' said Falcón. 'I can't compromise my position by giving out confidential information.'

'We don't know what he's going to be asked to do yet,' said Pablo.

'I didn't like the look of that word "betray",' said Falcón. 'That doesn't sound like they're going to be satisfied with my favourite colour, does it?'

Pablo shook his head at Gregorio.

'Anything else?' said Pablo.

'If they know about me, what's to say they don't know about the next step we've taken?' said Falcón. 'That I came over to make Yacoub one of our spies. He employs ten or fifteen people around his house. How do you know that he's "safe", that he's not going to be turned, and that they still think that I'm just a friend?'

'We have our own people on the inside,' said Pablo.

'Working for Yacoub?'

'We didn't just think this operation up last week,' said Gregorio. 'We have people working in his home, at his factory, and we've watched him on business trips. So have the British. He's been vetted down to his toenails. The only thing we didn't have, which nobody had, was access. And that's where you came in.'

'Don't think about it too much, Javier,' said Pablo.

'It's new territory and we'll take it one step at a time. If you feel there's something you can't do . . . then you can't do it. Nobody's going to force you.'

'I'm less worried about force than I am by coercion.'

35

That's what Flowers had said: 'You don't understand the pressure on these people.' Alone, now, Falcón gripped the arms of his chair in front of the dead computer screen. He'd only had a glimpse of it, but now he understood what Flowers had meant. He sat in his comfortable house, in the heart of one of the least violent cities in Europe and, yes, he had a demanding job, but not one where he had to pretend every day or cope with 'an initiation rite' that might demand 'betrayal'. He didn't have to cohabit with the minds of clear-sighted fanatics who saw God's purpose in the murder of innocents, who, in fact, didn't see them as innocents but as 'culpable by democracy', or the product of 'decadence and godlessness', and therefore fair game. He might have to face a moral choice, but not a life-or-death situation which could result in harm done to Yacoub, his wife and children.

Yacoub knew 'how their minds worked', that they would demand betrayal, because that would sever the relationship. They weren't interested in the low-quality information of a Sevillano detective. They wanted to

512

cut Yacoub off from a relationship that connected him to the outside world. Yacoub had been with the group for twenty-four hours and already they were setting about the imprisonment of his mind.

The mobile vibrating on the desktop made him start.

'Just to let you know,' said Ramírez, 'Arenas, Benito and Cárdenas have just left. Rivero, Zarrías and Alarcón are still there. Do we know what we're doing yet?'

'I have to call Elvira before we make a move,' said Falcón. 'What *I* want is for the two of us to go in there as soon as Rivero is alone and break him down so that he reveals *everybody* in the whole conspiracy, not just the bit players.'

'Do you know Eduardo Rivero?' asked Ramírez.

'I met him once at a party,' said Falcón. 'He's fantastically vain. Angel Zarrías has been trying to lever him out of the leadership of Fuerza Andalucía for years, but Rivero loved the status it conferred on him.'

'So how did Zarrías get him out?'

'No idea,' said Falcón. 'But Rivero is not a man to hand in his ego lightly.'

'It happened on the day of the bomb, didn't it?'

'That's when they announced it.'

'But it must have been coming for a while,' said Ramírez. 'Zarrías never mentioned anything to you about it?'

'Are you speaking with some inside knowledge, José Luis?'

'Some press guys I know were telling me there was talk of a sex scandal around Rivero,' said Ramírez. 'Under-age girls. They've lost interest since the bomb, but they were very suspicious of the handover to Jesús Alarcón.'

'So what's your proposed strategy, José Luis?' said Falcón. 'You sound as if you want to make yourself unpopular again?'

'I think I do. I've done a bit of work on Eduardo Rivero and I think that might be the way to make him feel uneasy,' said Ramírez. 'Lull him into a false sense of relief when we move away from the hint of scandal and then give him both barrels in the face with Tateb Hassani.'

'That *is* your style, José Luis.'

'He's the type who'll look down his nose at me,' said Ramírez. 'But because he knows you, and knows your sister is Zarrías's partner, he'll expect you to bring some dignity to the proceedings. He'll turn to you for help. I think he'll be devastated when you show him the shot of Tateb Hassani.'

'We hope.'

'Vain men are weak.'

Falcón called Comisario Elvira and gave him the update. He could almost smell the man's sweat trickling down the phone.

'Are you confident, Javier?' he asked, as if begging Falcón to give him some resolve.

'He's the weakest of the three, the most vulnerable,' said Falcón. 'If we can't break him, we'll struggle to break the others. We can make the evidence against him sound overwhelming.'

'Comisario Lobo thinks it's the best way.'

Falcón pocketed his mobile and a photograph of Tateb Hassani. He used his reflection in the glass doors to the patio to knot his tie. He shrugged into his jacket. He was conscious of his shoes on the marble flagstones of the patio as he made his way to his car. He drove through the night. The silent, lamp-lit streets under the dark trees were almost empty. Ramírez called to tell him that Alarcón had left. Falcón told him to send everybody home except Serrano and Baena, who would follow Zarrías once he'd left.

It was a short drive to Rivero's house and there was parking in the square. He joined Ramírez on the street corner. Serrano and Baena were in an unmarked car opposite Rivero's house.

A taxi came up the street and turned round by Rivero's oak doors. The driver got out and rang the doorbell. Within a minute Angel Zarrías came out and got into the back of the cab, which pulled away. Serrano and Baena waited until it was nearly out of sight and then took off in pursuit.

Cristina Ferrera had taken a cab back to her apartment. She was so exhausted she forgot to ask the driver for a receipt. She got her keys out and headed for the entrance to her block. A man sitting on the steps up to the door made her wary. He held up his hands to show her he meant no harm.

'It's me, Fernando,' he said. 'I lost your number, but remembered the address. I came to take you up on your offer of a bed for the night. My daughter, Lourdes, came out of intensive care this evening. She's in a room now with my parents-in-law looking after her. I needed to get out.'

'Have you been waiting long?'

'Since the bomb I don't look at the time,' he said. 'So I don't know.'

They went up to her apartment on the fourth floor. 'You're tired,' he said. 'I'm sorry, I shouldn't have come, but I've got nowhere else to go. I mean, nowhere that I'd feel comfortable.'

'It's all right,' she said. 'It's just another long day in a series of long days. I'm used to it.'

'Have you caught them yet?'

'We're close,' she said.

She put her bag on the table in the living room, took off her jacket and hung it on the back of the chair. She had a holster with a gun clipped to a belt around her waist.

'Are your kids asleep?' he asked, in a whisper.

'They sleep with my neighbour when I have to work late,' she said.

'I just wanted to see them sleeping, you know . . .' he said, and fluttered his hand, as if that explained his need for normality.

'They're not quite old enough to be left on their own all night,' she said, and went into the bedroom, unhooked the holster from her belt and put it in the top drawer of the chest. She pulled her blouse out of her waistband.

'Have you eaten?' she asked.

'Don't worry about me.'

'I'm putting a pizza in the microwave.'

Cristina opened some beers and laid the table. She remade the bed with clean sheets in one of the kids' rooms.

'Do your neighbours gossip?'

'Well, you're famous now, so they're bound to talk about you,' said Ferrera. 'They know I used to be a nun so they're not too concerned about my virtue.'

'You used to be a nun?'

'I told you,' she said. 'So what's it like?'

'What?'

'To be famous.'

'I don't understand it,' said Fernando. 'One moment I'm a labourer on a building site and the next I'm the voice of the people and it's nothing to do with *me*, but because *Lourdes* survived. Does that make any sense to you?'

'You've become a focus for what happened,' she said, taking the pizza out of the microwave. 'People don't want to listen to politicians, they want to listen to someone who's suffered. Tragedy gives you credibility.'

'There's no logic to it,' he said. 'I say the same things that I've always said in the bar where I go for coffee in the morning, and nobody listened to me then. Now I've got the whole of Spain hanging on my every word.'

'Well, that might change tomorrow,' said Ferrera.

'What might change?'

'Sorry, it's nothing. I can't talk about it. I shouldn't have said anything. Forget I even mentioned it. I'm too tired for this.'

Fernando's eyes narrowed over the slice of pizza halfway to his mouth.

'You're close,' said Fernando. 'That's what you said. Does that mean you know who they are, or you've actually caught them?'

'It means we're close,' she said, shrugging. 'I shouldn't have said it. It's police business. It slipped out because I was tired. I wasn't thinking properly.'

'Just tell me the name of the group,' said Fernando. 'They all have these crazy initials like MIEDO – Mártires Islámicos Enfrentados a la Dominación del Occidente.'

Islamic Martyrs facing up to Western Domination.

'You didn't listen.'

517

He frowned and replayed the dialogue.

'You mean they weren't terrorists?'

'They *were* terrorists, but not Islamic ones.'

Fernando shook his head in disbelief.

'I don't know how you can say that.'

Ferrera shrugged.

'I've read all the reports,' said Fernando. 'You found explosives in the back of their van, with the Koran and the Islamic sash and the black hood. They took the explosive into the mosque. The mosque exploded and . . .'

'That's all true.'

'Then I don't know what you're talking about.'

'That's why you've got to forget about it until it comes out in the news tomorrow.'

'Then why can't you tell me now?' he said. 'I'm not going anywhere.'

'Because suspects still have to be interrogated.'

'What suspects?'

'The people who are suspected of planning the bombing of the mosque.'

'You're just trying to confuse me now.'

'I'll tell you this if you promise me that that will be the end of it,' said Ferrera. 'I know it's important to you, but this is a police investigation and it's totally confidential information.'

'Tell me.'

'Promise me first.'

'I promise,' he said, waving it away with his hand.

'That sounds like a politician's promise.'

'That's what happens when you spend time with them. You learn too much, too quickly,' said Fernando. 'I promise you, Cristina.'

'There was another bomb that was planted in the mosque which, when it exploded, set off the very large quantity of hexogen which the Islamic terrorists were storing there. That's what destroyed your apartment building.'

'And you know who planted the bomb?'

'You promised me that that would be the end of it.'

'I know, but I just need to . . . I *have* to know.'

'That's what we're working on tonight.'

'You have to tell me who they are.'

'I can't. There's no discussion. It's not possible. If it came out, I'd lose my job.'

'They killed my wife and son.'

'And if they are responsible, they will face trial.'

Fernando opened up a pack of cigarettes.

'You'll have to go out on the balcony if you want to smoke.'

'Come and sit with me?'

'No more questions?'

'I promise. You're right. I can't do this to you.'

Falcón and Ramírez were ringing the bell as Zarrías's taxi turned out of Calle Castelar. Eduardo Rivero opened the door, expecting it to be Angel coming back for the notebook he'd forgotten. He was surprised to find two stone-faced policemen in the frame, presenting their ID cards. His face momentarily lost all definition, as if the muscles had been deprived of their neural drive. Geniality revived them.

'What can I do for you, gentlemen?' he asked, his white moustache doubling the size and warmth of his smile.

'We'd like to talk to you,' said Falcón.

'It's very late,' said Rivero, looking at his watch.

'It can't wait,' said Ramírez.

Rivero looked away from him with faint disgust.

'Have we met?' he asked Falcón. 'You seem familiar.'

'I came to a party here once, some years ago,' said Falcón. 'My sister is Angel Zarrías's partner.'

'Ah, yes, yes, yes, yes, yes . . . Javier Falcón. Of course,' said Rivero. 'Can I ask what you'd like to talk to me about at this time of the morning?'

'We're homicide detectives,' said Ramírez. 'We only ever talk to people at this hour of the morning about murder.'

'And you are?' said Rivero, his distaste even more undisguised.

'Inspector Ramírez,' he said. 'We've never met before, Sr Rivero. You'd have remembered it.'

'I can't think how I can help you.'

'We just want to ask some questions,' said Falcón. 'It shouldn't take too long.'

That eased the tension in the doorway. Rivero could see himself in bed within the hour. He let the door fall back and the two policemen stepped in.

'We'll go up to my office,' said Rivero, trying to reel in Ramírez, who'd gone straight through the arch to the internal courtyard and was brushing his large intrusive fingers over the rough head of the low hedge.

'What's this called?' he asked.

'Box hedge,' said Rivero. 'From the family Buxaceae. They use it in England to make mazes. Shall we go upstairs?'

'It looks as if it's just been clipped,' said Ramírez. 'When did that happen?'

'Probably last weekend, Inspector Ramírez,' said

Rivero, holding out his arm to herd him back into the fold. 'Let's go upstairs now, shall we?'

Ramírez snapped off a twig and twiddled it between thumb and forefinger. They went up to Rivero's office where he showed them chairs, before sinking into his own on the far side of the desk. He was irritated to find Ramírez examining the photographs on the wall: shots of Rivero, in politics and at play with the hierarchy of the Partido Popular, various members of the aristocracy, some bull breeders and a few local *toreros*.

'Are you looking for something, Inspector?' asked Rivero.

'You used to be the leader of Fuerza Andalucía until a few days ago,' said Ramírez. 'In fact, didn't you hand over the leadership on the morning of the explosion?'

'Well, it wasn't a sudden decision. It was something I'd been thinking about for a long time, but when something like that happens it opens up a new chapter in Seville politics, and it seemed to me that a new chapter needed new strength. Jesús Alarcón is the man to take the party forward. I think my decision has proved to be a very good one. We're polling more now than in the party's history.'

'I understood that you were very attached to the leadership,' said Ramírez, 'and that moves had been made before now to persuade you to hand over, but you'd refused. So what happened to make you think again?'

'I thought I'd just explained that.'

'Two senior members of your party left at the beginning of this year.'

'They had their reasons.'

'The newspapers reported that it was because they were fed up with your leadership.'

Silence. It always amazed Falcón how much Ramírez enjoyed making himself unpopular with 'important' people.

'I seem to remember that one of them even said that it would take a bomb to get you to give up the leadership and, I quote: "That would have the satisfying side effect of removing Don Eduardo from politics as well." That doesn't sound as if you were actively thinking about giving up your position, Sr Rivero.'

'The person who said that was expecting the leadership to be conferred on him. I didn't think he was a suitable candidate as he was only seven years younger than me. It was unfortunate that we fell out over the matter.'

'That's not what was written in the newspapers,' said Ramírez. 'They were reporting that these two senior members of your party were not pushing themselves forward but were, in fact, pushing for Jesús Alarcón to take over. What I was wondering was, what happened between then and now to bring about this sudden change of heart?'

'I'm quite flattered to find you so knowledgeable about my party,' said Rivero, who regained some strength by reminding himself that these men were homicide detectives and not from the sex crimes squad. 'But didn't you tell me you were here to talk about something else? It's late; perhaps we should press on.'

'Yes, of course,' said Ramírez. 'It was probably just malicious rumour anyway.'

Ramírez sat down, very pleased with himself. Rivero looked at him steadily over the rims of the gold specs he'd just put on. It was difficult to know what was burning inside him. Did he want to know what this rumour was, or would he prefer Ramírez just to shut the fuck up?

'We're looking for a missing person, Don Eduardo,' said Falcón.

Rivero's head whipped away from Ramírez to focus on Falcón.

'A missing person?' he said, and some relief crept into the corner of his face. 'I can't think of anybody I know who's gone missing, Inspector Jefe.'

'We're here because this man was last seen in your household by one of your maids,' said Falcón, who had spoken each word clearly and slowly so that he could watch the accumulation ease into Eduardo Rivero with the intrusiveness of a medical probe.

Rivero was a practised politician, but even he could not relax and animate himself through the progression of this sentence. Perhaps because it was a line that he'd dreaded hearing and had forced to the bleakest region of his mind.

'I'm not sure who you could be talking about,' said Rivero, clutching at the rope of hope, only to find frayed cotton threads.

'His name is Tateb Hassani, although in America he was known as Jack Hansen. He was a professor of Arabic Studies at Columbia University in New York,' said Falcón, who removed a photograph from his inside pocket and snapped it down in front of Rivero. 'I'm sure you'd recognize one of your own house guests, Don Eduardo.'

Rivero leaned forward and planted his elbows on the desk. He glanced down, stroked his chin and massaged his jowls with his thumb, over and over, whilst ransacking the furniture of his brain for the inspiration that would take him to the next moment.

'You're right,' said Rivero. 'Tateb Hassani was a guest in this house until last Saturday, when he left, and I haven't seen or heard of him since.'

'What time did he leave here on Saturday and how did he depart from these premises?' asked Falcón.

'I'm not sure when he left . . .'

'Was it daylight?'

'I wasn't here when he left,' said Rivero.

'When was the last time you saw him?'

'It was after lunch, probably four thirty. I said I was going to take a siesta. He said he would be leaving.'

'When did you wake from your siesta?'

'About six thirty.'

'And Tateb Hassani had already gone?'

'That is correct.'

'I'm sure your staff will be able to confirm that.'

Silence.

'When did you last see the cosmetic surgeon, Agustín Cárdenas?'

'He was here this evening . . . for dinner.'

'And before that?'

Silence, while monstrous abstractions boiled up, loomed, subsided and loomed again in Rivero's nauseated mind.

'He was here on Saturday evening, again for dinner.'

'How did he arrive for dinner?'

'In his car.'

'Can you describe that car?'

'It's a black Mercedes Estate E500. He'd just bought it last year.'

524

'Where did he park his car?'

'Inside the front doors, below the arch.'

'Did Agustín Cárdenas stay the night here?'

'Yes.'

'What time did he leave on Sunday?'

'At about eleven in the morning.'

'Were you aware of that car leaving your house at any time between Agustín Cárdenas's arrival and his departure on Sunday morning?'

'No,' said Rivero, the sweat careening down his spine.

'Who else was present at that dinner on Saturday night?'

Rivero cleared his throat. The water was getting deeper, winking at his chin.

'I'm not sure what this could possibly have to do with the disappearance of Tateb Hassani.'

'Because that was the night that Tateb Hassani was poisoned with cyanide, had his hands surgically removed, his face burnt off with acid and his scalp cut away from his skull,' said Falcón.

Rivero had to clench his buttocks against the sudden looseness of his bowels.

'But I've already told you that Tateb Hassani left here before dinner,' said Rivero. 'Maybe four hours before dinner.'

'And I'm sure that can be corroborated by the domestic servants on duty here at the time,' said Falcón.

'We're not accusing you of lying, Don Eduardo,' said Ramírez. 'But we must have a clear idea of what happened here, in this house, in the hope that it will explain what happened later.'

'What happened *later*?'

'Let's take it step by step,' said Falcón. 'Who attended the dinner, apart from yourself and Agustín Cárdenas?'

'That will shed no light on the disappearance of Tateb Hassani, because HE HAD ALREADY LEFT THIS HOUSE!' roared Rivero, hammering out the last six words with his fist on the desk.

'There's no need to upset yourself, Don Eduardo,' said Ramírez, leaning forward, full of false concern. 'Surely you can understand, given that a man was murdered and brutally dealt with, that the Inspector Jefe has to ask questions that may appear mystifying but which, we can assure you, will have a bearing on the case.'

'Let's go back a step,' said Falcón, to make it sound less unrelenting. 'Tell me who prepared Saturday's dinner and who served it.'

'It was prepared by the cook and it wasn't served. It was brought up to the room next door and laid out as a buffet.'

'Can we have those employees' names please?' said Falcón.

'They left straight afterwards and went home.'

'We'd still like their names and phone numbers,' said Falcón, and Ramírez handed over his notebook, which Rivero refused to accept.

'This is an infringement . . .'

'Tell us what happened after the dinner,' said Falcón. 'What time did it finish, who left and who stayed, and what did those who stayed do for the remainder of the night?'

'No, this is too much. I've told you everything that's relevant to the disappearance of Tateb Hassani. I've co-operated fully. All these other questions I consider to be outrageous intrusions into my private life and I see no reason why I should answer them.'

'Why was Tateb Hassani a house guest of yours for five days?'

'I told you, I'm not answering any more questions.'

'In that case, we must inform you that Tateb Hassani was suspected of terrorist offences, directly linked to the Seville bombing. His handwriting was on documents found in the destroyed mosque. You were therefore harbouring a terrorist, Don Eduardo. I think you know what that means regarding our investigation. So we would like you to accompany us down to the Jefatura and we will continue this interview under the terms of the antiterrorism –'

'Now, Inspector Jefe, let's not be too hasty,' said Rivero, blood draining from his face. 'You came here enquiring about the disappearance of Tateb Hassani. I have co-operated as best I can. Now you are changing the nature of your enquiry without giving me the opportunity to address the matter in this new light.'

'We didn't want to have to force your hand, Don Eduardo,' said Falcón. 'Let's go back to why you entertained Tateb Hassani as your house guest for five days . . .'

Rivero swallowed and braced himself against the desk for this next lap of the course.

'He was helping us to formulate our immigration policy. He, like us, did not believe that Africa and Europe were compatible, or that Islam and Christianity could cohabit in harmony. His particular insights into the Arabic mind were extremely helpful to us. And, of course, his name and stature added weight to our cause.'

'Despite the fact that he rarely visited his homeland,

had spent his entire adult life in the USA and that he had to leave Columbia University under the cloud of a sexual harassment case, which cost him his apartment and all his savings?' said Falcón.

'Despite that,' said Rivero. 'His insights were invaluable.'

'How much did Fuerza Andalucía pay him for this work?'

Rivero stared into the desk, terrified by this burgeoning demand for more and more improvisation. How was he ever going to remember any of it? Fatigue got a foothold in his viscera. He viciously shrugged it off. He had to hang on, like a fatally wounded man he had to keep talking, to overwhelm any desire he might have to give up. The flaws were developing inside him. His shell had been weakening from the moment that DVD had come anonymously into his possession and he'd had to view the hideousness of his indiscretions. The cracks had spread further when Angel had come to see him. He had listened, his white mane of hair gone wild and his face battered by excessive alcohol, as Angel had told him how he'd saved him. The rumour had been rife, like a wildfire consuming the tinder-dry undergrowth, gathering strength to leap up into an enormous conflagration. Angel had saved him, but it had come at a price. The time had come to step down or be destroyed.

That conversation with Angel had weakened him more than he knew. Over the days the flaws spread through him until every part of him was ruined. Every step now was a step down into the dark. Murder had come into his house and a desecration of the sanctity of the body. He could not think, after it had taken place, how such a thing could have happened to him in a matter of weeks. One moment brilliant and whole, the next corrupt, fractured, fissured beyond repair. He had to get a grip on himself. The centre must hold.

'You must remember what you had to pay for such invaluable advice,' said Falcón, who had been watching this immense struggle from the other side of the desk.

'It was 5,000,' said Rivero.

'Was that with a cheque?'

'No, cash.'

'You paid him with black money?'

'Even policemen know how this country works,' said Rivero, acidly.

'I must say, Don Eduardo, that I do admire your poise under these very stressful circumstances,' said Falcón. 'Had I been in your shoes and found out that the man I'd paid €5,000 for his advice on immigration had also been involved in a terrorist plot to take over two schools and a university faculty, I would be in a state of shock. That this man should also have been responsible for writing out those appalling instructions to kill schoolchildren, one by one, until their demands had been met would devastate me, if I were you.'

'But then again, you are a politician,' said Ramírez, smiling.

Sweat was raking down his flanks, his stomach was embarking on a ferocious protest, his blood pressure was screaming in his ears, his heartbeat was so fast and tight that his breathing had shallowed, and his brain gasped for oxygen. And yet, he sat there, tapping the side of his nose, bracing himself against the desk.

'I have to say,' Rivero said, 'that I cannot begin to think what this means.'

'So, you had this dinner on Saturday night,' said Falcón. 'It wasn't served, but was laid out as a buffet. How many people attended that dinner? So far, we have yourself and Agustín Cárdenas, but you'd hardly go to the trouble of a buffet for just two people, would you?'

'Angel Zarrías was there as well,' said Rivero, smoothly, thinking, yes, they could have Angel, he should go down with them, the little fucker. 'I quite often have buffets on Saturday nights, so that the servants can go home and enjoy dinner with their families.'

'What time did Angel arrive?'

'He was here around 9.30, I think.'

'And Agustín Cárdenas?'

'About 10 p.m.'

'Did he arrive with anybody else?'

'No.'

'He was alone in the car?'

'Yes.'

'You're saying there were only three people for dinner?'

Rivero didn't care about the lying any more. It was all lies. He stared into his desk and let them fall from his tongue, like gold coins worn to a slippery smoothness.

'Yes. I quite often have a buffet and whoever turns up . . . turns up.'

Falcón glanced at Ramírez, who shrugged at him, nodded him in for the kill.

'Do you know one of your staff called Mario Gómez?'

'Of course.'

'It was he who laid out the buffet in the next room on that Saturday night.'

'That would be his job,' said Rivero.

'He told us that he'd served Tateb Hassani with at least one meal a day since he'd arrived in your house, up here in these rooms.'

'Possibly.'

'He knew who Tateb Hassani was, and he saw you accompanying him upstairs to dinner with Angel Zarrías at 9.45 on Saturday night. Some hours later Tateb Hassani was poisoned with cyanide, horribly disfigured and driven from here, in Agustín Cárdenas's car, to be dumped in a bin on Calle Boteros.'

Rivero clasped his hands, drove them between his slim thighs and sobbed with his head dropped on to his chest. Released at last.

36

'Great news,' said Elvira, sitting at his desk in his office in the Jefatura.

'Nearly great news,' said Falcón. 'We didn't manage to force Rivero into revealing the entire conspiracy. He only gave us two names. It's quite possible that we can charge the three of them, but only with the murder of Tateb Hassani and not the planning of the bombing of the mosque.'

'But now we can get a search warrant for Eduardo Rivero's house and the Fuerza Andalucía offices,' said Elvira. 'We must be able to squeeze something out of those two places.'

'But nothing in writing. You don't draw this sort of stuff up in the minutes of a Fuerza Andalucía meeting,' said Falcón. 'We have a tenuous link between Angel Zarrías and Ricardo Gamero, but no proof of what they discussed in the Archaeological Museum. We have no idea of the connection of any of these men to the people who actually planted the bomb. Both José Luis and I think that there is a missing element to the conspiracy.'

'A criminal element,' added Ramírez.

'We're sure that Lucrecio Arenas and César Benito are in some way involved, but we couldn't persuade Rivero to even give us their names,' said Falcón. 'They could be the "other half" of the conspiracy. Arenas put up Jesús Alarcón as a candidate for the leadership, so we assume that he is involved. But did Arenas and Benito make contact with the criminal element who planted the bomb? We're not sure we'll ever find out who, or what, that missing element was.'

'But you can put Rivero, Zarrías and Cárdenas under enormous pressure . . .'

'Except that they know, with the clarity of self-preservation, that all they have to do is keep their mouths shut and we'll only be able to pin murder on one of them, and conspiring to murder on all three, but nothing more,' said Falcón. 'And as for Lucrecio Arenas, Jesús Alarcón and César Benito, we have no chance. Ferrera worked hard just to get that final sighting of Tateb Hassani. Once those few remaining employees left, the house was empty, which means we'll have a job to place Arenas, Benito and Alarcón there . . . that is, assuming that they turned up for the killing.'

'And if I was them, I'd have kept well away from that,' said Ramírez.

'The link to the bomb conspiracy is Tateb Hassani,' said Elvira. 'Work on the suspects until they reveal why Hassani had to be killed. Once they've admitted —'

'If it was *my* life that depended on it,' said Ramírez, 'I'd just hold out.'

'I can't speak for Rivero and Cárdenas, but I know Angel Zarrías is very religious, with a deep faith —

533

however misguided it might be. I'm sure he'll even find it in himself to be absolved of all his sins,' said Falcón. 'Angel is urbane. He knows what's tolerable in modern Spanish society, as far as expressing religious views is concerned. But I don't think we're talking about a mentality that's any less fanatical than an Islamic jihadist's.'

'Rivero, Zarrías and Cárdenas are going to spend the night in the cells,' said Elvira. 'And we'll see what tomorrow brings. You both have to get some sleep. We'll have search warrants ready in the morning for all of their properties.'

'I'm going to have to give my sister at least half an hour of my time,' said Falcón. 'Her partner has just been dragged out of bed and arrested in the middle of the night. There's probably a hundred messages on my mobile already.'

Cristina Ferrera slammed back into consciousness with dead-bolt certainty and sat upright in her bed, faintly swaying, as if moored by guy ropes in a wind. She only came awake like this if her maternal instinct had received a high-voltage neural alarm call. Despite the depth of the sleep she'd just abandoned, her lucidity was instantaneous; she knew that her children were neither in the apartment, nor in danger, but that something was very wrong.

The street lighting showed that there was nobody in her room. She swung her legs out of bed and scanned the living room. Her handbag was no longer in the centre of the dining-room table. It had been moved to the corner. She toed the door open to the bedroom she'd made up for Fernando. The bed was empty. The pillow was dented, but the sheets had not been drawn back. She checked her watch. It was coming up to 4.30 a.m. Why would he have come here just to sleep for a few hours?

She turned the light on over the dining-room table and wrenched open the neck of her large handbag. Her notebook was on top of her purse. She slapped it on the table. Nothing was missing, not even the € 15 in cash. She sat down as their conversation came back to her: Fernando badgering her for news. Her eyes drifted from her handbag to her notebook. Her notes were personal. She always kept two columns; one for the facts, the other for her thoughts and observations. The latter was not always tethered to the former and sometimes verged on the creative. She turned the notebook over. One of her observations jumped out at her from the page. It was alongside the names of the people who'd been seen by Mario Gómez going up with Tateb Hassani to the 'last supper'. In her observation column she'd scribbled the only possible conclusion to all the enquiries she'd made: Fuerza Andalucía planted the bomb. No question mark. A bold statement, based on the facts she'd gathered.

It was suddenly cold in the room, as if the air conditioning had found another gear. She swallowed against the rise of adrenaline. She headed for the bedroom, with the backs of her thighs trembling below the oversized T-shirt she wore in bed. She slapped the light on and opened the drawer of her dresser where she kept a vast tangle of knickers and bras. Her hand roved the drawer, again and again. She ripped it out and turned it over. She ripped out the other drawer and did the same. She thought she was going to faint with the quantity of chemicals her body was injecting into her system. Her gun was no longer there.

This was too big for her to manage on her own. She was going to have to call her Inspector Jefe. She hit the speed-dial button, listened to the endless ringing tone and reminded herself to breathe. Falcón answered on the eighth ring. He'd been asleep for one and a half hours. She told him everything in three seconds flat. It went down the line like a massive file under compression software.

'You're going to have to tell me all that again, Cristina,' he said, 'and a little slower. Breathe. Close your eyes. Speak.'

This time it came out in a thirty-second stream.

'There's only one person from Fuerza Andalucía who Fernando knows who isn't currently in police custody and that's Jesús Alarcón,' said Falcón. 'I'll pick you up in ten minutes.'

'But he's going to kill him, Inspector Jefe,' said Ferrera. 'He's going to kill him with my gun. Shouldn't we . . .?'

'If we send a patrol car round there he might get spooked and do just that,' said Falcón. 'My guess is that Fernando is going to want to tell him something first. Punish him before he *tries* to kill him.'

'With a gun he doesn't have to try very hard.'

'The concept is easy, the reality takes a bit more,' said Falcón. 'Let's hope he woke you up as he left your apartment. If he's on foot he can't be too far ahead of us.'

Fernando squatted on his haunches next to some bins on the edge of the Parque María Luisa. Only his hands were in the light from the street lamps. He looked from the dark at the blue metal of the small .38 revolver. He turned it over, surprised at its weight. He'd only ever held toy guns, made from aluminium. The real thing had the heft of a much bigger tool, condensed into pure efficiency and portability.

He emptied the bullets from the chambers of the revolver's cylinder and put them in his pocket. He clicked the cylinder back into place. He was good with his hands. He played around with the weapon, getting used to its weight and the simple, lethal mechanisms. When he was confident with it, he counted the bullets back into the chambers. He was ready. He stood and did what he'd seen people do in the movies. He tucked it into the waistband in the small of his back and pulled the Fuerza Andalucía polo shirt, given to him by Jesús Alarcón, over the top.

The wide Avenida that separated the park from the smart residential area of El Porvenir was empty. He knew where Jesús Alarcón lived because there'd been the offer of a room for as long as he wanted it. He hadn't accepted it because he didn't feel comfortable with their class differences.

He stood in front of the huge, sliding metal gate of the house. A silver Mercedes was parked in front of the garage. If Fernando had known that it was worth twice as much as his destroyed apartment it would have stoked his fury even more. As it was, the malignancy growing inside him was too big to contain. His rib cage creaked against his endlessly extending outrage at what Jesús Alarcón had done. Not just the bombing, but the purpose with which he'd set out to make Fernando, whose family he had personally been responsible for destroying, his close friend. It was treachery and betrayal on a scale to which only a politician could have been impervious. Jesús Alarcón, with all his authentic concern and genuine sympathy, had been playing him like a fish.

There was no traffic. The street in El Porvenir was empty. None of the people in these houses was ever up before dawn. Fernando called Alarcón on his mobile. It rang for some time and switched into the message service. He called Alarcón's house phone and looked up at the window he imagined would be the master bedroom. Jesús and Mónica in some gargantuan bed, beneath high-quality linen, dressed in silk pyjamas. A faint glow appeared behind the curtains. Alarcón answered groggily.

'Jesús, it's me, Fernando. I'm sorry to call you so early. I'm here. Outside. I've been out all night. They threw me out of the hospital. I had nowhere to go. I need to talk to you. Can you come down? I'm . . . I'm desperate.'

It was true. He was desperate. Desperate for revenge. He'd only ever heard tales of the monstrousness of this horrific emotion. He had not been prepared for the way it found every crevice of the body. His organs screamed for it. His bones howled with it. His joints ground with it. His blood seethed with it. It was so intolerable that he had to get it out of himself. He wanted stilts so that he could step over the gate, smash through the glass, reach into Alarcón's bed and pluck out his beautiful wife and throw her to the ground, break her bones, dash out her brains, tread his sharpened stilt into her heart and then see what Jesús Alarcón made of that. Yes, he wanted to be enormous, to drive his arm into Alarcón's home as if it was a doll's house.

He saw his hand ferreting around the bedrooms reaching for Alarcón's small children, who would run squealing from his snatching hand. He wanted Alarcón to see them crushed and laid out under little sheets in front of the house.

'I'm coming,' said Alarcón. 'No problem, Fernando.'

Had he known the hidden hunger behind the eyes staring through the bars of the gate, Jesús Alarcón would have stayed in his bed, called the police and begged for special forces.

A light came on outside the front of the house. The door opened. Alarcón, in a silk dressing gown, pointed the remote at the gate. Fernando flinched, as if being shot at. The gate rumbled back on its rails. Fernando slipped through the gap and walked quickly up to the house. Alarcón had already turned back to the front door, holding out an arm, which he expected to fit around Fernando's shoulders and welcome him into his home.

Moths swirled around the porch light, maddened by the prospect of a greater darkness, which never materialized. Alarcón was still too groggy to recognize the level of intent moving up on him. He was astonished to feel a fistful of his dressing-gown collar grabbed from behind and the front door reeling away from him as Fernando, with the hardened strength of a manual worker, swung him round. Alarcón lost his footing and fell to his knees. Fernando yanked him backwards and trapped his head between his thighs. He had the gun out of his waistband. Alarcón reached back, grabbing at Fernando's trousers and polo shirt. Fernando showed him the gun, poked the barrel into the socket of his eye so that Alarcón gasped with pain.

'You see that?' said Fernando. 'You see it, you little fucker?'

Alarcón was paralysed with fear. His voice, with his neck pulled taut, produced only a grunt. Fernando pushed the gun between Alarcón's lips, felt the barrel rattle across his teeth and sensed the steel mushing into the softness of his tongue.

'Feel it. Taste it. You know what it is now.'

He wrenched the gun out of his mouth, taking a chip of tooth with it. He jammed the barrel into the back of Alarcón's neck.

'Are you ready? Say your prayers, Jesús, because you're going to meet your namesake.'

Fernando pulled the trigger, the gun pressed hard against Alarcón's shaking neck. There was a dry click. A gasp from Alarcón and a stink rose up from behind him as he loosed his bowels into his pyjamas.

'That was for Gloria,' said Fernando. 'Now you know her fear.'

Fernando moved the gun round to Alarcón's temple, screwed it into the top of his sideburn so that Alarcón winced away from it. Another dry click and a sob from Alarcón.

'That was for my little Pedro,' said Fernando, coughing against the emotion rising in his throat. 'He didn't know fear. He was too young to know it. Too innocent. Now look at the gun, Jesús. You see the cylinder. Two empty chambers and four full ones. We're going upstairs now and you're going to watch me shoot your wife and two children, just so you know how it feels.'

'What are you doing, Fernando?' said Alarcón, finding his voice and his presence of mind, now that the rush of the initial onslaught was past. 'What the fuck are you doing?'

'You and your friends. You're all the same. There's no difference between you and any other politician. You're all liars, cheats and egomaniacs. I don't know how I fell for your stupid, fucking line. Jesús Alarcón, the man who will talk to you without cameras, without the photo opportunity, without his beautiful profile in mind.'

'What are you talking about, Fernando? What have I done? How have I lied and cheated?' said Alarcón, pleading.

'You killed my wife and child,' said Fernando. 'And then, because you needed me, you made me your friend.'

'How did I kill them?'

'I read it in the police notes. You were all in it. Rivero, Zarrías, Cárdenas. You planted the bomb in the mosque. You killed my wife and son. You killed all those people. And for what?'

'Fernando?'

He looked up. A different voice from beyond the gate. Female. Not in his head. The blood was simmering in his brain, bubbling and popping in such arterial rage that he'd become confused.

'Gloria?' he said.

'It's me, Cristina,' she said. 'I'm here with Inspector Jefe Falcón. We want you to put the gun down, Fernando. This is not how you resolve things. You've misunderstood . . .'

'No, no. That is not true. I have *finally* understood only too well. You listen. You listen to my "friend", Jesús Alarcón.'

Fernando knelt down by the side of Alarcón and whispered harshly in his ear.

'I am not going to shoot you or your family on one condition,' he said. 'The condition is that you must tell them the truth. They're the cops. They know what the truth is. You're going to tell them the truth for the first time with your gilded politician's lips. Tell them how you planted the bomb and you will live to see the rest of this day. If you don't, I will shoot you and, when you are dead, I will go inside and find Mónica and shoot her, too. Go on, tell them.'

Fernando stood up and prodded Alarcón in the neck with the gun. Alarcón cleared his throat.

'The truth,' said Fernando, 'or I'm sending you into the dark. Tell them.'

Alarcón crossed himself.

'He has asked me to tell you the truth about the bomb,' said Alarcón, his head hung on to his chest, his arms limp by his sides. 'If I fail to tell you the truth he says he will shoot me and then my wife. I can only tell you what I know, which may not be the whole truth, but only a part of it.'

Fernando stood back, arm straight. He rested the gun barrel on the crown of Alarcón's head.

'I had nothing to do with the planting of any bomb in that mosque, so help me God,' said Alarcón.

37

There was no gunshot. A force travelled from Alarcón's head, up the gun barrel, through Fernando's hand, arm and shoulder and into his mind. It made his upper body shudder so that the gun barrel drifted from its aim, and had to be retrained on to Alarcón's crown, not once or twice, but three times. His finger caressed the trigger with each retraining of the revolver. He blinked, took in huge gulps of air and looked down on the man, who a few moments ago had been the object of his deepest hatred. He couldn't do it. Alarcón's words had somehow drained all his resolve. It was the miracle cure for the malignancy of his revenge. He knew with absolute certainty that he had heard the truth.

At first light, with the sky turning from midnight blue to anil, Fernando dropped his arm and let it hang with the weight of the gun. Ferrera stepped forward and removed it from his slack grasp and holstered it. She moved him away from behind Alarcón, who fell forwards on to all fours.

'Take Fernando to the car,' said Falcón. 'Cuff him.'

Alarcón was dry retching and sobbing at the sudden

release of tension. Falcón got him to his feet and took him to where his wife was standing, wide-eyed, features rigid, by the front door. Falcón asked for the bathroom. The request brought Mónica Alarcón back to reality. She led Falcón and her husband upstairs to where the children were standing, one holding a fluffy tiger, the other a small blue blanket, uncomprehending of the adult drama. Mónica got the kids back into their bedroom. She joined Falcón in the bathroom where her husband was struggling to undo the buttons on his pyjamas. Falcón told her to strip her husband's clothes off and get him into the shower. He would wait downstairs in the kitchen.

Exhaustion leaned on Falcón like a big, stupid dog. He shut the front door and sat at the kitchen table, staring into the garden, with only one thought shuttling backwards and forwards through his mind. Jesús Alarcón was not part of the conspiracy. It looked as if he was their compliant and ignorant front man.

Mónica came back down to the kitchen and offered him a coffee. She was shaken, her hands trembled over the crockery. She had to ask him to work the espresso machine.

'Did he have a gun?' she asked. 'Did Fernando have a *gun*?'

'Your husband handled himself very well,' said Falcón, nodding.

'But Fernando and Jesús were getting on so well.'

'Fernando read something he shouldn't have done and misunderstood an observation as a fact,' said Falcón. 'Your husband's courage meant that it didn't end in tragedy.'

'We both admired Fernando so much for the way

544

in which he was managing his terrible loss,' she said. 'I had no idea he was so unstable.'

'He thought your husband had betrayed him, that he'd made him his friend to further his political career. And Fernando *is* unstable. Nobody can be called stable after losing their wife and son like that.'

Jesús appeared in the doorway. He'd lost the ashen look. He was shaved and dressed in a white shirt and black trousers. Falcón made him a coffee. Mónica went back upstairs to check on the children. They sat at the kitchen table.

'A lot has happened overnight,' said Falcón. 'Can you answer a few questions before we discuss that?'

Alarcón nodded, stirred sugar into his coffee.

'Can you tell me where you were on Saturday 3rd June?' asked Falcón.

'We were north of Madrid for the weekend,' said Alarcón. 'One of Mónica's friends got married. The wedding party was at a finca on the way up to El Escorial. We stayed there on Sunday and came back on the AVE train early on Monday morning.'

'Did you go to the Fuerza Andalucía offices in Eduardo Rivero's house during the week before that?'

'No, I didn't,' said Alarcón. 'On the advice of Angel Zarrías I was staying clear of Eduardo. Angel was still working on him to relinquish the leadership and he reckoned that for Eduardo to see the new young blade of the party around him might be construed as humiliation. So, I didn't see any of them, except Angel, who came here a couple of times to tell me how things were going.'

'When you say you didn't see any of them, who do you include in that?'

'Eduardo Rivero and the three main sponsors of the party, who are all my supporters: Lucrecio Arenas, César Benito and Agustín Cárdenas.'

'When did you last see Eduardo Rivero?'

'On the Tuesday morning, when he formally handed over the leadership.'

'And before that?'

'I think we had lunch around the 20th of May. I'd have to check my diary.'

'Have you ever seen this man before?' asked Falcón, looking at Alarcón as he pushed a photo of Tateb Hassani across the table. It was clear he didn't recognize the man.

'No,' he said.

'Have you ever heard mention of the name Tateb Hassani or Jack Hansen?'

'No.'

Falcón took the photograph back and turned it over and over in his hands.

'Has that man got anything to do with what Fernando was talking about?' asked Alarcón. 'He looks North African. That first name you mentioned . . .'

'He's originally a Moroccan who became a US citizen,' said Falcón. 'He's dead now. Murdered. Rivero, Zarrías and Cárdenas are under arrest on suspicion of his killing.'

'I'm confused, Inspector Jefe.'

'Don Eduardo told me a few hours ago that he paid Tateb Hassani a € 5,000 consultancy fee last week for his advice on the formulation of Fuerza Andalucía's immigration policy.'

'That's ridiculous. Our immigration policy has been in place for months. We started work on that last October when the EU opened the door to Turkey and all those African immigrants tried to jump the wire into Melilla. Fuerza Andalucía does not believe that a Muslim country, even with a secular government, can be compatible with Christian countries. Europeans have shown themselves to be consistently intolerant of other religions throughout history. We have no idea of the social consequences of introducing Turkey, whose membership will result in one fifth of the European Union population being Muslim.'

'You're not on the campaign trail now, Sr Alarcón,' said Falcón, holding up his hands against the avalanche of opinion.

'I'm sorry. It's automatic,' he said, shaking his head. 'But why are Rivero, Zarrías and Cárdenas accused of murdering a man who they'd just paid to help formulate policy? Why does Fernando think that Fuerza Andalucía is in some way responsible for planting a bomb in the mosque?'

'I'm going to give you an irrefutable fact and I want you to tell me what you construe from it,' said Falcón. 'You heard on the news that a fireproof box was found in the destroyed mosque, which included architect's drawings of two schools and the university biology faculty, with notes attached in Arabic script.'

'The ones giving the horrific instructions.'

'Those were written by Tateb Hassani.'

'So, he was a terrorist?'

Falcón waited, tapping the edges of the photograph, one after the other, on the table top, while the espresso machine fumed quietly in the corner. Alarcón frowned at the back of his hands as his brain worked through the permutations. Falcón gave him the other facts that were not in the public domain, as yet: Tateb Hassani's handwriting also matched that found in the two Korans, found in the Peugeot Partner and in Miguel Botín's apartment. He also told him about Ricardo Gamero's final meeting with Angel Zarrías and the CGI agent's subsequent suicide. Alarcón turned his hands over and looked at his palms, as if his political future was trickling away through his fingers.

'I don't know what to say.'

Falcón gave him a short life history of Tateb Hassani and asked him if that sounded like the profile of a dangerous Islamic radical.

'Why did they pay Hassani to make up documents that would indicate a planned terrorist attack when, as has been made clear by the discovery of traces of hexogen in the Peugeot Partner, Islamic terrorists were positioning material to carry out a bombing campaign?' asked Alarcón. 'It doesn't make sense.'

'The executive committee of Fuerza Andalucía did not know about the hexogen,' said Falcón, which opened up the story about the surveillance by Informáticalidad, the fake council inspectors, the electricians, and the planting of the secondary Goma 2 Eco device and the fireproof box.

Alarcón was stunned. He knew all the directors of Informáticalidad, whom he described as 'part of the set-up'. Only then did he finally understand how he'd been used.

'And I was positioned as the fresh face of Fuerza Andalucía, who, in the aftermath of the atrocity, would attract the anti-immigration vote, which would give us the necessary percentage to make ourselves the natural coalition partner of the Partido Popular for next year's parliamentary campaign,' said Alarcón.

The revelations drained what little energy remained in Alarcón and he sat back with his arms limp at his sides and contemplated the catastrophe in which he'd been unwittingly involved.

'I realize that this must be hard for you . . .' said Falcón.

'There are enormous implications, of course,' said Alarcón, with an odd mixture of dismay and relief spreading across his features. 'But I wasn't thinking of that. I was thinking that Fernando's madness has had the inadvertent side effect of allowing me to exonerate myself in front of the investigating Inspector Jefe.'

'Our range of interrogation techniques no longer includes mock executions,' said Falcón. 'But it has saved me a lot of time.'

'It wasn't what I had in mind for the extension of police powers in the handling of terrorists, either,' said Alarcón.

'You might have to work a little harder than that to get my vote,' said Falcón. 'How would you describe your relationship to Lucrecio Arenas?'

'I'm not exaggerating when I tell you that he's been like a father to me,' said Alarcón.

'How long have you known him?'

'Eleven years,' said Alarcón. 'In fact, I met him before that, when I was working for McKinsey's in South America, but we became close when I moved to Lehman Brothers and started working with Spanish industrialists and banks. Then he head-hunted me in 1997 and since then he's been a surrogate father . . . he's shaped my whole career. He's the one who has given me belief in myself. He's second in my life only to God.'

It was the response Falcón had expected.

'If you think *he* is involved in whatever this is, then think again. You don't know the man like I do,' said Alarcón. 'This is some local intrigue, cooked up by Zarrías and Rivero.'

'Rivero is finished. He was finished before this happened. He was walking with the fly-buzz of scandal about him,' said Falcón. 'I know Angel Zarrías. He's not a leader. He makes people into leaders, but he doesn't make things happen himself. What can *you* tell me about Agustín Cárdenas and César Benito?'

'I need another coffee,' said Alarcón.

'Here's an interesting link for you to think about,' said Falcón. 'Informáticalidad to Horizonte, to Banco Omni, to . . . I4IT?'

The coffee machine gurgled, trickled, hissed and steamed, while Alarcón hovered around it, blinking in this new point of view, matching it to his own bank of knowledge. Doubt threaded its way across his eyebrows. Falcón knew this wasn't going to be enough, but he didn't have anything more. If Rivero, Zarrías and Cárdenas didn't break down then Alarcón might be his only door into the conspiracy, but it was going to be a heavy door to open. He didn't know enough about Lucrecio Arenas to induce a sense of outrage in Alarcón at the way in which he'd been shamelessly exploited by his so-called 'father'.

'I know what you want from me,' said Alarcón, 'but I can't do it. I realize it's not fashionable to be loyal, especially in politics and business, but I can't help myself. Even suspecting these people would be like turning on my own family. I mean, they *are* my family. My father-in-law is one of these people . . .'

'That was why you were chosen,' said Falcón. 'You

are an extraordinary combination. I don't agree with your politics, but I can see that, for a start, you are very courageous and that your intentions towards Fernando were completely honourable. You're an intelligent and gifted man, but your vulnerability is in your professed loyalty. Powerful people *like* that in a person, because you have all the qualities that they don't, and you can be manipulated towards achieving their goals.'

'It's a marvellous world in which loyalty is perceived as a vulnerability,' said Alarcón. 'You must be a man made cynical by your work, Inspector Jefe.'

'I'm not cynical, Sr Alarcón, I've just come to realize that it's the nature of virtue to be predictable,' he said. 'It's always evil that leaves one gasping at its bold and inconceivable virtuosity.'

'I'll remember that.'

'Don't make me any more coffee,' said Falcón. 'I have to sleep. Perhaps we should talk again when you've had time to think about what I've told you and I've started working on Rivero, Zarrías and Cárdenas.'

Alarcón walked him to the front door.

'As far as I am concerned, I have no wish to see Fernando punished for what he did to me,' he said. 'My sense of loyalty also enables me to understand the profound effects of disloyalty and betrayal. You might have charges you wish to press against him, but I don't.'

'If this gets out to the press I'll have no option but to prosecute him,' said Falcón. 'He stole a police firearm and there's a good case for attempted murder.'

'I won't talk to the press. You have my word on it.'

'You've just saved the career of one of my best junior officers,' said Falcón, stepping off the porch.

He walked to the gate and turned back to Alarcón.

'I presume, after last night's meeting, that Lucrecio Arenas and César Benito are still in Seville,' he said. 'I would suggest a face-to-face meeting with one, or both, of them while the information I've just given you is still out of the public domain.'

'César won't be there. He'll be at the Holiday Inn in Madrid for a conference,' said Alarcón. 'Is seventy-two hours from inception to demise of a political future some kind of Spanish record?'

'The advantage you have at the moment is that you, personally, are clean. If you can retain that, you will always have a future. It's only once you join hands with corruption that you're finished,' said Falcón. 'Your old friend Eduardo Rivero could tell you that from the bottom of the well of his experience.'

Cristina Ferrera and Fernando were sitting in the back of Falcón's car. She'd cuffed his hands behind his back and he leaned forward with his head resting against the back of the front seat. Falcón thought that they'd been talking but were now exhausted. He turned to face them from the driver's seat.

'Sr Alarcón is not going to press charges and he won't talk to the newspapers about this incident,' he said. 'If I were to prosecute you I would lose one of my best officers, your daughter would lose her father and only parent and would have to be taken into care, or go to live with her grandparents. You would go to jail for at least ten years and Lourdes would never know you. Do you think that's a satisfactory outcome for a burst of uncontrollable rage, Fernando?'

Cristina Ferrera looked out of the window blinking

with relief. Fernando raised his head from the back of the passenger seat.

'And had your rage got the better of you, had your hatred been so dire that no reason could have appealed to it, and you'd actually killed Jesús Alarcón, then all the above would still be true, although your prison sentence would be longer, and you'd have had the death of an innocent man on your conscience,' said Falcón. 'How does that feel, in the dawn light of a new day?'

Fernando looked straight ahead, through the wind-screen, down the street growing lighter by the moment.

He said nothing. There was nothing to say.

38

'You didn't make it to our appointment last night,' said Alicia Aguado.

'I was in no condition,' said Consuelo. 'I left you, went to the pharmacy with the prescription you'd given me, bought the drugs and didn't take them. I went back to my sister's house. I spent most of the day in her spare room. Some of the time I was crying so hard I couldn't breathe.'

'When was the last time you cried?'

'I don't think I ever have . . . not properly. Not with grief,' said Consuelo. 'I don't even remember crying as a child, apart from when I hurt myself. My mother said I was a silent baby. I don't think I was the crying type.'

'And how do you feel now?'

'Can't you tell?' said Consuelo, twitching her wrist under Aguado's fingers.

'Tell me.'

'It's not an easy state to describe,' said Consuelo. 'I don't want to sound like some mushy fool.'

'Mushy fool is a good start.'

'I feel better now than I have done for a long time,' said Consuelo. 'I can't say that I feel good, but that terrifying sense of impending hideousness has gone. And the strange sexual urges have gone.'

'So, you don't think you're going mad any more?' said Aguado.

'I'm not sure about that,' said Consuelo. 'I've lost all sense of equilibrium. I can't seem to have just one feeling, I'm both extremes at once. I feel empty *and* full, courageous and afraid, angry and placid, happy and yet grief-stricken. I can't find any middle ground.'

'You can't expect your mind to recover in twenty-four hours of crying,' said Aguado. 'Do you think you could describe what happened yesterday morning? You came to some sort of realization which completely felled you. I'd like you to talk about that.'

'I'm not sure I can remember how it came about,' said Consuelo. 'It's like the bomb going off in Seville. So much has happened that it already feels like ten years ago.'

'I'll tell you how it came about afterwards,' said Aguado. 'Concentrate on what happened. Describe it as best you can.'

'It started off like a pressure, as if there was a membrane stretched across my mind, like an opaque latex sheet, against which someone, or something, was pressing. It's happened to me before. It makes me feel queasy, as if I'm at that crossover point between being merry and drunk. When it's happened in the past I'd make it go away by doing something like rummaging in my handbag. The physical action would help to reassert reality, but I'd be left with the sensation of the imminence of something that had not come to pass.

The interesting thing was that I stopped getting these moments a few years ago.'

'Were they replaced by something else?'

'I didn't think so at the time. I was just glad to be rid of the sensation. But now I'm thinking that it was then that the sexual urges started,' said Consuelo. 'In the same way that the pressure started during a lull of brain activity, so the urges would come, sometimes in a meeting, or playing with the kids, or trying on a pair of shoes. It was disturbing to have no control over when they appeared, because they would be accompanied by graphic images which left me feeling disgusted with myself.'

'So what happened yesterday?' asked Aguado.

'The membrane came back,' said Consuelo, palms suddenly moist on the arms of the chair. 'There was the pressure, but it was much greater and it seemed to be expanding at an incredible rate, so that I thought my head would burst. In fact, there *was* a sensation of bursting, or rather splitting, which was accompanied by that feeling you get in dreams of endlessly falling. I thought this is it. I'm finished. The monster's come up from the deep and I'm going to go mad.'

'But that didn't happen, did it?'

'No. There was no monster.'

'Was there anything?'

'There was just me. A lonely young woman in a rain-filled street, full of grief, guilt and despair. I didn't know what to do with myself.'

'When this happened, we were talking about someone you knew,' said Aguado. 'The Madrid art dealer.'

'Ah, yes, him. Did I tell you that he'd killed a man?'

'Yes, but you told me about it in a certain way.'

'I remember now,' said Consuelo. 'I told you about it as if his crime was greater than my own.'

'What does that mean?'

'That I believed that I had committed a crime?' said Consuelo, questioning. 'Except that I knew what I'd done. I had always faced up to the fact that I'd had the abortions, even the appalling way I'd raised the money for the first one.'

'Which had resulted in some confusion in your mind,' said Aguado. 'The graphic sexual images?'

'I don't understand.'

'This pain you mentioned when you watched your children sleeping, especially the youngest child – what do you think that was?'

Consuelo gulped, as the saliva thickened in her mouth and tears flooded her eyes and rolled down her face.

'You told me before that it was the love that was hurting,' said Aguado. 'Do you still think it was love?'

'No,' said Consuelo, after some long minutes. 'It was guilt at what I had done, and grief at what could have been.'

'Go back to that time when you were standing in the rain-filled street. I think you told me earlier that you were looking at some smart people coming out of an art gallery. Do you remember what you were thinking, before you decided that you wanted to be like them, that you wanted to "reinvent" yourself?'

There was a long silence. Aguado didn't move. She stared straight ahead with her unseeing eyes and felt the pulse beneath her fingers, like string untangling itself.

'Regret,' said Consuelo. 'I wished I hadn't done it, and when I saw those people coming out into the street I thought that they were not the sort of people to get themselves into this state. It was then that I decided I wanted to leave this pathetic, lonely, pitiful person on this wet street and go and be someone else.'

'So, although you've always "faced up" to what you'd done, there was also something missing. What was that?'

'The person who'd done it,' said Consuelo. 'Me.'

The search warrants for Eduardo Rivero's house, the premises of Fuerza Andalucía, Angel Zarrías's apartment and Agustín Cárdenas's residence were issued at 7.30 a.m. By 8.15 the forensics had moved in, the computer hard disks had been copied and evidence was being gathered and gradually shipped back to the Jefatura. Comisario Elvira, all six members of the homicide squad and three members of the CGI antiterrorism squad convened for a strategy meeting in the Jefatura at 8.45. The idea was that the nine-man interrogation team would interview the three suspects, with a few breaks, for a total of thirteen and a half hours. To prevent the suspects developing relationships or getting used to a certain style, every member of the team would interview each suspect for an hour and a half. While the first three interviewers worked the next wave would watch, and the third wave would rest or discuss developments. Lunch would be taken at 3 p.m. and there would be another tactical discussion. The next session would run from 4 p.m. to 10 p.m. and, if none of the suspects had cracked, there would be a break for dinner and a final ninety-minute session at midnight.

The point of the interviews was not to persuade the suspects to admit to the killing of Tateb Hassani, but to force them to reveal who had put Fuerza Andalucía in touch with him, why he was being employed, where the documents he'd prepared had been delivered, and who else had been at the dinner at which Tateb Hassani had been poisoned.

Exhaustion was the communal state. The meeting broke up with sighs, hands run through hair, jackets removed and shirt sleeves rolled up. It was agreed that Falcón would take Angel Zarrías first, Ramírez would handle Eduardo Rivero, and Barros would start on Agustín Cárdenas. Once they were told that the suspects were in the interview rooms they went downstairs.

Ferrera was due to follow Falcón interviewing Angel Zarrías. They stood in front of the glass viewing panel, looking at him. He was sitting at the table, wearing a long-sleeved white shirt, hands clasped, eyes fixed on the door. He seemed calm. Falcón began to feel too tired for this confrontation.

'You're going to find out that Angel Zarrías is a very charming man,' said Falcón. 'He especially likes women. I don't know him very well because he's the sort of man who keeps you at a distance with his charm. But there has to be a real person underneath that. There has to be the fanatic that wanted to make this conspiracy work. That's the man we want to get to, and once we've got to him we want to keep him there, exposed, for as long as possible.'

'And how are you going to do that?' said Ferrera. 'He's practically your brother-in-law.'

'I've learnt a few things from José Luis,' said Falcón,

nodding at Rivero's interview room, which Ramírez had just entered.

'Then I'll keep an eye on both of you,' said Ferrera.

Angel Zarrías's eyes flicked up as Falcón opened the door to the interview room. He smiled and stood up.

'I'm glad it's you, Javier,' he said. 'I'm so glad it's you. Have you spoken to Manuela?'

'I spoke to Manuela,' said Falcón, who sat down without turning on any of the recording equipment or following any of the normal introductory procedure. 'She's very angry.'

'Well, people react in different ways to having their partners arrested in the middle of the night on suspicion of murder,' said Zarrías. 'I can imagine some people might get angry. I don't know how I'd feel myself.'

'She wasn't angry about your arrest,' said Falcón.

'She was pretty fierce with your officers,' said Angel.

'It was after I'd spoken to her that she became . . . incandescent with rage,' said Falcón. 'I think that would be a fair description.'

'When did you speak to her?' he asked, unnerved, puzzled.

'At about two o'clock this morning,' said Falcón. 'She'd already left about fifty messages on my mobile by then.'

'Of course . . . she would.'

'As you know, she can be quite a daunting prospect when she's emotionally charged,' said Falcón. 'It wasn't possible for me to just say that you'd been arrested on suspicion of murder and leave it at that. She had to know who, where and why.'

'And what did you tell her?'

'I had to tell her by degrees because, of course, there

are legal implications, but I can assure you I only told her the truth.'

'What was this "truth" that you told her?'

'That is what *you* are supposed to tell *me*, Angel. You are the perpetrator and I am the interrogator, and between us there is a truth. The idea is that we negotiate our way to the heart of it, but it's not up to *me* to tell *you* what I think you've done. That's your job.'

Silence. Zarrías looked at the dead recording equipment. Falcón was pleased to see him confused. He leaned over, turned on the recorder and made the introductions.

'Why did you kill Tateb Hassani?' asked Falcón, sitting back.

'And what if I tell you that I didn't kill him?'

'If you like, for the purposes of this interview, we won't draw a distinction between murder and conspiring to murder,' said Falcón. 'Does that make it easier for you?'

'What if I tell you I had nothing to do with the murder of Tateb Hassani?'

'You've already been implicated, along with Agustín Cárdenas, by the host of Hassani's final and fatal dinner, Eduardo Rivero. You've also been identified as being present at the scene of the crime by an employee in his household,' said Falcón. 'So for you to say that you had *nothing* to do with Hassani's death would be a very difficult position to defend.'

Angel Zarrías looked deeply into Falcón's face. Falcón had been looked at like this before. His old technique, before his breakdown in 2001, was to meet it with the armour-plated stare. His new technique was to welcome them in, bring them to the lip of his deep well and dare them to look down. This was what he did to Angel Zarrías. But Angel wouldn't come. He looked hard but he never came to the edge. He backed off and glanced around the room.

'Let's not get bogged down in all the detail,' said Falcón. 'I'm not interested in who put the cyanide in what, or who was present when Agustín Cárdenas did his gruesome work. Although I *am* interested to know whose idea it was to sew Tateb Hassani into a shroud. Did you come up with any suitable Islamic orisons for him? Did you wash him before you sewed him up? It was a bit tricky for us to tell once we'd discovered him, bloated and stinking, with the shroud torn off, on the rubbish dump outside Seville. But I thought that was a nice touch of respect from one religion to another. Was that your idea?'

Angel Zarrías had pushed his chair back and, in his agitation, had started to pace the room.

'You're not talking to me already, Angel, and we've only just started.'

'What the hell do you expect me to say?'

'All right. I know. It's difficult. You've always been a good Catholic, a man of great religious faith. You even managed to get Manuela to go to Mass, and she *must* have loved you to do that,' said Falcón. 'Guilt is a debilitating state for a good man, such as yourself. Living in mortal sin must be petrifying but, equally, it's a daunting task to bring yourself to the confessional for the greatest of human crimes. I'm going to make this easier for you. Let's forget about Tateb Hassani for the time being and move on to something you're more comfortable with, that you should be able to talk about, that should loosen your vocal cords so that you will,

562

eventually, be able to come back to the more demanding revelations.'

Angel Zarrías stopped in his tracks and faced Falcón. His shoulders slumped, his chest looked like a cathedral roof on the brink of collapse.

'Go on then, ask your question.'

'Where were you on Wednesday, 7th June between 1.30 p.m. and 3 p.m.?'

'I can't recall. I was probably having lunch.'

'Sit down and think about it,' said Falcón. 'This is the day *after* the explosion. You would have received a phone call from someone who was desperate. I'm sure you'd remember that: a fellow human being in distress who needed to speak to you.'

'You know who it is, so you tell me,' said Angel, who'd started his agitated walking again.

'SIT DOWN, ANGEL!' roared Falcón.

Zarrías had never heard Falcón shout before. He was shocked at the anger simmering beneath the placid surface. He swerved towards the chair, sat down and stared into the table with his hands clasped tight.

'You were seen and identified by a security guard,' said Falcón.

'I went to the Archaeological Museum and met a man called Ricardo Gamero.'

'Are you aware of what happened to Ricardo Gamero about half an hour after you spoke to him?'

'He committed suicide.'

'You were the last person to speak to him, face to face. What did you talk about?'

'He told me he had developed feelings for another man. He was very ashamed and distressed about it.'

'You're lying to me, Angel. Why should a committed

563

CGI agent leave his office during the most important antiterrorist investigation ever to happen in this city, to go and discuss his sexual angst with you?'

'You asked me a question and I replied,' said Zarrías, without taking his eyes off the table.

Falcón pummelled Zarrías with questions about Ricardo Gamero for three-quarters of an hour, but could not get him to budge from his story. He accused Zarrías of telling Marco Barreda from Informáticalidad to offer up the same lie. Zarrías didn't even give Falcón the satisfaction of a flicker of recognition at this new name. Falcón made a show of ordering Barreda to be brought down to the Jefatura for questioning. Zarrías hung on grimly, knowing that this was the difference between life and a living death.

It was well past 10 a.m. when Falcón returned to the murder of Tateb Hassani. Zarrías looked pale and sick from maintaining his wall of deceit. One eye was bloodshot and his lower lids were hanging down from his eyeballs to reveal raw, veined and shiny flesh.

'Let's talk about Tateb Hassani again,' said Falcón. 'An employee, Mario Gómez, saw you, Rivero and Hassani going upstairs to the Fuerza Andalucía offices in Rivero's house to dine on a buffet that he'd just laid out. The time was 9.45 p.m. Rivero has told us that Agustín Cárdenas arrived a little later and parked his car underneath the arch of the entrance. Tell me what happened in the time between you going up the stairs and Tateb Hassani's body being brought down to be loaded into Agustín Cárdenas's Mercedes E500.'

'We drank some chilled manzanilla, ate some olives. Agustín turned up a little after ten o'clock. We served ourselves from the buffet. Eduardo opened a special bottle of wine, one of his Vega Sicilias. We ate, we drank, we talked.'

'What time did Lucrecio Arenas and César Benito arrive?'

'They didn't. They weren't there.'

'Mario Gómez told us that there was enough food for eight people.'

'Eduardo has always been generous with his portions.'

'At what point did you administer the cyanide to Tateb Hassani?'

'You're not going to get me to incriminate myself,' said Angel. 'We'll leave that for the court to decide.'

'How was Tateb Hassani introduced to you?'

'We met at the Chamber of Commerce.'

'What did Tateb Hassani do for you?'

'He helped us formulate our immigration policy.'

'Jesús Alarcón says that was already in place months ago.'

'Tateb Hassani was very knowledgeable about North Africa. He'd read a lot of the UN reports about the mass assaults by illegal immigrants on the enclaves of Ceuta and Melilla. We were incorporating new ideas into our policy. We had no idea how well-timed his help would be in view of what happened on 6th June.'

Falcón announced the end of the interview and flicked off the recorder. It was more important now that he prepare Zarrías for the next interview. There was plenty of evidence of decrepitude in his face, but he had retreated into himself, concentrated his powers into a nucleus of defence. Falcón had only achieved some superficial damage. Now he had to make him vulnerable.

'I had to tell Manuela,' said Falcón. 'You know what she's like. I told her that you'd had to murder Tateb Hassani because he was the only element outside the conspiracy and, therefore, the only danger to it. If he was left alive it would render Fuerza Andalucía vulnerable. Manuela wasn't prepared to deal in those sorts of generalizations so I had to give her the detail; how you'd employed him and where evidence of his handwriting was found. She knows you, of course, Angel. She knows you very well. She hadn't quite realized how far your obsession had gone. She hadn't realized that you'd gone from being extreme to fanatical. And she admired you so much, Angel, you know that, don't you? You helped her a lot with your positive energy. You helped me, too. You saved my relationship with her, which was important to me. I believe that she could have forgiven you this misguided attempt to finally grab a workable power, even if she didn't hold with your extreme beliefs. She thought, at least, that you were honourable. But there was something that she could not forgive.'

At last Zarrías looked up, as if he'd just come to the surface of himself. The tired, bruised and sagging eyes were suddenly alive with interest. In that moment Falcón realized something he'd never quite been sure about: Angel loved Manuela. Falcón knew that his sister was attractive, plenty of people had told him that they found her funny and that she had a great zest for life, and he'd seen her affect men touchingly by playing the little girl as well as the grown woman. But Falcón knew her too well and it had always seemed unlikely to him that anybody not related to Manuela could love her absolutely, because she had too many faults and dislikeable traits constantly on display. Clearly, though, she'd given something to Angel that he'd missed from his previous marriage, because there was no mistaking his need to know why she hated him.

'I'm listening,' said Zarrías.

'She could not forgive the way you talked to her that morning, when you'd already planned for that bomb to explode and she hadn't sold her properties.'

39

Yacoub was in the library in the group's house in the medina when they came for him. With no warning there were suddenly four men around him. They put a black hood over his head and tied his hands behind him with plastic cuffs. Nobody said a word. They took him through the house and out into the street, where he was thrust into the footwell in the back of a car. Three men came in after him and rested their feet on his supine body. The car took off.

They drove for hours. It was uncomfortable in the footwell, but at least they were driving on tarmac. Yacoub controlled his fear by telling himself that this was part of the initiation rite. After several hours they came off the good road and began labouring up some rough track. It was hot. The car had no air conditioning. The windows were open. It must have been dusty, because he could smell it even inside his hood. They spent an hour dipping and diving on the rough track until the car came to a halt. There was the sound of a rifle mechanism, followed by an intense silence as if each face in the car were being searched. They were told to carry on.

The car continued for another fifteen minutes until it again came to a halt. Doors opened and Yacoub was dragged out, losing his barbouches. They ran him across some rocky ground so fast that he stumbled. They paid no attention to his lost footing and hauled him on. A door opened. He was taken across a beaten earth floor and down some steps. Another door. He was hurled against a wall. He dropped to the floor. The door shut. Footsteps retreated. No light came through the dense material of the hood. He listened hard and became aware of a sound, which did not seem to be in the same room. It was a human sound. It was coming from a man's throat, a gasping and groaning, as if he was in great pain. He called out to the man, but all that happened was that the voice fell silent, apart from a faint sobbing.

The sound of approaching feet kick-started Yacoub's heart. His mouth dried as the door opened. The room seemed to be full of people, all shouting and pushing him around. There was the sound of screaming from the next room and a man's voice, pleading. They picked Yacoub up bodily, held him face down, and took him back up the stairs, outside, across rough ground. They dropped him and stood back. Whoever had been down-stairs in the cells was now out in the open with him, crying out in pain. A rifle mechanism clattered close to his ear. Yacoub's head was pulled up and the hood removed. He saw a man's feet, bloody and pulpy. His hair was grabbed from behind and his vision directed towards the man lying in front of him. A gunshot, loud and close. The man's head jolted and matter spurted from the other side. His bloody feet twitched. The hood was pulled back over Yacoub's head. The barrel of a gun was put to the back of his neck. His heart was thundering in his ears, eyes tight shut. The trigger clicked behind his head.

They picked him up again. They seemed gentler. They walked him away. There was no rush now. He was taken into a house and given a chair to sit on. They removed his plastic cuffs and black hood. Sweat cascaded down his neck and into the collar of his jellabah. A boy put his barbouches down by his feet. A glass of mint tea was poured for him. He was so disorientated that he could not even take in the faces of those around him before they left the room. He put his head down on the table top and gasped and wept.

After being inside the hood, his eyes were already accustomed to the darkness of the room. There was a single bed in the corner. One wall was covered with books. The windows were all shuttered. He sipped the tea. His heart rate eased back down to below the one hundred mark. His throat, which had been tight with hysteria, slackened. He went over to the books and studied the titles of each one. Most of them were about architecture or engineering: detailed tomes on buildings and machines. There were even some car manuals, thick manufacturer's plans for some four-wheel-drive vehicles. They were all in French, English or German. The only Arabic texts were eight volumes of poetry. He sat back down.

Two men came in and gave him a formal, but warm, welcome. One called himself Mohamed, the other Abu. A boy followed them, carrying a tray of tea, glasses and a plate of flat bread. The two men were both heavily bearded and each wore a dark brown burnous and army boots. They sat at the table. The boy poured the tea and left. Abu and Mohamed studied Yacoub very carefully.

'That is not normally part of our initiation procedure,' said Mohamed.

'A member of our council thought that you were a special case,' said Abu, 'because you have so many outside contacts.'

'He felt that you needed to be left in no doubt as to the punishment for treachery.'

'We did not agree with him,' said Abu. 'We did not think that anyone bearing the name of Abdullah Diouri would need such a demonstration.'

Yacoub acknowledged the honour accorded to his father. More tea was poured and sipped. The bread was broken and distributed.

'You had a visit from a friend of yours on Wednesday,' said Mohamed.

'Javier Falcón,' said Yacoub.

'What did he want to discuss with you?'

'He is the investigator of the Seville bombing,' said Yacoub.

'We know everything about him,' said Abu. 'We just want to know what you discussed.'

'The Spanish intelligence agency had asked him to approach me on their behalf,' said Yacoub. 'He wanted to know if I would be willing to be a source for them.'

'And what did you tell him?'

'I gave him the same answer that I'd given the Americans and the British when they'd made the same approaches,' said Yacoub, 'which is why I am here today.'

'Why is that?'

'In refusing all these people, who dishonoured me

by offering money for my services, I realized that it was time for me to take a stand. If I was certain that I did not want to be with them, then it should follow that my loyalties lay elsewhere. I had refused them because it would be the ultimate betrayal of everything my father stood for. And, if that was the case, then I should take a stand for what he believed in, against the decadence that he so despised. So when my friend left I went straight to the mosque in Salé and let it be known that I wanted to help in any way that I could.'

'Do you still consider Javier Falcón to be a friend?'

'Yes, I do. He was not acting for himself. I still consider him to be an honourable man.'

'We have been following the Seville bombing with interest,' said Mohamed. 'As you've probably realized, it has caused great disruption to one of our plans, which has demanded a lot of reorganization. We understand that some arrests were made last night. Three men are being held. They are all members of the political party Fuerza Andalucía, a party holding anti-Islamic views, which it wants to translate into regional policy. We have been watching them closely. They have recently elected a new leader, who we know little about. What we do know is that the three men they have arrested are being held on a charge of suspected murder. It is believed that they killed an apostate and traitor called Tateb Hassani. That is of no interest to us, nor are these three men, who we believe to be unimportant. We would like to know – and we think that your friend, Javier Falcón, will be able to help – who gave the orders for the mosque to be bombed?'

'If he knew that, then I am sure they would have been arrested.'

'We don't think so,' said Abu. 'We think that they are too powerful for your friend to be able to touch them.'

Falcón knew that his goading of Angel Zarrías would not help in any material way, but he hoped that it would cause some unseen structural damage, which might lead to a breakdown later on. Angel Zarrías had revealed himself, of course – how could he not? While he'd been squaring up to do battle with the corruptive powers of materialism and the ruthless energy of radical Islam, his partner, the woman he loved, was having a tantrum like some spoilt two-year-old, consumed by her pathetic needs and concerns. It represented to him all that was wrong with this modern existence that he'd grown to despise, which was how he justified employing equally corruptive powers and fanatical energy to bring the aimless world back to heel.

Falcón became quite concerned that the rage unleashed by his revelation of Manuela's comparative peevishness might result in a fatal embolism or lethal infarction. Angel's forty-five years of political frustration had finally erupted, producing spluttering admissions which indicated, beyond any doubt, his and Fuerza Andalucía's involvement in the conspiracy, but did nothing to help the investigation cross the divide into unknown areas.

By prior arrangement, Falcón was not going to be interviewing anybody between 10.30 and midday. He was going to attend the funeral of Inés Conde de Tejada.

He drove out to the San Fernando cemetery on the northern outskirts of the city. As he drew near he counted three television vans and seven camera crews.

Everybody from the Edificio de los Juzgados and the Palacio de Justicia was in attendance at the cemetery. Close to two hundred people were milling around the gates, most of them smoking. Falcón knew them all and it took him some time to work his way through the crowd to reach Inés's parents.

Neither of her parents was tall, but the death of their daughter had diminished them. They were dwarfed by its enormity and overwhelmed by the numbers of people around them. Falcón paid his respects and Inés's mother kissed him and held on to him so tightly it was as if he was her lifesaver in this sea of humanity. Her husband's handshake had nothing in it. His face was slack, his eyes rheumy. He'd aged ten years overnight. He spoke as if he didn't recognize Falcón. As he was about to leave, Inés's mother grabbed his arm and in a hoarse whisper said: 'She should have stayed with you, Javier', to which there was no answer.

Falcón joined the crowd walking up the tree-lined path to the family mausoleum. The camera crews were there, but they kept their distance. As the coffin was taken up the steps there was a great wailing from some of the women in the crowd. These occasions, especially with untimely deaths, were so emotionally lacerating that many of the men had their handkerchiefs out. When one elderly woman cried out, 'Inés, Inés,' as the coffin disappeared into the dark, the crowd seemed to convulse with grief.

The crowd dispersed after the short ceremony. Falcón

walked back to his car, head bowed and throat so constricted he couldn't respond to the few people who tried to stop him. Driving back alone was a relief, a great unknotting of strangled emotion. He arrived at the Jefatura and wept for a minute, with his forehead on the steering wheel, before pulling himself together for the next round of interviews.

By lunchtime they'd all discovered their fundamental problem. Not even Rivero, who was the weakest of the three, would give the interrogators the necessary link between Fuerza Andalucía and the bomb makers. Not one of them would even yield up the link to Informáticalidad, never mind to Lucrecio Arenas and César Benito.

In a conference between Elvira, del Rey and Falcón, in which they were trying to work out the most serious possible charges with which they could hold the three suspects, Elvira put forward the possibility that the link wasn't forthcoming because it didn't exist.

'They had to give Hassani's work to someone,' said del Rey.

'And I think we all believe now that the reason Ricardo Gamero killed himself was that the electrician's card, which would end up in the Imam's hands, via Botín, made him feel responsible,' said Falcón. 'Mark Flowers told me that the Imam was expecting more intrusive surveillance. In fact, he wanted the microphone planted in his office so that the CGI antiterrorist squad would find out about Hammad and Saoudi's plan. Obviously, none of them knew a bomb was going to be planted with that microphone. The point is that Gamero went back to the person who had given him the card, looking for an explanation. Who gave that card to Zarrías?'

'It's possible that Zarrías didn't know about the bomb either,' said Elvira. 'Perhaps he just thought this was an escalation of the surveillance carried out by Informáticalidad.'

'The person I would really like to see down here is Lucrecio Arenas,' said Falcón. 'He positioned his protégé, Jesús Alarcón, to take over the leadership from Rivero. He is a long-standing friend of Angel Zarrías and he has been involved with the Horizonte group, with whom Benito and Cárdenas are associated and who ultimately own Informáticalidad.'

'But unless these guys give him up, all you *can* do is talk to him,' said del Rey. 'You have no leverage. The only reason we've got this far is a lucky sighting of Tateb Hassani late on the Saturday night in Rivero's house, and Rivero's subsequent confusion and loss of nerve when you and Inspector Ramírez first spoke to him.'

Falcón was in the observation room for the next interviews, which started at four o'clock. At about five Gregorio appeared at his shoulder.

'Yacoub needs to talk,' he said.

'I thought we weren't due to "chat" until tonight.'

'In an emergency we've given Yacoub the possibility of making contact,' said Gregorio. 'It's to do with the initiation rite.'

'I haven't got the Javier Marías book with me.'

Gregorio produced a spare copy from his briefcase. They went up to Falcón's office and Gregorio prepared the computer.

'You might find there's more of a delay between each line of "chat" this time,' said Gregorio. 'We're using different encryption software and it's a bit slower.'

Gregorio gave up Falcón's seat and went over to the window. Falcón sat in front of the computer and exchanged introductions with Yacoub, who opened by saying he didn't have much time and gave a brief account of what had happened that morning. He wrote about the execution he'd witnessed, but wrote nothing of his own mock execution. Falcón reeled from the computer screen.

'This is out of control,' he said, and Gregorio read Yacoub's words over Falcón's shoulder.

'Steady him. Keep him calm,' said Gregorio. 'They're just warning him.'

Falcón started to type just as another paragraph came through from Yacoub.

'Important things in no particular order. 1) I was taken from the house in the medina at about 6.45 a.m. The journey was about three and a half hours long and then there was about forty minutes before I met the two men, who called themselves Mohamed and Abu. They told me they were following the Seville bombing very closely. 2) They said that the explosion had caused "great disruption to one of their plans which had demanded a lot of reorganization". 3) I was left in a room with books on one wall. The titles were all about architecture or engineering. There were also a number of manufacturer's car manuals for four-wheel-drive vehicles. 4) They knew about the arrest of three men from a political party called Fuerza Andalucía, who were suspected of murdering "an apostate and traitor" called Tateb Hassani. They also knew that this was in some way connected to the Seville bombing, but said that these men were "unimportant". 5) The information they want from you, Javier, is as follows: the identities of the men who were responsible for the planning of the bombing of the mosque in Seville. They know about the three arrests, and they believe that although you know who the real perpetrators are, they are too powerful for you to touch them.

'I don't expect you to reply immediately. I know you will have to talk to your people first. I need your answer as soon as possible. If I can give them this information I believe it will increase my standing with the council immeasurably.'

'That last bit I don't even have to think about,' said Falcón. 'I can't do it.'

'Just wait, Javier,' said Gregorio, but Falcón was already typing out his reply:

'Yacoub, it's completely impossible for me to give you that information. We have our suspicions, but absolutely no proof. I assume the leaders of this council are looking for revenge for the bombing of the mosque and that is not something I am prepared to have on my conscience.'

Falcón had to hold Gregorio back as he hit the send button. After about fifteen seconds the screen wavered and the CNI secure website disappeared to be replaced by the msn home page. Gregorio played about on the keyboard and tried to get back into the website, but there was no access. He made a call standing at the window.

'We've lost the connection,' he said.

After several minutes of listening and nodding he closed down the mobile.

'Trouble with the encryption software. They had to terminate the transmission as a precaution.'

'Did my last paragraph go through?'

'They said it did.'

'All the way through to Yacoub?'

'That I don't know yet,' said Gregorio. 'We'll reconvene at your house at 11 p.m. I'll have had a chance to discuss the meat of what Yacoub was saying and its implications with Juan and Pablo by then.'

40

On the way back down to the interview rooms Falcón ran into Elvira and del Rey in the corridor. They'd been looking for him. The forensics computer specialists had hacked into the Fuerza Andalucía hard disks. From the articles and photographs found on one of the computers they could tell that the user was compiling the raw material to be transformed into the web pages that would appear on the VOMIT website. From other material on the same hard disk, the user was evidently Angel Zarrías. Elvira seemed annoyed that this news didn't impress Falcón, whose mind was still reeling from the exchange with Yacoub.

'It's more leverage,' said Elvira. 'It places Zarrías and Fuerza Andalucía closer to the heart of the conspiracy.'

Falcón had no ready opinion about that.

'I'm not sure that it does,' said del Rey. 'It could be construed as a separate entity. Zarrías can defend it as a personal campaign. All he's done is use a Fuerza Andalucía computer to draft the articles, which he's downloaded on to a CD and given to some geek, to anonymously slap them up on the VOMIT website. I can't see the leverage we can extract from that.'

Falcón looked from one man to the other, still with no comment. Elvira took a call on his mobile. Falcón started to move away.

'That was Comisario Lobo,' said Elvira. 'The media pressure is at breaking point.'

'What has the media been told so far about these men being held?' asked Falcón, coming back down the corridor to Elvira.

'Suspicion of murder and conspiring to murder,' said Elvira.

'Has Tateb Hassani been named?'

'Not yet. Naming him would involve revealing too much about the nature of our enquiry at the moment,' said Elvira. 'We're still sensitive to the expectations of the people.'

'I'd better get back to work. I'm due to start on Eduardo Rivero in a few minutes,' said Falcón, looking at his watch. 'Tell me, have the forensics found any blood traces in the Fuerza Andalucía offices, yet? Especially in the bathroom?'

'I haven't heard anything on that,' said Elvira, moving off with del Rey.

All the interrogators were in the corridor outside the interview rooms. A paramedic in fluorescent green was talking to Ramírez, who caught sight of Falcón over his shoulder.

'Rivero's collapsed,' he said. 'He started gasping for air, getting disorientated, and then fell off his chair.'

Rivero was lying on the floor between two paramedics who were giving him oxygen.

'What's the problem?' asked Falcón.

'Heart arrhythmia and high blood pressure,' said the paramedic. 'We're going to take him to hospital, keep him under observation. His heart rate is up around 160 and completely irregular. If we don't bring it down there's a danger that the blood will pool and clot in the heart, and if a clot gets loose he might have a stroke.'

'Shit,' said Ramírez from the corridor. 'God knows how this is going to play out in the media. They'll tell the world we're running Abu Ghraib down here.'

All the interrogators thought that Rivero, of all the suspects, had been the least attached to the central conspiracy. He had only been important as the leader of the party and, given that the intention was to wrest that from him in order to install Jesús Alarcón, it would stand to reason that he would be kept the least informed. His collapse had occurred under persistent questioning from Inspector Jefe Ramón Barros about the real reason for his relinquishing of the leadership. The pressure of sticking to his story about old age, while the truth worked away at the flaws in his mind, had proved too much.

Just after 7 p.m. Marco Barreda, the Informáticalidad sales manager, was brought in. He'd been met at the airport having flown in from Barcelona. His mobile phone records were accessed but none of the numbers called corresponded to any of those owned by Angel Zarrías. Falcón made sure that Zarrías knew about Barreda's appearance in the Jefatura. Zarrías was unperturbed. Barreda was questioned for an hour and a half about his relationship with Ricardo Gamero. He didn't deviate from his original story. They released him at

8.30 p.m. and went back to Zarrías and lied to him about Barreda, saying he'd admitted that Gamero had said nothing about being in love with him and wasn't even a homosexual. Zarrías didn't buy any of it.

By 9 p.m. Falcón couldn't take any more. He went outside to breathe some fresh air, but found it hot and suffocating after the chill of the Jefatura. He drank a coffee in the café across the street. His mind was confused with too much going on between Yacoub and the interrogation of the three suspects. He drank some water to wash out the bitterness of the coffee, and Zorrita's words from last night came back to him

In the Jefatura he went down to the cells where he asked the officer on duty if he could speak to Esteban Calderón, who was in the last cell, lying on his back, staring at the back of his hands held above him. The guard locked Falcón in. He took a stool and leaned back against the wall. Calderón sat up on his bunk.

'I didn't think you were going to come,' he said.

'I didn't think there was much point in coming,' said Falcón. 'I can't help you or discuss your case with you. I'm here out of curiosity only.'

'I've been thinking about denial,' said Calderón.

Falcón nodded.

'I know you've come across a lot of it in your work.'

'There's no greater guilt than that of a murderer,' said Falcón, 'and denial is the human mind's greatest defence.'

'Talk me through the process?' said Calderón. 'The theory's always different to the reality.'

'Only in the aftermath of a serious crime, such as murder, does the motive for taking such disastrous measures suddenly seem ridiculously disproportionate,' said Falcón. 'So, to kill someone for, say, the paltry reason of jealousy seems like madness, an affront to the intellect. The easiest and quickest way to deal with the aberration is to deny it ever happened. Once that denial is in place, it doesn't take long for the mind to create its own version of events which the brain comes to believe with absolute certainty.'

'I'm trying to be as careful as I can,' said Calderón.

'Sometimes care is not enough to defeat a deep-seated desire,' said Falcón.

'That scares me, Javier,' said Calderón. 'I don't understand how the brain can be at the mercy of the mind. I don't understand how information, facts, things we've seen and heard can be so easily transformed, reordered and manipulated . . . by what? What is it? What is the mind?'

'Maybe it's not such a good idea to lie in a prison cell, torturing yourself with unanswerable questions,' said Falcón.

'There's nothing else to do,' said Calderón. 'I can't stop my brain from working. It asks me these questions.'

'Wish fulfilment is a powerful human need, on both a personal and a collective level.'

'I know, which is why I'm being so careful in examining myself,' said Calderón. 'I've started at the beginning and I've been admitting some difficult things.'

'I'm neither your confessor, nor your psychologist, Esteban.'

'But, apart from Inés, you are the person I have most wronged in my life.'

'You haven't wronged *me*, Esteban, and if you have I don't need to know.'

'But I need you to know.'

'I can't absolve you,' said Falcón. 'I'm not qualified for that.'

'I just need you to know the care with which I am conducting my self-examination.'

Falcón had to admit to himself that he was interested. He leaned back against the wall and shrugged. Calderón took some moments to prepare his words.

'I seduced Inés,' he said. 'I set out to seduce her, not because of her beauty, her intelligence or because of the woman she was. I set out to seduce her because of her relationship with you.'

'Me?'

'Not because of who you were, the son of the famous Francisco Falcón, which was what had made you interesting to Inés. It was more to do with . . . I don't know how to put this: your difference. You were not well liked in those days. Most people thought you cold and unapproachable, and therefore arrogant and patronizing. I saw something I didn't understand. So, the first way, the most natural way for *me* to understand you was to seduce your wife. What did this beautiful, much-admired woman see in you, that I didn't have myself? That's why I seduced her. And the irony of it was, she gave me no insight at all. But before I knew it, it was no longer just an affair as I'd intended; we became an open secret. She was always way ahead of me in public relations. She could manipulate people and situations with consummate ease. So, we became the golden couple and you were the cuckold, who people enjoyed laughing about behind your back. And I admit it now, Javier, just so that you know what I'm like: I enjoyed that situation because, although I didn't understand you, which made me feel weak, I had inadvertently got one up on you, and that made me feel strong.'

'Are you sure you want to tell me this?' said Falcón.

'The next item isn't so personal to you,' said Calderón, batting him down with his hands, as if Falcón was thinking of leaving. 'It's important that you know me for the . . . I was going to say "man" but I'm not sure that's appropriate now. Remember Maddy Krugman?'

'I didn't like her,' said Falcón. 'I thought she was sinister.'

'She's probably the most beautiful woman I never went to bed with.'

'You *didn't* sleep with her?'

'She wasn't interested in me,' said Calderón. 'Beauty – I mean, great beauty – for a woman is both her good fortune and her greatest curse. Everybody is attracted to them. It's difficult for normal people to understand that pressure. Everybody wants to please a beautiful woman. They spark something in everybody, not just men; and because the pressure is so constant, they have no idea who has good intentions, who they should choose. Of course, they recognize the poor, slack-jawed fools who drool on to their lapels, but then there are the others, the hundreds and thousands with money, charm, brilliance and charisma. Maddy liked you because you brushed aside her beauty . . .'

'I don't think that was true. I was as much affected by her beauty as everybody else.'

'But you didn't let it affect your vision, Javier. And Maddy saw that and liked it. She was obsessed with you,' said Calderón. 'Of course, I had to have her. She teased me. She played with me. I amused her. That was about it. And the worst of it was that we had to talk about you. I couldn't bear it. I think you knew that it was eating me up inside.'

Falcón nodded.

'So when we got into that final and fatal scenario with Maddy and her husband . . . I had to lie about it afterwards,' said Calderón. 'I perjured myself, because I couldn't bear your fearlessness. I couldn't stand the poise with which you handled that situation.'

'I can tell you that I didn't *feel* fearless.'

'Then I couldn't stand the way you overcame your fear and I was left sitting on the sofa, paralysed,' said Calderón.

'I've been trained for those situations. I've been in them before,' said Falcón. 'Your reaction was completely natural and understandable.'

'But it was not how I saw myself,' said Calderón.

'Then your standards are very high,' said Falcón.

'Inés was marvellous to me after the Maddy Krugman affair,' said Calderón. 'You couldn't have wished for a better reaction from a fiancée. I'd humiliated her by announcing our engagement and on the same day, I think it was, I ran off with Maddy Krugman. And yet she stuck by me. She picked up the pieces of my career and self-esteem and . . . I hated her for it.

'I stored up all her kindnesses to me and mixed them with my own bitterness into a rancorous stew of deep resentment. I punished her by having affairs. I even fucked her best friend during a weekend at Inés's parents' finca. And I didn't stop at affairs. I refused to look for a house. I made her sell her own apartment, but I wouldn't let her buy the sort of house she desperately wanted. I wouldn't let her change my apartment to suit her. When I started hitting her – and that was only four days ago – it was just the physical expression of what I'd been doing to her mentally for years. What made it worse was, that the more I abused her, the tighter she clung to me. Now there's a story of denial for you, Javier. Inés was a great prosecutor. She could persuade anybody. And she persuaded herself, totally.'

'You should have left her.'

'It was too late by then,' said Calderón. 'We were already locked in our fatal embrace. We couldn't bear to be together, we couldn't wrench ourselves apart.'

The key rattled in the door. The guard put his head in.

'Comisario Elvira wants to see you in his office. He said it's urgent.'

Falcón stood. Calderón raised himself with effort, as if he was stiff or under a great weight.

'One last thing, Javier. I know it will seem incredible after what I've just told you,' said Calderón, 'and I'm quite prepared to face the punishment handed down to me for her murder, because I deserve it. But I need *you* to know that I did not kill her. You might have spoken to that Inspector Jefe from Madrid, and he might have told you that I gave a very confused account of what happened that night. I *have* been in a fairly wild state . . .'

'So who did kill her?'

'I don't know. I don't know what their motive could have possibly been. I don't know anything, other than that *I* did not kill Inés.'

The Comisario was not alone in his office. His secretary nodded Falcón in. Pablo and Gregorio were there, along with the chief forensic pathologist. They all sat wherever they could except for the pathologist, who remained standing by the window. Elvira introduced him and asked him to give his report.

'The mosque is now empty of all rubble, detritus, clothes and body parts. We have conducted DNA testing on all body parts, fluids and blood that we've been able to find. That means we have tested every square centimetre of the available area in the mosque. We have all the results of these tests, except for the final two square metres closest to the entrance, which was the area containing the least DNA material and was the last batch to be sent off. We have been able to find matches to all DNA samples supplied by the families of all the men believed to have been in the mosque. We have also matched a DNA sample retrieved from the Imam's apartment with some in the mosque. However, we have been unable to match DNA samples taken from the Madrid apartment belonging to Djamal Hammad and Smail Saoudi with any found in the mosque. Our conclusion is that neither of those two men were in the mosque at the time of the explosion.'

41

Seville – Saturday, 10th June 2006, 07.00 hrs

Falcón woke up early, with renewed determination. Once the pathologist had left the night before, after his stunning revelation, they discussed what could possibly have happened to Hammad and Saoudi. Pablo updated Comisario Elvira on the intelligence they'd received from Yacoub, whose group believed that a total of 300 kilos of hexogen had been sent to Spain. The bomb disposal officer had thought, as a 'conservative' estimate, that 100 kilos of hexogen had exploded in El Cerezo on 6th June, which would leave between 150 and 200 kilos still at large. They all agreed that having secured the remaining hexogen, Hammad and Saoudi would have either gone to ground or left the country.

Elvira put a call through to the Guardia Civil about the route of the Peugeot Partner last seen at a service station outside Valdepeñas at 4 p.m. on Sunday, 4th June. There'd still been no sightings of the van on any of the main roads in the Seville, Cordoba and Granada triangle. There was now a huge operation underway, looking for sightings on the smaller routes, but it was an impossible task, given the anonymous quality of the vehicle and the fact that the journey was made nearly a week ago. Falcón sent Pérez and Ferrera back to El Cerezo to check with the residents that the Peugeot Partner had not been seen until the Monday morning of 5th June.

The meeting broke up with Elvira drafting a press release about Hammad and Saoudi and announcing the reinstatement of spot checks on vehicles coming into the city. This was to be aired on the TVE ten o'clock news and on Canal Sur. Gregorio had come back with Falcón to his house on Calle Bailén, where they made another unsuccessful attempt to reach Yacoub. They drafted a report about Hammad and Saoudi, including photographs, which Gregorio pasted into the clipboard of the CNI website to send to Yacoub later, in the hope that he could locate them in Morocco.

For one reason or another Falcón had not yet interviewed Agustín Cárdenas, and it had been decided that he would talk to him first thing in the morning while Ramírez tackled Zarrías for a second time. The rest of the squad would be up early to walk the streets around El Cerezo to see if they could get any confirmed sightings of Hammad and Saoudi either on Sunday evening/Monday morning, or after the explosion on Tuesday.

By 7.30 a.m. Falcón had called ahead to the Jefatura to make sure that Agustín Cárdenas would be waiting, ready to be interviewed as soon as he arrived. He stopped for a coffee and some toast on the way and was sitting in front of a still groggy Agustín Cárdenas by 7.50.

In his photograph, Agustín Cárdenas looked in his mid thirties, while his CV told Falcón he was forty-six

years old. By this Saturday morning he'd found his
way up into the mid fifties, which was somewhere he'd
never been before.

'You're not looking good, Agustín,' said Falcón. 'You
could do with a bit of nip and tuck yourself this morning.'

'I'm not a morning person,' he said.

'How long have you known César Benito?'

'About eight years.'

'How did you meet him?'

'I did some work on his wife and then he came to
see me himself.'

'For some work?'

'I removed the bags under his eyes and tightened
up his neck and jowls.'

'And he was happy?'

'He was so happy he got a mistress.'

'Were your clinics part of the Horizonte group at
this stage?'

'No, César Benito thought that Horizonte should buy
my business.'

'Which made you a lot of money,' said Falcón. 'Did
they give you stock options in Horizonte?'

Cárdenas nodded.

'And being a part of the group meant that you had
capital,' said Falcón.

'I expanded the business to nine clinics in Barcelona,
Madrid, Seville, Nerja and another due to open in
Valencia.'

'It's a shame that you've built up such a successful
business and you're never going to see the fruits of
your labour,' said Falcón. 'You're not protecting César
Benito just because he's made you this fortune that
you'll never enjoy?'

Cárdenas took a deep breath and stared at the table, thinking to himself.

'No,' said Falcón. 'It would have to be more than that, wouldn't it? There's your Hippocratic oath. César must have had quite a hold on you to be able to persuade you to not only poison Hassani at his last supper, but also to use your surgical skills to cut off the man's hands, burn away his face and scalp him. You didn't do all that for César just because he made you a rich man?'

More silence from Cárdenas. Something was eating away at him. Here was a man who'd done a lot of thinking and not much sleeping overnight.

'What can you offer me?' said Cárdenas, after some long minutes.

'In terms of a deal?' said Falcón. 'Nothing.'

Cárdenas nodded, rocked himself in his chair. Falcón knew what was working its way from Cárdenas's insides out: resentment.

'I can only give you César Benito,' said Cárdenas. 'He was the only person I had contact with.'

'We'll be happy with that,' said Falcón. 'What can you tell me?'

'One of the reasons I was not as wealthy as I should have been when I first met César was that I'd been a gambling addict for almost ten years,' said Cárdenas.

'Did César Benito know about that when he arranged for Horizonte to buy your cosmetic surgery clinics?'

'No, but he found out soon afterwards,' said Cárdenas. 'It was through him that I managed to get it under control.'

'And how did it get out of control again?'

'I went on a business trip with César down to the Costa del Sol in March. He took me gambling.'

'*He* did?'

Cárdenas nodded, looking at Falcón very steadily.

'That started me off again. But this time it was even worse. I was much better off than I had been the last time. My funds seemed to be limitless by comparison. By the beginning of May I owed over one million euros and I was having to sell things to make the interest payments on some of the loans I'd taken out.'

'And how did César find out?'

'I told him,' said Cárdenas. 'I'd had a visit from somebody I owed money to. They took me into the bathroom of my rented flat in Madrid and gave me the wet towel treatment. You know, you really think you're going to drown. They said they'd be back in four days' time. It scared me enough to go to César and ask for help. We met in his apartment in Barcelona. He was shocked by what I told him, but he also said that he understood. After three days of being completely terrified I was relieved. Then he told me how he could make this problem go away.'

'Are you a religious man, Sr Cárdenas?'

'Yes, our families go to church together.'

'How would you describe your relationship with César Benito?'

'He'd become a very close friend. That's why I went to see him.'

'When Benito told you that you would have to commit murder and gross disfigurement, surely you must have asked him for every detail of the conspiracy?'

'I did, but not on that occasion,' said Cárdenas. 'Once I realized what he was asking I decided on a safety strategy. The next time I met him was in my rented apartment in Madrid and I secretly recorded our entire conversation.'

'And where is that recording?'

'It's still in the apartment,' he said, writing down the address and telephone number. 'I taped it to the back of one of the kitchen drawers.'

When Lucrecio Arenas was at his villa in Marbella he liked to get up early, before the staff arrived, which on a Saturday was not before 9 a.m. Arenas put on a pair of swimming trunks, shrugged into his huge white bathrobe and slipped into a pair of sandals. On his way out of the house he picked up a large, thick, white towel and a pair of swimming goggles. He hated chlorine in his eyes and always liked to see clearly, even underwater. He walked down the sloping garden in the warm morning, pausing to take in the glorious view of the green hills and the blue of the Mediterranean, which at this time of day, before the heat haze had risen, was so intense that even his untouchable heart ached a little.

The pool had been built at the bottom of the garden, surrounded by a dense growth of oleander, bougainvillea and jasmine. His wife had insisted it be put down there because Lucrecio had wanted a 20-metre monster. They'd dynamited three hundred tons of rock out of the mountainside so that he could swim his daily kilometre in fifty lengths, rather than having the awful bore of turning just as he'd got into his stride. He reached the poolside and flung his towel on a lounger and let his bathrobe fall on top. He stepped out of his sandals and walked to the end of the pool. He fitted his goggles over his face and nestled the rubber into his eye sockets. He raised his arms and through the rose-tinted lenses of the goggles he saw something that looked like a postcard on the end of the diving board. He dropped his arms just as he felt two colossal thuds in his back, like sledgehammer blows but more penetrating. The third blow was to the neck and came down on him with the full weight of a cleaver. His legs would not support him and he collapsed messily into the water. The dense growth behind him rearranged itself. There was the sound of a small scooter starting up. The splendid day continued. The ice blue water in the swimming pool clouded red around the body. A speedboat nosed out into the blue morning, pursued by its white frothy wake.

The Holiday Inn on Plaza Carlos Triana Bertrán in Madrid was not one of César Benito's favourite hotels, but it had some advantages. It was close to the conference centre where he'd given a speech to Spain's leading constructors the night before. It was also near the Bernabeu Stadium and even when Real Madrid weren't playing he enjoyed being close to the beating heart of Spanish football. The hotel had a third advantage on this Saturday, which was that it was only twenty minutes to the airport and he had a flight to catch to Lisbon at 11 a.m. He'd asked for breakfast to be served in his suite as he hated looking at other people, who were not his family, early in the morning. The room service boy had just wheeled in the trolley and Benito was flicking through Saturday's *ABC* and chewing on a croissant when there was another knock at the door. It was so soon after the room service boy had left that he assumed it was him coming back for some reason. He didn't look through the spy hole. He wouldn't have seen anybody if he had.

He opened the door on to an empty corridor. His head was just coming forward to look out when the edge of a hand swung into him with rapid and lethal force, chopping across his Adam's apple and windpipe and making a loud cracking noise. He fell backwards into the room, spluttering flakes of croissant over the front of his bathrobe. His heels worked furrows into the carpet as he tried to draw air into his lungs. The door closed. Benito's feet slowed after a minute and then stopped working. There was a gargling rattle from his collapsed throat and his hands lost all grip. He didn't feel the fingers searching for a neck pulse or the light touch of the card placed on his chest.

The door of the hotel room reopened and closed with a *Do not disturb* sign swinging on the handle. The air conditioning breathed easily in the hush of the empty corridor, while unclaimed newspapers hung in plastic bags from other, indifferent, doors.

At 9.30 a.m. Falcón had taken a break from his interview with Agustín Cárdenas and called Ramírez out to give him the news of the recording Cárdenas had made, hoping it could be used to apply pressure on Angel Zarrías. Cárdenas was taken back down to the cells while Falcón went to his office to call Elvira to get the Madrid police to pick up the recording from Cárdenas's rented flat, while simultaneously arresting César Benito in the Holiday Inn.

It was Ferrera, calling him from a café on the Avenida de San Lázaro, who told him to look at the latest news on Canal Sur. Falcón ran through the Jefatura and burst into the communications room just in time to see a shot of Marbella disappear from the television screen, to be replaced by the newsreader who repeated the breaking news item: Lucrecio Arenas had been found by his maid floating face down in his swimming pool at 9.05 that morning. He had been shot three times in the back.

His mobile vibrated and he took the call from Elvira.

'I've just seen it,' he said. 'Lucrecio Arenas in his pool.'

'They got César Benito in his hotel in Madrid as well,' said Elvira. 'That's going to come through in the next few minutes.'

It took another five minutes for the Benito item to break. A TVE camera crew got to the Holiday Inn before Canal Sur reached Arenas's villa in Marbella. It took a further half an hour before their camera crew pushed a lens into the face of the maid, who'd only just recovered from the hysteria of finding her boss dead in the pool. The newsreaders jumped between the two dramas. Falcón called Ramírez out of the interview room to let him know, went back to his office and slumped in his chair, all the enthusiasm of the morning gone.

His first thoughts were that this was the end. It didn't matter what they found out now from Cárdenas and Zarrías, it was all immaterial. He stared at his reflection in the dead, grey computer screen and it started him thinking in a slightly less linear way about what had happened. He made some uncomfortable connections, which made him furious and then another idea came to him, which frightened him into calming down. He got the communications room to send a patrol car to Alarcón's house in El Porvenir. He called Jesús Alarcón. His wife, Mónica, answered the phone.

'You've heard the news,' he said.

'He can't speak to you now,' said Mónica. 'He's too upset. You know Lucrecio was like a father to him.'

'First thing: none of you are to go outside,' said Falcón. 'Lock all the doors and windows and go upstairs. Don't answer the door. I'm sending a patrol car round there now.'

Silence from Mónica.

'I'll tell you what it's about when I get there,' said Falcón. 'Did Jesús speak to Lucrecio Arenas yesterday?'

'Yes, they met.'

'I'm coming round now. Lock all the doors. Don't let anybody in.'

On the way to El Porvenir, Falcón called Elvira and asked for armed guards to protect Alarcón and his family. The request was granted immediately.

'There's more stuff coming out all the time,' said Elvira, 'but I can't talk about it on the phone. I'm coming in.'

'I'm on my way to see Alarcón,' said Falcón.

'Do we know where Alarcón was on the night of Tateb Hassani's murder?'

'He was at a wedding in Madrid.'

'So you think he's clean?'

'I know he's clean,' said Falcón. 'I've got a special insight.'

'Special insights, even *your* special insights, don't always look good in police reports,' said Elvira.

The street was empty of people and Falcón parked behind the patrol car, which was already outside the metal sliding gate of Alarcón's house. Mónica buzzed him in. Falcón had a good look around before he went through the front door, which he closed and triple locked. He went to the back of the house and checked all the doors and windows.

'We're just being careful,' said Falcón. 'We don't know who we're dealing with yet and we're not sure whether Jesús is on their list. So we're putting you under armed guard until we know.'

'He's in the kitchen,' she said, looking sick with fear. She went upstairs to sit with the children.

Alarcón was sitting at the kitchen table with an untouched espresso in front of him. He had his arms stretched out on the table, fists clenched, staring into space. He only came out of his trance when Falcón broke into the frame of his vision and offered his condolences.

'I know he was important to you,' said Falcón.

Alarcón nodded. He didn't look as if he'd slept much. He made light knocking noises with his fists on the tabletop.

'Did you speak to Arenas yesterday?' asked Falcón.

Alarcón nodded.

'How did he react to the information I gave you?'

'Lucrecio had reached the point in his life and business career where he no longer had to bother with detail,' said Alarcón. 'He had people who did the detail. I shouldn't think he'd seen a bill for the last twenty-five years, or read a contract, or even been aware of the tonnage of paperwork involved in a modern merger or acquisition. His desk is always clean. It doesn't even have a phone on it since he discovered that the only people he wants to talk to are on his mobile. He never learnt how to use a computer.'

'What are you telling me, Jesús?' said Falcón, impatient now. 'That the services of Tateb Hassani and his consequent murder were "details" that did not concern Lucrecio Arenas?'

'I'm telling you that he's the sort of man who will

listen to the business news, with all its astonishing up-to-the-minute detail, even a channel like Bloomberg, which is right on top of its subject, and laugh,' said Alarcón. 'Then he'll tell you what's *really* happening, because he is talking to the people who are actually *making* it happen, and you realize that the so-called news is just a bit of detail that a journalist has either picked up or been given.'

'So what did you talk about?'

'We talked about power.'

'That doesn't sound as if it's going to help me.'

'No, but it has been an enormous help to me,' said Alarcón. 'I'll be resigning from the leadership of Fuerza Andalucía and returning to my business career. My statement to the media will take place at eleven o'clock this morning. There's nothing left, Javier. Fuerza Andalucía is over.'

'So, what did he tell you about power?'

'That all the things that matter to me about politics, such as people, health, education, religion . . . all these things are details, and none of it can happen without power.'

'I think I can grasp that.'

'There's a saying in business, that what happens in the USA takes about five years to start happening here,' said Alarcón. 'Lucrecio told me: look at the Bush administration and understand that you only achieve power in a democracy with an enormous sense of indebtedness.'

'You owe favours to all the people who've made it possible for you to reach high office,' said Falcón.

'You owe them so much that you begin to find that *their* needs are shaping *your* policies.'

Three armed police arrived as Falcón left. Falcón drove back to the Jefatura, amazed at his naivety in thinking that Jesús Alarcón would be able to get anything approaching an admission from an animal like Lucrecio Arenas.

Elvira was alone in his office, standing by the window, peering through the blinds as if he was expecting insurgents in the street. Without turning round he told Falcón that he was going to have to prepare for a major televised press conference whose time, as yet, had not been set.

'The CNI will be here in a minute,' he said. 'Did you get anything from Alarcón?'

'Nothing. He's resigning later this morning,' said Falcón. 'He had a very unappetizing lesson on the nature of power from his old master.'

'Who seems to have met his nemesis,' said Elvira. 'A card was found on the diving board of his swimming pool. An identical card was found on César Benito's body in his hotel room. Arabic script. A quote from the Koran about the enemies of God.'

Elvira finally turned round when he sensed something thunderous developing behind him.

'Are you all right, Javier?'

'No,' he said, gritting his teeth. 'I'm not all right.'

'You're angry?' said Elvira, surprised. 'It's very dismaying, but . . .'

'I've been betrayed,' he said. 'Those bastards from the CNI have betrayed me, and it's cost us the possibility of a resolution to this entire investigation.'

A knock on the open door. Pablo and Gregorio came in. Falcón wouldn't shake their hands, got up and went over to the window.

'So, what's going on here?' asked Elvira.

Pablo shrugged.

'I recruited a Moroccan friend of mine . . .' started Falcón, and Gregorio tried to interrupt by saying this was all top-secret CNI business and not for public consumption. Pablo told him to sit down and shut up.

'My Moroccan friend has infiltrated the group which positioned Hammad and Saoudi with the hexogen in Seville. The group demanded that he show his loyalty by passing an initiation rite. This required him to ask me who was behind the Fuerza Andalucía conspiracy. I refused to do this. At which point there was a very timely breakdown in communication – "a problem with new encryption software". Since then, I have not been able to contact my friend. I do not think that the deaths of César Benito and Lucrecio Arenas are unconnected with what happened. I believe that my refusal to help was intercepted and replaced with the information my friend required. The fact that these two men were found dead with quotations from the Koran on, or near, their bodies seems to indicate that revenge has successfully been taken.'

Elvira looked at the CNI men.

'Not true,' said Pablo. 'It proves nothing, but we can show you the transcripts. It's true that your refusal to help did *not* go through before the system failed, but we did not replace it with anything else. The encryption software problem has still not been solved and we are now thinking of going back to the original software so that we can at least make contact with your friend. On the subject of the deaths of Arenas and Benito: the detectives and forensics on the ground in Marbella and Madrid have independently told us that they believe this to be the work of professional hitmen. They say that, whilst they have no record of any individual "hits" being taken out by Islamic jihadists, they do have records of professional hitmen using these methods.'

'Agustín Cárdenas had just given me César Benito,' said Falcón slowly.

'We know,' said Pablo. 'We spoke to Madrid. They've picked up the recording he mentioned in his interview with you.'

'You nailed him,' said Gregorio.

'For the murder of Tateb Hassani,' said Falcón. 'Don't you think the families of the people who died in El Cerezo deserve a bit more than that?'

'They might get it in court,' said Elvira.

'You said it yourself on Tuesday night,' said Pablo. 'Terrorist attacks are complicated things. You only have a *chance* at a resolution. At least in this one the perpetrators have all suffered.'

'Apart from the electrician who planted the Goma 2 Eco,' said Falcón. 'And, of course, the people who are so contemptuous of law and order that they will assassinate anybody who might make them vulnerable.'

'You have to be satisfied with what you've achieved,' said Pablo. 'You've prevented a dangerous group of Catholic fanatics from developing a power base in Andalucían politics. And in the process, through the actions of Hammad and Saoudi, we have uncovered an Islamic jihadist plot. Juan doesn't think that that is such a terrible outcome.'

'Which brings us back to the business in hand,' said Elvira. 'Hammad and Saoudi. Their faces have been all over the news and there's been a terrific response. Unfortunately, there have been sightings from all over Spain. They've been seen on the same day, at the same time, in La Coruña, Almería, Barcelona and Cádiz.'

Elvira took a call on his mobile.

'Chasing Hammad and Saoudi is a waste of time,' said Pablo. 'It's been four days. They'll have done whatever needed to be done and got out. The only thing that will help us now is intelligence.'

Elvira came back into the conversation.

'That was the Guardia Civil. They've had a confirmed sighting of Hammad and Saoudi, early on Monday morning 5th June, on a stretch of country road near a village called El Saucejo, about twenty-five kilometres south of Osuna.'

'And how do we know this is a bona fide sighting?' asked Pablo.

'They were changing the back tyre, driver's side, on a white Peugeot Partner,' said Elvira.

42

'We thought we'd lost you back there,' said Pablo.

'*I* thought you'd lost me,' said Falcón.

'Are you still with us?'

'I'm tired, I'm shocked that my sister's partner is so deeply involved in this; I've been disturbed by what's happened to Yacoub and, because of these two assassinations, I've lost the possibility of a resolution to my investigation,' said Falcón. 'Maybe you're used to this in your world, but in mine it feels lurid.'

'I told Juan when we first came up with the idea of using you that we were expecting too much,' said Pablo. 'Operating in two worlds, the real and the clandestine, is the quickest way to paranoia.'

'Anyway, I'm out the other side now,' said Falcón. 'I think we should go to El Saucejo.'

'I can't,' said Pablo. 'Juan's just recalled me to Madrid. There's a lot of internet "chatter" and now there's been some movement as well. He can't spare me down here to help you . . .'

'So what are you going to do about Hammad and Saoudi, the other quantity of hexogen, the "hardware"

606

that didn't arrive and the "disruption to a plan which has required a lot of reorganization"?' said Falcón. 'Isn't that what you'd call intelligence? Yacoub has been frightened half to death to get this stuff for you.'

'I don't know what you're expecting to find in El Saucejo,' said Pablo. 'Hammad and Saoudi sitting on some hexogen, helping people pack it into the "hardware" and carrying on with the plan? I don't think so.'

Falcón paced the room, chewing on his thumbnail.

'This hardware . . . that keeps getting referred to. It doesn't sound as if it's easily available, not something you go down to the shops and buy,' said Falcón. 'For some reason it sounds to me as if it's been custom made for a certain task.'

'It could be. Keep having ideas. Keep feeding them to Yacoub and see if he can come back with something relevant. That's all we can do.'

'You said the only thing that would make you sit up and get interested in our investigation was if we found that the Imam, or Hammad and Saoudi, were not in the mosque when it exploded,' said Falcón. 'And now you don't seem to give a damn.'

'Things have moved on. I've been recalled to Madrid. I'm being asked to look at other scenarios.'

'But don't you think it's significant that the original hexogen was brought to Seville, that there's additional hexogen out there, that Hammad and Saoudi are alive and well, and we know that there's an intention to attack?' said Falcón. 'Doesn't all that add up to . . . something?'

'Given the level of security around all major buildings, the announcement made last night of the re-instatement of spot checks and the police presence on the streets, I think it unlikely that they'll launch anything in Seville.'

'That sounds like an official communiqué,' said Falcón.

'It is,' said Pablo. 'The truth is, we have no idea. On Tuesday afternoon they were checking all vehicles going in and out of Seville, by Wednesday evening they were doing spot checks because people were complaining about traffic jams, on Friday they stopped all checks because people were *still* complaining, now they've reinstated them and you'll see what happens. Life goes on, Javier.'

'That sounds as if you're saying that *we* shouldn't worry too much if the population are so unconcerned,' said Falcón. 'But they don't know what we know – that there's more hexogen, that there is an intention to attack, *and* there was a twenty-four-hour break in the spot checks on vehicles.'

'All that information is in Juan's hands, and he's called me back to Madrid because what is going on there is more "significant" than anything that could happen here,' said Pablo.

They went to El Saucejo: Gregorio and Falcón in the front and a bomb squad officer and his dog in the back with Felipe the forensic. In Osuna they were met by the Guardia Civil, who led them up to El Saucejo in their Nissan Patrol. They stopped in the village and picked up two men and continued in the direction of Campillos. The rolling hills around El Saucejo were either given over to endless olive trees or had been ploughed up to reveal dun-coloured earth, with chalk-white patches. The Nissan Patrol stopped outside a ruined house on the right-hand side of the road, which had a view over the shimmering verdigris of the olive trees up to some distant mountains. The entrance and a section of the verge on the opposite side of the road about twenty-five metres down towards El Saucejo had been taped off as a crime scene.

The Guardia Civil introduced the owner of the house and the man who'd spotted Hammad and Saoudi changing the rear tyre early on Monday morning. Felipe started work on the tyre tracks on the side of the road and confirmed that they matched those of the Peugeot Partner in the police compound. He then examined the tyre tracks going into and out of the courtyard to the left of the ruined house.

After half an hour Felipe was able to tell them that the Peugeot Partner had come from the direction of Campillos, which was to the east, entered the court-yard and then exited it sustaining a puncture, which was repaired twenty-five metres down the road.

Inside the courtyard the bomb squad officer released the dog, which ran around for a few minutes before sitting down under some secure roofing near the main house. The officer then made some tests on the dry, beaten earth under the roofing and confirmed that there were traces of hexogen.

The owner of the house said it hadn't been lived in for over thirty years because it was too isolated for most people and there was a problem with water. He'd rented it out to a Spaniard with a Madrileño accent for six months. There was no contract and the man had paid him 600, saying he just wanted to use it occa-sionally for storage. The man who'd spotted Hammad and Saoudi changing the tyre said he drove past the house every day and had never seen anybody using it. He hadn't even seen the Peugeot Partner coming out of the courtyard. It was already on the side of the road, with one of the guys changing the tyre.

'What's important,' said Falcón, 'is: did anybody see a car going into or out of this courtyard at any time since Tuesday morning?'

They shook their heads. Falcón drove back to El Saucejo. They talked to as many people as they could find in the village, but nobody had seen any vehicle using the ruined house. They left the problem with the Guardia Civil.

On the way back to Seville, Gregorio took a call from the CNI communications department, saying that they had reinstalled the old encryption software and the system was now up and running. They had made the Hammad and Saoudi file available to Yacoub, but he had not, as yet, picked it up.

By 2.30 p.m. they were back in the Jefatura, sitting in front of the computer. They saw immediately that Yacoub had now picked up the file. A prearranged signal email was sent to him and he came online.

'The men you know as Hammad and Saoudi are already back in North Africa,' wrote Yacoub. 'They have been here since Thursday morning. I only know this because there was much cheering and clapping when the satellite news announced that it was now known that the two men had not been in the mosque when it exploded.'

'We've found the place where they stored the remaining hexogen but have no idea when it was picked up or where it has gone.'

'It has not been talked about here.'

'The two men who were assassinated earlier today, Lucrecio Arenas and César Benito, were the answer to your initiation test. Their killings were made to look like the work of Islamic militants.'

'A denial has already been issued to Al-Jazeera.'

'Have you heard anything more about the "hardware" that was supposed to be made available for the original consignment of hexogen?'

'It has not been discussed.'

'Since yesterday there has been an increase in internet "chatter" and also some cell movement here in Spain. Can you comment?'

'There's nothing specific. There's a sense of excitement here and there's talk of one or more cells being activated, but it's nothing definite. Nothing I am told by the group who meet here in the house in the medina can be relied on.'

'Can you spend some time thinking about what you saw when you were taken out of Rabat to be given your initiation test? You mentioned the architectural and engineering books and some car manuals.'

'I'll think about it. I have to go now.'

After lunch Falcón arranged for Zarrías to be brought up to the interview room.

'I'm not going to record this,' said Falcón. 'Nothing we say to each other now will be used in a court of law.'

Zarrías said nothing, he just looked at the person who could have been his brother-in-law.

'My Inspector has already told you that Lucrecio Arenas was shot three times in the back,' said Falcón. 'The maid found him face down in the pool. Do you want the people who did that to Lucrecio to get away with it?'

'No,' said Zarrías, 'but I can't help you, Javier, because I don't know who he was involved with.'

'Why was César Benito important to this?' said Falcón. 'Do you think it was something to do with his construction company?'

Zarrías looked troubled, as if this question had brought something into the frame that he hadn't considered before.

'I don't think this was about money, Javier,' said Zarrías.

'On your part,' said Falcón. 'In a discussion between Lucrecio and Jesús yesterday your old friend told him that power in a democracy does not come without a great sense of indebtedness.'

Zarrías's head snapped back, as if he'd just been kicked in the face.

'Maybe you were working at cross purposes, Angel,' said Falcón. 'While you and Jesús were in it to make this world into what you consider to be a better place, Lucrecio and César just wanted pure power and the money that comes with it.'

Silence.

'It happened in the Crusades, why shouldn't it happen now?' said Falcón. 'While some were out there battling for Christendom, others just wanted to kill, pillage and conquer new territory.'

'I cannot believe that of Lucrecio.'

'Maybe I should get Jesús to come down here and he can talk you through *his* disappointment,' said Falcón. 'I didn't see it, but he told me he was going to resign at eleven this morning and resume his career in business. I've never seen a man's idealism so emphatically extinguished.'

Angel Zarrías shook his head in denial.

'Didn't you stop to think, Angel, about the nature of the forces you were joining?' asked Falcón. 'Was there not one moment, after you'd poisoned Tateb Hassani and you knew that Agustín Cárdenas was amputating his hands, burning off his face and scalping him, that you thought: "Are these the extremes to which one must go to achieve goodness in the world?" And if it didn't happen then, what about when you saw the shattered building and the four dead children under their school pinafores? Surely then you must have thought that you had inadvertently teamed yourself with something very dark?'

'If I did,' said Angel quietly, 'it was too late by then.'

The press conference took place at 18.00 in the Andalucían Parliament building. Falcón had prepared a statement on his investigation, which had been incorporated into the official press release, to be delivered by Comisario Elvira. Falcón and Juez del Rey were attending the conference, but only to answer any questions on which Elvira didn't have the specific information. They were told to keep their replies to an absolute minimum.

The conference lasted about an hour and was a subdued affair. Elvira had just reached the point where he was looking to wrap up the event when a journalist at the back stood up.

'A final question for Inspector Jefe Falcón,' he said. 'Are you satisfied with this result?'

A brief silence. A cautionary look from Elvira. A

woman leaned forward in the front row to get a good look at him.

'Experience tells me I might have to be,' said Falcón. 'It is the nature of all murder investigations that, the more time passes, the less chance there is that fresh discoveries will be made. However, I would like to tell the people of Seville that I, personally, am *not* satisfied with this outcome. With each act, terrorism reaches new depths of iniquity. Humanity now has to live in a world where people have been prepared to abuse a population's vulnerability to terrorism in order to gain power. I would have liked to have provided the ultimate resolution to this crime, which would have been to bring everyone, from the planners to the man who planted the device, to justice. We have only been partially successful, but, for me, the battle does not end with this press conference, and I want to assure all Sevillanos that I, and my squad, will do everything in our power to find all the perpetrators, wherever they may be, even if it takes me the rest of my career.'

From the end of the press conference until 10.30 p.m. Falcón was in the Jefatura, catching up on the monumental load of paperwork that had accumulated in the five days of investigation. He went home, took a shower and changed, and was ready for the evening transmission to Yacoub when Gregorio came round at 11 p.m.

Gregorio was nervous and excited.

'It's been confirmed, from several different sources, that three separate cells are on the move. A group left Valencia last night by car, a married couple left from Madrid, in a transit van, early this morning and another group left from Barcelona, some together, some alone, at various times between Friday lunchtime and early this morning. They all seem to be heading for Paris.'

'Let's see what Yacoub makes of it,' said Falcón.

They made contact and exchanged introductions.

'I have no time,' wrote Yacoub. 'I have to leave for Paris on the 11.30 flight and it will take me more than an hour to get to the airport.'

'Any reason?'

'None. They told me to book my usual hotel in the Marais and that I would receive my instructions once I arrived.'

Falcón asked about the three cells activated in Spain since Friday, all heading for Paris.

'I've heard nothing. I have no idea if my trip is connected.'

'What about the "hardware"?'

'Still nothing. Any more questions? I have to leave now.'

Gregorio shook his head.

'When you were taken to the GICM camp for your initiation, you wrote about a wall of books – the car manuals. Have you remembered anything about them? It seems a curious thing to have.'

'They were all four-wheel-drive vehicles. I remember a VW insignia and a Mercedes. The third book was for Range Rover and the last I had to check my memory of the insignia on the internet. It was Porsche. That's it. I will try to make contact from Paris.'

Gregorio got up to leave, as if he'd just wasted his time.

'Any thoughts on that?' asked Falcón.

'I'll talk to Juan and Pablo, see what they think.'

Gregorio let himself out. Falcón sat back in his chair. He didn't like this intelligence work. Suddenly everything was moving around him at an alarming pace, with great urgency, but in reaction to electronic nods and winks. He could see how people could go mad in this world, where reality came in the form of "information" from "sources", and agents were told to go to hotels and wait for "instructions". It was all too disembodied for his liking. He never thought he'd hear himself say it, but he preferred his world, where there was a corpse, pathology, forensics, evidence and face-to-face dialogue. It seemed to him that intelligence work demanded the same leap of faith as religious belief and, in that respect, he'd always found himself in a twilight world, where his belief in a form of spirituality couldn't quite extend itself to the recognition of an ultimate being.

The three notebooks he'd filled during the course of the investigation sat on his desk, next to a pile of paperwork he'd brought home with him. He took a sheet of paper from the printer and opened up the first notebook. The date was 5th June, the day he'd been called to view Tateb Hassani's corpse on the rubbish tip outside Seville. He saw that he'd semiconsciously written *El Rocío* next to the date. Perhaps there'd been something on the radio. It was always reported when the Virgen del Rocío had been successfully brought out of the church and paraded on Pentecost Monday. As he doodled out the shape of one of the painted wagons that was so typical of the pilgrimage, he realized how El Rocío had become almost as important an event to tourists as Semana Santa and the Feria. It had always drawn thousands from all over Andalucía, and they had now been joined by hundreds of tourists, looking for another Sevillano experience. His brother, Paco, had even started providing horses and accommodation on his bull-breeding farm for an agency specializing in more luxurious forms of the pilgrimage, with magnificent tents, champagne dinners and flamenco every night. There were luxury versions of everything these days. There was probably a caviar version of the walk to Santiago de Compostela. Decadence had even got into the pilgrimage trade. Below the drawing of the wagon he wrote: *El Rocío. Tourists. Seville.*

More flipping through the random notes and jottings. When he did this he couldn't help but think of artists and writers with their notebooks. He loved it, in the great retrospective of an artist, when the museum showed the notebook sketches, which eventually became the great, and much recognized, painting.

A single line he'd written on the reverse side of a sheet of paper caught his eye: *drain the resources of the West through increased security measures, threaten economic stability by attacking tourist resorts in southern Europe and financial centres in the north: London, Paris, Frankfurt, Milan.* Who had said that? Was it Juan? Or perhaps it was something Yacoub had written?

There was a map of Spain on the wall next to his desk and he crabbed across to it on his chair. Was Seville the obvious place to bring explosives together to launch attacks on the tourist infrastructure of Andalucía? Granada was more central. The Costa del Sol was more accessible from Málaga. Then he remembered the 'hardware'. To create panic in a tourist resort needed nothing more than a pipe bomb packed with nuts, bolts and nails, so why go to the trouble of special hardware and procuring hexogen? Back to the desk. Another note: *hexogen – high brisance = explosive power, shattering effect.* Exactly. Hexogen had been chosen for its power. A small quantity did a lot of damage. And with that thought his mind slipped back to the important buildings of Andalucía: the regional parliament in Seville, the cathedrals in Seville and Cordoba, the Alhambra and Generalife in Granada. Pablo was right, it would be impossible to get a bomb anywhere near those places with the whole region on terrorist alert.

His computer told him it was midnight. He hadn't eaten. He wanted to be out and amongst people. Normally he would have relied on Laura to fill his Saturday night, but that was over now. He'd allowed himself that morbid thought and it led him back to Inés's funeral. Her parents, lost as children, in the sea of people. He snapped out of it and was walking aimlessly from his study to the patio when he remembered Consuelo's call. He hadn't expected her to be so thoughtful. She'd been the only person to call him about Inés. Not even Manuela had done that. He dug out his mobile. Was this a good time? He retrieved her number, punched the call button, let it ring twice and cut it off. It was Saturday night. She'd be in the restaurant, or with her children. Two or three images of their sexual encounters shot through his mind. They'd been so intense and satisfying. He had a rush of physical and chemical desire. He punched the call button again and before it even started ringing he could hear himself trying to smother his desire with inept small talk. He cut the line again. This was all too much for one week: he'd split up with a girlfriend, his ex-wife had been murdered and now he wanted to rekindle a love affair which had burnt out after a matter of days nearly four years ago. Consuelo had called him about Inés as a friend would. It was nothing more than that.

It was warm outside and there was life in the streets. Human beings were resilient creatures. He walked to El Arenal and found the Galician bar, which did wonderful octopus and served wine in white porcelain dishes. As he ate, he saw himself appear on the news, answering that last question put to him by the journalist at the press conference. They showed his answer in its entirety. The waiter recognized him and wouldn't take money for the food and instead sloshed more wine into his white porcelain dish.

Out in the street he was suddenly exhausted. The hours of adrenaline-filled work had caught up. He bought a *pringá* – a spicy, meat-filled roll – and ate it on the way home. He fell into bed and dreamed of Francisco Falcón, back in this house, knocking down a wall to reveal a secret chamber. It woke him in the intense dark of his bedroom, with his heart pounding in his ears. He knew that he would not sleep for at least two hours after that.

Downstairs he flicked through the endless satellite channels, looking for a movie, anything that would quieten down his brain activity. He knew why he was awake: he'd heard himself on the news making that promise to the people of Seville. He still had Hammad and Saoudi on his mind. The hexogen they'd stored in the ruined house outside El Saucejo. The great deal of 'reorganization' that 'the disruption' of the bomb had caused to the GICM's plan.

The TV screen was filled with the face-off between two colossal armies in some recent swords-and-sandals epic. He'd seen it before and it had made no lasting impression on him apart from the designer's vision of what the wooden horse would have looked like if the Greeks had built it, as he supposed they had, out of broken-up triremes. He had to wait for more than an hour for the horse to be given its roll-on part and, as he lay on the sofa, drifting along with the plot, he wondered at the power of myth. How an idea, even one with faulty wiring in the logic, could worm its way into the psyche of the Western world. Why *did* the Trojans drag the damn thing inside their city walls? Why, after all they'd been through, weren't they in the least bit suspicious?

Just as he'd reached the point of wondering whether there would ever be a generation of kids that didn't know about the wooden horse, the beast hove into view on the screen. The sight of it triggered something in his brain and all the random thoughts, notes and jottings of the past five days came together, jolting him off the sofa and into his study.

43

The Hotel Alfonso XIII was, in terms of size, probably Seville's grandest place to stay. It had been built to impress for the 1929 Expo and had a mock *mudejar* interior, with geometric tiles and Arabic arches, around a central patio. It was dark in the reception and the strong scent of the lilies in the huge flower arrangement struck a funereal note.

The manager arrived a few minutes after eight. Falcón had dragged him out of bed. He was shown into the office. The manager glanced at the police ID as if he saw them every day.

'I thought it was a heart attack,' he said. 'We get plenty of those.'

'No, nothing like that,' said Falcón.

'I know you. You're investigating the bomb,' said the manager. 'I saw you on the news. What can I do for you? We haven't got any Moroccan clients here.'

People saw the news, thought Falcón, but they only listened to what they wanted to hear.

'I don't know exactly what I'm looking for. It could be a block-booking for a minimum of four rooms made

621

by some foreign tourists, possibly French, maybe from Paris. The booking would have been made for El Rocío,' said Falcón. 'It could possibly be for more rooms, but the crucial thing is that they would have four-wheel-drive cars, driven down from Northern Europe rather than hired locally.'

The manager spent time at his keyboard, shaking his head as he entered variations on Falcón's data.

'Around the time of El Rocío I've got large tour groups in coaches,' he said. 'But there's nothing in the smaller block-bookings of between four and eight rooms.'

There were roadworks where the metro was being built outside the Hotel Alfonso XIII and Falcón decided that this was not the sort of place they'd stay in. He'd had a look at the Porsche Cayenne on the internet, and he reckoned that the owner of a car like that would be looking for exclusivity. Somehow the Alfonso XIII's grandeur made it passé. It was a conservative person's hotel.

He tried the Hotel Imperial. It was hidden away down a quiet street and overlooked the gardens of the Casa Pilatos. He had no luck there either. His epiphany of last night was beginning to take on the luridness of an early-morning idea that looked absurd in the cold light of day.

The first indication that his creative instincts hadn't gone completely awry was at a boutique hotel where the receptionist remembered a woman from London, calling in March, asking for four rooms before and after El Rocío with parking for four vehicles. The hotel had no parking and only two rooms for the dates she'd wanted. The woman had asked to hold those rooms for twenty-four hours to see if she could find another two elsewhere. The receptionist showed an email from a UK company, which had arrived after the call, from a woman called Mouna Chedadi making the booking on behalf of Amanda Turner. Falcón was certain that he'd found what he was looking for.

He started working his way through a list of local hotels, asking for a booking made by Amanda Turner. Thirty-five minutes later, he was sitting in the manager's office of the Hotel Las Casas de la Judería.

'She was lucky,' he said. 'A group had just cancelled ten minutes before she called and she got her four deluxe suites together.'

'What about their cars?' asked Falcón, giving him Mouna Chedadi's name to make the search through the hotel email database.

'They had four cars,' said the manager. 'And I see here, she was asking if they could leave them in the hotel while they went on the pilgrimage to El Rocío.'

'Did you let them?'

'The garage isn't big enough to hold four cars for people who aren't current clients of the hotel at that time of year. They were told that there were plenty of car parks in Seville where they could leave them.'

'Any idea what they did with their cars?'

The manager called the receptionist and asked her to bring in the hotel registration forms for the four rooms. She confirmed that the eight people had arrived in taxis from wherever they'd parked their cars.

'They stayed here on 31st May,' said the manager, 'and left the following day to go on the pilgrimage.

They came back on 5th June and left again on 8th June.'

'I remember they were going to Granada for a night,' said the receptionist.

'They came back here on 9th June and left . . . have they left yet?'

'They paid their bill last night and left at seven thirty this morning, when the garage opened.'

'So they *did* leave their cars here when they came back from Granada?' said Falcón. 'Do you know the models?'

'Only the registration numbers.'

'What do they give as their professions?'

'Fund managers, all four of them.'

'Did they leave any mobile phone numbers?'

Falcón asked for photocopies of the forms. He went outside and phoned Gregorio, gave him the four UK registration numbers and asked him to find which models they belonged to. Back in the hotel he asked to speak to the bar staff who'd been on duty the night before. He knew what English people were like.

The bar staff remembered the group. They tipped very well, like Americans rather than English people. The men drank beer and the women drank manzanilla, and then gin and tonics. None of the bar staff knew enough English to understand anything of their conversation. They remembered a man who'd had a short exchange with them and then left soon after and there was another couple, some other foreigners, who'd joined them for drinks. They'd all gone out for dinner afterwards.

The other couple were identified as Dutch, and were called down to reception. Falcón worked on identifying the lone man who'd had a brief chat with the group before leaving. The bar staff said he looked Spanish and spoke with a Castellano, rather than Andaluz, accent. The receptionist remembered him and said that he'd paid his bill last night as well. She dug out his registration form. He'd given a Spanish name and ID card. He'd arrived on 6th June and had parked a car in the hotel garage as well. Falcón asked them to scan the ID and registration form, paste it into an email and send it to Gregorio.

The Dutchman appeared looking hungover. They'd had a big night out with the English, who they'd met on the pilgrimage to El Rocío. They hadn't got to bed until two in the morning and yet the English said they were leaving early.

'Did they say where they were going?'

'They just said they were going back to England.'

'What about their route?'

'They were staying in paradors, then going via Biarritz and the Loire to the Channel Tunnel. They all had to be back at work a week tomorrow.'

Falcón paced the patio, willing his mobile to start vibrating. Gregorio called back just before 10 a.m.

'First of all, that Spanish ID card was stolen last year and we haven't got a visual match for his face in any of our files. His car was a Mercedes and was hired in Jerez de la Frontera on Monday, 5th June in the afternoon, and it was returned at 9.15 this morning. I've told them not to touch the car until they hear from us. Are you going to tell me what this is about?'

'What about the car models of UK registrations?'

'They're coming through now,' said Gregorio, reading

them off. 'A VW Touareg, a Porsche Cayenne, a Mercedes M270 and a Range Rover.'

'You remember the car manuals Yacoub saw?'

'Let's meet in your office now. I can get secure phone lines there.'

Forty-five minutes later Falcón was still waiting in his office, making notes as the complications to the scenario multiplied in his mind. Gregorio called from Elvira's office and told him he'd set up a conference call with Juan and Pablo, who were in Madrid.

'The first thing I want to hear is the line of logic in all this,' said Juan. 'Gregorio's talked us through it, but I want to hear it from you, Javier.'

Falcón hesitated, thinking there were more important things to discuss than the workings of his brain.

'This is urgent,' said Juan, 'but we're not in a panic. These people are going to take their time travelling back and it's going to give *us* time to find out what we're up against. I've sent some people from the bomb squad to take a look at the Mercedes in the car-hire company down in Jerez. Let's get the information first and plan our action afterwards. Tell me, Javier.'

Falcón talked him through last night's thought processes, the transmission with Yacoub and the car manuals, the notes he'd looked over about El Rocío, the high brisance of hexogen, the idea of crippling the EU with attacks on tourist resorts and financial centres. Juan was irritable and interrupted frequently. When Falcón happened to mention seeing himself on television, Juan was sarcastic.

'We saw it here, too,' he said. 'Very *nice*, Javier. We don't allow ourselves to get too sentimental in the CNI.'

'People need hope, Juan,' said Pablo.

'They get enough bullshit rammed down their throats by politicians, without having to listen to the police version.'

'Let him talk,' said Gregorio, rolling his eyes at Falcón.

'I went to bed and woke up a few hours later. I watched a movie called *Troy*,' said Falcón, and added a little jibe for Juan. 'You know the story of Troy, Juan, don't you?'

Gregorio shook his hand, as if this was getting hot.

'The Greeks packed a wooden horse full of soldiers, left it outside the gates of Troy and faked a retreat. The Trojans pulled the horse inside and, in doing so, sealed their fate,' said Juan, at speed.

'The first thing that occurred to me was: how in this high-security age could Islamic terrorists get a bomb into a significant building in a major city's financial centre?'

'Ah!' said Pablo. 'You'd get the people who work in the city centre to take it in there for you.'

'And how would you do that?' asked Juan.

'You'd pack someone's car full of high explosive while they were unaware,' said Falcón. 'Tourists going to El Rocío stay in Seville before and after the event. The main celebration of the pilgrimage finished on 5th June. Hammad and Saoudi brought the hexogen to Seville on 6th June with the intention of packing it into "hardware" and fitting it into these people's cars, so that they would drive it back to the UK and into the heart of the City of London.'

'The first, and possibly the most important thing, about this scenario,' said Juan, reasserting his control

627

over the call, 'is that the terrorists have intelligence. The four guys who own these cars all work for the same company: Kraus, Maitland, Powers. They manage one of the City's largest hedge funds, specializing in Japan, China and Southeast Asia. The relevance of that is they are all wealthy men. They all live in big houses outside London, which means that they drive into work every day, and they don't get stuck in traffic because their work day starts at 3 a.m. and finishes at lunchtime. Their cars are guaranteed to be in the building in the heart of the City at rush hour. Their office is in a landmark building known as the Gherkin.'

'Where did you get all that information?' asked Falcón.

'MI5 and MI6 are already involved,' said Juan. 'They are now looking for various candidates who could have given the terrorists their intelligence.'

'What about this woman, Mouna Chedadi – the one who made the bookings for Amanda Turner?' asked Falcón.

'They're looking at her records now. She is not a known terrorist suspect. She lives in Braintree in Essex, just outside London. She's Muslim, but not particularly devout and definitely not radical,' said Juan. 'She's only been working for Amanda Turner's advertising agency since the beginning of March. She would, of course, have known everything about their holiday arrangements.'

'But possibly not very much about Amanda Turner's boyfriend and his colleagues working in the hedge fund,' said Pablo. 'Which means the terrorists probably have two or more sources of intelligence.'

'But we don't know who they are, so we cannot talk to anybody in any of the companies associated with these eight people,' said Juan.

'We've also consulted with the British, and they agree that we cannot talk to the people in the cars either,' said Pablo. 'Only a highly trained soldier would be capable of behaving normally whilst driving a car known to be packed with explosives.'

'Which brings us to the final problem,' said Juan. 'Because the "hardware" has been kept separate at all times from the high explosive and seems to be from different provenance, the British are concerned that the core of the hardware might contain something toxic, like nuclear waste. They are also assuming that the cars will be shepherded back to their destination. This means that the option of getting the people away from the cars is not a viable alternative.'

'You've got a call on line four, Juan,' said Pablo in Madrid.

'Hold on a moment,' said Juan. 'No talking while I'm gone. We all need to know everything that's said.'

Gregorio looked for an ashtray but it was a no-smoking office. He went into the corridor. Falcón stared into the carpet. One of the advantages of the clandestine world was that nothing ever achieved reality for these people. Were any of them to actually see Amanda Turner, sitting in the passenger seat of the Porsche Cayenne as it ripped past the Spanish countryside, it might be a different matter. As it was, she'd become an element in the video game.

Juan came back to the conference. Gregorio crushed his cigarette out.

'That was the bomb squad from Jerez de la Frontera,'

said Juan. 'They've found traces of a hexogen plastique mix in the boot of the rented Mercedes. They've also found two air holes drilled through from the boot into the back seat, and evidence of food and drink. It looks as if he drove into the hotel car park with the bombs and one or two technicians in the boot. They were left overnight to install the devices in the British tourists' vehicles.'

'I don't think we need any more confirmation than that,' said Pablo.

'But now we have to find these tourists,' said Juan, 'without creating a national police alert.'

'How long have they been on the move?'

'They left Seville just after 7.30 a.m.,' said Falcón. 'It's now 10.45. The Dutch couple said the British were heading north to spend a few nights in paradors.'

'The slow route would be via Mérida and Salamanca,' said Gregorio. 'The fast route via Cordoba, Valdepeñas and Madrid.'

'We should call the Paradors de España central office and find out where they made their bookings,' said Pablo. 'We can have a bomb squad waiting for them. They can disable the devices overnight and the tourists can continue on their way without knowing a thing.'

'That should give us their route, too,' said Gregorio.

'OK, we'll start with that,' said Juan. 'Any news from Yacoub?'

'Not yet,' said Gregorio.

'Am I needed for this?' asked Falcón.

'There's a military plane waiting for the two of you at Seville airport to bring you to Madrid,' said Juan. 'We'll meet in Barrajas in two hours' time.'

'I've still got a lot to do here,' said Falcón.

'I've spoken to Comisario Elvira.'

'Have you put anybody on Yacoub in Paris?' asked Gregorio.

'We've decided against it,' said Juan.

'And what about the three activated cells heading for Paris?' asked Falcón.

'They're looking more like decoys now,' said Pablo. 'The DGSE, French intelligence, have been alerted and they're following their progress.'

They closed down the conference call. Gregorio and Falcón drove straight to the airport.

'I don't understand why you're involving me in this,' said Falcón.

'It's the way Juan works. This was your idea. You follow it through to the end,' said Gregorio. 'He's annoyed that one of us didn't pick up on the piece of information that unlocked the scenario, but he always performs better when he has something to prove.'

'But it was pure luck that I picked up on an inconsequential bit of information.'

'That's what intelligence is all about,' said Gregorio. 'You put someone like Yacoub into a dangerous situation. Nobody has any idea what he's supposed to be looking for. We have a vision of a developing scenario, which he cannot see. He tells us what he can. It's up to us to translate it into something meaningful. You managed to do that. Juan is annoyed because he was left looking at the decoy but, then again, he couldn't afford to ignore it.'

'Are you worried about Yacoub being sent to Paris?' said Falcón. 'If he was part of the diversion, that would mean the GICM know, or at least suspect, he's spying for us.'

'That's why Juan is leaving him alone. He won't even tell the DGSE about him,' said Gregorio. 'If the GICM are looking at him they'll see someone completely clean. That's the beauty of what's happened. *They* put Yacoub into the position where he found the information, even though he didn't know what those car manuals represented. It means he hasn't had to expose himself in any way. When their operation breaks down, they won't be able to point the finger at him. Yacoub is in a perfect position for the next time.'

'Am I being stupid in asking why, if you know so much about the GICM, you don't just take it out?' asked Falcón.

'Because we need to take out the whole network with it,' said Gregorio.

They landed at Barrajas airport in Madrid at 1.15 on a hot afternoon, with the air crinkling above the tarmac. A car met the plane and took them to an office at one end of the terminal building where Juan and Pablo were waiting for them.

'We've had some developments here,' said Juan. 'The Parador central office has records of bookings in Zamora for tonight and Santillana del Mar for tomorrow night. Pablo called both hotels and found that the British cancelled their bookings four hours ago.'

'MI5 are trying to work out why they've changed their plans,' said Pablo. 'It could be a family matter. Two of the women are sisters. Or it could be work. The only problem is that they don't have anybody vetted on the inside of the hedge fund company. There hasn't been any seismic movement in the Far East markets. They're talking to City people now to see if there's talk of a buy-out, or a take-over.'

'Have you found the cars yet?' asked Falcón.

'If they cancelled four hours ago they were already well on their way, so we still have no idea whether they're heading north via Madrid or Salamanca.'

'What about the ferries?' asked Gregorio.

'We've checked both Bilbao/Portsmouth and Santander/Plymouth and they've made no bookings. Their Channel Tunnel booking still stands, with no alteration to the date,' said Pablo. 'That's the Interior Minster's line, Juan.'

Juan took the call, making notes. He slammed down the phone.

'British intelligence have now been in touch with French intelligence,' said Juan. 'Amanda Turner has just changed the Channel Tunnel bookings to Monday afternoon – tomorrow – so it looks as if they're driving to northern France non-stop. Neither the French Ministry of the Interior nor the British Home Office want those cars going through the Channel Tunnel. The French have said that they don't want those cars going through France. Their route north will take them close to nuclear reactors and through densely populated areas. The cars are on Spanish soil. We have areas of low population density. We're going to have to deal with it here. He's given us direct access to special forces.'

'It's about 550 kilometres from Seville to Madrid,' said Gregorio. 'It's 200 kilometres from Seville to Mérida. If they changed their plans four hours ago they could have still switched to the quicker route north, via Madrid.'

'So if they went to Madrid directly they should already be past us, but if they changed their route they should be around Madrid now.'

Pablo called the Guardia Civil and told them to watch the NI/E5 heading north to Burgos and the NII/E90 heading northeast to Zaragoza, emphasizing that they only wanted a report on the cars; there was to be no pursuit and definitely no general alert.

Juan and Gregorio went to the map of Spain and studied the two possible routes. Pablo contacted special forces and asked them to have two cars ready, a driver and two armed men in each unmarked vehicle.

At 14.00 the Guardia Civil called back with a sighting of the convoy on the Madrid/Zaragoza road, just outside Guadalajara. Pablo asked them to put motorbike police in all the service stations along the route and to report if the convoy left the road. He went back to special forces, gave them the route information and told them to watch out for the convoy's shepherd. Their two cars left Madrid at 14.05.

At 14.25 the Guardia Civil called to say the convoy had left the road at a service station at Kilometre 103. They had also noticed a silver VW Golf GTI, whose registration number had shown it to be a hire car from Seville, which had come off at the same time as the convoy. Two men had got out. Neither of them had gone into the service station. They were both leaning on the back of the Golf, one of them was making a phone call on a mobile.

While Pablo relayed that information to the special forces vehicles, Gregorio called the car-hire company in Seville. It was closed. Falcón called Ramírez and told him to get it open as soon as possible. Juan ordered a helicopter to be ready for immediate take-off. He gave the Interior Minister an update on the situation and told him that at some point they would have to close the mobile phone network down for an hour on the Madrid/Zaragoza road between Calatayud and Zaragoza.

'Special forces are going to have to take out the shepherd vehicle over one of the mountain passes,' he said. 'That way, if they're using mobile phone technology to detonate the devices, the network will be down and if they're using a direct signal there's less chance of a good connection.'

At 15.00 Ramírez called back from the car-hire company. Gregorio gave the registration number of the silver Golf GTI. The car-hire company gave them the ID card of the driver. Gregorio checked it on the computer. Stolen last week in Granada.

The helicopter tilted and rose up into the cloudless sky above Barrajas airport. Falcón hadn't wanted the privileged seat next to the pilot. It had been ten years since he'd been in a helicopter. He felt exposed to the elements and had an unnerving sensation of lightness of being.

They tracked the NII/E90 autopista from Madrid to Zaragoza and in less than an hour they were up above the mountains around Calatayud.

'We don't often get to see this,' said Juan, over the headphones. 'The denouement of an intelligence operation, I mean.'

Even now, as they raced towards the culmination

of months of work and days of intensity, it hardly felt real. Spain tore past under his feet and men somewhere below made their final preparations as the convoy of four-wheel-drive vehicles, full of real, live people, sped north unknowing and unconcerned at this vast and complicated mechanism moving into action behind them.

The pilot gave him binoculars and pointed down at the section of road where he watched as a silver Golf GTI was overtaken by a dark blue BMW. The BMW braked so sharply that puffs of smoke came out of the wheel arches. The Golf GTI slammed into the back of it, but the soldiers were out, their guns ready, arms jerking with the recoil. The helicopter swooped down on the scene. Two men were being dragged from the car; its windscreen was shattered, the front crumpled, steam pouring out from under the bonnet.

The helicopter hopped over to the other side of the mountain pass where the tourists' convoy had been pulled over on to the hard shoulder by other armed special forces travelling in a forward car. The helicopter turned and hovered as the four couples got out and ran away from their cars.

To see it all played out with no sound – or rather, too much sound from the thumping blades thrashing the air – added to the unreality. Falcón felt faint at the thought that this final operation had all happened as a result of his hunch. What if reality yielded no bombs in the vehicles and a Golf GTI with two injured innocent men? He must have been looking bewildered and lost, because Juan's voice came on in his head.

'We quite often think that,' he said. 'Did this really happen?'

The helicopter banked away from the distant city of Zaragoza, which bristled under the heat and a stagnant smog. The pilot muttered his position and direction as the brown, hard-baked mountains settled back into the late afternoon.

CODA

Falcón was sitting in the restaurant at the back of the bar in Casa Ricardo. It was almost four years to the day that he'd last been in this place and it had been no accident. He took a sip of his beer and ate an olive. He was just cooling off after the walk in the atrocious heat from his house.

There had been no time for anything in the last month. The paperwork had achieved surreal dimensions, from which he broke away to re-enter a world he'd expected to find changed. But the bomb had been like an epileptic fit. The city had suffered a terrible convulsion and there had been much concern for its future health, but as the days passed and there were no further outbreaks, life reverted to normal. It left a lesion. There were families with an unfillable space at the table. And others, who regularly summoned their courage to face another day at waist height to people they'd always looked in the eye. There were the forgotten hundreds who looked in the mirror every morning to shave around a scar, or smooth foundation on to a new blemish. But the one force greater than

638

the terrorist's power to disrupt was humanity's need to get back into a routine.

The debrief on the intelligence operation had lasted four days. Falcón had been relieved when four explosive devices had been found in the British four-wheel-drive vehicles. Each device was a small marvel of engineering, as each bomb's aluminium casing had been built to fit in the car as if it was an integral piece of the structure. Falcón couldn't help but think that the bombs were like terrorism itself, fitting so perfectly into society, its sinister element indistinguishable. His relief had been that they existed. They weren't a figment of his, or the intelligence world's, imagination. And there had been no 'dirty' element in the core as the British had feared.

Since returning from Madrid, Falcón had been working with Juez del Rey to bring the case against Rivero, Cárdenas and Zarrías to court although, since Rivero had suffered a stroke and been left unable to speak, it was really against the last two. The case was being prepared in another surreal dimension. Del Rey had decided to prosecute the two men for the murder of Tateb Hassani first because he wanted to proceed step by step towards proving their involvement in the greater conspiracy. What the public knew about Hassani was that he had written the horrific instructions attached to the plans of the schools and biology faculty. Somehow, through a collective blindness, these instructions had been separated from the fiction that the conspiracy had attempted to establish. The result was that large sections of the public thought of Cárdenas and Zarrías as folk heroes.

Yacoub had made contact on his return from Paris.

The GICM high command had given him no instructions. He thought that they suspected him and had therefore made no attempt to contact the CNI. He had wandered about in public places, afraid to stay in his hotel room in case there was a knock he couldn't bear to answer. He returned to Rabat. He attended the group's meetings in the house in the medina. There was no mention of the failed mission.

Calderón's case was due to be tried in September. Inspector Jefe Luis Zorrita and the instructing judge, Juan Romero, were convinced of his guilt. Their case was rock-solid. Falcón had not seen Calderón again, but had heard that he was resigned to his fate, which was to spend fifteen years in prison for the murder of his wife.

Manuela had been a worry to Falcón. He'd thought that the vacancy left by Angel's removal would leave her lonely and depressed, but he'd underestimated her. Once the horror, rage and despair at his crime had burnt out, she found a renewed vitality. All those lessons on positive energy from Angel had paid off. She did not sell the villa in Puerto de Santa María; the German buyer came back to her and she found a Swede to take the other Seville property. She also didn't lack for dinner invitations. People wanted to know everything about her life with Angel Zarrías.

There had been other positive developments in the aftermath to the bomb. Last Sunday, while sitting on a park bench in the shade of some trees in the Parque María Luisa, Falcón had found his eye drawn to a family group. The man was pushing a wheelchair occupied by a young girl and he was talking to a small blonde woman in a turquoise top and white skirt. Only when two kids sprinted up to join them did Falcón recognize that the children belonged to Cristina Ferrera, who put her arm around her son while her daughter reached over and helped the man push the wheelchair. It was only then that he realized that he was looking at Fernando Alanis.

Falcón had arrived too early in the Casa Ricardo. He finished his beer and asked the passing waiter to bring him a chilled manzanilla. The waiter came back with a bottle of La Guita and the menu. The dry sherry misted the glass as it trickled in. He fanned himself with the menu. He was on a different table to the one he'd been at four years ago. This one gave him the perfect view of the door, which drew his attention every time someone came in. He couldn't bear the teenage anxiety creeping up on him. At times like this his mind would gang up on him and he'd find himself thinking about the other thing that made him anxious: that promise he'd made to the people of Seville to find the ultimate perpetrators of the bombing. The sight of himself on the television in the Galician bar came back to him again and again, along with Juan's sarcastic comment. Had that been a crazy thing to do or, as Juan had said, just sentimental? No, it hadn't been, he was sure of it. He had his ideas. He knew, when he had more time, where he was going to start looking.

It's always the way that, just as your mind engages elsewhere, the person you've been waiting for all this time arrives. She was over him before he knew it.

'The pensive Inspector Jefe,' she said.

His heart leapt in his chest, so that he sprang to his feet.

'As usual,' he said, 'you're looking beautiful, Consuelo.'

125,-